TRULY MADLY
Montana

Fiona Lowe

BERKLEY SENSATION, NEW YORK

BERKLEY
SENSATION

An imprint of Penguin Random House LLC
375 Hudson Street, New York, New York 10014

TRULY MADLY MONTANA

A Berkley Sensation Book / published by arrangement with the author

ISBN: 978-0-425-27696-9

PUBLISHING HISTORY
Berkley Sensation mass-market edition / July 2015

PRINTED IN THE UNITED STATES OF AMERICA

10 9 8 7 6 5 4 3 2 1

Cover art by Aleta Raftan.
Cover design by George Long.
Interior text design by Kelly Lipovich.

Penguin
Random
House

*To Kari Lynn, who puts Montana for real
in the Medicine River series. Thank you so very much!
I couldn't have done it without you.*

Praise fo...

M...

"In the first Me... little town of Bear Paw, Montana, hosts delightful characters whose interactions feel deep and real . . . The witty conversations, family drama and accurate (but never maudlin) descriptions of loss and grief will have the reader laughing out loud, wiping away tears and eagerly awaiting future books." —*Publishers Weekly* (starred review)

"This is a funny, sexy and heartwarming novel that I feel is a must-read and a keeper. It made me laugh. I loved each character, and wish I could visit Bear Paw."
—Catherine Anderson, *New York Times* bestselling author of *Silver Thaw*

"Lowe's latest is a humorous story full of likable, distinct characters set in the small town of Bear Paw, Montana. Josh is charming and sexy, and his chemistry with Katrina ignites the pages. Lowe's beautiful storytelling sets up a heartwarming romance between two relationship-challenged people who are reluctant to give their hearts. This is a delightfully modern read." —*RT Book Reviews* (★★★★)

"Fiona Lowe has a gift for creating small towns that have both a certain quirkiness and a dimensional realism. That gift is at its polished best in *Montana Actually*, the first book in her Medicine River series. This is a book filled with humor, poignancy, sizzle and heart." —*The Romance Dish*

"This is a well-rounded contemporary that hit all the points I look for in a romance, including a good combination of humor and emotional content." —*Smexy Books*

Acknowledgments

When I write a book, my characters often take me to places I never expected to go, and I find myself reaching out to people who are experts in a variety of fields. *Truly Madly Montana* could not have been written without a lot of help from many people, so please let me count the ways. Huge thanks go to Kari Lynn (karilynndell.com) for her photographs, information about the Blackfeet Reservation and for putting me in contact with Deb. Thank you to Deb for all her information about small-town policing in Montana, from the type of gun officers carry to the county fuel credit card. Your e-mails were invaluable. The Cut Bank Area Chamber of Commerce was also very generous with information. I still think those bear paws on the sidewalk would make a cool town tour!

Thanks go to Preston, @Night_ER_Ninja on Twitter, for talking me through the administration of D50. Any mistakes in the telling are mine. A collective thanks to the medical community who like to play and share on Twitter. Your tweets are both hilarious and heartfelt and a great source of story ideas.

Fortunately for me, the diabetes community is filled with keen bloggers and vloggers. Special thanks go to Reva (typeonederful .com) for her informative blog, her honest reflections on being a young woman with type 1 diabetes and for talking me through how insulin pumps and CGMs work. Thanks to Kerri (sixuntilme .com) for explaining CGM in the cloud, the smart watch, and how all the devices work together as well as giving me an insight into the constancy of being a diabetic. The character of Millie is a montage of the many different challenges diabetics face.

Thank you to Steph and Lianne for their kickboxing information. I've learned enough about it to know I never want to do it! Once again, Lee came to my aid with information about rescue helicopters and how mind-bogglingly expensive they are to operate. To the AWESOM gals for lunches, laughs and understanding the highs and lows of the "biz," thank you, and to my dear family, who put up with me and this crazy writer's life, I love you all very much.

I'm very appreciative of my beta reader, Doris, who continues to cope with me sending her large chunks of the book and only a short time to read it. Of course, this book wouldn't exist without the support of my wonderful agent, Helen; my editor, Wendy; my cover designer, George (I adore this cover, thank you!); my go-to person, Katherine; and all the other Berkley staff who are involved in getting this book into a bookstore near you. And then there's you. A big bouquet of thanks to all my wonderful readers. I know the choice of books available for you to buy is large and often your book budget is not so big. I appreciate very much your choice in purchasing this book with your precious and hard-earned book money. Happy reading!

Chapter 1

As Millie Switkowski drove into Bear Paw for the first time in months, it seemed both ironic and fitting that her continuous glucose monitor, Dex, started beeping wildly. It was like a mocking welcome home message: *You're back where it all started, baby.*

"Okay, Dex," she said to the machine with which she shared a love-hate relationship. "Simmer down. I'm pulling over."

She'd been late leaving Bozeman because last night instead of packing, she'd panicked and had done last-minute cramming for her microbiology final. As it turned out, the extra study hadn't been necessary, and she would have been far better spending the time loading the car as per her original idea. For five years she'd worked at making her life a series of well-thought-out plans, and she knew she really needed to trust them more. If she'd had more faith in her study program, today's road trip would have been divided up into ordered and necessary scheduled breaks rather than her rushing to get to Bear Paw by six and risking a sugar crash.

Parking next to the enormous twenty-seven-foot-high, ten-thousand-pound concrete penguin, which confidently declared that Bear Paw was the coldest spot in the nation, she smiled at the incongruity of it as she often did. She'd always wondered how the brain trust behind the black-and-white statue had both cheerfully disregarded Alaska and the fact that penguins weren't found in the northern hemisphere. Geography was obviously not their strong suit. She pricked her finger and tested her blood sugar—predictably low—before rummaging through her enormous tote bag until she found a juice box and some fruit snacks.

The last thing she needed was to arrive at Dr. Josh Stanton's bachelor party with plummeting blood sugar. She didn't need the drama of feeling like crap. She surely didn't need the drama of people hovering or, worse still, some well-meaning person telling her parents she'd arrived back in town looking pale and shaky. No, she was striding into Leroy's and the party like any normal twenty-six-year-old woman just back from grad school.

Truth be told, most normal twenty-six-year-old women probably weren't invited to their former boss's bachelor party, but Josh, like everyone else in town, never seemed to notice she was a woman. She was just Millie. Practical, sensible, dependable Millie—one of the guys. Someone who could shoot pool and throw darts with the best of them.

She checked her appearance in the rearview mirror. Pale face, crazy curls springing everywhere and some freckles on her cheeks left over from spring break in Mexico. Without the time or the inclination to spend an hour with a hair straightener, she knew her hair was beyond help. At least in a few minutes the sugar would hit and pink up her cheeks.

She glanced down at her Montana State sweatshirt and gave thanks it didn't have a ketchup stain on it from the hot dog she'd grabbed when she'd filled up on gas in Great Falls. She gave herself points for clean jeans, kinda clean boots and a clean, baggy T-shirt—the perfect attire for a boys' night at Leroy's.

Millie, honey, there's nothing wrong with wearing a dress from time to time.

She quickly swiped on some lip gloss, as if that show of femininity was enough to silence the memory of her mom's often sad and critical voice. Her mom had wanted a girlie-girl daughter to share her love of clothes. Instead, she'd gotten a son who loved fashion and football with equal fervor and a daughter who couldn't tell the difference between a Gucci and a Gabbana. Millie was far more Old Navy, last season and on sale, and she felt way more at home in jeans, fleeces and T-shirts. Her brother, Evan, did his best to make up for Millie's fashion shortcomings and took their mom shopping whenever she visited him in California. Of course, he also took their dad to the football game, so really, he was the perfect adult child. Millie, on the other hand, knew her overriding contribution to the family was a constant source of parental worry.

She drained the juice box with a slurp and sent a text to her mom and dad, who were out of town.

Got home safely. Tell Uncle Ken happy birthday from me. Millie x

With the job of reassuring-the-parents done, she checked her blood sugar. Eighty-six and rising. Awesome. And real food was coming. As Josh's best man, she'd ordered up big on the hors d'oeuvres—BBQ meatballs, layered Mexican dip, stuffed mushrooms, bacon-wrapped Jalapeño poppers and buffalo wings. If they weren't serving food when she arrived, she'd ask them to start.

The good and the bad thing about Bear Paw was that most of the older residents and anyone she'd gone to high school with knew she was diabetic. They didn't comment if she ate at a different time from them, although they often had an opinion about what she ate. As a result, in her life outside of Bear Paw as a medical student, she only shared her lack of a functioning pancreas with people on a strictly need-to-know basis. She made sure that need didn't arise very often at all, because she had a PhD in horrified and pitying looks, or worse yet—over-intrusive interest from people who saw her as a training specimen. All she wanted was to be known as Millie—although she wasn't exactly certain who that was, but tonight wasn't the time to tackle that particular chestnut.

Throwing the car into drive, she shoulder-checked, pulled out onto the road and drove the last mile to Leroy's. The parking lot was almost full, and some smart-ass cowboy had fashioned a rope noose and hung it over the door next to a banner that said,

Another good man all tied up. Ducking to miss it, she pushed open the door, and a wall of noise and the malty scent of beer wafted out to greet her.

"Millie!"

"Millie's here!"

A welcoming roar went up from the cowboys and assorted businessmen who were gathered around the bar. They turned and raised their drinks to her.

She grinned and tipped her imaginary hat. She knew all of them, either having treated them at the clinic when she'd worked there as a nurse or having bested them here at pool and darts. "Hey, guys. It's good to be back."

"Millie, welcome home." Ethan Langworthy, the librarian, greeted her in his quiet and gentle way.

"Hey, Millie." Josh gave her a warm hug and a perfunctory kiss on the cheek. It was a sharp contrast to the buttoned-up city doctor who'd arrived in Bear Paw just over a year ago. "It's great to see you."

She hugged him back. "And you. Getting nervous?"

"About the wedding?" He shook his head. "Not at all. About my parents spending a week in Bear Paw, yes. Katrina's dad offered to host them out at Coulee Creek ranch, which probably means I owe him our firstborn child."

She punched him lightly on the arm. "They can't be worse than when you first arrived in town with your fancy coffee and stinky French cheeses."

He gave a good-natured smile. "Your parents always greet me with open arms when I place my monthly gourmet food order."

"I can't argue that, then, especially as by default you're likely contributing to my generous birthday and Christmas presents." She raised her hand toward the bar and gave the bartender a wave. He'd started at Leroy's not long before she'd left for medical school. "Sparkling water, please, Shane."

"It's a bachelor party, Millie. Moose Drool is mandatory," he said, filling a glass with the amber liquid. "You can worry about your weight tomorrow."

And you're home. Her gut tightened. Half of her was grateful Shane didn't know about her diabetes, while the other half of her hated that she'd just taken a hit about her weight. She wasn't obese, but then again, she was hardly willow thin, either. She knew this sort of banter was how guys talked to one another, and she'd never expected them to treat her any differently before. Tonight wasn't the night to go all girlie on them.

"A beer and pass the buffalo wings, Shane," she said brightly. As for the alcohol, she'd have to bolus insulin for the carbs and make that one beer last the entire night. Turning back to Josh, she asked, "How's Katrina?"

"She says to say hi and told me to tell you that you're not to party too hard tonight because she wants you in good shape at her girls' night tomorrow."

"Is that code for me to stay sober so I can keep an eye on you?"

He grinned. "Maybe, although I don't think I've ever seen you even a little bit buzzed."

And you won't. She'd been there, done that, years before he'd come to town, and it just wasn't worth the health risk. She still carried the guilt, and that weighed her down enough.

Pushing the past back where it belonged, she slapped him on the back in typical guy-style. "As the best man, it's my job to make sure you don't get injured when you inevitably fall off the mechanical bull, to guarantee no cowboy takes you outside and sits you backward on a horse and, as the designated driver, to get you home in one piece by midnight."

He slung his arm around her shoulder, the touch easy and friendly. "And that's why I chose you to be my best man."

"That and the fact you couldn't ask Ty Garver no matter how much you want him standing next to you," she said sadly, thinking about the cowboy who'd fallen in love with Katrina years ago.

"Well, yeah, there is that." Josh sighed with heartfelt understanding. "And Will Bartlett's not available. He couldn't get anyone to cover him at MontMedAir for the weekend."

And there is a God. Not that she didn't like Will; she did. In fact, last year, she'd liked the Aussie MontMedAir doctor just a little too much. Heat burned her cheeks at the embarrassing recollections. Having a crush at sixteen was normal; crushing on a work colleague at twenty-five probably got a listing in the *DSM-5*. The memory of last spring and summer was still excruciatingly embarrassing, given he'd barely noticed her other than as one of many people he came into contact with through work.

Will was laid-back, easygoing and charming, and he had a way of making people feel appreciated and part of a team. That had been her undoing—being appreciated was powerful stuff, and Floyd Coulson, Bear Paw's hospital administrator, could learn a thing or two from him. Given all that, she'd read way too much into Will's generous praise, especially as he often said, "You're the best, Millie," when she'd accompanied him on Mont-MedAir retrievals.

Following him on Twitter and pretending it was because of his #FOAMed tweets—free open access meducation—was borderline stalker behavior, although totally educational. What the guy didn't know about emergency airway management wasn't worth knowing. At least she'd come to her senses before clicking on *Add Friend* on his Facebook account, and for that, she was both proud and grateful. Sadly, she'd undone that bit of clear thinking after a traumatic medical evacuation last August.

It was the fifth time she'd been the accompanying nurse out of Bear Paw, and they were airlifting two badly injured tourists who'd been involved in a motor vehicle accident. They'd flown out between two storm fronts, and the pilot had given her the all clear to check the patients' vitals. She was out of her seat when the plane hit an air pocket, and she'd been thrown sideways, landing face-first in Will's lap. She still got a hot and cold flash whenever she thought about it.

He'd gripped her arms, lifted her up and checked she was okay before hitting her with his devastatingly gorgeous smile—the one that radiated from his full lips, creased his tan cheeks and crinkled the edges of his unusual dark blue eyes. He'd quipped something about things moving fast for a first date, which had disarmed her all-consuming embarrassment and made her crush-filled brain totally misunderstand what he meant. When they landed and had handed over their patients to the Seattle hospital staff, she'd suggested they have a drink.

"Great idea, Mils," he'd said with his sexy Australian diphthong, sounding as if he truly believed the words. Her heart had soared, flipped and high-fived all at once only to plummet to her feet when he'd continued with, "but I'll have to take a rain check."

Of course he would.

A rain check that never came. A rain check that made her puce with embarrassment whenever she thought about it.

With his surfer-dude good looks, he was likely very used to nurses—heck, probably all women with a pulse—throwing themselves at him. Only she wasn't usually one of those nurses or women, because she knew he was so far out of her league it wasn't worth playing the game. She still blamed the fog caused by low blood sugar along with the addition of a post-emergency adrenaline rush for her out-of-character invitation, because she'd stopped asking out guys *in* her league a long time ago.

As a twenty-first-century woman, she knew she had the right to ask a guy out, but since giving up her party lifestyle and casual hookups, things had changed and dating had gotten difficult. After a series of flat-out no's, a few disastrous dates and two truly awful one-night stands, she'd learned from her mistakes. She didn't ask guys out, period. As a result, her current dating average was zip.

"It's too bad Will can't make it, Josh," she said, trying to sound more sincere than relieved. "But I'm pumped to be your best man, and I promise to get you to the church on time."

"You're a good friend," he said sincerely.

That's me. Everyone's good buddy. "Hey, it's way too early to be getting all touchy-feely on me," she said, climbing onto a chair as much to start the party as to run from her thoughts. Sticking her fingers in her mouth, she blew hard and the piercing whistle silenced the bar.

"Aw, Millie," a voice from down near the pool table called out, "you're not gonna make a speech, are you?"

"Hey, Doc, I told you not to choose a chick to be your best man," Trent Dattner said on a long-suffering sigh.

"Millie's not a girl," Dane Aitken heckled before turning and giving Trent a high five.

"Ha-ha." Millie rolled her eyes, surprised by the dull ache that spread through her. "And to think that Comedy Central hasn't signed you up yet. For that smart-ass comment, Dane, the bull gets set on high for you."

The cowboys in the room cheered, knowing full well the sanitation worker wouldn't last three seconds in the saddle.

She raised her glass. "We've got food, we've got beer and

we've got a bull. Let's give Josh a Bear Paw bachelor night to remember."

———

DR. Will Bartlett was on a mission. He was used to missions—he'd flown a lot of miles doing emergency medical air retrieval in both Australia and Montana, but this particular mission was very different. It was also proving to be a hell of a lot harder than intubating a critical patient at twenty thousand feet.

"Brandon, mate, we're talking twenty-four hours."

The physician tapped a medication order onto the tablet computer in his hand. "You know better than anyone that a lot can happen in twenty-four hours."

A lot could happen in twenty-four seconds—hell, his life had been irreversibly changed in less time than that. Convincing Brandon to swap shifts was his last hope, as everyone else who could have possibly covered his schedule had ironclad commitments. The key, though, was making it look like he was doing Brandon McBain a favor, not the other way around, because if people sensed weakness, they zeroed in on it.

"Only last week you were whinging"—at Brandon's blank look, Will immediately translated the Australian—"whining to me that you were sick of treating patients with the flu and prescription drug addicts trying to get meds. You said you wanted more of a challenge and this is it." He tapped his own chest twice with his fist. "I'm offering you the chance of heart-pumping, adrenaline-racing trauma, the crack cocaine of all emergency physicians."

"It's tempting."

Yes!

". . . but I just got a date for tonight with that pretty brunette from Orthopedics."

Will knew the intern—he'd enjoyed flirting with her at a party, but she had the look in her eyes of a woman seeking commitment. That was his red card, so he hadn't pursued it any further. "Jenna will understand. That's the whole point of dating inside the medical community—they get that work interferes. Promise her a rain check."

Brandon snorted and shot Will a scowl. "That's your line, not mine. I actually like her and I want to date her. Unlike you, with your weird accent that seems to make every woman in this hospital think you're Jesse Spencer and Hugh Jackman rolled into one, I had to work damn hard to get her to say yes." He walked toward the nurses' station. "Anyway, I thought you didn't like weddings."

He easily matched the shorter man's stride. "I haven't got anything against them as long as I'm not the groom. Josh Stanton's a good bloke and I'd like to be there. How about I work your next two weekends? That's more than fair. Whad'ya say?"

"I dunno." Brandon stowed the tablet in the charger. "What if Jenna sees changing the date as a chance to cancel?"

He tried not to sigh. Brandon was a good doctor, but he was hopeless with women, and his dating strikeout rate in the hospital was legendary. Maybe Will could get his swap by sweetening the deal and helping the guy out. "You know, if you tell Jenna that you're delaying your date to help me attend a wedding, you'll automatically be more attractive to her."

Brandon finally gave Will his full attention. "How do you figure that?"

"All women love weddings, so by helping me get there you're doing your bit for love. Plus, I'll pay for the flowers you're going to send her as an apology for changing the date and I'll get you a table at Annie's. I know the maître d'."

"Oh, that's good." Brandon's eyes lit up with a calculating light. "If you throw in dating tips so I get a second date with Jenna, I'll swap."

"Jeez, McBain. I've already given you more than you deserve."

Brandon casually opened a candy bar. "Exactly how much do you want to be the best man at this wedding?"

The thought of discussing dating's do's and don'ts with Brandon was up there with sitting in the dentist's chair with the sound of the drill buzzing in his ears. Was getting to this wedding really worth it?

You know it is. Josh Stanton was a good mate—one of the few people he'd really connected with this last year in Montana. Even though Josh was a Yank, he totally related to Will's feelings of discombobulation when he'd arrived from Australia to work in Montana. He'd told Will that for a guy from New York and Chicago, small-town Montana was as strange and different for him as if he'd been the one to move countries.

Plus, they shared a passion for emergency medicine, and with Bear Paw's proximity to Glacier National Park and accident-prone tourists, they'd worked together a lot. Being at the wedding was an act of friendship that he wanted to make.

Knowing he'd probably live to regret it, because McBain would likely continue to seek him out for dating advice long after the favor was done, he clapped his hand on the clueless doctor's shoulder. "Brandon, the first rule of dating is making it all about her and leaving your neediness at the door."

"But I can tell her how grateful I am that she came on the date, right?"

"Yeah . . . no." He shook his head and swallowed a sigh, already tasting regret. "Your job is to ask questions and listen. Be attentive."

Brandon pulled out his phone. "What sort of questions?"

Spare me. The MontMedAir pager thankfully chose that moment to beep loudly, and he pressed it into Brandon's hands. "This is your call, McBain. If I leave now, I'll just make it to Bear Paw for the wedding."

"You're driving on no sleep?"

He knew it wasn't ideal, but he didn't have a choice. "I'll drive with the windows down and the music blasting," he replied, walking to the door.

"Text me the questions," Brandon called after him.

"Later." As much as Will respected Josh as a friend, he hoped one of Katrina's bridesmaids was going to make his weekend worth the frustrations of being McBain's date doctor.

———

MILLIE took the short but familiar walk from what had once been her parents' guesthouse at the bottom of the yard, up toward the main house and her childhood home. Over the last few years, the guesthouse had become her apartment whenever she was living in Bear Paw. She appreciated her parents' generosity, especially now that she was studying to become a doctor and was required by her scholarship to spend her summers working in Bear Paw.

Through the window, she could see her folks dressed and ready for the wedding and chatting in the kitchen. She'd spent more time than usual getting ready herself, and she thought she looked pretty sharp. As she stepped through the door, she called out, "Hi," before clicking her fingers and executing a soft-shoe shuffle across the kitchen floor. She finished with a twirl in front of them. "Ta-da."

Her mother, Susie, dressed in a gray silk shift dress gathered in at the waist with a matching cummerbund and secured with a diamanté broach, stared at her, horrified. "Why are you wearing a tuxedo?"

"Because, Mom . . ." Millie smiled, already prepared for the question. "I'm the best man."

"You're the best person," Susie said in a long-suffering tone, "and in my experience, the women who stand up with their guy friends always wear a dress."

Stay calm. "I'm sorry you're upset, Mom, but I did tell you I was wearing a suit."

"And I assumed you meant something classic like a Chanel."

She laughed, hearing the tightness in the sound and wishing it wasn't there. "A Chanel suit is way out of my price range, and besides, it wouldn't have all these awesome pockets for my stuff."

"That's what a purse is for."

Millie looked at her mother's tiny clutch purse—the one that perfectly matched her shoes and frock. It was barely big enough to hold a phone, let alone her continuous glucose monitor handset and her test kit. "You know I need more room than that."

Conflicting emotions warred on her mother's face, and she let out a sigh. "Yes, honey, but if you'd let me take you shopping, I'm certain we could have found the perfect dress and purse."

I doubt it. "Mom—"

"You look terrific, Millsy," her father said, finally stepping into the conversation as he always did just as it was getting uncomfortable. "You'll put all the other guys in the shade."

"Thanks, Dad." She kissed him gratefully on the cheek. "I better get going or Josh will beat me to the church. I'll see you guys there."

"At least wear some color," Susie said, pressing a pretty wine-stained lipstick into her hand. "You look pale. Are you sure you're feeling okay?"

As a redhead, she was frequently pale, but that wasn't what her mother meant. "I'm fine, Mom. My blood sugar is my friend today. I promise you that I'll put on the lipstick just before I go into the church, I'll spritz on some perfume and I'll pinch my cheeks, but seriously, all eyes will rightly be on Katrina and Josh, not me."

Thank goodness. As her fingers closed around the door handle, her father asked, "You've got everything you need, right?"

For the briefest moment, she rested her forehead on the door-jamb. She loved her parents dearly, but their constant concern wore her down. Everyone's constant concern wore her down. She patted her pockets. *Dex, keys, test kit, snack.* "Yep. Bye."

It wasn't until ten minutes later when she was parking next to Josh's positively gleaming sports car that she realized she'd left her phone back at the guesthouse resting on the charger. Oh well, she was at the church now, and if Josh needed anything, he could tell her in person. Feeling naked without her heavy tote bag on her shoulder, she hurried over to the steep-pitched, maroon-roofed building. Stepping out of the bright afternoon sunshine and into the dimness of the changing room, her eyes were slow to adjust, and she fuzzily made out the shape of a guy with his back to her.

"Hey, Josh," she said, moving in for a big hello hug. "Fifteen minutes 'til showtime." As her arms went firmly around his shoulders, she caught the flash of dark blond hair, the sharp zip of citrus cologne and the glint of amused dark blue eyes.

Josh had brown hair, wore woodsy cologne and his eyes were silvery gray. And as tall as Josh was, her cheek was usually closer to his shoulder than this, and she didn't remember him feeling quite this broad. Who exactly was she body-hugging?

She was about to step back when she heard, "Hey, Millie." Josh's voice filled with gentle amusement. "On my wedding day, you're supposed to be making a fuss over me, not Will."

Will?

Her brain melted at the exact same moment as her body. *No way! Not possible.* Will wasn't even coming to the wedding. But as she glanced up into familiar dancing eyes—eyes she'd spent way too much time daydreaming about last year—she knew.

Dear Lord, she had her arms wrapped tightly around Will Bartlett.

Shock dried her mouth and embarrassment made her arms drop away fast from his wide shoulders. She stumbled backward, wishing desperately that she could teleport anywhere as long as it was far, far away from here and Will Bartlett.

Be cool. Be calm. Be disinterestedly detached. "H-Hi-ello, Will."

Oh yeah, so smooth.

"G'day, Millie." A cheeky grin lit up his perfectly symmetrical face, and she saw the precise moment he recalled exactly their last meeting—the time she'd fallen into his lap. "We have to stop meeting like this."

Chapter 2

The wedding reception was in full swing, and Will took advantage of the band's break to disengage himself from a group of well-dressed women in their forties who'd cornered him on the dance floor. According to Katrina's brother, Beau, they were Bear Paw's notorious book club, and all men under thirty-five were fair game. It wasn't like Will to be caught unawares by any woman, but lack of sleep must be catching up on him, because his bum had been pinched by more than one manicured hand, his chest stroked, and during one dance, he'd detected definite rubbing.

Charlie would love it.

He blew out a breath as the accurate thought took hold of him. His twin would have been in his element tonight, and despite the fact they were in their early thirties, he would have dragged Will into a fun plan that would confuse the hell out of these bold women. Back in the day at a function like this, they'd used their mirror-image likeness of each other to fool girls. For years in their dusty, country childhood town where no one could tell them apart, they'd caused chaos. Their mother was the only person who could recognize their minute physical differences, while their father relied on personality when assigning blame for a prank discovered. Sadly, his father didn't need to do that anymore.

Hey, bro, lighten up! Charlie's voice floated across his mind. *It's a wedding.*

He really should e-mail the grief counselor the hospital had made him see and tell him that his advice about time lessening loss and his comment that Charlie's voice would fade was total BS. Taking his twin's advice, he grabbed a glass of champagne left over from the toasts and wandered out of the tent to find some entertainment.

The evening was warm and balmy—even the wind had dropped, and *that* miracle had to be in honor of the newly-weds, because usually it took a great deal of effort to stand upright in Bear Paw. Will blinked as the horizon seemed to tilt. He shook his head, realizing he was far wearier than he thought. The fatigue was worth it, though—he was very glad he hadn't missed the wedding.

Josh had worn a goofy grin on his face from the moment he'd turned to see Katrina walking down the aisle toward him on her father's arm. Will was no expert on wedding dresses, and if he'd been pressed on what the bride wore, he'd have replied, *A dress with a lace thing over it*, but he also would have added that she glowed with happiness. Josh had told him that Katrina's mother had died just under a year ago, and her death had hit the family really hard. Knowing that, it was great to see the McCades coming together for a happy occasion and having fun.

Sadly for Will, his plans for a night of fun with one of the bridesmaids had taken a solid beating. As it happened, there was only one bridesmaid, and as delectable as Megan McCade was—and she truly was in that red, figure-hugging dress—she was also Katrina's baby sister. At twenty-two, she was the classic male fantasy of a nubile college girl, and maybe, if he'd been on vacation, he could have justified a mindless fling, but an annoying voice in his head kept reminding him she was way too young. Adding that to the fact that her father, brother and newly minted brother-in-law would likely frog-march him from the ranch if he dared try anything, and that it would damage his friendship with Josh, he'd been well behaved.

Not that Megan hadn't been game. She'd openly flirted

with him during the bridal waltz, and he'd been momentarily tempted to disregard the decade that lay between them, but then her father had cut in and sanity had prevailed. For some reason, sanity had been prevailing a lot lately, and it was getting in the way of him getting much or any action. He'd been hoping to rectify that sorry state this weekend, but here he was, hiding out from cougars and Lolitas, and he wasn't certain there were any other possible candidates.

None that he'd noticed, anyway, but he consoled himself that there was still some evening left. He'd been having regular sex since he was sixteen, and this current dry spell was as atypical as it was confusing. It wasn't like he was short on offers—that never changed—it was just lately, none of the offers tempted him. With the last couple of women he'd been with, he'd felt like he was going through the motions. Given he had no plans to see them again, it didn't seem fair to only give them average sex, so he'd stopped. He'd thought a few weeks off would fix things, only the weeks had bled into months and not a lot had changed.

Everything's changed.

He glanced up to see the moon rising and casting its silvery glow over the pasture and the guests. With the flickering flames of the tiki torches and the white light of the stars starting to pierce the canopy of inky darkness, the night had a magical quality to it. He loved the outdoors, but Charlie loved it just that little bit more.

Just like at home in the outback of Australia, Montana offered Will the great outdoors in spades, only here there were even more opportunities for extreme sports. The mountains offered hiking, biking, rafting, snowboarding, rock climbing—the list was endless. It was also part of the reason he'd stayed longer in the States than he'd intended, but just recently, the call of home had started to deafen him. For some inexplicable feeling he felt farther away from Charlie here, which was crazy, because no matter where he lived or worked, Charlie was unreachable.

Recognizing exactly where his train of thought was heading and fast, he knew he needed to cut it off at the pass with some company. He glanced around at the clusters of people—some standing, some sitting—looking for someone he knew. A group of giggling nurses from the Bear Paw Hospital waved at him, and he automatically gave them a wave in return. They immediately advanced on him, wobbling on high heels that sank into the soft earth with every step they took.

Idiot! Why did you wave? He'd left the tent because he'd had enough of being superficially charming and keeping women at bay. *Find someone, ideally a bloke you know, and avoid this gaggle of women.*

He turned his head quickly and the ground tilted again. He swayed, and as he steadied, he spied Josh's nurse practitioner, Millie, and his fellow groom's person. *What was her surname? Doesn't matter.* She was sitting alone at a table with an empty chair opposite her, and she had her head down looking at something in her hand. He assumed it was her phone. He loved social media as much as the next person, but it bothered him how many people spent their time at social functions live tweeting them rather than talking to the people present. It probably answered the question as to why she was sitting alone. Still, she was his save from the attentions of the hammered and giggly nurses. "Mind if I join you?"

Her head shot up so fast that her kamikaze curls bounced across her eyes, which, although mostly green, had an unusual ring of coppery brown around each iris. She quickly slid the device she was holding into her pocket, and he caught a flash of pink in the glow from the cluster of tea lights on the center of the table. Funny. He'd never have picked Millie for a pink girl. Come to think of it, he'd never thought about her in terms of femininity at all. Millie was just . . . Millie. Unprepossessing. Ordinary, even.

A flash of a memory from last year flared. *Not totally ordinary. She's got a dimple-cute smile.*

Only, she wasn't smiling now. In fact she looked slightly taken aback. "Really? You want to sit?"

The nurses were bearing down on him fast. "Really."

"Okay, I guess."

It wasn't the most welcoming invitation he'd ever received, but he took it anyway. As his bum hit the chair, he heard a loud and collective sigh behind him.

"Doctor Bartlett, you tease," Cassidy Blund cooed.

"We thought you were coming to talk to us," said another nurse who Will thought might be called Marissa. Or it could be Larissa—he really didn't remember nor did he really care, but he'd never let her know that.

He pulled his mouth into a broad smile and turned his face toward the buzzed group. "And I was coming straight over to you until Millie, here, reminded me that we have official secret wedding business to attend to before Katrina and Josh leave."

Millie made a definite snorting sound.

He ignored her, choosing instead to press on with the nurses and appease them. "Sorry, ladies. Rain check?"

"I guess." Cassidy squeezed his shoulder. "But only 'cause you're cute."

"So very cute." A woman he'd never met before gave him a dreamy smile.

"We'll be on the dance floor," 'Issa instructed firmly. "Come find us."

They smiled and giggled before wobbling their way back toward the tent, and he turned back to face Millie.

Her previous wide-eyed surprise had morphed into a narrow gaze. "Secret wedding business?"

"Incredibly secret." He grinned at her, expecting his smile to soften the critical look she was currently spearing through him. He leaned in conspiratorially and dropped his voice to a low burr that had gotten him places with women in the past. "So secret that if either of us speak of it, weddings as we know it will never be the same again." He tapped his nose with his finger. "It's just not worth the risk."

Instead of laughing, she leaned back slightly, reestablishing the previous space between them. If she'd wanted to smile at what he'd just said, she was doing a great job of hiding it. "Just so you know, Will," she said matter-of-factly, "the Bear Paw nursing department is known to hold a grudge."

"No worries. I'll bring cake and chocolates next time I'm in town."

She blinked and then shot him an irritated look. "I should turn you in."

He broadened his smile. "But you won't. We're brothers-in-arms."

Something flickered in her eyes. "How do you figure that?"

"Well, we're Josh's groomsmen, or in your case, groom's person."

She lifted her chin. "Actually, I'm the best man."

He laughed. "I don't think so. I'm the best man."

She shook her head so hard that her dark auburn curls brushed her creamy cheeks. "I arranged the bachelor party."

With a jolt of surprise, he realized she was pissed off at him. "And I appreciate that," he said, starting to regret his decision to avoid the tipsy nurses.

Her spearing look sharpened. "Exactly what did you do apart from arrive at the last moment and look better in a suit than me?"

Ouch. What had he done to make her so snarky? And why the hell was she wearing a suit anyway? He really didn't know Millie very well. Sure, they'd done a few emergency retrievals together last summer, and she'd always been easy to work with—she seemed to know what she was doing and she just got on with the job. She'd always been competent and friendly but without crossing the professional line, and for that he'd been grateful. No matter how great his male colleagues thought it was to have women openly coming on to him at work, it got old fast. Millie had never shown any interest in him, not even the time she'd lost her balance and face-planted in his lap.

He'd helped her up and she'd just laughed, called herself a klutz and gone back to work. Every other woman he knew either would have been massively embarrassed and apologetic or would have used the situation to make a double entendre with a promise of what could happen at a different time and place. Her lack of sexual subtext was both refreshing and a relief. He found it a constant juggle to keep up the status quo at work, because some women got really upset if he refused their invitations, and could go on to make a shift hell. As a result, he was charming to everyone and he'd developed some strategies that avoided a straight-out no and disappointed no one.

Millie had always been friendly, but right now she looked anything but. Why was she so insistent she was the best man and what was with the crack about him looking better than her in a suit? His head spun from fatigue and ached with the task of trying to work out what was going on. Women always had an agenda that came with a bewildering number of emotional items that he usually found as clear as mud. Give him a medical emergency any day—at least it had a logical process.

Before tonight, he'd only ever seen Millie in baggy, shapeless scrubs, and now she was attending a wedding wearing a tuxedo. In the months since he'd last seen her had she come out as a man? In the yellow glow of the tea lights he could make out the gloss of lipstick on her surprisingly pretty lips. Although he was no expert on transgendered people, he was almost certain that if she was now living as a man, she wouldn't be wearing lipstick. Still, he supposed that didn't exclude her from being a butch lesbian. Not that he knew much about the lesbian community, either, except from the dissertation he'd been served once by a lesbian feminist patient. His takeaway from that had been that as a heterosexual male he was automatically in the wrong. He'd found the attitude bewildering, because wasn't it equally as prejudiced?

He'd always considered himself open-minded, and he wanted to try and understand, especially as he liked Millie and, unlike right now, she was usually fun to be around. He added up the evidence in front of him and came to the conclusion that butch or not, she obviously still liked pink and lipstick, and why not? Sexuality was a complicated beast, and in a town this size, her coming-out must have taken a huge amount of courage. He wanted to acknowledge that. "Don't underestimate yourself, Mils. With your height, you can carry a suit well and you look pretty good."

Her plump lips pursed. "I don't need you to flatter me, Will."

Yup. Automatically in the wrong. "I wasn't trying to flatter you, Millie. You've probably got a girlfriend for that, right?"

His left eye chose that moment to twitch with exhaustion, and Millie's eyes rounded as wide as an owl's. *Shit.* She probably thought he'd just winked at her. He swallowed a groan. So much for trying to be totally PC and showing support.

He tried to cover the faux pas by raising his glass to her. "Sorry. Girlfriend or not, good for you for being out and proud."

OH. My. God. Will Bartlett thought she was gay.

Millie didn't know whether to laugh or cry, be shocked and offended or, in some perverse way, relieved. Irrespective of her scattered emotions, it was without doubt the frosting on the cake of an evening that had gone downhill from the moment she'd inadvertently thrown herself at Will. Josh had been understandably thrilled at Will's unexpected and last-minute arrival, and he'd kept slapping Will on the back, saying over and over how great it was and didn't Millie think it was great, too.

So great . . . not. She'd felt more than a twinge of jealousy at Will being here, and she hated that. It made her feel needy—like she'd fallen well short of the mark of being a good best man for Josh. In her rational moments, she knew she was being silly. Of course Josh valued her and of course he'd want one of his male friends to stand next to him if they were available. Only all her insecurities screamed louder than her logic and, damn it, while she was left feeling like chopped liver, the only thing missing from Will's arrival was the white charger and a hero's welcome.

When she'd left home this afternoon wearing the tux, she'd felt happy and just a little bit smug. She looked good—she knew she did, and it wasn't often she felt that way. Usually at formal occasions she was stressing about her insulin pump—could it be seen, was it ruining the line of the dress—but the suit gave her a freedom she'd embraced. With Will's arrival, that feeling had faded fast, and by the time she was standing at the front of the church, she'd just felt plain silly and was berating herself for not wearing a dress.

It was one thing to be Josh's only attendant and have some fun with the whole *the best man's a woman* and wear a penguin suit. It was another thing entirely to stand next to Josh and Will in the suit. Of course, they both looked devastatingly handsome in their starched white shirts and black bow ties. She'd just felt lumpy and ridiculous and had longed to swap sides and be a bridesmaid.

The lovely wedding service had passed in a blur because her mind had been totally taken up with Will, and her thoughts and emotions had ricocheted wildly like a racquetball. First there was fury—how dare he turn up without notice. Then acute embarrassment—good grief, she'd body slammed him with a huge hug. Followed by blissful memories—he'd felt so solid and amazing pressed up against her, and finally humiliation when she'd stuttered like a total fangirl.

The stuttering bothered her the most, because she'd been convinced she was over her crush. For goodness' sake, she had to be over it. She was twenty-six years old, an experienced RN and one quarter of the way toward becoming a doctor. People expected her to be sensible, mature and upstanding. Crushing on Will was as far removed from sensible as sticking a fork into a toaster.

The guy might be the poster-boy of every woman's fantasy, but he barely noticed her. She'd accepted that, or at least she thought she had, because, hell, a lot of guys didn't notice her, but this was the first time anyone had thought she was gay. She felt a hysterical laugh rise in her throat. Will had the wrong Switkowski. Granted, her brother hadn't announced he was gay, but there were some fairly strong indicators that he might be. Millie had been waiting for Evan to say something ever since he'd moved to California, but a year and a half had passed without a murmur.

Set Will straight.

Sure! Like that won't be embarrassing. At. All. She could just imagine the confusion flaring in his eyes when she said, *Actually, I'm not gay.* It would immediately be followed by pity. The whole episode would be right up there with the time a couple of years back when she'd been carrying some extra weight and a pregnant patient had touched her arm, excitedly asking her if she was pregnant, too.

No, it was just easier to let the whole thing slide. What did it matter, anyway? The wedding was almost over—there was only the throwing of the bouquet and the waving off of Katrina and Josh as they left for their honeymoon. After that, she'd say good night, and if there was any justice in the world, the good folk of Bear Paw would be healthy, not require an emergency evacuation to a bigger hospital, and she'd not have to run into Will Bartlett all summer. And even if she did, she'd be androgynous in scrubs like she always was at work, and he'd never think twice about his assumption.

Decision made, she gave a silent apology to all the lesbians in the world, picked up her glass of sparkling water and clinked his already-raised champagne glass. "Oh yeah, totally out and proud, but can we please not talk about it?"

"Are you sure?"

"Believe me, I'm very sure."

Two worry lines appeared between his eyes. "It's just, I don't want you to think I'm uncomfortable about it or judging you in any way, because I'm not."

Shoot me now. She swallowed a sigh. "No, I get it. You're an ally."

A look of relief slipped across his model-worthy face. "So we're good, then?"

"We're totally good." At that moment she wished she had vodka in her glass.

He smiled that devastating, toe-curling smile of his and then casually reclined in the chair, all loose limbed, relaxed and totally gorgeous. Every muscle in her body slackened, and her mouth opened slightly, emitting a tiny pant.

Stop that. Right now.

She immediately jerked her head back and gazed up into the night sky, desperate to look anywhere other than at Will. Her body moaned in disappointment at the loss of the tantalizing visuals, and her befuddled, lust-filled mind staged a revolt, emptying on the spot of all conversation starters. All it could offer up was moon, star, star, black sky, star.

It suddenly occurred to her that as an Australian, he'd be used to a different night sky, so she started pointing out the constellations that she knew—all three of them. "That's Polaris, the North Star, and that's the Big Dipper, which the Blackfeet call the Bear."

Will didn't say anything, so she swung her arm wide and kept talking. "And somehow those faint stars are supposed to look like a giraffe." She gave a tight laugh. "And now I've totally maxed out my astronomy knowledge."

Still, Will didn't comment, so she glanced at him. His head had fallen forward, his eyes were closed and he looked to be fast asleep.

Fan-freakin'-tastic. Not only did he think she was she gay, but extremely boring, too. Hurt and frustration collided in a hot, hard mass in her chest, and she pushed her foot forward, intending to nudge him awake. Unfortunately, the toe of her boot connected with his shin.

"Bloody hell." His eyes flew open—dazed and unfocused. "What was that?"

"What was what?" she asked innocently, squashing down her guilt.

He rubbed his now shadow-stubbled jaw. "It felt sharp, like something just bit me."

"Probably a mosquito. They're big out here with a vicious bite," she said airily, despite the fact the wind usually kept them far, far away. An idea hit her that might just make Doctor Charming feel ill at ease and go some way to matching how'd she'd felt most of the evening. "Then again, it might have been a scorpion."

His now focused eyes gave her a long and assessing look. "I thought the only scorpions in Montana were in the southeast."

Damn, how did he know that?

"Millie, there you are. Your dad and I have been look—" Her mom's voice trailed off as she caught sight of Will, who was now bending forward, rubbing his leg. She supposed it exposed the curve of his behind, which she knew was impressive and capable of rendering a woman speechless. She really needed to start searching hard for flaws on his body.

Her cheeks burned at the thought. "Hi, Mom. Have you met Will, Josh's groomsman?"

In a fluid movement—one Millie begrudgingly conceded was impressive—Will rose to his feet, his height dwarfing her mother. He extended his hand. "Pleased to meet you, Mrs. . . . ?"

"Call me Susie," her mother almost purred. "How special for Josh that you were able to take a break from saving lives and be here tonight."

No, Mom! Not you, too. All night long she'd watched just about every female guest—from the cute-as-a-button six-year-old flower girl to Mrs. van Dyke, who was ninety-three years young—bat their eyes at the man. And she'd watched Will effortlessly charm them all. Charm everyone except her. With her, he didn't even try.

"I'm honored to be here, Susie," Will said, "and it's delightful to meet you."

Her mother giggled. "Charming and handsome. Millie, if Will's the example of how perfect Australian men are, perhaps a trip Down Under is in order."

Will glanced between her and her mother, looking momentarily perplexed.

Her stomach flipped. *Do something. Do it fast. He can't find out I'm as straight as he is.* "Daddy might be a bit put out if you run off, Mom."

Before her mother could reply, she was saved by the *boom-tish* of the band's drummer—their sign it was time to return to the tent for an official part of the evening. Slipping her arm through her mom's, she said, "Sounds like it's time for the throwing of the bouquet."

When they entered the tent, they found everyone gathered around the dance floor—the women at the front and the guys standing behind. Her mom drifted off to join her father, leaving her and Will standing at the back.

Katrina, radiantly beautiful in a strapless A-line lace dress complete with a cathedral train, called out to everyone, "Are you ready?"

Cassidy held up her arms. "I was ready three weddings ago."

"Practice makes perfect, Cassie," one of the cowboys said, raising his longneck in her direction.

Will leaned in close to her ear. "You're not going to hustle for it?"

She badly wanted to hold on to her annoyance with him, but had she been gay, he'd just shown her a sign of solidarity. "There's no point. Gay marriage isn't recognized here. Besides," she said, having some fun, "I'm saving myself for the garter catch."

He grinned at her, his deep blue eyes twinkling. "Good call."

Her insides liquefied, and shimmering heat swooped through her from tip to toe, making her knees go weak and leaving her slightly breathless. *Noooooo.* She wanted to sob. Her head might be telling her she was over her crush, but her body had missed the memo. Right now it was telling Will she was ready, willing and oh so very able.

She knew her pupils would be dilated, her cheeks bright pink, and she could already feel the tingling ache in her breasts as they strained against her bra with her nipples standing to attention. Somehow—but only just—she managed to stop from licking her lips.

Will suddenly slipped off his jacket. "It's warm in here."

"Yeah. It is." She removed her jacket, too, and for the very first time it was a relief that Will thought she was gay. It was beneficial, even, because it effectively hid from him the physical signs of her unwanted but undeniable attraction to him.

Josh counted down, "Five, four, three, two, one," and Katrina gave her bouquet a pitcher's toss, sending it sailing over the heads of the leaping and squealing women.

Roses and tulips came barreling straight at Millie like a lethal weapon. If she caught the bouquet, the jokes about her getting married would start, and Will would find out fast she wasn't gay. If she didn't catch the flowers, she'd be hit in the face by a pack of sturdy stems and risk a black eye.

A split second before she ducked, Will's hand shot out, firmly grasping the bouquet and stopping it from slamming into her. The men laughed. The women sighed.

Will held it aloft like a trophy. "Hey, Katrina, how about you throw it again?"

"No, Will," the bride said smiling at him. "It clearly chose you, and you have to keep it. Looks like you're next to get married."

The women sighed again.

"I'd have preferred the garter," he said laconically.

"No flirting with my wife, thank you very much," Josh said good-naturedly, taking Katrina by the hand. "Thanks, everyone. It's been a great night."

With a big wave, they ran from the tent and out to Josh's car, which Beau and Katrina's younger brother, Dillon, had decorated with cans and a *Just Married* sign.

Everyone followed, clustering around the car and waving good-bye. All the while, the band kept playing, and as Josh and Katrina drove across the pasture, some of the crowd returned to the dance floor while others drifted away, heading home for the night. When Millie walked back into the tent, women once again surrounded Will. His handsome face was impassive, but when he caught her gaze, it was the look in his eyes that struck her.

Did he need rescuing?

She shook away the crazy thought. Will Bartlett no more needed rescuing than she needed a hole in the head.

"Hey, Millie."

She swung around to see Megan carrying a tray. "Did you get some wedding cake? Shannon made it and it's to die for?"

Millie knew exactly how great a cook Beau's wife was,

having eaten lunch at the Big Foot diner most workdays last year. "What sort of cake is it?"

"Rich vanilla frosted with chocolate ganache." Megan smiled. "You know you want it."

Dex had been remarkably quiet tonight, which meant that she'd managed the juggle of bolusing insulin versus food intake without any unexpected rises or falls. It was no mean feat at a function like this.

Don't risk it.

She no longer took stupid risks, and although eating a piece of the cake wasn't stupid, it wasn't totally wise, either. But she could handle it, and after everything that had gone down tonight, she needed cake. And chocolate. "It sounds perfect."

Chapter 3

"Thanks for helping out, Millie," Dillon said as he tied the last trash bag and dropped it on top of the pile of post-wedding debris.

"I was happy to help." She'd stayed back to give the McCades some assistance packing up, because after eating that decadently rich and wonderful cake so late in the evening, there'd been no point going home to bed.

She wasn't going to get much sleep, because Dex would be beeping at her on and off all through the night as she tried to stabilize her blood sugar. She already had the heavy feeling that came with a high reading—lead weight limbs and a sensation she was hauling herself through chest-height snowdrifts. Plus she was thirsty as hell and needing to pee every thirty minutes.

Told you that cake wasn't worth it.

Shut up! It was seriously worth it. The ganache was as close to an orgasmic experience as she'd come in a very long time.

"You coming to the barn?" Dillon asked. "Megan's planned an awesome after-party."

"Thanks for the invitation, Dillon, but it's time for me to call it a night."

"You sure?" Dillon was looking at her as if he didn't believe what he was hearing. "Legend has it that at college you were the queen of the after-party and always the last to leave."

And she had been until she'd landed up in the hospital scaring her family and frightening herself. She smiled. "I'm handing over my crown to Megan."

"Drive safe, then."

"Will do. Good night, Dillon."

"Night." He gave her a wave before disappearing into the dark.

She glanced around the now empty tent and wondered at the deconstruction of what had been, only an hour before, a wedding wonderland. The band had packed up and driven away, all the guests were gone, the tables and chairs were neatly stacked and the white tablecloths stuffed into laundry bags ready for collection tomorrow. Megan and her father, Kirk, had carried the wedding presents to the ranch house, and all that was left of a great wedding reception were trash bags, one abandoned high-heeled strappy sandal, a pretty evening purse and a black suit jacket.

She took a closer look. A suit jacket with a boutonniere that matched hers.

As Josh had left the wedding wearing his jacket, this had to be Will's. She hadn't seen him since he'd been talking with Brittany, one of Megan's friends. Actually, talking was a stretch—it had been full-on flirting. Brittany's back had been pressed up against one of the marquee supports, and she'd been gazing up at him. Will's left arm had been raised and his hand flat on the support above her head. With his collar unbuttoned and bow tie untied and draped around his neck, he'd been leaning in and Brittany had been laughing at whatever he was saying. The next time she'd looked for him, he'd been nowhere to be seen and neither had Brittany.

Apparently they'd been so enthusiastic to go someplace more private, Will had left his jacket behind. As she picked it up, she heard a jangle and checked the inside pocket. Car keys and his wallet. He wouldn't have gotten far without either of those things. Still holding the jacket, she walked outside, wondering if he'd gone to the barn party. As she walked between the back of the big tent and the food service area, she saw a silhouette of a man standing yet leaning, his forehead resting against the corner metal upright of the tent. Everything from his height to the shape of his body left her in no doubt as to his identity.

Was he sick? Drunk? She marched over to him. "Will, are you okay?"

He didn't move. She walked up to him, reached out and touched his forearm. His warmth radiated through the soft cotton of his shirt, tickling her fingertips. It felt so good—he felt so good—and her heart rate instantly kicked up.

Don't do this. Don't think hot and hard solid forearm. Think flexor carpi radialis, extensor digitorum muscle—

Sensational idea! Use him as an anatomy lesson. I bet his rectus abdominis muscles are incredible.

The image of what his abs might look like slammed her brain, and she swallowed against a dizzy rush of arousal. Okay, so maybe using Latin names wasn't such a great idea after all.

Coming out of her fog of lust, she realized he still hadn't moved. This time she gave his arm a shake. "Will?"

His only response was a gentle snore. She couldn't believe it—he'd literally fallen asleep on his feet.

"Will, wake up. The wedding's over. Time to go home."

Still, he didn't stir. He'd fallen asleep at the table earlier, and now he'd done it again. She knew about fatigue—she'd worked long hours and back-to-back shifts, and sometimes she'd been so tired she couldn't see straight—but she'd never fallen asleep standing up. She tried again, giving his hand an extra hard shake. Nothing. The poor guy must be zonked, because he was totally out. She knew she couldn't leave him here, but moving him on her own would be tricky. If only she had her phone with her, she could call someone for help.

Use his phone. Pleased with her idea, she searched his jacket again, but his phone wasn't there, which meant it was somewhere on his person. As formal shirts didn't have pockets, that left his pants. *Just slide your hand into his trouser pockets.* The thought thrilled her way more than it should, because the reality was that touching up an unconscious guy was unconscionable. If a man did the same thing to a woman, he'd be accused of sexual assault.

Think of him in terms of a patient. Pat his pockets and find his cell phone. Slide hand in, slide hand out. Do it fast.

Flexing her fingers, she was just about to pat down his left pocket when Dex started beeping incessantly, telling her that her blood sugar was skyrocketing.

Will's head shot up, his eyes glazed. "Emergency packs! Let's go."

"Ah, Will, it's me, Millie, and—"

He grabbed her arm and started running. "We have to get to the airport."

Okay then. Now she had six feet, one inch and one hundred eighty pounds of walking, talking, sleepwalking Will, who obviously thought Dex was his emergency pager and that they were needed at a MontMedAir emergency. As his hand was firmly gripping her arm, she had no choice but to jog along beside him.

Think! She ran through her options. Waking up a sleepwalker wasn't dangerous, but it wasn't pleasant for the victim because it left them disoriented and unpredictable. Also, it wasn't always possible to wake them, as she'd just learned. That left sticking with him to make sure he didn't injure himself.

"The vehicle's this way," she said, pushing him in the direction of her car. At least if she got him inside the car, he'd be safer than running around a dark pasture. He hauled open the passenger side door and got in, sticking his hands out in front of him as if seeking the steering wheel. She remembered that Australians drove on the left-hand side of the road, and in his sleepwalking state he'd reverted to what he was most used to.

She turned on the ignition. "I'll drive, Will."

His unfocused eyes moved right then left, and he slammed his hand on the dash. "Chopper's waiting. Go."

She eased her car down the rutted ranch road, bumping and bouncing until they reached the relatively smooth blacktop of the highway. As she turned right, she noticed that Will's head had fallen back against the headrest and his eyes were closed.

With no clue where he'd checked in to stay the night in Bear Paw, and not wanting to risk him rushing into the lobbies of the two motels in town yelling, *Incoming*, she decided the safest thing to do was drive home. She was grateful the guesthouse had a rear entrance, because explaining to her folks that she had Will in the car would only get their hopes up.

She still hadn't quite recovered from the excruciating conversation with her mom three years ago when Susie had sat her down with a glass of wine in her hand. Things had gone down-hill from there, fast. Susie had told her she wasn't a prude and she understood that at twenty-three, Millie was an adult with sexual needs just like the next woman. She wanted Millie to know that if she ever wanted to bring a guy back to the guesthouse, she and her father would be okay with it.

Millie had died a thousand deaths on the spot and had mumbled something like, *Good to know*, and had immediately tried to change the subject. Fast. Very fast. Only Susie, who was by then enjoying her second glass of wine, had hinted that since Millie and Evan had moved out, she and her father's sex life had improved tremendously.

The temptation to break her relative sobriety that night, wrench the bottle of wine off of her mother and down the contents fast had burned hot and strong. One part of her appreciated her parents' open-mindedness, but another part knew it wouldn't be that simple. When her mom said a guy, she really meant a keeper. She did not mean some random guy she might hook up with for occasional sex. On the infrequent occasions Millie did have sex, she made sure it always happened out of town, because Millie had never met a keeper, and Will was certainly not one. A keeper would swim shark-infested waters for her. A keeper wouldn't assume she was gay.

She killed the engine and dropped her head onto the steering wheel with a sigh. If her mother ever discovered Will thought she was gay, she knew she'd be taken directly to Seattle without passing go and be forced to buy a closet's worth of dresses. Sitting back, she checked Dex. Her blood glucose was still too high, which bothered her because she'd been confident she'd already given herself plenty of insulin to deal with the cake. If she gave herself more, she risked crashing, and yet the double arrows continued to point ominously upward, demanding she give herself more.

As she pressed the buttons to bolus insulin, Will, who'd been breathing deeply and steadily beside her for the last twenty minutes, sat bolt upright.

"It's okay, Will. We're here. We're at—" But he was already out of the car before she could say, "my place."

She shoved her pump in her bra and jumped out, too, running after him, worried he was going to run out onto the road, but he was heading toward her porch like a moth drawn to the light, bending low as if he was approaching a helicopter. "Will, wait."

He didn't. He opened her unlocked door and disappeared inside. She found him crawling on his hands and knees. "Will, what are you doing?"

"Keep low. We're almost there."

Where? She wished he'd wake up, but it seemed that was increasingly unlikely. Hoping to direct some of the play, she got down on all fours so she was at his level. "This way." She led him toward the bedroom, wondering how she could stop what was clearly, for him, a nightmare. She climbed onto the bed and crossed her fingers. "Here."

Will immediately kneeled on the bed, running his hands up and down her long bolster pillow. "Twenty-five-year-old male, explosion victim, burns to seventy percent of his body, fractured pelvis, stridor and pulse-ox eighty-two."

That was a pretty low pulse-ox, making her pillow critical. Did she join in or not say anything? She had no clue, so she decided to see if treating it like an ER situation would work. "One hundred percent oxygen by non-rebreather mask?"

"No, the risk of laryngeal swelling's too high. Always think ABC. Airways, breathing, circulation. I need to tube him and then insert a central line."

She remembered her burns' lectures. "Putting up lactated Ringer's solution."

"Call the burns unit."

Crazily, her heart hammered fast, as if this was a real medical emergency. Dex beeped again and she glanced at the screen. Yay! Her blood sugar was finally starting to fall.

"Shit, he's crashing." Will's hands started rhythmically compressing the pillow, giving it CPR. "Push epi and atropine."

Millie silenced Dex and set it to vibrate, realizing that every time Dex went off, it seemed to set off Will.

"Come on. Stay with me." Will's arms pumped up and down, furiously willing the pillow to live. "Asystole. Damn it, no!"

She put her hand over his, hoping he'd stop now. "It's time to call it, Will."

As his hands gradually stilled, a long, slow sigh shuddered out of him. "Time of death, 3:05."

On one level, she knew this wasn't real, but on another it was very real to him. No one found it easy to lose a patient, and she had a strong urge to try and comfort him. "He was in really bad shape, Will. You did everything you could."

"It sucks. I hate nights like this." He ran his hand through his hair, sighing again. "And I'm so bloody tired . . ."

This was her cue. "Lie down and sleep."

"Can't. I'm on call."

She plumped a pillow. "No, the schedule's changed. You're off."

His glazed gaze stared off in the distance. "I'm off? Thank God." He swung off the bed, kicked off his shoes and, dropping his left arm behind his head, tugged at his collar. Raising his right shoulder, he pulled his shirt off in one fluid movement.

Her mouth dried at the sight of his naked chest with its delineated pectoral muscles, dark nipples and dusting of light brown hair. Her gaze slipped lower, and a thrill shot through her as she noted that his rectus abdominis were indeed as awe-inspiring as she'd imagined.

Distracted by the sight, she was caught by surprise when he shucked his trousers. Now he stood before her in gray trunks—trunks that fit him perfectly, outlining an impressive package that left little to the imagination.

Oh. My. God. She couldn't deny that the sound coming out of her mouth was a high-pitched squeak. So much for being an experienced nurse and a trainee doctor who was unfazed by body parts. She always had a certain detachment when it came to seeing half-naked and fully naked men, but right now it had deserted her.

Does he sleep naked? her crush asked, bouncing up and down. *Let him sleep naked, please.*

She pressed her hands to her face to block the view. *He's asleep. I'm not looking—that would be perving.*

Oh please. You know this is your only chance so go ahead and take it.

She heard the rustle of the covers, and when she peeked through her splayed fingers, she saw Will had gotten into the bed, laid down his head and was instantly asleep. Then again, this whole time he'd never actually been awake. She stood for a moment, gazing at him, soaking him in. She watched the slow and steady, rhythmic rise and fall of his chest, studied the way his thick, chocolate milk lashes brushed his cheeks and how his day's-end blond brown stubble shadowed his square jaw.

Her gaze lingered on the sensual curve of his mouth. Oh, what a mouth—thick, full lips that peaked across a wide philtrum—it should come with its very own parental guidance warning. Even with a faint, jagged scar on his chin and his top lip being slightly larger than his bottom one, he was, without doubt, a truly beautiful specimen of humankind. She wondered about the collision of DNA that had given him such dusky skin and contrasting light-colored hair. It was an unusual combination, as were his deep sapphire blue eyes. Either way, she knew she could gaze at him for hours.

A yawn bubbled up and out of her, and she glanced at the clock on her nightstand: 1:45 A.M. Bed was calling. *Where are you going to sleep?* Technically, she could place the bolster pillow between her and Will, and with the width of the king-size bed, it meant they'd be unlikely to touch each other.

Good plan! Let's do that! her crush cheered. *You never know, he might roll over the bolster.*

Dex vibrated. She checked the reading and sighed before pricking her finger and confirming the result. Having finally started to fall, her blood sugar was now tumbling way too fast. As she'd feared, that last unit of insulin had been overkill, and now, even though she wasn't remotely hungry, she needed to go eat and eat a lot. She knew Dex would alarm if she hit the danger zone at either end of the spectrum, and as the beeps seemed to send Will into emergency physician mode, that dictated she spend the night on the sofa.

Just fabulous. Between Dex beeping, her trying to get comfortable on the too-short sofa and knowing that Will was so close in the next room, she doubted sleep was going to happen. Come morning, though, she knew exactly what was going to happen. Will was leaving and leaving early. The only way she could keep her secret was to push him out the door as fast as possible and put a one-hundred-mile safety buffer between them.

WILL slowly became aware of sunlight penetrating his eyelids, but he didn't open them, because that would mean he was awake, and right now, he was warm, relaxed and cozy. He wanted to stay that way.

The earthy scent of musk, mint and lemon circled him, reminding him of the flowering eucalypts at home. Smooth, soft sheets stroked his body, and he rolled over just so he could feel their silky touch sliding against him. These sheets didn't feel anything like the ones in the on-call room. Come to think of it, the bed was way more comfortable, too—it was wider and his feet didn't poke out the end. He wiggled his toes, and that's when it hit him. He wasn't in the on-call room. He was in Bear Paw, and this was the Glacier Park Inn.

He cocked one eye open, and as the wallpaper came into focus, he quickly opened his other one. Although he'd only spent half an hour in the motel room before the wedding, grabbing a shower and a shave, he didn't recall the walls being decorated with silver and gray wallpaper that outlined white, skinny trees. He sat up and took in the rest of the room. Instead of the ubiquitous brown motel nightstands, these were white. There was also a white dresser divided up by five drawers and with a mess of stuff on the top, a white closet and a heap of clothes cascading out of a white wicker laundry hamper.

Where the hell was he?

He scrubbed his face with his hands as if that would help him think more clearly. All it told him was it had been hours since he'd shaved. The last thing he remembered was making the decision to return to the motel. He'd extracted himself from Brittany before gifting Mrs. van Dyke with the wedding bouquet and walking out of the tent to find his car. Why the hell wasn't he at the motel? He glanced to his left at the vacant side of the bed. More importantly, who the hell had he slept with last night?

Shit. He had no recollection and he should remember. He hadn't been hammered—hell, he'd only had a few drinks—and yet he had no clue whose bedroom he was in. He groaned, suddenly horrified. Surely he hadn't given in to Brittany? *Please, no.* How could he have had sex and not remember a thing about it?

Had he been roofied? *Nah.* He didn't have any of the known side effects of the drug, and if a woman had spiked his drink, it would have been to her disadvantage because Rohypnol would have rendered him unable to perform. Then again, he couldn't remember even trying to perform. His brain spun and stalled, trying to find a way through what was a blank space in his memory.

You can work this out. Just take it step by step.

He definitely remembered Mrs. van Dyke and her look of delight when he'd presented her with the bouquet. It was after saying good-bye to her that things got fuzzy. To add to his confusion, he had a strong feeling he'd gone to work, which made absolutely no sense at all.

He glanced around, looking for obvious clues in the room—things that would tell him where he was, such as photos, a discarded formal dress, but there were no people pictures and the only clothes on the floor were his. Faced with more questions than answers, he had little choice but to get dressed and go charm his way out of this mess. He was about to throw back the covers when his nostrils detected the aroma of bacon and eggs. His stomach growled.

The bedroom door opened partway, as if the person on the other side was peeking in to see if he was awake. Taking the bull by the horns, he said, "G'day." It was the first word he'd spoken for the day, and it came out husky and deep. He cleared his throat. "Come in."

The door opened all the way, and a ginger and white cat shot in, jumping onto the bed and giving him a long and disapproving stare as if to say, *Who the hell are you?*

Far more used to dogs than cats, he reached out his hand to pat its head. "Ouch." He pulled his hand back fast as the bloody thing tried to bite him.

"Hey, sleepyhead." Millie walked in carrying a tray.

Millie? Relief slid through him that it was her and not any of the other women who'd been chasing him at the wedding. Laughter followed, rocking out of him as he realized all his fears about what might have happened in this bed last night were totally unfounded. He'd dodged a hell of a bullet.

As she set the tray down on the other side of the bed, she raised her brows at his chuckle. "Something funny?"

He leaned back on the pillows. "You've just solved a mystery for me."

"Oh?"

He smiled at her, knowing she'd appreciate the joke. "I was

having a lot of trouble remembering what happened last night, and I wasn't exactly certain who was going to walk through that door."

She folded her arms across her green singlet pajama top. "You weren't expecting it to be me, were you?"

"Put it this way: I'm very glad it's you."

Her mouth grimaced on one side, and he got the impression he'd somehow insulted her. She spun abruptly on her heel and walked over to the dresser, bending down to pull open the bottom drawer.

His gaze followed her. He'd only ever seen Millie in long pants, but today she was wearing blue and green striped pajama shorts and her long legs were bare. Very bare. Gloriously bare and showing acres of creamy, smooth skin that wasn't stretched taut over solid muscle, but then again, it wasn't flabby, either. It looked enticingly soft. For the first time in weeks, his body reacted, and he had an overwhelming urge to test if her thighs felt as good as they looked.

Jesus, what's wrong with you? She's gay.

I'm just window-shopping.

He pressed his fingers against the indisputable itch in his palm and pulled his gaze away.

Rising, she threw a T-shirt at him. "This was my brother's before I commandeered it. It should fit."

He raised a hand and caught it. "There's a dress code for breakfast?"

"There is if you want bacon."

"Consider me dressed." He promptly pulled the faded maroon Montana Grizzlies T-shirt over his head, acknowledging this had to be the first time a woman had ever asked him to cover up.

He moved the tray across his lap and picked up a piece of whole wheat toast golden with butter. Placing two pieces of crispy bacon on top, he took a big bite, savoring the flavor of salt and pork as he chewed and swallowed it down. "This is amazing. Thank you."

"You're welcome." She poured coffee from a pot, pilfered a piece of bacon off his plate and then sat facing him, cross-legged, at the end of the bed.

"So last night . . . ?" he asked around mouthfuls of the best breakfast he'd had in a long time, hoping she'd fill him in on how he'd landed in her bed.

"Was interesting," she said with a smile that trailed all the way from her pert, pink lips up to her eyes, making the green and brown flecks sparkle.

"Definitely interesting." He matched her smile with one of his high-wattage ones—a smile that generally made women talk—before he realized with a gut-dropping thud that none of his usual techniques would make a damn bit of difference with Millie.

She leaned back on the bed end. "You don't have a clue what happened, do you?"

He chose honesty. "Not really, no." He wiped the runny yolk from the poached egg off his chin with a napkin. "I know I gave Mrs. van Dyke a kiss good-bye and I left the tent. That's a very clear image, but what happened next is vague. I don't remember arriving here, but I have this strong feeling I attended a MontMedAir emergency, which is crazy, right?"

She smiled an indulgent smile over her coffee mug. "Not totally crazy."

Man, he really was losing it. "I worked last night?"

"You thought you did." She took a slug of the fragrant brew. "You do know that you sleepwalk, right?"

"No, I don't," he said as a prickle of indignation ran up his spine.

"Yeah, you do."

"I did as a kid, but I grew out of it years ago."

Her chestnut brows rose mockingly. "You sure about that?"

"Yes." The word came out short and sure. "Mum said I only ever sleepwalked when I was overtired and . . ." Memories of last night—the tilting sensations, the dizzy spells, the fact he'd fallen asleep sitting down—came rushing back, filling him with a sinking feeling. "Please tell me I didn't?"

Her burst of laughter rained over him, confirming his worst fears. "Oh, you really did, and you did it on a spectacular scale," she said, looking as if she was relishing the idea of telling him the full story. "I found you asleep standing up after everyone had left. When I tried to wake you, you thought you were needed at MontMedAir and you insisted we go to the airport. Fortunately, I steered you toward my car, and lucky for me you sat in the passenger seat. If you hadn't, you probably would have driven the car. When we got back here, you tried to resuscitate my bolster pillow." Her gaze dropped to her coffee.

"What?" He had a feeling he'd done something bad. Perhaps something that had upset her.

Her head shot up, but she didn't meet his eyes. "Then you got undressed and got into bed."

His gut rolled again. He always slept naked, and it was one thing to get naked with a willing and appreciative woman, but Millie wasn't either of those things. With a sinking feeling, he raised the sheet. His eyes glimpsed the black band of his jocks, and relief slid into him. "Thank God."

"Exactly," she said with a wry tilt to her lips.

Her very kissable lips. Why hadn't he ever noticed them before?

What the hell? The moment you find out she's gay and there's no chance she's ever going to be into you, you decide she's sexy? He shook the thought away but then he heard Charlie say, *That's sick, mate. You need help.*

"So you slept . . . ?"

"On the sofa, but sleep is a relative term."

He noticed the dark shadows that smudged the delicate skin under her eyes. "Sorry. What can I do to make it up to you? Lunch? A picnic? After all, I owe you one for not letting me drive my car asleep."

She stretched out her long legs before swinging them to the floor, and the itch in his hand intensified. Picking up the obstreperous cat, she hugged it close to her. "I thought you were due back in Great Falls?"

He moved the tray off his lap as his brain started to kick into gear. He had no reason to race back to Great Falls to an empty apartment and a pile of dirty washing. With Josh gone on his honeymoon, Millie would be good substitute company. "It's all good as long as I'm back by eight tonight." He reached for his pants.

"I'll leave you to get dressed." She walked quickly to the door.

He was shoving his left leg into his trousers when it hit him. "Millie, wait."

She turned toward him, her eyes widening, and then she hurriedly turned back and faced the door. "What?"

"Where's my car?"

She gently banged her forehead against the door. "It's still at the Coulee Creek ranch."

"My shower can wait if it's easier for you to drive me out there now." He zipped his fly closed and pulled on his socks before shoving his feet in his shoes. "Ready when you are." It wasn't until he'd picked up his jacket and located his wallet and keys that he realized she hadn't said anything. "Millie?"

"Sorry, Will. I've got plans."

"At 10 A.M. on a Sunday morning?"

"Yes." The word shot out defensively. "Is that so unexpected? I do have a life, Will."

He held up his hands in a show of peace. "Of course you do," he said in a placating tone, surprised by her emphatic reply. Although he wasn't a regular churchgoing bloke, he'd learned soon after arriving in Montana that most churches had 11 A.M. services. The hour of power usually meant an hour of peace in the ER—the walking wounded tended to arrive after lunch.

"Is there any chance your plans could include dropping me out at the ranch first? You've got an hour before church, and it would be your good deed for the day." He tilted his head and gave what he hoped was both a flattering and encouraging smile. "Please."

She sucked in her lips as if she was stopping herself from speaking. "Give me your phone."

He handed it over and watched her plug in what he assumed was her number so they could catch up later. When she gave it back to him, she said, "That's the number for the Bear Paw cab. Well, it's more of a minivan. If you call Don now, he can take you out to Coulee Creek before he starts the church run."

"What about the picnic? Surely there's a national monument around here an Aussie should see?"

Her plump lips didn't even crack a smile. "It was good to see you, Will. Drive safe."

As she closed the door behind her, he realized he'd just been fobbed off and his invitation soundly rejected. It wasn't a familiar scenario. Usually he was the one saying, *I'll be in touch* or *Can I take a rain check?* Not the other way around. Hell, she hadn't even offered up the oldie but goodie of *Another time, perhaps?* She hadn't even sounded apologetic.

That ticked him off. When he didn't want to accept an

invitation, he at least made it sound like he was sorry so as not to hurt the invitee's feelings. An irrational disappointment spread through him, and *that* was unexpected. Why the hell should he be disappointed that Millie was busy?

Because you don't want to spend the day alone.

He sighed. Coming to Montana was all about getting used to being alone. It was a much-needed change in a new place where he and Charlie had never spent any time together. He still had another year on his visa, but just lately, Charlie's voice was getting louder and he'd been having intense moments of homesickness. This bothered him, because the point of being in Montana was to learn how to live as a twinless twin. Surely going home would just make things harder?

When homesickness struck and he missed the red dirt, the golden sands, the aquamarine sea of the West Australian coast, and the sweet taste of a jam-filled Lamington, he found getting active and doing stuff outdoors helped. The vast expanse of the intense blue Montana sky was the same as home, only without the heat-haze shimmer. Having company helped, too. A picnic with Millie had held appeal because it was outdoors and she was fun and really easy to be around.

Do I need to say it again? She's gay.

Exactly!

The last time he'd had a female friend he'd been ten. Once puberty hit, everything had changed. He'd learned that no matter what women told him about wanting to be friends, they inevitably wanted more, and that's when things got complicated. If he had sex with them, the friendship failed. If he didn't have sex with them, the friendship failed. Feelings always got in the way and always got hurt. But with Millie, sex wasn't an issue. She had all the qualities of the perfect female friend—fun, uncomplicated and with no hidden agenda.

His phone beeped with an incoming message.

Floyd Coulson here. Just following up on last night's conversation. Can we meet at the Big Foot diner this morning before you leave town?

Last night's conversation? Will wracked his memory, but other than Katrina introducing him to Bear Paw's jolly and florid hospital administrator and a brief conversation about the influx of tourists in the town during summer, he couldn't recall anything that required a follow-up. Then again, he couldn't remember giving Floyd his cell number or much else about parts of the evening. There was every chance he'd momentarily fallen asleep, and as his head had fallen forward, Floyd had taken it as an assenting nod.

Now the guy wanted to meet. Well, he had a day to kill, so why not? Intrigued, he texted back, Yes.

Chapter 4

Tara Ralston checked she had everything ready for work. Polished leather boots? Check. Leather belt? Check. Handcuffs? Check. Whip? No, there was no mounted police division in Montana. Pen. Notepad. Taser. Handgun. Check. Check. Check. Check.

She took a last gulp of coffee, draining the mug, and immediately rinsed and upturned it on the drainer before glancing around her small and sparsely decorated apartment. Her gaze settled, as it often did, on the framed photo of her mother standing outside one of the many trailers that had constituted home when Tara was a kid. She remembered very clearly the day the photograph had been taken—it was her mother's thirtieth birthday and her twelfth.

There'd been chocolate cake from the grocery store bakery with her name written on it in pink frosting and the gift of a new pair of jeans and a T-shirt from K-Mart. Tara had been over the moon, because new clothes hadn't been common in her childhood. Her mother had also given her a necklace, and she'd worn it every day until it had fallen apart a year later along with the clothes. But the real reason that day had been so special was because her mother was happy, sober and had stayed awake past seven. They'd cuddled up on the couch watching TV in the way she'd always imagined normal families did. It was one of the highlights of her childhood. Everything had gone downhill fast not long after.

She grabbed her Ike jacket and headed out the door, walking the short distance to the station. *LEC, remember.* She smiled to herself, thinking that Hollywood was unlikely to start having movie cops say, "Bring him down to the Law Enforcement Center for questioning," but she hadn't mentioned that thought to the county officials who'd employed her. They were justifiably proud of the new purpose-built facility that included the police station, pods, holding cells and the city court. However, Mitch Hagen, the sheriff and her boss, rolled his eyes every time he heard the letters *LEC*.

While she walked she made a call. "Hey, boss, how's it going this fine Monday morning?"

"How the hell do you think it's going, Ralston? This frickin' cast itches worse than poison ivy."

Mitch had broken his leg a week ago falling out of a tree while trying to rescue Bethany Jacobs's cat. The cat had climbed down unscathed. Tara wondered how Mitch had spent years as a country cop without learning that along with his gun and his Taser, his other must-have weapon for law and order was a can of tuna fish.

"Sorry to hear that. Do you have a ruler? They make good scratching sticks."

He grunted. "You on top of things?"

Was she? She was Bear Paw's first female police officer, and although that shouldn't be an issue, people often made it one. As a woman on active duty in the military, she'd had to perform better than her male counterparts before she'd been taken seriously. She had no clue what the Bear Paw residents thought about her appointment, but she was holding her breath until after her introductory interview by the local press hit the stands and the Internet tomorrow. Folks who didn't know the county had appointed a woman would read it for themselves, and she imagined there might be the odd discussion about it over at the bakery, the bar and every other place in town.

Meanwhile, after nine days in Bear Paw and seven on the job, she'd suddenly found herself in charge of the department now that Mitch was on sick leave. Not that she had to worry about managing staff—she was the deputy and she usually did what she told herself to do, and police-wise, there was no one else at the moment until the county made another appointment. Judy Sharp ran the office the way she'd done for years, and what she didn't know about the town and the department wasn't worth knowing.

"Compared to Afghanistan and a year in Detroit, Sheriff, Bear Paw's a walk in the park."

"There are snipers and unexploded mines here, too, Ralston," Mitch said, his tone serious. "Only they have different guises from what you're used to. Don't get sloppy thinking nothing happens here."

"No, sir," she said, trying hard not to roll her eyes as she glanced up and down a virtually empty street. The only action she could see was a squirrel holding a possibly stolen acorn and running up a tree with it.

"And, Ralston, you've been thrown in at the deep end, so if anyone gives you a hard time, you let me know."

I don't think so. She liked Mitch. He was one of the good guys—the complete opposite of the men her mother, Lexie, had been attracted to. Lexie had introduced a variety of men into their lives, and their legacy had stayed on long after their departure. Part of her appreciated Mitch's concern for her, but she'd been looking after herself for a very long time, and she wasn't going to start depending on anyone now.

"I'm a big girl, Sheriff, and I'll be just fine. You go back to watching daytime TV." Laughing, she cut the call on his outraged expletive.

She spent the first couple of hours of the day trying to clear paperwork. Her only interruptions were a tourist needing a police report for an insurance claim after she'd lost her wedding ring in the campground shower house and Peter Wengham, an intellectually disabled teen who'd gotten separated from his independent living skills class. He'd come to the station because he was lost.

Tara made a couple of calls and located the class and Peter's mother. "Come on, buddy, I'll take you back."

The boy grinned at her. "You've got boobs."

"I have, and I'm a police officer," she said, thinking that men with far greater IQs had made the same remark, only theirs had intended offense. If she had testicles, the uniform alone would give her respect, but because she had a set of double Ds, too many men underestimated her and tried something. They always regretted it.

"I like boobs," Peter said, his cheeks pinking.

She tried not to smile at his pubescent wonder. "Most men do, Peter. It's fine to think in your head that you like boobs, but you don't say it out loud because it can upset women."

"My mom says that."

She smiled. "And your mom's right."

He followed her to the patrol car and got inside, his fingers running over the dash and his eyes wide at the console buttons and lights. "Cool. Turn on the siren?"

Tara wasn't used to police work like this. In Detroit, the kids that ended up in her patrol car had usually been picked up for graffiti, breaking and entering, drug use or motor vehicle theft. She opened her mouth, ready to say, *Keep your hands by your sides*, but instead she closed it.

New job, new procedures. Could she break procedure and let the siren whoop for two beats? Her heart rate picked up at the thought.

"What's this?" Peter pointed to the dash, his round face alight with interest and the siren forgotten.

"It's the radar unit. It tells me how fast someone's traveling."

Peter kept up a barrage of questions that matched the inquisitive interest of a four-year-old, and over the course of the short journey she named almost everything in the vehicle from the mobile data terminal to the spotlight arm. How hard was life with a disabled kid? Her mother had struggled to raise her, and she'd been able to dress herself, cook and get to school all on her own. Truth be told, she'd raised herself.

She pushed away the sadness that threatened to sneak in whenever she thought about that and instead concentrated on the job at hand like she always did. She enjoyed the order of things, and most work tasks could be completed in full without the messy or unfinished business that tagged the rest of her life.

Parking in front of the community center, where the daily living skills class had walked to from the grocery store, she delivered Peter to his group. They were learning how to cook eggs, but everyone seemed far more interested in Tara's gun, her badge and her favorite color than how to heat a pan. If she'd thought Peter had asked a lot of questions, he had nothing on a group of eight. A jittery sensation buzzed in her chest, and she made a hasty retreat back to her patrol car.

She leaned against it, sucking in a few long, slow deep breaths. Had she really signed on for this? It had seemed like a good idea when she'd seen the advertisement for the job. When the interview panel had asked her why she wanted to work here, she'd said confidently that she was more than ready for a change and was seeking a slower pace. Only small-town policing was proving to be very different from what she'd imagined. She just wanted to lock up offenders and keep the peace. She didn't ever want to answer questions about herself.

As she clicked her seat belt into place, her stomach rumbled loudly, reminding her it was time for lunch. Before she could go to the Big Foot diner, though, she needed to do a town patrol. This would include a drive past Mitch's house, otherwise he'd be texting her and asking what was happening. The man had no clue how to relax.

And you do?

Years of structure in the forces didn't allow for relaxation. In a war zone, a soldier, like a cop, was on duty even when he or she technically wasn't. Modern warfare meant snipers were just as likely to kill soldiers on R & R as they were those out in the field. She immediately reminded herself she was in Bear Paw, the gopher capital of Montana, where there hadn't been a murder in thirty-five years and people didn't lock their doors unless they had something to hide.

Why are we here again? The quiet voice that questioned her decision to relocate to Bear Paw was gaining volume with each passing day. *It's so damn quiet.* She refused to answer and instead cruised up and down the quiet streets of her newly adopted town.

Bear Paw was basically one mile long by one and a half miles wide. She'd read in her orientation handbook that it had sprung up when the most northern railroad in the country had come through in 1888. The distinctive concrete grain elevators dominated the town where no other building was more than two stories high, and the closer the street was to the railroad yards, the older the housing.

The mellow early June sunshine warmed her through the windshield as she made her way up and down the numbered streets and avenues until she was in the newer part of town. *New* was a relative term. The houses were twenty years old, and the area backed onto the steep ridge of the creek, which lay way below. Here the houses were a combination of brick and clapboard, and they had neat gardens with the obligatory blue spruce growing in the front yard and a lilac tree where the front path joined the sidewalk. The trees were in stark contrast to older parts of town where rusted-out vehicles rather than concrete gnomes and ceramic frogs featured. Tara was familiar with "sculptures" hewn from the fine color of rust and decorated with tall grass. As a kid, they'd been her play spaces.

Here in the newer part of town there was no view of industry, just the vista of the country club, and farther out across the grassy plains, the silhouette of the majestic Rocky Mountains. She reached a dead end, although a very faded sign proclaimed more land was for sale. Bear Paw wasn't growing, but then again, it had missed the bubble and bust of the non-prime housing debacle. Executing a U-turn, she was tempted to text Mitch and tell him all the criminals and troublemakers were obviously taking an early lunch.

As she signaled and took a left turn, something flickered in her peripheral vision. She immediately tensed, slowed and turned her head toward the movement, her eyes quickly taking in the scene. An old truck with a swinging license plate was parked in the driveway of a large house with a well-maintained garden, and a pair of legs stuck out of a basement window. Legs clad in rust-colored trousers that were swinging widely as they shimmied over the windowsill.

Don't get sloppy, Ralston, thinking nothing happens here.

Yes! Finally, some action. She was out of the patrol car in an instant, her booted feet pounding across the thick and spongy lawn before she threw herself down on the ground and grabbed two ankles with a vice-like grip. "Stop. Police."

———

ETHAN Langworthy, PhD, felt the firm grip of fingers biting into his ankles and stilled. It was turning out to be a hell of a birthday, and it was only twelve noon. For the hundredth time, he berated himself for not telling the German backpacker who'd bunked in his spare room last night not to lock the doors when he'd left to catch the train out of town. Ethan never locked his house, so it had been a shock to arrive home from the library for lunch and find the doors and almost all the windows bolted. Those Germans were nothing if not efficient.

The small basement window was the only one that Jürgen had missed closing, and although Ethan wasn't a big and burly guy, he wasn't small, either, and he barely fit through the tiny space. Now, along with the fingers digging into his skin, came the pain of the windowsill cutting into his belly. Basically, it was pain all around, given he'd hit his head on the raised sash when he'd tried to push through. He was still seeing silver spots from that slam, but even so, he'd swear he just heard a voice say, *Stop. Police.*

It was unlikely. In fact, it was far more likely to be the bored Aitken twins joking around. "Ha-ha. Very funny, guys."

"Move yourself back onto the lawn, now." The voice sounded feminine, but then again, the twins' voices did tend to go up and down with the vagaries of puberty. He remembered that excruciating time only too well. Late to the puberty party, he'd been short and weedy at fifteen with his voice squeaking and cracking at inopportune times. It had firmly established his nerd status—one that had dogged him all through school. Who was he kidding? A part of him was still dogged by it, only he'd turned it into a profession.

"Guys, cut the crap."

The hands didn't move.

"Now," he added in his best authoritative voice, which always silenced the pleasers but the naughty kids mostly ignored.

Suddenly, his body jerked back as his legs were tugged hard and his belly scraped roughly over the sill in a jag of pain. "Jesus. Let go of me."

"And let you disappear into the house? I don't think so," the definitely feminine voice replied before yanking his body backward again.

His hands gripped the sill to stay her momentum, his arms burning in their shoulder sockets. His shirt pulled away from his trousers, and he immediately felt the edge of the window grazing the thin layer of skin stretched tight over his vertebrae.

He gasped at the whipping and stinging sensation, and his fingers lessened their grip. Her pull won out, and with a thud that expelled the breath from his lungs, he landed facedown in the garden bed with his favorite pair of retro cat-eye spectacles cutting into his face.

Before he could suck in a breath or try to move, his arms were suddenly wrenched roughly behind him, and he felt cold metal pressing against his wrists. God damn it, had he just been handcuffed? He tried to move his hands, and that was when his brain finally caught up with events. Fury blew through him, and he rolled fast onto his side. Looking up, he met a pair of blue green eyes, the color of Saint Mary Lake on a clear and sunny day.

"What the hell are you doing?"

The woman's expression was neutral. "My job."

"The hell you are." In one swift movement he'd learned from years of martial arts, he rolled onto his knees and pushed up onto his feet until he was facing her. He registered her momentary look of surprise as it raced across her cheeks.

Despite the severity of her almost puritanical hairstyle that had her golden blond hair pulled straight back off her face and tightly braided, she was stunning. Her dazzling eyes were ringed with licorice black lashes, and her smooth and even skin stretched over ski-jump cheekbones. Not even a utilitarian uniform shirt could disguise that she also had a hell of a rack. She reminded him of an avatar—the perfect visualization of every male gamer's imagination.

Who was she? Her uniform looked real, but that made no sense, because he'd never seen her before and he knew almost everyone in town. Besides, Bear Paw didn't have a female police officer, and he couldn't imagine a woman this attractive wanting to work in law enforcement.

The memory of a conversation that had taken place two weeks ago at Leroy's after a county in-service drifted back to him and gave him a clue about what was going on. Damn it, but those guys at the county never took *no* well, and every time he thought he'd shucked off his past and reinvented himself, something like this happened. Hell, they'd probably been the ones to lock him out of the house and not the pedantic German.

He glanced around, fully expecting to see the guys from

sanitation, EMS and road maintenance pop up from behind the trees and shrubs in the garden, yelling, *You've been pranked*. "Okay, guys," he called out. "You win. Come on, show yourselves."

The woman, who was tall for her sex but the same height as him, wrapped her hand around his arm and in her undeniably throaty voice said, "I'm taking you down to the station."

"Sure you are." He wanted to add *sweetheart*, but let's face it, he wasn't that type of guy. Some guys could say it with confidence and make it sound sexy. When he tried, it came out strangled. Truth be told, whenever he was faced with a truly beautiful woman, his mind generally went to mush. "Look, I know this is all part of my birthday roasting and the guys from the county hired you and sent you here to humiliate me because I said I didn't want a stripper for my thirtieth birthday. Mission accomplished. Consider your job done, and please return the uniform before you leave town."

"I can assure you this is no joke," she said, her voice dropping to a register that would snap freeze peas, trees and everything in its path. "I'm an officer of the law, and you're under arrest for breaking and entering. You have the right to remain silent. If you do say anything, what you say can be used against you in a court—"

"This isn't a Juilliard audition." Just his luck to get the wannabe-serious-actress stripper. "I know the guys are late and all this fine acting is going to waste, so I tell you what? How about you take a photo of me handcuffed and pussy whipped, which is all the guys want to see anyway, and then you can finish up early and get a jump on the long drive back to Great Falls."

She tapped the black box on her shirt. "All of this is being videoed."

What? It was one thing for the guys to use a photo to have some fun on Twitter, but a video was the next level, and he was putting a stop to it now. "Here's the thing. I don't need the lap dance or anything else they've paid for. I'll throw in an extra hundred for the footage. You can't get fairer than that."

Her beautiful face hardened to granite. "Walk. To. The. Car."

He sighed. She was determined to play this thing out to the

end. Well, tough. He'd just about reached his limit of what he was prepared to put up with in the indignity stakes. He'd drawn that line in the sand in middle school when Rudy Baker had pantsed him. She was mighty close to hitting that line. He wondered if the stripper spent time working as a dominatrix, because being pushed facedown in the garden bed was in his mind way over the top of what the guys would have intended as payback for him not giving them the party they wanted for his birthday. Fuck it. He was sick of this. Where the hell was everyone anyway?

With no movement in the garden, he turned to face the street, and the first thing he saw was the Bear Paw patrol vehicle. His stomach lurched, uncertain whether to rise to his throat or fall to his feet. Holy crap. The guys might have "borrowed" a spare uniform, but they sure as hell wouldn't have been able to use the car. This woman really was a cop, and somehow in the deluge that was his post-vacation e-mail inbox, he'd missed the city hall memo.

The fact he had right on his side and she'd jumped the gun arresting him on his own property didn't lessen the fact that he, the county's librarian, IT guy and equal opportunity officer, had just accused the newest member of the police force of being a sex worker.

———

"I got your text," Judy said as she walked back into the station waving a brown paper sack from the Big Foot diner.

Tara glanced up from her paperwork, pleased to see the older woman. Judy had been out for lunch when she'd brought the perp back to the station and placed him in the holding cell. From the moment he'd seen the patrol vehicle, he'd gone virtually silent, which had pleased her because she'd had more than enough of his crass comments about her being a stripper.

In the rearview mirror on the short ride from the crime scene and now from the cell when she'd caught him looking at her, she couldn't help but notice the intelligence in his cinnamon brown eyes. Not that criminals couldn't be intelligent. Heck, there were some brilliant crimes pulled off by masterminds, but this guy had been attempting petty theft in broad daylight, which wasn't so masterful. Even so, Tara had an uneasy feeling scuttling in her veins, which was ridiculous, because although she might second-guess her personal decisions, she never second-guessed work.

Granted, this guy with his rust chinos, blue collared shirt with its fashionable faded floral pattern, suede buck shoes and retro glasses didn't match the profile of the usual home burglar, but neither did he match the profile of most of the men she'd met in town so far. They'd fallen into distinct categories—swaggering cowboys, intense first responders, tradesmen and construction workers and jelly-bellied businessmen. This guy didn't fit the white-trash look, either, although his truck sure did. She quickly reminded herself that thieves came in all shapes, sizes, intelligences and dress codes. This one was moderate height, lithe and surprisingly strong.

"Thanks for buying the sandwich, Judy. He's not saying anything except that he's hungry."

"No problem and it's exciting. It's been a long time since I've had to buy food for a prisoner. The last time was at Christmas when Fred Eisenberg was sleeping off a bender." She dropped the bag beside Tara, her face alight with interest. "So, who've you got?"

Tara sighed and tapped her pen. "I don't know. He's got no ID on him, and the name he's giving me belongs to the owner of the house he was burglarizing."

"So who's he saying he is?"

She double-checked the name she'd written down. "Ethan Langworthy. Do you know the real Ethan Langworthy? He's not answering his cell."

"Sure do, and this guy's gotta be lying because Eth would be the last guy you'd be locking up." Judy picked up the lunch sack and headed toward the holding cells.

Relieved to hear that bit of information, Tara stood and followed her with the swipe card for the cell. She'd only taken five steps when she heard Judy's laugh—high-pitched, loud and long—echoing down the hallway.

"Yeah, it's hilarious, Judy," she heard the prisoner say, his tone a perfect deadpan. "And a hell of a birthday present. So pass me lunch and then go tell the overzealous officer who I am."

A whoosh of sickening adrenaline shot through her, making every cell shiver with dread. *Oh God. What had she done?*

Forcing herself to keep walking, she went and stood next to Judy, who was now doubled over with laughter and clutching the bars of the cell for support.

"Tara," she spluttered between fits of giggles. "This is the funniest thing that's happened in the department in ten years." Another burst of laughter rocked her. "You've just locked up . . ."—she collapsed in raucous laughter—". . . Bear Paw's librarian for . . ."—she fanned herself with her hand as she tried to suck in a breath in between rafts of hysterical chortling—". . . breaking into his own house."

Please, no. Tara wanted to go back in time to the moment before she'd seen a pair of long legs sticking out of a basement window. To a time before she'd let her own gut be overshadowed by the sheriff's warning that crime was alive and flourishing in Bear Paw. To a time when she wasn't begging for something to happen in this too-quiet town that let her own thoughts get too loud, but flights of fantasy didn't solve a damn thing, and she'd known that since she was twelve. She'd screwed up big-time.

Show no weakness. Despite not wanting to, she found herself raising her gaze to Ethan's, expecting to read triumph and revenge. Instead, she saw relief and something else that was a lot less defined. It involved wariness, but there was an element of warmth to it as well. That shocked her. If she was in his position, she'd be furious and wanting blood.

Judy's laughter slowly subsided, and just as Tara was sliding the swipe card to open the cell door, she noticed Judy had her phone in her hand.

"What are you doing?"

Judy didn't look up, but her fingers flew across the smartphone's keyboard. "Putting this on Twitter."

"No!" she yelled as Ethan's equally emphatic but deeper objection rolled over hers.

Judy looked genuinely surprised at their chagrin. "But it's funny. Besides, Ethan's used to this sort of thing going up on Twitter, aren't you, Eth?"

To the untrained eye, the librarian didn't react to the question, but Tara noticed the almost imperceptible ripple of tension roll through his body. His jaw, which was surprisingly square, stiffened slightly. And then it was gone.

"It's not me I'm worried about, Judy," he said in an even and well-modulated voice that reminded Tara of the soft touch of velvet. "But is it fair to Officer . . . ?" He glanced toward her name badge, which was pinned just above her breast, and then, as if staring at her chest was an offense, he snapped his head away so fast Tara thought she heard a click. "I don't believe you introduced yourself when we met."

His polite apology was laced with irony and rebuke. "Ralston," she offered briskly, wondering if she was going to get written up for her many mistakes in the last hour.

"Yes, Officer Ralston's been overenthusiastic in her upholding of the law in her first week, but if this gets out, you know it's going to make it impossible for her to be taken seriously by the town."

Tara had to stop her mouth from falling open. She couldn't believe after what she'd done to him that he was stepping in to pinch hit for her. No one did that. Ever.

"That's true, but . . ." Judy gave Tara a conflicted look. "This is just too delicious not to spill. It's going to kill me to stay quiet."

I'll kill you if you post it, Tara thought, gearing up to give a warning about confidentiality and risking losing the goodwill of the one person she needed on her side. "The sheriff won't want the department to be seen in a bad light."

"Okay." Judy sighed. "I won't put it on social media."

Her words did little to reassure Tara, because in a town this size, gossip flew around fast anyway. Social media only sped things up by about twelve hours.

Ethan took off his glasses and then, as if he was in pain, rubbed the bridge of his nose before sliding the frames back on his face. "What if I give you a replacement story with a promise that you keep this one completely confidential?"

Judy laughed. "Eth, we already know all of your dumb stuff."

"You only know what happens in Bear Paw."

Judy's eyes sparkled at his quiet and resigned words. "Tell me."

His Adam's apple moved slowly up and down his firm throat. "Last week when I was on vacation and visiting my cousin in Missoula, I was the emergency player on his soccer team."

Judy burst out laughing all over again. "Oh, I can feel this is going to be good." She turned to Tara and by way of explanation said, "Eth's not the most coordinated person when it comes to sports. How many times did you get hit by the ball in Little League?"

Tara clearly remembered how he'd gone from facedown and handcuffed in the dirt to standing on his feet without any assistance. Ball sports may not be his area of expertise, but he was far from uncoordinated.

"Do you want the story?" Ethan asked with the barest hint of heat in his voice.

"Of course I do," Judy said, returning her attention to him.

"I have video footage of me kicking a goal, pulling up my shirt and doing, among other things, a victory airplane lap in front of my bewildered team before the umpire pointed out that I'd kicked it in our goal."

Judy clapped and said to Tara. "Now *that's* a perfect Ethan story." As she hurried off to answer the now ringing telephone, she called back, "E-mail it to me as soon as Tara releases you."

That left Tara alone with the man she'd wrongfully arrested and feeling excruciatingly uncomfortable. She wasn't used to feeling that way, because at work she always knew what she was doing. There were rules. There were protocols. Today, none of those gave her any guidance, and Ethan wasn't helping.

She'd been expecting a complaint from him—one against her for wrongful arrest. She still did, and this video thing just muddied the waters, making her suspicious. None of it made any sense, so she made a preemptive strike.

"I wish to apologize for the misunderstanding, Doctor Langworthy. Where I come from and based on my experience, people don't generally break into their own homes."

"I don't generally break into mine," he said, his tone softly ironic. "I guess it was my lucky day that the one time I got locked out, you were driving past."

He rubbed the light brown short beard stubble on his jaw in a contemplative way and his warm and gentle gaze caught hers. "Now that you're working in Bear Paw, I must remember that the hour between twelve and one is a dangerous time of day."

She had a crazy urge to smile, but she squashed it. This was serious. This was work, and she still hadn't figured him out. "You're free to leave whenever you wish, Doctor Langworthy."

"And here I was thinking how nice it would be to spend the

rest of my birthday in a cell." His lips twitched before his mouth curved into a wry smile.

How had she missed that he had such a friendly mouth?

You were too busy being outraged that he'd called you a stripper.

Oh yeah, there was that.

"Many happy returns, sir."

"Call me Ethan."

"I'm on duty, Doctor Langworthy," she said, retreating behind the badge like she always did with men. With everyone.

"Well, when you're off duty, please call me Ethan." He looked at her expectantly, as if he was thinking she'd say, *And you can call me Tara.*

That wasn't going to happen. Life had taught her to be cautious with people, and she was Officer Ralston until she got to know them. Really know them. She didn't know Ethan Langworthy from Adam. Granted, she'd run a routine check on him and the worst thing she'd discovered was that he'd been issued a speeding ticket four years ago. He'd paid it on time. Still, there were three other levels of checks she could still do to find incriminating evidence.

Feeling discombobulated under the scrutiny of his open and friendly gaze and wanting him to leave, she picked up the bagged lunch Judy had left on the floor when she'd dissolved in laughter. She thrust it at him. "Please enjoy lunch courtesy of the department."

"I'm overwhelmed with the police department's generosity," he said with a smile in his voice as he accepted the bag.

He turned as if he was about to walk past her, and she breathed in the odor of garden mulch and pure soap that emanated from him. Flutters of relief moved through her that he was finally leaving.

He didn't move. "It's my birthday . . ."

What do you want? "So you said, Doctor Langworthy," she said coolly.

"I want you to know that's the reason why I said you were . . ." His gaze fell to the floor before he hauled it back to her face, the wariness back in place. "Why I jumped to conclusions about you and added to the craziness of the last hour."

The genuine regret in his voice was unexpected. "I think we're both guilty of that today."

"We are," he said in his quiet and musical voice, his wariness vanishing. "I've been on vacation, and I didn't know the town had hired a new police officer."

"The 'Welcome to Bear Paw' interview appears in the paper tomorrow."

"Timing," he said wryly.

"Exactly." She didn't know what else to say.

He ran his hand across the back of his neck, as if he was working out what to say next. "Given you're new to town and it's my birthday, you're very welcome to come to Leroy's tonight, which I can promise you is a stripper-free zone." His eyes warmed to the rich color of toffee. "A few of us are getting together for a quiet—and I do stress *quiet*—celebration, and a buddy of mine, Ty Garver, is playing guitar. It's casual and relaxed and it would be an opportunity for you to meet a few people."

Keep a professional distance. "Thank you for the invitation, but with the sheriff on sick leave—"

"Of course," he said hurriedly, as if he didn't want to hear the rest of her explanation. Something flickered in his compelling eyes, and his friendly smile dimmed as he raised the sandwich sack in salute. "I best get back to work and leave you to yours. Good afternoon, Officer."

As he walked away from her, and despite all her misgivings, she had the crazy urge to call out, *Tara.*

Chapter 5

"So, Millie, dear, any nice young men studying medicine with you?" Doris Peterson was at the clinic having the dressing changed on what was a very recalcitrant ulcer on her lower leg.

It was Friday afternoon, almost a week after the wedding, and Millie was coming to the end of her first week back at the clinic. For the last four and half days, she'd been fielding many different versions of the same question from her patients, whether they be her contemporaries, her parents' colleagues or Bear Paw's significant senior population. Everyone was keen to hear if she'd met someone while she was at grad school. "There are some perfectly nice young men, Doris."

Doris sighed. "But not one for you."

Millie shook her head in silent answer as she tried to shift from her mind the picture of a shirtless Will propped up on pillows in her bed eating bacon and eggs. Eating them slowly and savoring each mouthful like it was ambrosia. It was only a short, sharp and quick leap from that delectable visual to her wondering if his mouth savored a woman's mouth in the same slow yet thorough way.

A flash of heat zipped through her from head to toe, and

she swallowed hard, giving herself an imaginary slap before pulling her concentration back to Doris. Five days had passed since she'd lied to Will about having plans and had virtually pushed him out of the guesthouse. The only plan she'd had was to avoid spending any more time with him. This meant she'd stayed hiding in the guesthouse until Bethany had tweeted in the midafternoon, *Aussie doctor has left Bear Paw.* Did the woman have a camera on the city limits sign? Given her next tweet—*Who got lucky last night?*—she fortunately didn't have a camera or a spy in Millie's part of town.

"Doris, you've got some pink skin at the edges, here and here." She indicated with the tip of the dressing forceps.

The older woman peered where she was pointing. "Is that good?"

"It's better than good. It means we're winning and we've got this ulcer on the run."

"We'll run it far out of town," Doris said with relief before countering with, "It's not that I don't like coming in to see Doctor Josh and the other nurses each week . . ."

"But you've got better things to do with your day," Millie said, finishing the dressing. "Make another appointment for next week. Bethany can book you on the clinic bus if you need transportation."

Doris's cheeks pinked up. "Actually, Herb Jeffries has been driving me."

"All Hands Herb?" In her surprise, the nickname for the gropey senior slipped out before she could censor herself.

"Those hands are quite talented, Millie, dear." Doris's eyes twinkled as she patted her on the arm. "What he can do with his thumbs is pure magic, and I hope you find someone with similar skills very soon." She picked up her purse. "I'll keep an eye out for you."

The rushing sound of blood filled Millie's ears and her jaw sagged. She managed to pull it closed and then tried to speak, but nothing came out. As she closed it again, she knew she must look like a flapping trout, but for the love of all that was utterly unfair, Doris, at seventy, was getting more action than she was.

"Thank you," she finally managed to splutter weakly, "but I'm fine." She tacked on hastily, "Really, fine," and instantly regretted it.

Doris gave her a kind but disbelieving smile and another hand pat before walking down the hallway back to reception. Millie swore she heard her muttering something that sounded like *clueless.*

"Millie." Floyd Coulson, the good-humored hospital administrator, strode toward her, his round and florid face wreathed in a smile. "Just thought I'd stop by and see how you're doing."

Why? Last year when she'd worked full-time as an RN at the clinic, Floyd had never taken any notice of her. In fact, he'd taken to walking in the opposite direction whenever he saw her, and he'd completely ignored her repeated requests for a transfer to the ER. Yet, here he was today acting like he cared about her.

"It's Friday and I've survived my first week back at the Bear Paw clinic, so it's all good."

"Excellent. That's just what I want to hear from Bear Paw's future doctor." His voice deepened with sincerity. "We want to offer you the best experience we can."

Huh? She was tempted to hit herself upside the head and clear her hearing, but then everything suddenly lined up. As an RN she'd had little clout, but now, as a medical student and a TRUST—Targeted Rural and Under Served Track—scholar, Floyd was obviously courting her with a view to the future. He was hoping she'd eventually return to Bear Paw as a doctor when she was qualified.

This was an unexpected turn of events, but before she decided to milk it to her advantage, she'd best check that her understanding of the situation was the same as his. "With Josh on his honeymoon, my TRUST rotation can't start until July 1 when he gets back. This month, I'm working as a nurse practitioner in the clinic."

"That's what I wanted to talk to you about." Floyd gave her a fatherly glance. "I know last year you were disappointed not to be working in the ER."

Hope took a tentative soar. "You're giving me nursing shifts in the ER?"

"I think you'll find it's much better than that."

Better than working in the ER? She stared at him, trying to think what could possibly be better than that. "I'm intrigued."

Floyd's pale green eyes creased around the edges. "We

hope you'll be more than just intrigued. Josh's arrival a year ago has had a big impact on the hospital, and we're busier than we've ever been. Over the winter, he set up links with some of the Great Falls specialist physicians, and with the Board's approval, we've started a trial visiting doctor program. So far we have an ob-gyn and a general surgeon, and they stop by once a month for a couple of days for consultations and surgery. We're hoping to expand the program this fall to include an internist with an interest in endocrinology and, given our mini baby boom, a pediatrician."

"Wow, that *is* exciting." As a teen, she'd spent hours of her life commuting to Great Falls and sometimes to Billings to see her endocrinologist. "But how does this affect me?"

He clapped his hands as if heralding great news to a large crowd. "Last year there was an unprecedented number of emergency retrievals, with most of them coming out of Glacier National Park, because tourists seem to get themselves into all sorts of trouble on vacation. Great Falls has a level two trauma center, but it's farther away, so they want to partner with us this summer and base their helicopter here. It's got something to do with what the doctors call the golden hour."

Millie knew all about it. "The sooner a critical patient receives medical care post-trauma, the greater their chance of survival."

"That's it," Floyd said, nodding his agreement. "Anyway, it means that Bear Paw Hospital is doing the emergency retrievals and transfers. You're going to be part of the team starting Monday."

A squeal of delight left her lips, and she had the overwhelming urge to hug the big man. "Thank you so much, it's . . . I . . . I can't believe it. I thought my TRUST rotation was going to be the best part of summer, but this . . ." She still couldn't wrap her head around it.

Floyd shook his head indulgently. "Millie, this *is* your TRUST medical experience."

Her gut took a sharp dive toward her toes as disappointment socked her hard. As a nurse practitioner, she could do this job no problem, but not as a medical student. "Floyd, for it to be my TRUST experience, I need a supervising physician."

"The board knows this, and you have one." Again, Floyd

grinned at her, his face pink with enthusiasm. "I've arranged for that Australian doctor to come work with us. You know, the one who was at the wedding?"

"Will?" His name shot out on a high-pitched squeak as her lungs froze in shock. Her head spun crazily in the exact same way it did whenever her blood sugar plummeted. "Will Bartlett?"

Will, who turned her mind to mush with one smile. Will, who thought she was gay.

"Yes." Floyd hitched up his trousers, which constantly battled against the downward pressure of his belly. "I spoke with him at length at brunch on Sunday, and he's enthusiastic about the job. He said he was especially looking forward to working with you and being your TRUST supervisor." Floyd gave her an expectant look—one that said, *Congratulate me because I've done something amazing for you.* "So, what do you think?"

She stared at him. "I . . . it's . . . I . . ."

Floyd laughed. "It's not often I see you speechless, Millie, so I'm sure glad you're so excited about the opportunity. Rest assured, the hospital board wants to do everything to make your TRUST experience with us a positive one."

Somehow she managed to engage her brain and stutter out her thanks and appreciation. Floyd, happy with her response, walked away, calling over his shoulder that he'd send her an e-mail with all the details but to be ready to meet Dr. Bartlett at eight on Monday morning.

Forcing her wobbly legs to carry her to the treatment room, she sank onto the chair the patients used when they were having blood drawn. She dropped her face into her hands and let out a long, dismal groan. *What a mess.* On paper it was the most incredible opportunity for her, and one she would normally have almost killed to get. It would certainly make some of her fellow medical students in the University of Washington's WWAMI—Washington, Wyoming, Alaska, Montana and Idaho—regional medical program green with envy. Working in retrieval medicine was one big adrenaline ride—a ticking clock, split-second decision-making and a rush that made the Tower of Terror look like a walk in the park.

There was just one problem. One big problem. Why did the supervising physician have to be Will?

Because he's the best.

And there was no disputing that. He had a phenomenal body of knowledge with world-class experience working with the Australian flying doctors, and the fact she had access to all of it was an incredible opportunity.

A slither of logic broke through her shock. *Forget Will. Focus on the amazing teaching opportunity.*

There was just one teensy-tiny problem with that. Her mind tended to melt when she was around him, making the learning conditions less than ideal. Still, she'd be foolish to waste this chance, and she needed to make the most of it. All she had to do was focus totally on the learning and a lot, lot less on the lusting.

She could do that. *Easy. Right.*

Her only reply was a mocking laugh that echoed wildly in her head and was fast followed by, *Now you have to tell him about the gay thing.*

No. A ripple of guilt washed up against her resolute decision not to tell him the truth about her sexuality. She fried it faster than a mosquito landing on a bug zapper. Will's leap to an incorrect conclusion was his problem not hers, and she planned to take advantage of it. As long as he thought her a lesbian, it would hide from him any of her momentary lust lapses. After all, she needed all the help she could get.

Seriously? remnants of her Sunday-school-self asked her in a disappointed tone. *You cannot keep up that pretense for a month or more.*

Oh yes, I can. She didn't have a boyfriend, and the town had long given up on her getting one, so no one was likely to suggest Will as a possible candidate. There was also the added advantage that all the other single women in town would be throwing themselves at Will and they wouldn't even view her as competition. Will was unlikely to ask her if she had a girlfriend, and even if he did, she'd just say no. So nothing had to change—all she had to do was live her life as normal, and neither Will nor the town would be the wiser.

"Millie!" Bethany's strident voice boomed out of the intercom. "Get your ass into gear. Herb Jeffries is waiting to see you. He's complaining of pain in his thumb and wrist."

What he can do with his thumbs is pure magic.

Millie choked on her incoming breath, knowing immediately why Herb had that particular injury and wishing she didn't. At least working with Will would save her from sex-obsessed septuagenarians.

It won't save you from sex-obsessed thoughts about Will.
Word.

MILLIE had strapped Herb's wrist and had found herself blushing furiously while she reluctantly answered his questions on which vibrator might replicate his special skills to give the inflammation of his tendon time to subside. It wasn't a conversation she'd ever expected to have with a patient, let alone a man in his twilight years, and it bit that he knew more about the silicone devices than she did. He'd given her a similar look to the one Doris had used, inferring that despite being in her twenties, she was the old and out-of-touch person in the conversation.

She'd responded tartly that if he didn't want a frozen thumb he'd best follow her treatment instructions, which included ice, splinting and ibuprofen. Locking the clinic behind him, she breathed a sigh of relief he was the final patient of the day and the weekend was officially starting. She tested her blood sugar, grabbed her tote bag and walked over to Leroy's.

Even before she stepped inside the low, squat building, the aroma of hot fat and fish hit her nostrils, making her smile. Nothing said Friday more than a fish fry, and Leroy's did it to perfection. Friday nights at the bar were a tradition for her whenever she was in town, and she pushed open the door, ready to kick off her weekend.

"Millie!" The guys at the pool table raised their beers in her direction. "We're racking up. Wanna game?"

"I've gotta eat first, but after that, you're on." She walked up to the bar. "Hi, Shane. One fish fry and a diet soda, please. Is the kitchen running on time?"

The bartender tapped the order into the computer. "Sure is, Millie. You go sit and I'll find you."

"Thanks." Knowing by heart the carbs in the meal, she bolused insulin in preparation, shoved her pump into her bra and wandered over to the small stage where Ty Garver and Ethan Langworthy were fiddling with amplifiers. Ty often performed on a Friday if he wasn't busy with ranch work, and June was his quieter month, wedged firmly between the frenetic spring calving, branding and trailing of cows and the July haying. "Hi, guys. How's your week been?"

Ty gave her a quick nod, and she immediately regretted the question. Less than a week ago, he'd watched the woman he'd loved for years marry someone else and kill any lingering hopes he may have harbored that the marriage wouldn't come to pass. "Sorry, Ty, I didn't think."

"On a happier note," Ty said, tuning his guitar, "Eth got even more fame with some incriminating footage on YouTube. He kicked a goal for the opposing team in soccer."

She stared at her good friend, the mild-mannered, bespectacled librarian and computer geek. During her years of wild summers, he'd always kept an eye out for her, and he'd been the one to call 911 on the night her life changed. Eth had a lot of great qualities, but ball sports weren't one of them.

Laughter bubbled up in her chest. "Soccer, Eth? Seriously? Had you been drinking?"

"You know me. I live to entertain," he said quickly. "Are you . . ."

His voice trailed off, and Millie turned, following his gaze, which was fixed on the door. Tara Ralston, the new policewoman, strode into Leroy's, her long legs clad in slim-fit jeans and her well-endowed chest covered in a rainforest green sleeveless silk shell. The color was a perfect match for her blond hair, which, although she was out of uniform, was still braided just as tightly.

Millie wasn't surprised Ethan had looked—the woman was beautiful in a take-no-prisoners kind of way. The thought crossed her mind that if Tara Ralston and Will Bartlett ever got together, they'd create beautiful babies who'd grow into traffic-stopping adults.

She clicked her fingers in front of his face. "Earth to Eth."

He gave a sheepish look. "Sorry, what were you saying?"

She laughed. "You've got it bad, buddy." *And I totally understand.* "You were the one who was talking."

Ty slapped him on the back. "She'd freeze your balls off with one glance from those glacier green eyes, pal. Come on, we've got a set to play."

"Millie," Shane called out, holding her plate of food aloft and pointing to a table.

"Catch you guys later." She made her way over to the table and sat down just as the microphone threw Ethan's well-modulated voice around the room. "Who's got Friday on their mind?"

Ty played a riff.

The gathering crowd whistled and hooted, and Ethan picked up his instrument. "Let's do this."

The electrifying sound of cello and guitar burst into the air—the music of a Pink Floyd cover raining down, and the expectant crowd erupted. As Millie bit into her fish, she was once again amazed at how two of the nicest guys she'd ever met could play such badass music.

While she ate, she noticed Tara was standing off to the side of the bar slightly apart from the rest of the relaxed Friday patrons. Millie hadn't actually been introduced to her, but the woman looked so tightly strung and emanated waves of "I'm a cop, don't step out of line" that she doubted anyone, male or female, would dare approach her. Bear Paw wasn't used to unfriendly cops, or female ones, for that matter.

Wanting to be friendly and show some solidarity from one young woman to another, she stood up and waved in Tara's direction, hoping to catch her attention. At that precise moment, the police officer leaned in toward Shane, who appeared to be asking her a question. A guy a little farther down the bar turned, putting him in her direct line of vision.

Her hand faulted, turning the wave into a jerky Saint Vitus' dance as her entire blood supply dropped to her feet. Will Bartlett, who was not even supposed to be in Bear Paw until Monday, had a friendly smile on his face and was waving right back at her.

Her mouth dried, her tongue thickened and her eyes fused to the image of him walking toward her. Light chinos moved across his thighs, and his white and blue polo shirt clung to the musculature of his chest, the royal blue shade lightening his dark eyes. Casually dressed Will was as jaw-dropping as formally dressed Will. Why was she even surprised? Half naked or fully clothed, he had the same effect on her—an effect she had to get a handle on. Hell, now he was her boss, she had to crush it flat like the compactor did to the cars at the dump.

"G'day, Millie." His intriguing accent swirled around her. "How's it going?"

She gave him a weak smile as she willed her heart to pump some blood back to her head so she could get her brain and tongue to coordinate. "Great." It came out low and husky instead of the upbeat she'd aimed for.

His head tilted as he set down his plate and beer. "Have you come down with a summer cold?"

She shook her head and cleared her throat before taking another shot at sounding normal. "No."

If he'd noticed the rising inflection that ended on a cracked squeak, he didn't comment on it as he sat down. "Good to hear."

He flashed her that smile again, and she worked at blocking the blissful sigh that always rolled through her.

"Thanks for inviting me over, Millie. It's always nicer to eat with a friend than on your own."

We're friends? "Right." She plunged her fork into her fish. "Yes. Sure." *Any chance we can string more than one word together?*

He gave her an odd look before glancing at the section of the bar where he'd been sitting. His eyes landed on Tara and instantly widened in the exact same way as every other man's in the bar had done when they noticed her. He turned back to Millie with a silly grin on his face. "You weren't waving at me, were you?"

It took her a second to decode his expression, and then surprise whooshed through her. *Duh, he thinks you're hitting on Tara.*

This is perfect. You have to work with him and the only way to survive that is for him to think you're gay. Just play along. "Ah, no, I wasn't waving at you. Sorry." At least that part was the truth.

His face took on a hint of concern. "Do you really think you have a shot with her?"

A spurt of indignation ran up her spine fast and hot. Sure, Tara was the female equivalent of Will—blessed with a genetic cocktail of facial symmetry that cast lesser mortals like herself in the shade. And straight or gay, Tara may not notice her, but the fact that Will thought this was yet another insult on a growing pile. First, he'd never flirted with her like he did with just about every other woman he met, then he'd assumed she was gay without any real evidence and now he was saying she couldn't pull any tail . . . if that's even what a gay woman would think. God, this was harder than she thought it would be.

And yes, given her track record with men, she probably couldn't get a gorgeous woman to notice her, but jeez, that wasn't the point! She lifted her gaze to his, her chin jutting tight and sharp. "Are you saying I'm not good enough for her?"

"No." His shoulders stiffened and he looked insulted that she'd suggested it. "Of course I'm not, it's just . . ." He took a healthy gulp of beer.

"What?" She didn't care that her question was making him uncomfortable.

His long fingers toyed with the coaster, spinning it between his thumb and forefinger. "It's just . . ." His voice took on a gentle and kindly tone. "She doesn't look gay."

But you think I do? The kernel of hurt that he'd sown in her at the wedding cracked open. "Will, you can't always tell from one glance."

"I guess." He looked toward Tara again and back at Millie. "Is she gay?"

No clue. Probably not.

You can't say that. You have to act like you're interested in her.

Sweat pooled on her palms. "She might be. You came over before I could talk to her and . . ." *And what?* She toyed with her salad. What would a lesbian say? ". . . um, gauge the vibe."

"Look at you, all nervous and rattled," he said with an indulgent smile.

You have no idea. Drama class had never been a strong subject of hers, and Mrs. Baugh, her long-suffering teacher, had eventually assigned her to set painting.

"Let's just find out," he said.

"Find out what?" She pulled her mind back fast from high school memories.

"Find out if she's the one for you." He pushed back his chair.

No! She shot out her hand, fear and anxiety making her palm grip his warm, wide forearm like a vice. "What are you doing?" she hissed. "You can't just go over and ask her if she's gay."

His sapphire eyes darkened to navy and he sat down. "Give me a little credit, Millie. I know I'm not experienced with the whole gay dating thing, but I *am* experienced in dating. If I invite her over, we can shoot the breeze over a variety of topics and you can see if there's any interest or spark."

She glanced at Tara and back at Will, wondering why he was so keen to make this happen, and then understanding dawned. "You mean so *you* could see if she has any interest in you."

"Nah. She's not my type."

Millie snorted. "What's that expression you sometimes say? Pull the other one, it's made of rubber?"

He laughed, his face creasing into familiar, faithful and often-used lines. She could watch him smile 24-7. Watch how the scar on his chin danced, how his teeth appeared whiter than other people's against his dusky skin and how his smile carved into his stubble-strewn cheeks. The rumble of his laughter faded, and the brackets around his mouth suddenly smoothed out. For the first time, she noticed he had some permanent lines etched in deeply around his eyes.

He leaned his forearms on the table and laced his fingers. "I'm serious, Millie. I'm not in competition with you here. I'm happy to be an extra person in the conversation while you see if she bats for your team and if she's interested." He raised his glass to her, his handsome face filled with camaraderie. "Consider me your wingman."

Her wingman? Good grief, he was deadly serious. Why was this happening? Pretending to be a non-dating lesbian was supposed to have been easy—identical, even, to her normal state of being a non-dating heterosexual. She was fast coming around to believing she'd been cursed. It was the only answer she could come up with to explain why the guy she was ridiculously attracted to thought she was gay and now wanted to set her up on a date. Oh yeah. Her life just kept getting better and better.

Her stomach cramped as all the permutations and combinations of his offer hit her. If she didn't take him up on his suggestion, she'd look bitchy, but it would save her from the risk of the town finding out about her deception. She really didn't want to join Ethan as Bear Paw's number one source of amusement. On the other hand, if she did take Will up on his offer, it would help her keep up the necessary protective charade. After all, he knew she'd tried to get Tara's attention, so she couldn't hide from that.

The cogs of her mind went into overdrive. Here in the bar, her talking to Tara and Will wouldn't raise an eyebrow, but it did mean she was accepting his offer of being her wingman. This would unwittingly make Will think she was happy for his help again. Was he going to spend the entire summer pointing out potential dates for her? Oh God. Just the idea of it threatened to send her into therapy for years to come.

Perhaps during the conversation, she could suggest she and Tara get coffee sometime, and hopefully she'd say yes. After all, Tara was new to Bear Paw and didn't know many people, and if Will knew they were catching up in the future, he wouldn't be suggesting other dates. It might just work.

She sent up a general apology to all the LGBT people she was probably inadvertently offending by doing this. "Okay, but let me invite her over. I don't need you dazzling her with your beauty."

He rolled his eyes and then his gaze fell to her breasts. Her nipples instantly tightened and tingled before launching lust bombs, which detonated with fizzes and booms all around the rest of her body. *No, this isn't happening.* But it was, and it took all her control not to cross her arms over her chest.

When Will finally spoke, his words came out raspy. "Is that your phone in your bra?" He cleared his throat. "It's giving you a lopsided look."

It's my pump. "I'll move it." She delved into her tote bag, mostly to hide her now burning cheeks, but if she was pretending to pick up Tara, she had to pretend to take as much interest in how she looked as Will was doing. Her fingers passed over the bag of fruit snacks, blood sugar test sticks, thirty discarded tissues with a dot of blood on them, a pen she knew didn't work, a tape measure, because you never knew when you might need one, a notepad, her Bozeman bus pass, a juice box, her phone, spare batteries for her pump and an insulin pen, until finally she found her lip gloss. She swiped some on and then finger-combed her hair.

Will smiled approvingly. "You look good, although next time, probably best to change out of your scrubs."

Ouch. "If we're doing this, I draw the line at fashion advice. I have my mother for that."

He held up his hands in mock surrender, but his expression was sincere. "Sorry, I was only trying to help."

And she knew he was, which complicated things even more. Right now he was being well-meaning and considerate, and that made it really hard to dislike him for not ever noticing her as a woman.

He's allowed to do that.

And on an intellectual level, she understood, but it didn't make it any easier to accept.

You deserve a man who wants you, she said loudly over the top of the traitorous voice that was muttering, *That's never going to happen. At least this crush makes me feel alive.*

The problem was, as much as she wanted to maintain a quiet rage toward him, Will Bartlett was showing he had unexpected depths. Sure, she'd always known he was a great clinician, but his laid-back manner with everyone didn't necessarily hint at him ever getting involved with anything beyond the superficial. Yet right now he was being kind and thoughtful.

"You ready?" he asked, with an encouraging smile.

"Here goes nothing." She stood up and walked over to Tara.

Chapter 6

Will watched Millie walk toward the woman. Despite wanting to help her, he had a crazy urge to grab hold of her, pull her back toward him and say, *Don't do this.* He'd met women like the one Millie was admiring—women who were beautiful to look at but ice-cold to touch. This one had an aura about her that said, *Don't even think about it*, and he'd bet his bottom dollar she was as heterosexual as he was. That was the reason he wanted to pull Millie back. He didn't want her getting hurt.

Really? That's bullshit and you know it.

He drained his beer and signaled to the waitress for another, trying to forget that a few moments ago he'd stared at Millie's breasts with all the grace and style of a horny fifteen-year-old. Worse than that, he'd felt a definite stirring. Man, who was he kidding? He'd gone hard.

It had all started out innocently enough. Despite Millie being in baggy, shapeless scrubs, he'd wanted her to look her best if she was going to give it a shot with the ice queen. Only, he'd gone from noticing the bump of her phone pushing the neckline of her scrubs off-center to imagining the soft and creamy flesh hiding behind the utilitarian blue cotton. Imagining ivory orbs crowned with dusky pink, pert nipples that rose to hard nubs under the brush of his thumb. The flick of his tongue . . .

Shit. It was happening again. He poured himself a glass of cold water and downed it in one gulp. What the hell was wrong with him, and why, when he could have almost any woman he wanted, was his body wanting Millie?

His internal therapist sighed. *We've talked about this, Will. It's the allure of the unobtainable, the fantasy of making her want you, because normally all you have to do is flash that winning smile of yours and women fall into your arms.*

Tough shit, mate—it's never going to happen. Somewhere along the way, the therapist's voice had become Charlie's. *At least you can still get laid, bro.* The memory of his brother's voice held a slight edge. *Quit your whinging, stop being pathetic and go shag a willing woman.*

Guilt ran through him, jagged like the cut of a blunt knife, before settling under his ribs with a dull ache. Charlie was right. Whatever the hell it was that had been dogging him for the last few months, he had to shake it off. He owed it to Charlie. He saw Millie walking back to the table with a bright smile on her face that somehow made her nose look cute. She was giving him the two-thumbs-up sign and the other woman was following her.

"Will, I'd like you to meet Tara. She's our deputy sheriff and new to town just like you."

He rose to his feet and extended his hand, wondering why Millie was introducing him in a way that provided a connection and almost indicated that he was the one interested in dating her. "G'day, Tara. What can I get you to drink?"

She shook her head, her face tight. "I can't stay long."

Okay. He automatically pulled out a chair for her, as Millie had already sat down. "Beer, wine or are you a soda drinker like Millie?"

"A Coke, I guess," she said, accepting the seat but glancing around as if looking for the nearest fire exit.

Oh yeah. This had success written all over it.

The waitress arrived with his beer and took Tara's drink order, and by the time Millie had asked her how she'd found her first week in Bear Paw—*quiet but fine*—if this was her first job as a deputy—*yes*—and where had her last job been—*Detroit*—the Coke had been delivered.

Millie's usually happy expression had dimmed slightly at the litany of closed answers, and Will felt a jolt of annoyance at the policewoman's reticence. If she hadn't wanted to talk, why had she even come over? He caught Tara giving the stage a quick glance, and he tilted his head to Millie as if to say, *Try music*. Millie, obviously not on his ESP wavelength, continued to sip her drink.

"That guy can totally rock the cello," Will said, using his social smile.

"I never knew a cello could be played like that," Tara said with the faintest thaw in her aloof demeanor. She turned away slightly so Will now got a view of the back of her shoulder, and she focused her attention on Millie. "You said you worked at the hospital?"

"I'm an RN during the summer and a medical student the rest of the year. Will's an emergency medicine physician, so if there are any disasters or road traffic accidents, it's probably him you'll be dealing with."

Millie, what the hell? Why was she turning the conversation back to him? "I've only just arrived in town, so Millie's the one who's familiar with the county's disaster and emergency services plan," he countered, hitting the conversation ball straight back the other way.

"The hospital, the EMS and the police department work together well," Millie added. "We have a yearly mock-disaster for training. It's been thirty years since the big flood, but every spring we hold our breath. Mind you, with a disaster like that, MOOSE step in."

"Excuse me?" Tara asked, a stunned look on her face.

Will laughed. "Do they carry people on their backs through the flood waters?"

"They'd be more likely to charge and drown them," Millie said with a grin, the coppery ring around her irises burnishing to gold. "MOOSE is the acronym for Montana Operations and Observation Systems Environment."

The music came to an end, and the guy who'd been playing the cello said, "We're taking a short break, folks."

Tara immediately pushed back her chair. "I have to go."

"Oh, that's a shame." Millie jumped to her feet.

Will rose, too, planning to tell Millie the moment Tara was out of earshot that she'd be better off looking for someone else instead of wasting any more of her time on the arctic heiress.

"Tara, would you like to catch up for a coffee sometime?"

The policewoman's hand paused on her purse, and she stared at Millie for a moment as if she was having trouble interpreting the question.

"I mean . . . that's if you'd like to," Millie rushed on.

Tara ducked her head as if she was embarrassed, and Will held his breath, knowing heartache was an arrow heading straight toward Millie. An arrow he very much wanted to stop.

"That sounds great, Millie," Tara said before marching toward the door. "Call me at the station to set it up."

As Tara disappeared through the exit, Millie turned and faced him. With her eyes open wide and shining, her cheeks red and rosy, and her plump, soft, kissable lips parted slightly in surprise, she glowed from the tip of her curly hair to the bottom of her sensible work shoes.

It was the oddest combination—erotic and innocent and for some reason as sexy as hell. He wanted to be happy for her, he really did, but all he could think about was that he wished he could have been the one to light her up like that.

"I did it," she said breathlessly, sounding totally awestruck.

"You did." He tried to sound enthusiastic. Hell, he even raised his hand for a high five, but as she slapped his palm, he felt the pull and strain in his cheeks as he forced himself to smile.

———

MILLIE wanted to pinch herself. She couldn't believe that she'd pulled it off and Tara had accepted her invitation. She buzzed with the same gut-tingling excitement she got whenever she aced a test.

"You all set for Monday morning?" Will asked, sitting down again and kicking out her chair for her with a lazy flick of his foot. The action said, *Take a seat.*

She sat. At least talking to him about work was safe. "I am. Floyd only told me a couple of hours ago that you're my new TRUST supervisor."

"I was the natural choice."

It was a proud statement, but she guessed he had the right to make it. "Because of your medical experience?"

He gave a wry smile and shook his head. "Because I don't have family or any real connections in Great Falls."

He sounded slightly wistful, and not for the first time she wondered if the man who was always surrounded by women was actually lonely. Was that why he'd wanted to spend last Sunday with her? Why he'd insisted on being her wingman?

"Besides," he continued, "everyone else in the department refused to summer in Bear Paw, and to avoid a ballot, I put up my hand. It's close to the mountains, and I love to hike and rock climb, so I'm looking forward to it."

Once again he surprised her. "The town's pretty quiet."

He shrugged. "I grew up in a small town on the edge of the outback. We had more flies and grains of red dust than we had people, and Murrinwindi makes Bear Paw look positively cosmopolitan. This band, for instance"—he gestured with his hand—"I doubt the pub at home's ever seen an electric cello."

"Not many bars in rural Montana have, either. We're lucky Eth didn't give it up in middle school." She was interested in hearing more about Will's hometown. "So what sort of music did you have at the . . ."—she tried to sound Australian—". . . pub?"

He laughed. "Good try, but you sound British. The Lascelle brothers played a mean amplified didgeridoo."

"What's that?"

"A hollowed-out tube of wood that you play using circular breathing. It's really hard to master, and I spent more time making grunting noises than music, so in fairness to those around me I gave it up."

She smiled, enjoying his self-deprecating storytelling. "My parents banned me from the violin, the clarinet, the trumpet and the drums due to the stress the strangled sounds I made caused the pets."

"Crikey," he said with mock horror. "That's an epic fail in all four orchestra instrument groupings."

"Not to mention the fact the pets came first," she quipped. "I have no innate musicality."

"We share that in common."

His accompanying smile raced across his cheeks and up

into his eyes, which sparkled at her like the white light of the moon dancing on dark water. The slow simmer she'd kept a lid on since he'd walked toward her suddenly boiled over. Everything inside her melted until she felt like she was floating on a wide river of molten desire and all she wanted to do was lean back in her chair and let out a long and blissful sigh.

Leave. Now. The key to surviving working with Will this summer is to do just that. Only see him at work.

"I promised the guys a game of pool," she blurted out as she stood on weak-kneed legs.

"You play pool? Are you any good?"

There were many things about herself she second-guessed, but this wasn't one of them. "Does the pope have an art collection?"

"Good to see you're not hiding behind a facade of humility," he said with a laugh. "And if we're boasting, I'll have you know, I've got my name on a couple of trophies back in Murrinwindi. Fancy a game?"

The thought of watching Will lean over a pool table, with his soft chinos hugging his delectable behind, was more than she could handle. "I—"

A woman screamed.

"Millie," Ethan shouted down the microphone, his left arm pointing in the direction of the distressed woman.

"He's choking," a distraught voice called. "Someone help him. Please."

Millie moved, barely recognizing Ellen Hanson's voice, which was usually so cool and controlled but was now vibrating with fear. She could feel Will immediately behind her.

She reached Wayne Hanson, the overweight car dealer, first. He was seated at a table, and his flabby cheeks were flushed fire-engine red, his two chins wobbling and his stubby fingers gripping his throat as if that would help him breathe. "What happened?"

"He was eating the steak and he laughed at a joke I'd made," Ellen wailed, wringing her hands. "The next minute, he was like this. I hit him on the back, but it didn't work."

She didn't tell the almost hysterical woman that may have forced the meat farther down his trachea. Putting all her weight behind the big guy, she pushed Wayne forward so his chest pressed hard into the edge of the table. She fervently hoped the pressure caused by the momentum would be enough to dislodge the obstruction.

Come on. Fly out of his mouth.

Nothing happened.

Ethan appeared next to them. "Can I help?"

"Grab my medical bag from the black Jeep parked outside," Will said authoritatively as he moved in front of Wayne.

"Wayne, this is Doctor Bartlett," Millie said, giving thanks that Will was here. She'd have struggled to lift Wayne on her own.

"Mate, try and stay calm," Will said in his laconic drawl, putting a hand on Wayne's shoulder.

Unable to talk, Wayne's hugely terrified eyes locked with Will's, as the desperate, guttural sound of his retching left nothing unsaid.

"I'm going to put my arms under yours and force that lump of meat out of your throat." He hauled Wayne to his feet.

"Here." Millie gripped Wayne's shoulders and helped Will turn the heavy and panicking man around so he could grab him from behind.

Will formed a fist with his left hand, pressing it thumb-side in just above Wayne's belly button. Then he covered his fist with his right hand. Pulling his fist upward and inward, his strong arms pressed in hard, increasing the pressure on Wayne's airway to expel the obstruction out of his trachea.

Millie watched Wayne's mouth and held her breath, willing the meat to appear. The only thing that happened was Wayne's lips turned a dusky blue.

Will repeated the maneuver two more times and then he suddenly staggered backward, his brow knitted tightly with worry. "He's down. Where the hell's my bag?"

"Oh my God, Wayne." Ellen sobbed in an uncharacteristic show of emotion, her blond bob swinging wildly.

"We need a sharp knife, a pen or a straw. Now!" Millie yelled to no one in particular as she grappled to support Wayne while Will regained his balance. Together they lowered their patient to the ground.

"We've got two minutes," Will said quietly, his breath warm against her ear.

"Here's your bag," Ethan said, panting as he slid it toward them.

"Call 911," Will said, "and tell the dispatcher we need the MontMedAir helicopter."

Millie reached for the bag, but he batted her hand away. "There's no time for you to try and find what we need in here when I know exactly where everything is. I'll assist you."

She stared at him half terrified, half excited. "You want me to do a tracheotomy?"

"Cricothyroidotomy," he said briskly, one hundred percent the emergency physician. "Put your fingers on the Adam's apple and then go down two and half centimeters—sorry, an inch," he translated from the metric as he threw a pair of gloves at her. "You'll feel a soft spot. That's the cricothyroid membrane."

She snapped on the gloves. With trembling fingers, she followed Will's instructions as he sloshed antiseptic over Wayne's throat before ripping open a scalpel blade.

The ambient noise of the room faded, and all she could hear was the roar of blood in her ears. In what seemed like forever but was probably only about ten seconds, her fingers finally detected the soft spot. "Got it." *I think. I hope.* "Are you sure I should do this?"

"Stabilize the larynx and then cut one inch vertically just through the skin." He passed her the scalpel before grabbing the endotracheal tube from his bag.

She swallowed hard and pressed down, remembering how tough skin actually was, until she felt a loss of resistance. "There's not much blood? Have I gone deep enough?"

"That's normal and good. Means you missed blood vessels." He handed her a pair of hemostat forceps. "Pull the edges apart and check you've totally missed the thyroid gland."

"Okay." She did exactly that.

"Now, puncture the cricothyroid membrane and widen the forceps so I can insert the ET tube."

She pushed down. Nothing happened and panic scuttled through her. "It's not working."

"Use more pressure," Will said calmly. "He's a big guy with a thick neck."

How could he sound so unfazed when she'd never done this before and the clock was ticking down fast. Every second was one more that deprived Wayne of oxygen and brought him closer to a cardiac arrest. If she was the teacher, she'd be grabbing the forceps and taking over.

She tried again and this time felt the shift. A thrill ran through her. "I've got it." She widened the forceps to allow for the ET tube.

"That's one hell of a way to kick off your TRUST experience. Well done." Will gave her a quick smile of acknowledgment before he advanced the ET tube between the jaws of the forceps, carefully avoiding tearing the tube's cuff. "Now hold it there, check his pulse and then secure the ties," he instructed firmly before leaning down to puff air into the tube.

His hair brushed her fingers, and the clean, fresh, masculine smell of him enveloped her. Gripping the tube with her right hand, she sought Wayne's carotid pulse in the deep folds of his neck with her left. Her fingers delved and probed—desperately seeking. *Where the hell was his pulse?* She located his windpipe and slipped her fingers sideways, the thumping of her own heart loud in her ears. Had she been too slow? Had he arrested? The faintest movement beat against the tips of her fingers. "Very weak and thready."

"But there," Will said, relief infusing his words. "I'll take that for a win. Wayne, mate"—he shook the big guy's shoulders—"can you hear me?" The car dealer's eyes stayed closed. "I'll bag him," he said, attaching the small cylinder of oxygen to the bag and valve before connecting it all to the ET tube.

She leaned in close to his ear. "Was I too slow?" she asked softly.

He shook his head firmly.

"I thought he'd come to the moment he got air."

"Not always. He might just need time and oxygen." He gave her a meaningful look. "It's nothing you did or didn't do. You did great. As soon as you've secured the tube, check his pupils and start a HIC chart. There's a torch in the outside pocket."

She understood the acronym for the head-injury chart, but *torch* confused her. "You mean *flashlight*, right?" she asked, querying the Australian word. It seemed highly unlikely Will had an open flame in his bag.

"Is he going to be okay?" Ellen whispered, the soft sound as loud as an explosion in the now deathly quiet bar.

The question jolted Millie. She'd been so engrossed in saving Wayne she'd forgotten there was a crowd of fearful people gathered around them.

"He's still unconscious," Will said, immediately looking up at Ellen, "but the important thing is we've bypassed the obstruction and Wayne's now getting the oxygen he needs." His long, wide fingers rhythmically squeezed the valve bag. "Does your husband have any underlying health issues we should know about, such as diabetes or any cardiac problems?"

"No," Ellen said, shaking her head quickly. "What about the meat? It's still in his throat. How are you going to get it out?"

"My job's to get him to Great Falls where a respiratory physician will remove it."

"And then he'll be fine?" Her questions peppered Will. "Then he'll wake up?"

"I hope so," Will said sincerely but without promising Ellen a thing. "We'll know more when we get him to the hospital."

"Oh, Wayne." The woman who'd so brazenly pinched Will's ass at the wedding sank to her knees beside her prostrate husband. "Honey, open your eyes. Please."

Millie heard the vestiges of long-lost affection in Ellen's now brittle voice. A near-death experience did that to people. Made them remember. Made them think. Made them question things they didn't even know they'd been running from. At least that's what she'd discovered. She suddenly felt desperately sad for the woman.

The deafening roar of the whizzing helicopter's rotors sounded above them, and she realized it was preparing to land at the hospital. Where were the paramedics? They needed an ambulance to transport Wayne the half mile up the road. Thinking of transport, she said, "Ellen needs someone to take her to Great Falls and stay with her."

Sally Walters, one of Ellen's book club friends, stepped forward and put her hand under the anguished woman's elbow. "Honey, I'll take you."

"He'll need . . . pajamas," Ellen said hollowly.

"I'll help you pack a bag," Sally replied.

"The paramedics are here," Ethan called out.

Everything sped up again. Millie took over the bagging while Will and the guys maneuvered Wayne onto the gurney and wheeled him outside to the waiting ambulance, only it wasn't there. The parking lot was empty of all vehicles.

Millie stared at the enormous red and black twin-engine Dauphin helicopter. "How did this happen?"

"Ethan got us to move our cars," someone said.

"Hand over the bagging to the paramedic and get on board," Will instructed before climbing in behind her. She'd flown with him on a plane before, but this was the first time on a chopper. The first time she'd ever been on a chopper.

As she watched the legs of Wayne's gurney neatly collapse so it could be stowed in the helicopter, Will passed her a red headset. "Put this on, because in two minutes, you won't be able to hear a thing."

"Got it." By the time she'd adjusted the headphones over her ears and moved the mic in front of her mouth, the stretcher was inside the mobile intensive care unit. She sat beside her patient and took over the bagging from the paramedic.

Will wrapped the blood pressure cuff around Wayne's arm, slipped the pulse-ox monitor onto his finger, applied the EKG dots and studied the readout. "I'll be happier when I see his blood work," he said as the paramedics closed the doors.

The pilot began talking through his checks, and she heard the rotors start with a low whir that built slowly over a few minutes until they hit a screaming crescendo. The noise was deafening.

"Testing Millie, one, two, three. Can you hear me?"

Her head jerked around at the unexpected intimacy the headphones gave Will's voice. It was deep and mellow, its timbre vibrating through her and startling her with its intensity. Her eyes met his and he smiled at her—a combination of general inquiry and friendliness.

A bubble of lust tried rising to the surface. *Not here! I'm at work.* She forced it back by focusing on squeezing the bag and filling Wayne's lungs with air. "Hearing you loud and clear."

There was a change in the sound of the engines, and excitement as bright as the dancing northern lights on a summer Montanan night flared in the depths of Will's dark eyes. "This is it. Here we go."

The cabin swayed disconcertingly from side to side as the helicopter rose, and then it tilted forward, moving fast and smooth up into the sky. It all happened so quickly, and then they were banking in a sweeping turn as the pilot headed the chopper southeast to Great Falls. She glanced back at Will, who looked like an awestruck six-year-old taking his first helicopter flight instead of a seasoned veteran.

He met her gaze with an enthusiasm that grabbed her and held her tight. "Medicine and flying, Mils," he said, his voice filled with wonder as he leaned forward and checked Wayne's pupils. "It's a combination that never gets old."

Chapter 7

*It's going to be another glorious day in northern Montana.
The perfect weekend weather with clear and sunny skies.*

"There's no *going to be* about it," Will said to the pretty
television newsreader with the immaculately straight, white
teeth. "It already is."

Bright summer sunshine flooded his room at the Glacier
Park Inn, cheerfully blasting through the thin curtains as if
they weren't even there. He couldn't believe it was only 5:45 A.M.
What sort of a crazy place was it where the last light lingered
until ten at night and returned less than eight hours later? And
if that was the case, why the hell didn't the motel have decent
drapes?

The high-pitched squeal of a child snuck in under his door,
immediately followed by the pounding of feet in the hall. The
sun had risen, and with it so had every kid under the age of six.
In celebration of a new day, they were having relay races outside his room. Where were their parents? They'd probably
tipped them out of the room so they could keep sleeping. He
sighed. Good luck with that.

Not that he wasn't used to being up early, but there was

something particularly galling about being up at this hour on a Saturday when it wasn't required and when he could have been having a rare sleep-in. What the hell was he going to do? It was too early even for breakfast, and if the motel restaurant wasn't open until six, then he doubted anywhere else in town would be. The thought of two months of living at the motel sucked at his soul.

The clanking of water pipes shuddered in the walls and was immediately followed by the whooshing sound of water—the guest in the room next door was up and in the shower. He really didn't like being this close to the intimacies of other people's lives. When Floyd Coulson and his boss had asked him to work the summer in Bear Paw, he'd been thinking about the welcome challenges of the job, about Millie and Josh, and about how being in Bear Paw might ease the bouts of soul-sucking loneliness that continued to plague him no matter where he was living.

He hadn't factored into the equation that he'd be living in a motel without his stuff. Not that he had a lot of stuff in his Great Falls apartment, but over the last year he'd collected some books and framed some of his photographs, and slowly a collection of knickknacks he'd purchased from places he'd visited had started to grow. He also had a kitchen and one of those devices that chopped and blended and cooked while he drank wine or worked out or wrote journal articles.

His sister, Lauren, had made a crack about *boys and their toys* when he'd sent her a Snapchat of him and the first meal he'd made. Sure, it was a toy, but at least he was using it and cooking some of his own meals. He hadn't told her that the aromas reminded him of the times Charlie had taken to watching *MasterChef* with great gusto and had spent hours re-creating many of the meals with his typical enthusiasm and *have a go* approach to life.

Being in the motel meant Will wouldn't be cooking for the next two months. He looked up at the only wall decoration—matching framed prints of two spectacular, craggy mountains—and read *Sinopah Mountain and Lone Walker Mountain, Glacier National Park, Montana.* There was a folder of tourist information on the desk, a bible in the nightstand drawer and a flyer about pizza delivery. He suddenly missed his apartment, which, although sparsely furnished and barely decorated, seemed warm and a lot less lonely than the motel.

The image of Millie's untidy bedroom flashed unbidden into his head, and with it the memory of her sitting at the end of the bed with her bare, creamy legs crossed and her curly hair bouncing around her face. He wondered what she was doing. Would she be having coffee with Tara?

Duh! It's 5:50 A.M., you drongo. She's asleep.

All right, smart-ass. I meant, I wonder what she's doing today?

He should have asked her last night on the return flight, which had been relaxed compared with the one out to Great Falls. He'd kept Wayne Hanson sedated on the short flight, and they'd both been busy with checks and ventilating him. Despite Will having thrown Millie in at the deep end, she'd shown she had a knack for emergency medicine. She hadn't panicked or shied away from doing a tricky procedure for the first time; instead she'd taken that leap of faith and stepped out of her comfort zone.

He'd seen the moment the rush of a good save had hit her. He'd recognized the look—the thrill and the euphoria that the addictive, feel-good adrenaline blast always gave. His colleagues had told him they could always tell how close a save it had been by the width of his smile. Last night, Millie's smile had been huge, dimple-filled and enticing.

On the flight back, after her excitement had faded, she'd suddenly morphed into a tour guide, pointing out rivers, breaks, buttes and the Two Medicine fight site. She'd told him about the Blackfeet Nation and the Lewis and Clark Expedition. As the weather conditions had been perfect, Jay, the pilot, had happily hovered over the winding river and the emerald green floodplains so he could get a clear view in the summer-evening light. Like most places where a violent incident had taken place a long time ago, it now looked peacefully benign.

Just like Murrinwindi with its line of shady trees that divided the main street in half and the wide verandas that protected the stores from the sun.

He hauled his mind away fast from that particular thought, distracting himself by checking his messages on his phone.

Floyd Coulson had sent him a work schedule, his boss at Great Falls had attached the pro forma for him to document all the cases he flew out of Bear Paw as part of the golden hour study and Brandon McBain had texted:

> Jenna agreed to second date but said, "Surprise me." How?

Bloody hell, McBain, he thought as he texted back:

> It's summer. Take her to a market, buy fresh produce and a bottle of wine. Have a picnic. Pack bug spray.

As he pressed send, his phone made the sound of a train—the tone he'd assigned to his mother—and a photo appeared of his father windsurfing. The accompanying text said:

> Dad with his birthday present. Saw a guy wave boarding and thought of you. We miss you and hope you're happy. Do you have something planned for the anniversary? I'm worried you'll be on your own. Mum Xx

The anniversary. The day everything had changed for his parents. The day everything had changed for him and for his sister. The day normal had become a foreign state that was heavily fortified with border protections he could never breach.

Hey, dickhead. Charlie's voice crashed into his head. *You gonna sit here all day or race me on that new road bike of yours? You know I'll win.*

Will threw his phone onto the bed, jumped to his feet, found his key fob and headed out to the parking lot to unpack and assemble his bike.

———

MILLIE started the day by having a leisurely breakfast with her parents, and then, as it was gloriously sunny, she'd walked to the library. Her plan was to spend the rest of the day lazing by the pool and reading. The inground pool was her father's pride and joy, and he tended to it lovingly—tinkering with the pump, testing the PH and juggling the combination of salt and acid to get it just right. The crystal clear water sparkled invitingly, but icy experience had taught her that it took another couple of weeks before she considered it warm enough for swimming.

Unable to choose between two novels, she checked out both, and sliding her sunglasses back on her face, she stepped out into the warmth of the day. Thankfully, Dex hadn't made a peep since breakfast, which made her happy, because as important as exercising was, it sometimes played merry hell with her numbers. So many random things she couldn't control, along with the time of the month, could screw her numbers big-time.

A black Jeep with a bike rack on the back and a Canadian canoe on the roof pulled up next to her, and a tinted window wound slowly down. Will's face appeared, his eyes filled with momentary surprise before his mouth curved into an easy, and friendly, smile.

Will, the heartthrob who wanted to be her buddy.

A shimmer spun through her, setting up a throb at the apex of her thighs. *What is it that you don't understand about the word* friend? she rebuked her recalcitrant body.

"G'day, Millie."

"Ah, hey, ah, hi, Will," she said, feeling her cheeks burn. She had to get better at trying to be casual with him. "You look . . ."—*good enough to eat*—". . . like you're ready for an active weekend."

He laughed. "I've already done a thirty-mile bike ride."

"But it's only ten thirty," she said faintly, double-checking her watch.

The left side of his mouth tweaked up wryly. "I got a jump start on the day courtesy of the preschool brigade at the motel. I've also followed the trail of yellow and purple bear paw prints painted along the footpath and walked the town tour."

"There's a town tour?"

"Sure is. It takes you past the schools and churches, out to the hospital and over to the park for the view across the Medicine River ravine. There's even a pop quiz at the end." His eyes danced. "I aced it, and Lorelei at the visitors' center gave me a lollipop." He held up a candy on a stick before opening the car door. "Hop in."

"My mother warned me about men with sweets," she teased

as her head seemed to toss of its own accord. A curl landed in her mouth, sticking to her lips.

What are you doing? You can't flirt with him.

She blew the curl out of her mouth. *Very smooth. I rest my case.*

"What did your mum say about men with picnics?" He indicated a backpack on the backseat. "Shannon packed it for me when I asked her about places to canoe. She suggested I drive out to Medicine Lake."

Trying to keep her eyes off the way his upper arm bulged out of his T-shirt as he pressed his arm on the passenger seat, she focused on being a tourist guide. She'd done the same thing last night when she'd been sitting close to him in the helicopter and he'd been leaning in to look out the window. Every nerve ending had fizzled and popped so hard she'd thought her entire central nervous system would short out.

"Two Medicine Lake? There are three lakes with medicine in the name, but you can only canoe in two of them, unless you want to portage five miles. Remember to take a camera with you, because the views are spectacular."

"I thought you might like to come, too?"

The causal invitation caught her by surprise and instantly sent her into a tailspin. Spending the day with Will in the close confines of a car and a canoe without the distraction of work would be a delicious but dangerous hell. She'd barely survived the patient-less return helicopter flight, and she could just imagine what disasters might ensue if her body went into a lust-fest meltdown at an inopportune moment. She'd probably capsize the canoe.

Don't say no. Her body begged her, already preening. *Please, don't say no.*

"Thank you for the invitation," she said excessively politely, "but I was planning on having a relaxing day."

"What's more relaxing than mucking about in boats?"

"Sitting by the pool."

His cheerful expression lost some of its dazzling wattage. "This weekend is going to be inordinately long without some company, and I could do with some local advice on choosing the lake. Please come."

If he'd given her his devastating *do this for me* smile she'd seen him use on the nurses at work and all the women at the wedding, she could have resisted. Heck, she would have resisted. But the tilt of his head, along with his sincere plea that was tinged with loneliness, had her body softening faster than butter in the sun. She locked her knees against the sensation so she didn't slide onto the sidewalk. If he kept turning to her for company, she knew it was a fast track to insanity. She needed to encourage him to broaden his social horizons.

Opening her mouth with the intention of suggesting to him that Cassidy, Marissa or Megan would all love to go canoeing, she was surprised to hear herself say, "Do you have enough food for two?"

He threw open the car door and patted the passenger seat. "Does a kangaroo jump?"

His accompanying grin totally distracted her from saying *yes*.

———

THE sun shone warm on Will's back as he sat behind Millie in the Canadian canoe. An A-shaped mountain—all jagged edges and steep sides—rose dramatically out of the water, awe-inspiring in its dominance of the lake and taller than Australia's best effort of Mount Kosciuszko. Even so, Millie had told him it wasn't the tallest mountain in the park.

Despite being almost mid-June, patches of snow still clung to its windswept cliffs, and its sheer majesty should have acted as an eyeball and camera magnet, commanding his unwavering and awestruck gaze. The problem was, he couldn't shift his eyes from Millie. Sitting behind her in the canoe was necessary for balance and power, but for concentration, it was a seriously bad idea.

There was something hypnotic about the way she gripped the silver pole—her knuckles gleaming almost translucent—and how she decisively dipped the black tip of the paddle into the water, breaking the smooth, still surface and sending ripples racing back toward him. The swinging movement as she crossed the paddle over her chest made her thick, curly ponytail swish back and forth across her back like the pendulum of a clock. The action was mesmerizing, because every time the ponytail moved over the T-shirt, it revealed the outline of her bra. The place where the straps hooked together stood out like a red, flashing beacon declaring, *I'm the gateway guarding great bounty.*

Gateway? He puffed out a breath. Given the chance, he knew he could flick those hooks open in a heartbeat.

Yeah, but you're never going to get the chance.

"Hey, we've slowed down," Millie called out without glancing back. "You slacking off back there, partner?"

They were on their way back to the launching place after paddling out to a pebbly beach on the opposite side of the lake. They'd had an interesting start when Millie had totally surprised him by insisting on bringing that enormous tote bag she always lugged around. Of all the women he knew, Millie was the one he'd assumed could cope without a handbag.

"Surely you can do without your lip gloss for a few hours."

She'd laughed at him. "I do without lip gloss most of the time. This is all about a good nurse being prepared," she said, shoving it into the ironically named wet bag, which kept things dry.

He didn't get it. "What's in there that's useful for canoeing? Does it double as a flotation device?"

She'd given him a long-suffering sigh. "What if I said I've got bear spray?"

That made him pause. He came from a country that hosted the most venomous snakes, spiders and jellyfish in the world, but he knew how to deal with them. Bears, on the other hand, were totally foreign, and if he was honest, he never wanted to meet one other than in a zoo with him very much on the outside of the enclosure. "Do you?"

A sheepish expression crossed her face. "No, but I probably should have. There's lots of bears around here."

Great. "Your bag weighs a ton. Do you really have to bring it?"

"It goes or I don't."

Her unusually steely tone and total intransigence had surprised him. All too late, he'd realized with some discomfort that she probably had her period and he'd just gone and embarrassed her. "I guess it better come along, then."

Her good humor had instantly returned, and they'd made a pretty good canoe team, squabbling good-naturedly over direction and speed. Even though Millie was a local and Glacier

National Park was her backyard, she seemed to enjoy the scenery as much as he did. She'd certainly spent a lot of time gazing at it.

When they'd arrived at the beach for lunch, Millie had unpacked and inspected every item of food—turkey and salad subs, chocolate chip cookies and apples—as if she was checking for things she wouldn't eat. Given she'd scoffed a handful of nuts, seeds and dried fruit before they'd set out, he figured she was a bit of a health food fiend. Then she'd rummaged through her bag and produced hand sanitizer, a little black purse and some tissues.

"Just as well I brought this along after all," she'd said, tossing the antibacterial gel bottle at him before disappearing into the bushes. Yup, she had her period and he'd felt like a dick.

There were moments when he forgot Millie was a woman— she was just Millie, fun, easy to be with, his mate—and then there were times like right now in the canoe when he couldn't stop thinking about the fact she was every inch a woman.

"Will?"

This time her voice was louder, and she turned around, her copper-and-green-flecked gaze filled with inquiry. "Why have you stopped paddling?"

He immediately grabbed his camera with his free hand, trying to hide the fact he'd been so busy fantasizing about her boobs that he'd forgotten to paddle. "One more photo, okay?"

"Sure." She gazed up at the mountain. "Take as many as you want. The Blackfeet called this area the 'Backbone of the World.'"

"I can see why," he said, taking another photo without really seeing the view. He swung the camera back and focused it on the back of Millie's head. "Hey, Millie."

She turned around, hair flying and cheeks pink from exertion and the sun. "Yes?"

He pressed the shutter button. "Gotcha."

"No fair," she said indignantly. "Delete it. I've probably got my mouth open and my eyes closed."

He peered at the screen and into the face of a woman with a snub nose and an extra-wide mouth. A woman who wasn't pretty in the classical sense, but there was definitely *something* about her. Something he'd missed seeing last summer, but now, this nebulous thing was grabbing him by the throat and taunting him with, *You can look but you can't touch.* "You look great. Like you're having a fun time out on the water."

"Yeah, right." She rolled her eyes. "I bet I look like a lobster after it's been cooked. I should have brought a hat."

"Thought you'd have one in that bag of yours," he said with a grin and immediately ducked as she splashed water at him. "Hey, watch the camera."

"Wimp." Laughing, she faced the front again. "Come on. Get paddling."

"Want to hike up to the falls when we get back?"

"No." Her incredulity at the suggestion rang out over the lake.

"Why not?"

"I've earned the right to lie on the beach and do nothing. You should try it sometime."

Do nothing. He wasn't good at doing nothing. He had two lives to live and no time to waste.

———

"ONE, two, three, lift," Millie said with a grunt as she hefted one end of the deceptively heavy canoe onto the top of the car. "Man, this weighs a ton."

"Almost there," Will said encouragingly.

Millie didn't dare look at the shirtless Will with muscles bunching as he easily lifted his end of the canoe, in case she dropped her end.

"Can you boost it a little bit higher?"

"Trying," she gasped as she pressed up. "My arms are on fire."

"That's good. Now slowly down."

Millie's arms gave out and the canoe landed hard on the roof rack.

"That works, too," Will said, flinching slightly as the canoe bounced.

"Sorry. For such a gentle paddle, my arms are telling me I've got muscles I didn't know I had."

He threw rope over the top and quickly tied some securing knots. "Start lifting weights, because next time we're going white water rafting."

Next time? Dear God, she had to find the man another friend before he assumed she'd join him hang gliding.

If he did, you'd say yes.

And more fool her, she knew that was true. She'd really enjoyed the canoeing. It had been fun, and what wasn't to love about spending a cloudless, sunny day in world-class scenery?

Will's world-class scenery, too, only you won't let us even peek at him, her eyes and the rest of her body whined.

She'd worked out that if she avoided looking directly at him and she focused on everything else around her, her body was relatively well behaved. Late morning, when they'd been cheerfully scrapping over the best way to hold a paddle—in the exact same way as people who'd been friends for years did—she'd finally relaxed around him. There were even moments when she was facing forward in the canoe and not being hammered by the glorious visual that was Will that she believed they could actually manage to be friends. Unlike a lot of doctors she'd met, he didn't take himself too seriously, and his sense of humor was as dry as a glass of Californian chardonnay.

Of course, he had this whole Energizer Bunny thing going on with the need to be constantly physically active. Already today he'd cycled and paddled, and now he was ready for a hike. She was ready to take a nap.

Her stomach rumbled. How could she possibly be hungry after the enormous lunch she'd eaten?

"Drink?" Will grabbed two bottles of water from the car and passed one to her before twisting the top off his.

"Thanks." She'd just gotten hers open when he raised his to his lips and drank it down fast, his throat moving rhythmically up and down.

Her eyes just about bugged out of her head as they sent the visual to her brain. It promptly emptied. Her heart raced, her chest panted and barrages of hot, bone-melting need hit her, making it hard to stay standing upright. So much for not looking at him.

If he does this sort of thing after exercising, we are so going white water rafting. Heck, we're going cycling and running and mountain climbing with him, because he totally has to drink after all of those things.

No, we are not, because I will lose my mind.

Killjoy. The pout of a teenage girl had nothing on the one her body was currently giving her.

"You okay, Millie?" Will's forehead creased in concern. "You look really hot and bothered."

"Oh . . . um . . . I . . . do I?" Her hand automatically fanned her flushed face in embarrassment as she tried to pull her brain out of the vat of arousal it was currently soaking in. She needed it to stop feeling dizzy and start working, stat. "I'm fine."

Will picked up a baseball cap from the back of the Jeep that read, *Grizzly Triathlon, Missoula, Montana.* Of course it did. The man wouldn't have a cap that said anything as slothful as *I'd rather be drinking beer.* "Here." He slapped it on her head, pulling the brim down so low it occluded her vision.

He pointed toward a stand of lodgepole pines. "Let's go sit in the shade while you drink the water."

Sitting next to Will and having him watch her intently wasn't going to help her get her equilibrium back. Besides, she needed to be on her own, because she had to test her blood sugar. "How about me and my water go sit in the shade while you hike up to the falls."

He tilted his head. "You sure?"

"Totally sure." She started walking toward the trees. "I'll be right here napping when you get back."

He gave her a wave and took off at a jog, heading up the well-worn path that most tourists walked and walked slowly.

Her butt hit the soft mass of pine needles, and she checked Dex. Despite the huge lunch she'd eaten, her numbers weren't as high as she expected. Perhaps she wasn't as hopeless around Will as she thought and the dizziness wasn't one hundred percent caused by him.

Nice try, but your blood sugar's not that low.

Still, she needed something to eat to stop it from falling any further.

She reached for her tote bag and groaned, realizing it was still on the backseat of the car, where she'd put it before stowing the canoe. Pushing herself back onto her feet, she walked to the car, placed her fingers under the door handle and pulled. It didn't open. She tried again. Nothing. She tried all four doors and the back—every one of them stayed firmly shut with her tote bag tantalizingly out of reach on the other side of the glass. *Damn it.* Will must have locked the car when she was distracted with that hat.

She slowly jogged to the trailhead, cupped her mouth with her hands and yelled, "Will." She waited in hopeful anticipation for a return call.

It didn't come. Of course it didn't come—the man was probably sprinting the trail. She surveyed the parking lot, hoping to go beg a sugary treat from someone, but the two cars that had been there earlier must have driven out while they'd been loading the canoe. It was just her luck they'd come to a quieter part of the park. If they'd been at Lake McDonald, she'd have been set.

Puffing out a breath, she weighed her options. It wasn't time to panic yet. She could stay here, wait and hope that Will didn't linger at the top soaking in the view or she could go find him and get the key fob. The second option was more appealing, because at least she had some control. She started up the gravel path, walking quickly and calling out his name.

The path was thankfully in shade, because she was feeling hot and a little bit dizzy. With her auburn hair and pale skin, she knew better than to be out in the sun all day without a hat, but the force field that was Will sucked a lot of common sense out of her brain. She drank down the cool water until her thirst was quenched, and then she poured some into her hand and splashed her face. It felt so refreshing that she pulled the cap off her head and dumped the remains of the water over her hair, welcoming the coolness seeping through her. Using the cap as a fan, she kept walking and calling.

A hawk shrieked overhead, and she glanced up into the clear, blue sky, hoping to see it. Her foot hit a tree root and she stumbled. Adrenaline shot through her, making her legs tremble, and she stood, waiting for the shaky feeling to pass. She kept waiting, only it stayed with her.

Crap. She knew this sensation. With a sinking feeling, she pulled Dex out of her waistband just as it started beeping. She'd set the device on vibrate for the day, because she hadn't wanted to have the *I'm a diabetic* conversation with Will, but now her low blood sugar had activated the hypo alert and it was beeping loudly. Forty-two and falling.

Double crap. She needed sugar fast. She frantically looked at the foliage around her. Why was it that on almost every hike she'd ever been on, she came home with red stains on her shirt from brushing against berries she never noticed, but right now when she needed their glucose there were none to be found?

"Wi-il," she yelled, elongating his name and trying to keep the simmer of panic that bubbled in her chest from exploding into a full-scale boil. Freaking out didn't help, but neither did Dex's constant beeping and the accompanying double arrows that kept pointing ominously downward.

Keep going. She pushed forward on rubbery legs as sweat poured off every part of her. Her fingers slackened on the brim of the cap, and she was vaguely aware of it falling from her hand. Nausea joined in with the dizziness, spinning into her and making her gag. She struggled to see as the path danced in front of her, swinging up and dropping away as if it was a roller coaster. Her feet stilled and she squinted, trying to bring everything back into focus.

A tall tree with black bark jumped onto the path up ahead. *No, that can't be right.* She rubbed her eyes, but when she took her hands away, she couldn't remember what she'd been looking at. She wanted to sit down, but her legs wouldn't move and she couldn't work out how to get them to bend so that her butt was on the ground. More than anything, she wanted to sleep.

"Millie."

Will's surprised but pleased voice sounded like it was coming from a long way away. Was he in a tunnel?

"Cool. You decided to come after all."

Will. She could hear herself saying his name in her head, but her jaw seemed disconnected from her mouth, and her tongue felt swollen and wouldn't make the sound.

"Millie!"

Will's voice no longer sounded happy but worried. She felt the pressure of his fingers on her shoulder blades and his thumbs on her clavicle. It almost hurt, and then his handsome face swam in and out of focus as he peered at her. "What's going on? What's that noise?"

Hypo. "Hy." Her tongue wouldn't cooperate, and the edges of her mind clouded with black.

"Hi?" Will sounded puzzled. "Millie, what's wrong?"

"Hy." She swallowed and tried again. "Hypo."

"Hypo as in you're a diabetic hypo?"

She managed a nod.

"Shit."

His expletive sliced through the air with unexpected vehemence, and a thought crossed her fuddled mind that she'd never heard him really swear before. She started to laugh but she didn't know why.

"Millie, I'm picking you up."

"Too heavy," she said as his arms came around her.

"Rubbish."

Her feet left the ground, and suddenly she was pressed up against hot skin and hard muscle, and she wanted to put her arms around his neck but they were too heavy for her to lift. He smelled like peppermint, sunshine and sweat, and his heart pounded hard and fast against her chest in a solid and reassuring beat.

Her head, which had been wobbling like the top scoop of ice cream in a cone, fell gratefully onto his shoulder, resting in the crook of his neck, and she sighed. *You feel amazing.*

"Try and stay with me, Millie."

Her eyes fluttered closed. *I'm not going anywhere.*

Chapter 8

Will ran, sending up a vote of thanks they weren't far from the car and at the same time blocking all unnecessary thoughts like, *Jesus, Millie, why the hell didn't you tell me you were diabetic?* Those could come later when she was capable of stringing a coherent sentence together.

"Millie, I'm putting you down so I can get my bag out of the car. Can you stay upright?"

"Shh-ure," she slurred.

He lowered her down to the ground and propped her up against the side of the car. She listed to the left. "Dex."

He had no clue what she was trying to say, and he didn't have time to find out. She was close to blacking out, and the risk of fitting was way too high. He wrenched open the back of the car, pulled out his medical kit, unzipped a compartment and hauled out an IV set.

The incessant ticking sound of a bomb so very close to exploding echoed in his head. He primed the IV tubing, willing the fluid to fill the plastic fast, because he needed to catch her before the fall. Sliding the tourniquet up her arm, he tightened it with a tug and pressed his fingers against her hot and sweaty skin, feeling for a vein. *Come on, come on, find one.*

Millie stared at the tourniquet groggily with a bewildered expression on her face, and then she was fumbling with her T-shirt. The next minute she'd pulled it up high enough so he caught the swell of the undersides of her breasts, which were covered—if *covered* was really an accurate description—in a sheer lace, mauve-colored bra. "Juz."

He jerked his gaze away from the delectable curves and down to her soft, white belly where her insulin pump and her continuous glucose monitor were inserted into her skin. She'd tucked the handsets of both devices into the elastic waistband of her shorts. The pink one, which was her CGM, was now beeping and flashing in red the word *LOW* and the ominous number twenty-four. "Too late for juice, Millie." It was a miracle she wasn't unconscious right now.

He swept the swab down her arm, steadied the vein with his finger and pierced the skin with the large bore cannula. Millie sucked in a breath through her teeth at the sting and frowned at him as if he was a badly behaved child.

He knew it would have hurt, because the needle was a big sucker, but he didn't have a choice. Fifty percent dextrose solution was as viscous as a thick shake, and he needed all the help he could get to administer it fast and drive up her virtually nonexistent blood sugar. Taping the cannula firmly in place, he connected the drip, hung the bag from the car door and ran it fast to check the line. Millie needed sugar, but she didn't need necrotic skin, which was what would happen if he shoved an ampule of D50 into a pierced vein.

Gripping the enormous plastic syringe, he pinched off the line above the port and inserted the needle, pushing down hard to move the tenacious and sticky gel into the vein. "You're going to feel better really soon."

She was shaking so hard he wasn't sure she'd heard him. Her limbs trembled uncontrollably as each and every cell in her body fought to find the glucose it desperately needed to function. As soon as he'd administered all of the D50, he sat down next to her, throwing his arm around her shoulder. Pulling her close, he tried to absorb some of her violent shakes. Her head lolled and came to rest under his chin.

She smelled of almonds and the fresh, crisp scent of pine needles, and a curl tickled his nose. It seemed the most natural thing in the world to press his face into her hair and breathe in deeply. Her curls cushioned his cheeks, and her scent raced up his nostrils, imprinting itself on his brain.

Whoa! What are you doing? Patient, remember? He reluctantly lifted his head just as her right hand splayed across his chest, the heat of her fingers branding him.

She looked up at him with those unusual-colored eyes of hers with their ring of coppery gold, and he could see her struggling to focus. Two deep creases of concentration etched themselves between her eyes, and a moment later they faded as she smiled.

He'd seen her smile lots of times—ironic smiles, guarded smiles, bemused smiles, teasing smiles and at work the occasional nervous smile—but this one was different. It was free of all restraints, and it broke over her cheery, round cheeks in an open, joyous, deeply dimpled beam. "You're wonderful."

Her husky and breathy words shot into him, firing his blood and arcing it straight to his groin. He gazed down at her, desperate to kiss her. He wanted to capture those pink, plump lips with his and own them. He wanted to trace the place where her top lip, with its enticing peak, joined her lush bottom lip, and then explore it all the way from one side to the other. He wanted to feel her lips open, inviting him in.

A shot of heat fired deep inside him at the thought. He wanted to explore her mouth slowly, millimeter by millimeter—feel the scrape of her teeth, the yielding softness of her cheeks, the raunchy roughness of her tongue, and more than anything, he wanted to be flooded with her sweet and salty taste. He wanted to kiss her until she moaned into his mouth with that guttural, base tone that said, *I want you, too.* He wanted to feel her hands gripping his head so hard that her fingers dug into his scalp, leaving crescent moon marks—branding him as hers. Her legs would wrap around him and she'd haul her body up his chest, her breasts caressing him with her hard, peaked nipples until she was sitting on his lap, her ass gyrating hard against him, and then she'd push him to the ground and kiss him in return.

His breathing kicked up, and his blood, already hot and heavy, pulsed around his body with aching, throbbing need, seeking and demanding satisfaction. He was beyond hard, and hell, he was ready. Ready like he hadn't been in a very long time.

You know you want it so take it. Kiss her.

His head fell forward, lips tingling, his entire body desperate to connect with hers.

Charlie's image rose up sharply in his mind, standing in a doorway with his long arms high above his head and his fingers gripping the doorframe. *Exactly how many times do I have to tell you this, mate? It's never going to happen. She's not that into you. Hell, she's not into you or your gender at all. More importantly, she's barely conscious.*

Charlie shook his head back and forth slowly and meaningfully as if he couldn't believe what his twin was about to do. *It's creepy, bro, seriously creepy. The only reason she thinks you're wonderful is because she's disoriented from lack of sugar and you're her attending doctor.*

Her doctor.

An adrenaline blast shot Will's blood back to his brain, and this time he pulled back from Millie so hard and fast he wrenched his neck. He winced as the stinging, brutal pain burned hot and radiated to his shoulder. It was a metaphorical slap across the face from a woman who wouldn't welcome his advances. Only worse, because to hit on a woman socially was one thing. To hit on a patient was another thing entirely.

First, do no harm. What the hell was wrong with him? Jesus, not once in his career had he come close to doing anything so unethical. In her current hypoglycemic state, Millie was incredibly vulnerable, and he'd been half a second away from kissing her. On a logical level, it didn't make any sense at all. A. She was Millie. B. She was a mate. C. She was gay. It was as if his body had completely separated from his brain, and he wasn't used to it doing that. He always had a very cerebral approach to women—he chose from the many who offered themselves to him, but lately he hadn't been accepting any offers. Was this the problem?

He was in the midst of a long dry spell, and he'd been fine with that right up until now. If not having sex for a few months meant he was fantasizing over Millie and almost jeopardizing his medical license, then he was officially losing his mind. He had to prevent this from ever happening again, and that meant he had to end this self-imposed dry spell and fast. The next will-ing woman he met whom he liked and whose company he enjoyed, he was jumping into bed with her. He hoped he met her really soon.

That's more like it. Charlie's image faded away, and Will was stuck by the irony of Charlie being the one to step in and be moral guardian. It wasn't a role he'd attributed to his brother, who'd pushed the boundaries of what he could get away with every day of his life.

Millie's limbs still trembled against him, although the vio-lent shaking had lessened somewhat. He eased her fingers off his chest. "I have to do a blood sugar check, Millie, okay?"

"Hmm." She moved her head, and he got another face full of coconut-and-almond-scented hair, her springy curls clinging to his stubble as stubbornly as the tentacles of an octopus.

His nostrils flared and he blew the hair away as a zip of arousal tried to wreak havoc. *Millie is a patient. Millie is a mate. Millie is a lesbian. Millie is a lesbian mate, and patient.*

His blood cooled. *There you go. Remember that combina-tion.*

Millie still needed him for support, but he dropped his arm from around her shoulder and let her lean against him as he found the lancet and glucose monitor. "You'll feel a jab." He released the lancet into the side of her fingertip and gently squeezed, watching a red droplet form, staining the white of her skin.

"It better have some sugar in it," Millie said wryly as she struggled to sit up.

Thank God. It was the first full and coherent sentence she'd spoken since he'd found her. The D50 was working. "You coming back to the land of the living?"

"I guess I am." She rubbed her eyes as if she'd been sleep-ing rather than battling a deadly low blood sugar. "What's the number?" she asked as the monitor beeped.

"Seventy-one."

She checked her CGM and then fingered the cannula in her arm. "Dex shows double arrows pointing up, so time to take this baby out."

"No." He shook his head hard as if to emphasize the word. "You were damn near dead five minutes ago and I don't want to risk a rebound hypo."

"I'm the diabetic," she said, her tone defensive and irritable. "If that IV bag is five percent dextrose and you leave it in for too long, I'm going to spike way too high. I already feel like crap without adding that into the mix."

So much for him being wonderful. He knew her grumpiness was part and parcel of the hypo, but he didn't like the glint in her eye that said he was suddenly the bad guy. "What you need is a proper meal. How far away's the closest restaurant?"

She took a moment, as if thinking was still hard. "Just outside the park gates."

"That tiny joint we drove through with the Native American designs painted on the buildings? The one you said was part of the Blackfeet Reservation?" She nodded and he started calculating. "So, it takes what? Twenty-five minutes to drive there?"

"Yes, which is why we need to take the IV out now."

They'd eaten all of the lunch, and he didn't have any snacks in the car. "Do you have any food?"

Her fingers started peeling back the tape around the cannula. "I've got a granola bar in my bag."

"Wait." He realized he was grinding his teeth. "Is your pump still giving you insulin?"

Her gaze was still slightly unfocused and her movements clumsy. "I'll check." She pulled out the pump and fiddled with the settings. "I'll leave it off until we're at the restaurant, so now can you take the drip out?"

"After you've eaten and I've checked your blood sugar again."

"*I'll* test it." She picked up her CGM, fiddled with the settings and checked the screen. "Dex says sixty, so we're heading in the right direction. I usually feel best around one hundred ten." She suddenly lurched to her feet, and her already-pale face drained of all remaining color.

"Bloody hell, Millie." He sprang to his feet and caught her by the waist. She sagged against him, hot, soft and curvy. The thought of hugging her close tempted him more than most things in the last few weeks, but he wasn't letting his body set the agenda again. He set her back from him, still holding her upright but allowing cool air between them.

"Is it at all possible for you to follow any of my advice? You're not ready to stand up."

"I'll be fine," she said, her quivery tone not quite matching up with the words. "I'll sit in the car and eat while you drive us for food."

He wasn't used to patients bargaining with him. "Millie, ten minutes ago you were almost unconscious, and your blood sugar still isn't optimum. That affects your judgment, so how about you let me make the decisions?"

Her soft and pretty mouth flattened into a mulish line. "I've been making decisions about my diabetes for ten years."

Half of him understood her need to be in control of her diabetes, but she'd just scared the living daylights out of him. One minute she was fine, and the next minute she'd been fast heading toward death—just like Charlie—leaving him to deal with everything. Every part of him tensed. If he had to deal, then he wasn't going to negotiate or argue. That could come later when she'd recovered. "I'll change the bag to saline to keep the line open, and you put Dex on the hypo repeat setting," he said tersely, using her nickname for the device. "I want to hear the moment anything changes."

Her eyebrows rose. "How come I never noticed how bossy you are with the patients?"

He swung her up into his arms and dumped her unceremoniously on the passenger seat. "Because I'm only bossy with the difficult ones."

———

MILLIE sat in a booth studying the menu and raised her eyes above the edge of the black folder. "They serve great huckleberry pancakes here," she said conversationally, breaking the thick silence that had descended between them the moment Will had strapped her into the car seat.

He lowered his menu and stared at her, his gaze stern and critical, pretty much like it had been since they'd driven out of the parking lot at Two Medicine.

Oh please, don't give me that look. She huffed out a breath of exasperation, already missing the fun Will. "I only mentioned the pancakes because they're a local treat just like the huckleberry pie. As a Montanan, it's my duty to make sure you taste our delicacies. Of course, I'll be having the grizzly bait."

"The salmon?" he said without a trace of humor. "Sensible

choice." Glancing around, his gaze landed on the waitress and he clicked his fingers. "Miss?"

The waitress walked over, pad in hand and looking ticked off. "Are you ready to order?"

Will gave her a distracted smile. "We'll have the Indian taco to share, the salmon and I'll have the buffalo burger. Can the taco come out straightaway please, because my friend's diabetic and it's important that she eat as soon as possible."

Red flames of anger and betrayal flared and burned behind her eyeballs. *What the hell, Will? What about privacy?*

"Sure." The waitress threw her a sympathetic yet glad-that's-not-me look. "Do . . . you . . . want . . . the . . . soup . . . or . . . the . . . salad?" She spoke slowly and carefully as if having diabetes meant that not only did Millie's pancreas not work but her brain didn't, either.

"The soup," Millie managed to say calmly, although she wanted to hit both the waitress and Will upside the head with the menu. "And I'll have the vegetables with the salmon and a diet soda."

The waitress read back the orders before collecting the menus and retreating to the kitchen. Millie opened her mouth to blast Will about violating her privacy with the waitress when he suddenly folded his arms tightly across his chest and gave her an accusatory look.

"Why didn't you tell me you were a diabetic?"

She folded her arms right back at him. "I tell people on a need-to-know basis."

His chestnut brows hit his hairline. "And you didn't think that going canoeing, where you'd be exercising, counted as"—he made air quotes with his fingers—"a need-to-know situation?" Incredulity dripped off his words.

"That's correct," she said crisply, as if she was in the witness stand and he was the questioning prosecutor.

He made a definite snorting sound. "I think the fact you almost lapsed into unconsciousness is a conclusive argument as to why you *should* have told me."

"What happened today hasn't happened in years." She was still feeling jittery from the severe hypo, and his doctor-knows-best tone got under her skin. He didn't know best. Sure, he knew the theory, but he didn't know what it was like to dance every day on the tightrope that was diabetes, nor did he know the immense effort she put in to staying well. "When you left for the falls, my blood sugar was seventy. If I'd eaten something, then I'd have been fine." Despite her best efforts, the post-hypo wobblies made her voice waver. "Only I couldn't do that because *you* locked my purse in your car."

His head jerked back against the booth as if she'd struck him, and then his shoulders rolled back and his spine straightened. "You're blaming me for the hypo?"

Her throat was thick. "It was an accident."

"It was totally preventable," he ground out in a low and cutting tone. "If you'd told me you were diabetic, I wouldn't have locked the car. Jesus, Millie." He suddenly cleared his throat. "What if I'd decided to stay at the falls longer?"

Millie, this is serious. Millie, we're worried about you.

His anger at her wasn't dissimilar to that of her parents, and old memories washed up against her. The times she'd scared them. The times she'd disappointed them. The constancy of their concern for her despite the fact she now lived a sensible and stable life. She hated the guilt and self-reproach those memories brought up, but most of all she hated that her diabetes meant she was the one who was always expected to say sorry.

She didn't want to be sorry, and she couldn't stop the dismissive teenage shrug of her shoulders. "But you didn't stay longer."

Will's inky eyes widened to huge, dark pools in his tan face. "That's not a defense, Millie. You should have told me and then none of this would have happened. I mean, hell, you should have told me a long time ago. What if you'd had a hypo in the air?"

Her breath caught in her throat. Was he going to go all squirrelly on her and pull her from working with MontMed-Air? It teetered on discrimination, but even so, the thought that he might cite medical grounds and pull her off the team made her both panic and seethe.

Breathe in, breathe out, in, out. Think.

She moved the sugar pourer toward her and added it to the condiment lineup in the middle of the table, as if it marked a battle line between them. *Stay calm. Speak slowly.* "I've flown with you six times, Will, and I've never come even close to having a hypo, because I handle my diabetes. I've been handling it for years, and usually I'm never away from my tote bag. It's my survival kit. In my book, that's a conclusive argument as to why I didn't have to tell you about my diabetes. I'm sure there are things in your life you keep private."

His chiseled jaw stiffened, and he suddenly looked as if he was working really hard at controlling his temper. But he didn't yell or thump the table; instead, he suddenly raised his hands to his stubbled cheeks and rubbed his palms against them. When he dropped his hands away, he looked straight at her. "You scared me."

His quietly spoken words packed a punch of culpability straight to her solar plexus. *I didn't mean to. I didn't want to. I didn't have a choice.* All too clearly she remembered her panic and disorientation on the trail, and she opened her palms outward. "I scared me, too." She licked her dry lips. "Thank you for being there."

"Yeah." The word came out hushed on an exhale, and deep lines creased the edges of his eyes. He looked exhausted, as if he'd been the one fighting the hypo, not her.

She always felt shattered afterward, like a wrung-out rag, which was exactly how she felt now. All she wanted to do was curl up and sleep, but she had to stay awake. She had to eat. She had to monitor her blood sugar until she was sure it had stabilized. It was draining, and on top of struggling to stay awake, she kept getting flashes of memory, only she couldn't tell what was hypo-induced hallucinations and what was real. She remembered Will picking her up on the trail and the burning sting of the IV piercing her skin. After that, things got hazy.

There were definite moments when she'd felt safe, warm and cocooned, but then there was a vibrant memory of Will gazing down at her with naked desire bright in his dark, fathomless eyes. *That* was definitely a hallucination—her sugar-deprived brain spinning pure fantasy. Still, it had been an amazingly wonderful 3-D make-believe, and she planned to revisit it in quiet moments when she was alone with her vibrator. It was as close as she was ever going to get to Will actually wanting her.

The waitress arrived, breaking the strained silence between them, and they concentrated on rearranging the table to make room for the plate of Indian taco. The flat fry bread was heaped with chili, lettuce, tomato, onion, cheddar cheese, sour cream and salsa. Millie tested her blood sugar at the table, because now that Will knew about her diabetes, there was no need for her to go somewhere private like she'd done at lunch.

"What is it?" Will asked, leaning forward.

"All good," she said lightly, not looking at him as she pulled out her insulin pump. Truthfully, her blood sugar was still on the low side of ideal, and she didn't want to give herself too much insulin and have her blood sugar tumble again.

She was in the middle of calculating the carbs and allowing for the fact the sour cream and cheese would slow down the carbs' absorption when Will said, "Err on the side of caution with the insulin."

She glanced up from her pump, and he gave her an earnest and encouraging smile. The entertaining, Energizer Bunny Will, with his friendly, laid-back grin, was nowhere to be seen. In his place was Dr. Bartlett, emergency physician, and he was looking at her with a worried diagnostic gaze, as if he expected her to self-destruct before his eyes at any given moment. It was written clearly on his handsome face that he no longer saw her as Millie the medical student or Millie the RN or even Millie his friend.

She stifled a hysterical laugh that rose in her throat, and she pursed her lips to stop it from breaking free. Never in her wildest dreams had she thought she'd yearn for a time when Will thought about her as Millie, his lesbian friend. No, now she was Millie the diabetic. A dull ache took up residence in her chest, throbbing slowly in a tattoo of loss.

Chapter 9

Ethan closed the library door behind the last stroller as toddler story time, which supposedly finished at eleven thirty, had once again spilled into his lunch break. He didn't mind. If parents took the time to ask his advice on book suggestions for their kids, he wasn't going to say no.

"Tahlee, can you shelve those board books for me, please?" he asked his new but lazy intern as he grabbed a folder off his desk. "I've got a family fun day meeting and then I've got to go to city hall and wrangle with them to release our Ready 2 Read Goes Wild! funding. I'll miss the seniors' bus, so if you need any help, you can get me on my cell."

"A minibus of seniors?" The twenty-year-old rolled her heavily kohled eyes as she inspected her black nail polish for chips. "I think I can cope."

Tahlee had no idea how busy that hour between two and three on a Wednesday afternoon could be or that her lackadaisical work ethic was about to get a thorough workout like it never had before. Doris would want her to find a particular book, but the only details she'd be able to give would be something as vague as *It's about the woman whose husband fought in Vietnam*. Rolf, whose arthritis wouldn't allow him to bend, always found a book he wanted on the lower stacks; Leo Ratzenburger would need help with logging on to the Internet, because he had far too many passwords and a habit of accidentally turning the caps lock button on; and at least three of the rest of the bus crowd would need some reminding on how to use the self-checkout kiosk. Guaranteed, someone will have forgotten their card.

Yup, Tahlee's studied indifference was going to be well and truly frazzled. He smiled at the thought. "I'll bring you back a coffee."

She shrugged. "What evs."

What evs? Had he ever been that disinterested in life? Not even as a teen. His total lack of coolness and his definite nerdiness had meant he'd had dollops of enthusiasm for the specific things he enjoyed and he'd thrown himself into them wholeheartedly. He still did. His self-imposed challenge was that by the end of the summer he'd have helped Tahlee find something that floated her boat and got her involved in the community. Perhaps he could let her loose on the Friends of the Library?

No, those fine people didn't deserve that. He smiled to himself, hatching a plan—the scary women of the Bear Paw book club were another matter entirely.

He cut across the park, making his way toward the Big Foot diner, waving to the moms who'd just left the library and were having a picnic lunch on the grass near the playground. His head was full of plans for the Fourth of July family fun day. It was a chance to showcase the library to the greater community. Not that memberships were down; in fact, with the current Bear Paw baby boom, they were growing steadily, and story and music time was always full, but he wanted to reach the families and teens who really needed the services the library offered.

He wanted to target the families who didn't have a novel in their home. He wanted to introduce the joy of audiobooks to families who found reading hard—after all, who didn't like being read to? He wanted to reach families who lacked access to computers and the Internet and families who needed a place to meet people and expand their world. He was toying with the idea of a father and kids night, because separated fathers often had no clue what to do with their children on access visits.

With ideas bouncing in his head, he found himself inside the diner without really noticing that he'd run up the steps and pushed open the door.

"Hey, Eth. Come join us."

He swung around and couldn't help but see Millie. Everyone could see her—hell, she was probably visible from the Hubble Space Telescope. For some reason, she was wearing vivid berry purple scrubs—the color in stark contrast to her usual more muted greens and blues. She'd risen from the booth seat and was waving at him as if she were taking part in a Mexican wave. Things must be quiet at the hospital if some of the staff had made it over to the diner for lunch.

"You're very bright today," he said, walking toward her.

"The hospital laundry service had a mix-up, which is why I look like an advertisement for grape juice," she said with a smile that wasn't quite as wide as it could be. "Sit with us. You've met Tara?"

His butt had already hit the bench seat before he realized that he wasn't sitting next to someone from the hospital. He hadn't spoken to Tara in several days—not since he'd been released from custody—but he'd seen her from a distance last Friday at Leroy's. He turned to face her and got hit by her beautiful but coolly serious blue green eyes, which stared straight at him. A zap of pure lust rocked him from head to toe.

God, you're absolutely gorgeous. "I . . . yes . . . we've met. Hi again."

The one part of him that always tried to be self-assured around stunning women—the one part that was frequently embarrassed by the rest of him—slapped his palm to his face. *Jeez, can you at least try to be cool.*

"Actually," he said, concentrating extremely hard at being casual, "we . . ." He leaned back, forgetting precisely how close his butt cheeks were to the edge of the bench seat. He suddenly felt air underneath him, and his fingers frantically gripped the edge of the table. No way in hell was he landing on his ass in the diner in front of a group of people who always had a phone and therefore a camera in their hand. Especially not today just as the roasting he'd gotten about the soccer video had died down.

Where the hell was the sticky table that stuck to you like

glue when you needed it? Today he got the one slick with some sort of oil on it, and his fingertips skated across the surface, unable to grip. In a desperate attempt to save himself from bouncing onto the floor, he used his martial arts, upper body strength to throw himself forward. His head hit Tara's shoulder hard—his forehead colliding with her collarbone with a nauseating and bone-cracking thwack.

Tara made a soft gasping sound and instantly recoiled into the booth.

"Sorry." He straightened up but not before her scent had locked on to him, reminding him of the sweet perfume of a bouquet of spring flowers. It was a soft and almost unworldly scent—the total opposite from what he'd expected. Innocence and naïveté didn't match up with an officer of the law.

"You seeing stars, Eth?" Millie asked with a sympathetic *I cannot believe you just did that but I totally get it* look in her eyes. "I'll get you some ice."

He was seeing stars, but he doubted it was from the knock on the head. It didn't matter that Tara wore a uniform shirt buttoned up to the neck, a tie and a name badge; for one brief moment his face had been pressed into the blessed softness of the top of her right breast. Pillow soft. Sheer heaven. He wouldn't forget that in a hurry.

Forget the boobs.

Are you serious? That's as close as we've gotten to any action in a while.

Dude, people are looking.

The fog of arousal vanished under the immediacy of reality. What he needed was containment, not a fuss. Ice meant people would notice he'd done something embarrassing, so he gave his askew glasses a tap with his fingers—viewing life in focus was always a help—and he shot for macho. "I don't need ice, Millie."

"I think you might," Tara said stiffly, her gaze staring distastefully at his forehead. "You've got a lump."

His fingers automatically probed his brow, and he felt the egg-size bump rising under his tips. *Just perfect.*

Millie, who'd cheerfully ignored him, handed him ice cubes wrapped in a cloth. "Here you go. Press it to your forehead for ten minutes. Tara, do you need ice, too?"

"Hey, Eth," Dane Aitken said, phone in hand and raising it toward his face. "Looking good." The phone clicked—the photo would be on Twitter in seconds.

He raised the ice pack in a salute and then turned his back on him. "So, Millie, you working at the first aid tent on the Fourth?"

"I am and—" Her phone started vibrating across the table, and then it emitted the screaming sound of a siren. She jumped to her feet. "Sorry, gotta go. I'll grab a ready-made sandwich, so when my turkey club arrives, Eth, you eat it. Sorry, Tara. Bye."

Millie scooped up her phone and ran to the door, leaving Ethan sitting next to Tara. "And that was the purple flash," he quipped, hoping to elicit a smile.

Her left palm pressed down on the table. "I should go, too."

Leaving before you've eaten the lunch you ordered. Okay, so she definitely didn't want to shoot the breeze with the guy who'd just whacked her with his head. Just like she'd left Leroy's on Friday the moment he'd finished the set, put down his cello and glanced in her direction. He was detecting a trend.

Most guys would try and talk her out of leaving, but he recognized only too well the *I'm not interested in you* vibe. He'd honed his skills detecting that particular vibe in college. At thirty, he was done punching above his weight with beautiful women—it wasn't worth the angst and the emotional put-downs. Sure, he'd like a girlfriend. Heck, he'd love a life partner, kids, a white picket fence, the whole nine yards, but he knew it was never going to happen with a woman who looked like Tara. Glamazons were for fantasy only, not for real life.

He was about to rise to allow her the freedom to leave the booth when Hunter Bauer arrived holding a red basket and a large dish. "One turkey club sandwich with extra salad, no fries, and a chicken Caesar salad."

"Thanks, buddy," Ethan said, accepting the sandwich. Over the winter, Hunter had been coming to the library regularly with his stepfather, Beau McCade, and borrowing books. It had surprised him, because Hunter was a skater kid, but then again, Ethan knew all about diverse interests.

An idea pinged into his head. "Hey, Hunter, if I set up a LAN gaming night, do you reckon some of the teens would come to the library to play?"

Hunter's eyes lit up momentarily, but his expression was cautiously dubious. "Maybe."

"Good to know." He'd take the spark of enthusiasm in the boy's eyes as a sign that the idea was worth pursuing. "Can you bring me a chocolate shake, and I think Officer Ralston wants her salad to go."

"Sure." Hunter reached for the salad.

Tara put her hand on the plate, stalling its movement. "That's okay. I'll eat it here."

Hunter shrugged as if he didn't care either way and then headed back to the kitchen to make the shake.

She's staying. Ethan set down the ice pack as a deluded spurt of happiness washed through him. "I'm glad you changed your mind."

Something flickered across her face that said she wasn't as equally glad. "Doctor Lang—"

"Ethan."

She sighed as if addressing him by his first name was stretching things. "Ethan."

"There you go." He threw her what he hoped was an encouraging smile but feared it probably came off as goofy. Her mouth immediately tightened, and he saw the policewoman firmly in control.

"I need you to move."

Do what now? She was staying for lunch but she wanted him to move?

He tried to read her impassive face but got nothing except *police officer on duty, do as you're told, now!* He was instantly reminded of the White Witch in Narnia, whose ice-cool beauty was both intoxicatingly tempting and frankly terrifying. If she offered him a hot drink or Turkish delight, he'd run a mile. Sadly, he was slowly moving toward agreeing with Ty that this woman was absolutely capable of emasculating him as fast and as efficiently as a cowboy with a knife at branding time.

His shock at her request for him to move must have registered on his face, because her high, smooth forehead furrowed slightly and she tilted her head toward the other side of the booth. "It's easier if you sit across from me."

Ah! He guessed that made sense. Kind of. He pushed his

sandwich basket across the table, stood, and then slid along the bench seat on the other side.

"Thank you," she said crisply.

"You're welcome." He tried not to sigh.

She picked up her silverware, her face still set in its serious lines. Did she ever smile? He had a foolish desire to see if he could make that happen. "No problem. After all, I'm hardly going to say no to a woman carrying a gun."

A pained expression followed, and she silently turned her attention to her salad. She ate with such single-minded focus it was as if she thought her meal might vanish from in front of her at any moment.

Strained silence hung over the booth like a threatening black rain cloud. *Careful what you wish for, pal.* As much as the thought of having lunch with Tara had been welcome, the reality was far from comfortable. The woman didn't do small talk. Heck, she didn't seem to do talk at all. It would have been a hell of a lot easier for both of them if she'd boxed her lunch and left.

———

TARA felt the beads of sweat forming in her hair and pooling at the back of her neck. What was drilled into every soldier and cop? *Stick to the MO!* So why had she changed her mind at the last minute and stayed for lunch when she'd had the chance to leave?

Because you left on Friday before you spoke to him and you still have to have this conversation, her practical-self told her.

Because you can still feel the softness of his hair on your face, her far-from-sensible-self added.

When Ethan had slammed into her, his hair had caressed her jaw, and the wintergreen scent of his shampoo had rushed her. Every part of her had clenched then sighed. The clenching part was expected. The sighing was not. The sighing bothered her. It bothered her a lot.

Ethan Langworthy was not her type of guy. Even if he had been, she wasn't interested, because her type meant heartache every single time, and she'd promised herself she wasn't going down that road again. For the first time in two years she was officially single, and she planned to stay that way. God knows, she'd earned it, and more importantly, she damn well deserved it. Besides, Langworthy had already caused her enough disquiet over the last nine days that she didn't need to add to it.

She'd spent most of the last several days on tenterhooks, anxiously waiting for the story of how she'd mistakenly arrested him to break all over town. She'd expected him to change his mind and lodge a complaint with Mitch and for Judy to give in to the temptation of the story and tweet it, but nothing had happened. Not even a whisper. Last Friday afternoon when Mitch had called her and congratulated her on a great first week and told her he'd been impressed by the nice haul of money she'd earned the department from her radar blitz on speeding tourists entering the town, she'd finally accepted that she'd gotten away with her biggest-ever career faux pas.

Relief had poured through her, making her jittery and light-headed, and she'd hit the couch with a rum and Coke to celebrate. Perhaps because right up until that moment she'd never believed the incident could stay a secret, she'd not watched the video that Judy had uploaded and tagged #OnlyEthan. But that night she did. The first time she saw it, she'd laughed so hard tears poured down her cheeks. Halfway through her second viewing, it hit her that this impression of fifty percent Brazilian soccer player, fifty percent "Chicken Dance" and one hundred percent goofball had opened him up to the town's ridicule.

Why? Why had he done this? What was his deal? It bothered her. It had bothered her at the station, but now that she'd seen the video it bothered her even more. It had propelled her off the sofa and out to the bar to find him and to ask him exactly what his deal was. People *always* had an agenda. Nobody expected something for nothing—everyone exacted a price eventually. She'd learned that growing up, and she had no intention of living in Bear Paw with this hanging over her. She'd intended to clear the air and get rid of this feeling that she owed him. She didn't want to owe anyone anything.

Only the moment she'd arrived at Leroy's, she'd felt out of place. Some people did the whole social scene easily. Tara did not—she was always the cop. And Ethan Langworthy in black boots, black skinny jeans, a slim-fit black Henley T-shirt and those black cat-eye glasses hadn't made being in Leroy's any easier. All that was missing from the ensemble was the leather jacket.

She'd found herself looking at him more than once. Truth be told, she'd looked about ten times. He didn't have the build of a biker, and despite the short beard look, he lacked the breadth and menace. His mouth was too friendly, his brow too tall and his hair too thick and wavy. His intelligence cloaked him like a black academic gown, but when he'd rocked that cello, he'd totally rocked her. It had scared her rigid, and she'd left without speaking to him.

Now he sat in front of her in blue jeans, a white T-shirt and a light gray cotton cardigan that was pushed up his very muscular and delineated forearms. Most of her had asked him to sit opposite her because every soldier wanted the enemy where she could see him, and having him next to her in her peripheral vision made her jumpy. Anyone in her peripheral vision made her jumpy. The rest of her had asked him to move because she needed a break from him being so close. Unlike the day she'd arrested him, he no longer smelled of garden mulch. Instead he had the musky scent of a man, and for some reason it was making it very hard for her to concentrate.

Just do it. She drew in a long, slow breath. "I watched the video."

The slightest ripple of movement crossed his shoulders. "I hope it gave you a laugh."

"It confused me."

"Oh?"

"Why would you publicly embarrass yourself for me when you don't even know me?"

He shrugged. "We all deserve one get-out-of-jail card. This was yours."

He'd done her a favor, and it bristled, because her experience with favors was bad. They always came back to bite her. They always had strings attached. "Thank you, but you didn't have to do it. I'm more than capable of taking care of myself."

"I'm more than sure that you are," he said mildly before taking a sip of the shake Hunter had delivered to the booth.

She dragged her gaze away from the way his lips closed around the straw and how, when he sucked, his cheeks indented, deeply outlining his prominent cheekbones. Wayward and unwanted thoughts beamed through her brain, and she cut them off briskly. Unfortunately, that briskness carried over into her voice. "As long as you know that."

He set down the damn cheek-sucking shake and raised his toffee-colored eyes to hers in an unflinching stare. "This is your first job in a small town, isn't it?"

She speared a piece of chicken with her fork, unnerved that he'd worked that out. "Maybe."

His gaze softened. "I'm taking that as a yes. Look, Bear Paw's a decent town, which is why I came back here to live, but parts of it can be a bit like high school. Believe me, you do one dumb thing here and you own it forever."

She thought about the guy who'd just taken the photo of Ethan with the ice pack on his forehead. If it had happened to her, she would have grabbed the man's wrist and removed the phone instead of sitting by aiding and abetting yet another humiliating photo. "And you're the voice of experience."

"I have a PhD in it as well as in Library and Information Science."

He didn't sound unhappy—if anything, his tone was one of mild resignation. She didn't understand why he allowed the town to do this to him. "And you have a hashtag."

"I do. It's a term of endearment."

He took another suck of the thick shake, and she looked down at her salad, hoping the cos lettuce and mayonnaise would offer her some respite from her unwelcome tangential thoughts about how his lips would feel on her body. The fact that notion even occurred surprised her. Sex wasn't something she thought about very often, and she had no intention of starting today.

"Do you have any experience in community policing, Tara?"

"Some." *Not really.* Her thoughts shied away from the weekly meetings—*shuras*—she'd attended with local Afghan women in Afghanistan as a stab of guilt hit her that she'd gotten out and they were still living in a war zone. Her time in Detroit had been more about locking up criminals than community liaison.

His fingers toyed with a folder that he'd brought in with him. "It takes a while to find your feet in a new job and a new town. The best way is to get involved in local events. You know, give people a chance to get to know you." His eyes lit up. "I've got an idea, and if you're worried that you owe me about the other day, then this will make us even."

Finally! They'd reached payback time. This was *exactly* what she'd been expecting from him for nine long days. At long last, she was on solid ground with him. "You do realize, Doctor Langworthy, that blackmailing a police officer is an offense."

His mouth widened in a smile, and with a flash of white teeth, he threw back his head and laughed. It was a rich, genuine sound that trickled through her veins, making promises she didn't want—promises she certainly didn't trust. She felt her lips clamp together hard and the accompanying sweep of tightness pull across her jaw, travel along her neck and shoot down her spine, until her entire body was ramrod stiff.

He suddenly stopped laughing, and his face shifted gears, settling into grim and unfamiliar lines. Not even when she'd mistaken him for a thief, handcuffed him and placed him in a holding cell had he given her a look like this.

"You're deadly serious, aren't you?"

She kept her chin tilted up. "I never joke about the law."

"Faa-rrr out." He dug his fingers into his scalp. "I can't believe this. What exactly did you think I was suggesting?"

"Well, I . . ." Her absolute conviction that he wanted something reprehensible from her started to wobble on its foundations.

"Don't stop there." He leaned back, folding his arms. "Tell me. I'm utterly fascinated."

"It doesn't matter." She reached for her hat, which was sitting on the table.

Ethan got to it first, holding it hostage. "Actually, it does matter, Tara. I'm sick of you making snap judgments about me. First I was a thief and now I'm supposedly blackmailing you?"

"You said I owed you and this would make us even. That sounds like blackmail to me."

His brow creased as his thoughts clicked over—thoughts that were illuminated in his intelligent eyes. "I was talking about you joining the Fourth of July family fun day committee."

"Oh." It came out softly on a whoosh of air that left her breathless and winded.

"*Oh* is right." He fingered the brim of her hat. "You know, last week I wanted to help you out, so your first day didn't dog you for your entire time in Bear Paw. Right now, I'm rethinking the whole nice-guy thing."

She was still floundering, desperately trying to hold on to anything that would make sense of this. "Can you honestly sit there and tell me that you had no other agenda in putting up that video other than helping me out?"

He rubbed his jaw and gave a wry smile. "You're a very attractive woman, Tara, and okay, maybe on some level I wondered if helping you out might make you view an invitation for a date favorably."

Her finger slammed into the middle of the table. "That's exactly what I'm talking about."

His eyes flashed burnt butter, and his deep but usually calm voice took on an edge. "No, that is not it at all. Had I asked you out and you'd given me the expected *no*, I would have accepted it, no questions asked." He leaned forward, his voice low. "Look, I have no clue where you've come from or what sort of people you've been associating with, but most of us here are decent folk. And you can relax, because hell would freeze over before I ever asked you out."

Before she could say a word, he pushed her hat back toward her and rose to his feet. "You have no clue how to work in a small town, Tara, and I'm done helping. You're on your own now."

Without saying good-bye, he strode across the diner, pausing only when a little girl jumped to her feet and called his name. She started singing and doing the "Chicken Dance" for him. He joined her for one round before twirling her back to her mom. The patrons clapped and wooted, and he did an ostentatious bow before walking out the door.

Her chest tightened. Who was this guy? She'd never met anyone quite like him. Had she got it all wrong? Had she just accused a good man of something immoral based on him doing something relatively selfless? Had she lost so much faith in humanity over the years that she'd just offended a decent guy who'd been trying to help?

"You want coffee or pie?" Hunter said, appearing next to her and removing the now empty salad plate.

"No, thanks, I'm good." She laid down some bills for him

and rose to leave. Halfway across the diner, her phone rang and she checked the caller ID as she made for the door. "Hey, Chief. How's the itching?"

"The least of my problems," Mitch grumbled down the line. "I'm in Great Falls and the physician isn't happy. He wants to replace the plaster."

"Sorry to hear that," she said as the afternoon heat hit her.

"Yeah." He sighed. "It's gonna kill my afternoon."

She almost said, *It's not like you were doing anything,* but he kept on talking. "I've been going to some town meetings so you didn't get overloaded, Ralston, but you're gonna have to do this one for me."

"Okay. What and where?"

"City hall in fifteen. Doc Langworthy, Ethan, the librarian. You met him yet?"

Somehow, she managed to force a strangled *yes* out of her spasming throat.

"Good. He's the convener of the family fun day on the Fourth. Can get a bit overenthusiastic, so your job's making sure whatever he suggests is safe in a crowd situation. Think traffic control for the parade and around the park where the festival takes place. If it's not safe, just tell him. Got that?"

She tried to speak, but her lunch was back, filling her mouth.

"Ralston?"

She forced her salad back down her throat. "The thing is, sir, I was doing further investigations on the theft of a cattle truck this afternoon. Can't you just respond to the written minutes?"

"No." She'd never heard Mitch Hagen sound so emphatic. "They'll come up with some half-assed plan, and we'll be left to clean it up. We don't want another disaster like 2010. You've got to be there."

"Yes, sir." She had no clue what had happened in 2010, but right now this meeting was shaping up to be a total disaster for her.

Chapter 10

William's day had been a series of treat 'em and street 'em, and he was hanging out for when Josh got back from his honeymoon, because the bulk of the people he'd seen today were not ER situations. He'd prescribed antihistamines and calamine lotion for mosquito bites and suggested the hapless camper buy bug spray from the pharmacy. He'd also recommended to the young woman who thought she was pregnant that she take a visit to the drugstore, pointing out that the test he would use was identical to the one she could buy there at a considerably cheaper price.

There'd been one case of bad sunburn; a cowboy with a deep laceration to his arm when he'd come off second best in an argument with a barbwire fence; and a forty-five-year-old bloke with a suspected heart attack that had thankfully turned out to be heartburn. Will had prescribed avoiding Leroy's "challenge meal" of an eighty-ounce steak, baked potato, salad, roll and twenty-two-ounce beverage, even if it did come with a T-shirt.

Bored, he glanced at the clock, willing the last few minutes of his shift to hurry up and finish or bring in something exciting. It was a shocking thing to wish harm on anyone, and he didn't, but he was going stir-crazy. He needed a jolt of adrenaline, a rush of invigorating panic, a blast of healthy fear—something to make him feel alive. Something to fill the void that was now part of him since Charlie's death.

"Will," Millie called out as she walked through the door waving a sheaf of papers.

Goose bumps rose so fast on his skin that his arm hair stood to attention. *Bloody hell.* Over the last six days he'd done his best to honor the vow he'd made to himself to meet a woman who interested him, have sex with her and shift this crazy reaction to Millie. He'd taken all the ER nurses out to dinner at Leroy's for team bonding and had talked to each and every one of them. They were a great crew, but there was no spark between him and any of the single women or, thankfully, the married ones. He'd jumped online and met a woman who lived in Cut Bank, the next closest town to Bear Paw. She'd been pleasant enough, but he kept finding himself comparing her to Millie, which made no sense, because this woman was heterosexual and available and Millie was neither of those things.

This whole Millie thing was driving him around the bend. On top of trying not to think about her in any way other than as a medical student—and failing miserably, especially at 3 A.M. when visions of what he imagined she might look like naked swam into his mind—there was dealing with the real Millie every day. When he'd accepted this job, he'd done it because he was craving friendship and Millie on paper was the perfect friend, but ever since her hypo on Saturday, she'd been different. He couldn't put his finger on exactly how, but he'd definitely noticed.

Now she leaned against the nurses' station in green scrubs, which made the green flecks in her fascinating eyes darken, making him think of the lush rain forests of far north Queensland. Her top sported a brown stain of antiseptic from when the burly cowboy with the barbwire laceration had fainted, knocking the bottle from her hand. Her scent was a combination of antiseptic and lemons—clean, sharp and fresh—a hint of home.

It took him back to his childhood when he and Charlie had rushed inside with cuts and scrapes and his mum would hoist them onto the kitchen bench and sit them next to the fruit bowl to tend to their wounds. The wooden bowl, made from Tasmanian Huon pine, always had lemons in it picked fresh from their tree. With a start, he realized he hadn't seen a lemon tree since arriving in Montana, and a shot of homesickness fizzed in his gut.

He cleared his throat, which suddenly seemed tight. "What have you got there?"

"I need you to sign these doctor release forms."

He noticed she had faint black smudges under her eyes. "You okay?" he asked as he signed the documents. "Blood sugar behaving?"

"I'm fine." Her emphatic and almost fierce tone reverberated around the quiet department. "You?"

"Bored."

"I told you Bear Paw was quiet."

"Wednesday wasn't," he said, thinking of the bus of band camp kids from Calgary who'd all come down with food poisoning and had arrived in the ER vomiting and worse. Millie, who for some reason had been wearing bright purple scrubs that day that surprisingly suited her, had dashed about dispensing antiemetics, antidiarrheals and a lot of TLC.

"You can't have that sort of excitement every day," she teased him with a flash of the old Millie. She was quiet for a moment, her expression thoughtful. "Seeing you're craving the buzz, let's go white water rafting tomorrow."

The offer tempted him way more than it should, and he almost raised his hand for a high five, but then he remembered the deadweight of her in his arms and how terrified he'd been when her blood sugar had crashed to dangerously low levels. It was one thing for that to happen on land—it was another thing entirely if it happened in a raft on churning, pulsating, white river water. What if she got tipped out? What if she got sucked under and he couldn't reach her. His chest got tight just thinking about it. "I don't think so."

She sucked in her plump and pretty and oh-so-kissable lips. "You're not squirming out of an invitation, are you? Not when the weather forecast is perfect for rafting?"

"I was thinking of a hike instead."

Enthusiasm zipped across her face. "Sure, that'd be cool. You said you wanted to do the Mount Brown Lookout? If we leave early, we could manage it, and with the clear weather the views will be amazing. There's one patch of huckleberries on the trail"—she elbowed him gently in the ribs—"so I'll bring the bear spray and a whistle."

Bears aside, Mount Brown Lookout was a tough hike with a long, upward, five-mile slog. It was a physical challenge for fit people who had a pancreas that worked, let alone a diabetic. "Actually, I was thinking of staying closer to home. Lorelei at the visitor information center told me there's a pretty hike along the creek that starts under the trestle railway bridge."

Millie's eyes narrowed. "Really? You, who thinks a thirty-mile bike ride is a warm-up to any event, want to hike a wheelchair-friendly trail that's less than a mile? You wouldn't even break a sweat."

She had an uncanny way of reading him, and he wasn't used to women seeing much more of him than good looks and friendly, flirting charm. "Apparently the water hole's pretty and there's a fire pit. I could be the quintessential Aussie bloke and bar-becue you snags." She didn't look convinced, and she didn't even ask him what a snag was. In fact, she looked extremely pissed off, so he lied outright. "And it's close to Bear Paw in case I get called in."

She folded her arms across her chest, and her breasts rose, hinting at a generous cleavage that her scrubs top normally hid. "I thought Great Falls covered your days off?"

"They do, but McBain's sick and I'm on call. So, are you in?" He waited for her dimple-cute smile to break across her face and confirm the arrangement.

She pushed off the desk. "I'll think about it."

Disappointment socked him. He tried to throw it off, but what remained unsettled him. "Fair enough. I understand. You're leaving things open in case you get a better offer. I don't want to get in the way of you dating."

She rolled her eyes. "Who knew you were so thoughtful."

He'd seen Tara in the foyer of the ER late on Wednesday after they'd dealt with the puking kids. She'd looked slightly less together than usual, as if something had gotten to her and blow-torched the edges of her frosty personality. Then again, it might just have been the acrid stench of vomit that had permeated the entire ER. He'd assumed she had a public health question for him about the roadhouse twenty miles away that had given the kids

E. coli. When he'd enquired, she'd said *no* in that official clipped tone of hers and had asked if Millie was free. He'd even wondered if perhaps he'd been wrong about Tara's sexual preferences.

Nah! He didn't get that type of thing wrong.

He pulled deep, wanting to make his next question for Millie sound casual. "Had that coffee with Tara yet?"

"Yup."

Good? Bad? Her expression gave him nothing. "And?"

She stood up and pointed to the clock. "And we're done here for the day. How about you come to Leroy's and I bust your ass at pool."

He laughed, relieved that for the first time this week, the old Millie was back. "Yeah, right. I'd like to see that."

She tossed her head, sending curls bouncing in every direction. "Oh, you'll see it all right."

He loved a challenge, and feeling the happiest he had all week, he followed her across the road, anticipation thrumming.

———

SEETHING, Millie racked the balls on the green felt of Leroy's pool table. Will Bartlett might be the pool champion of his hometown, but she was Bear Paw's, and she planned to wipe the floor with him and then tell him to take a hike—preferably off a cliff.

He'd been giving her odd looks on and off all week, and when it was his turn to bring in food for the staff, instead of the traditional frosted donuts, he'd provided almonds, celery sticks with peanut butter, cherry tomatoes, cheese and crackers and baby carrots. Everyone had put it down to him being Australian, but Millie had a sneaking suspicion the platter was meant for her. And it would have been a kind and thoughtful gesture if it hadn't been for those long, penetrating looks. Looks that said, *You're diabetic* and *What's your blood sugar reading?*

She knew she had a tendency to get mad not only at her diabetes but also at the way people treated her because of it, so she'd decided to run a check to make sure she wasn't over-dramatizing and misreading the situation. The invitation to go white water rafting was a test. A test he'd failed miserably, and she was furious with him.

Be fair. He probably is on call and can't be too far away.

But she didn't want to be fair. She remembered how he'd behaved with her before he'd found out she was diabetic and how he'd behaved since. It both irked and hurt.

Will grinned as he spun a quarter into the air. "Heads or tails, Mils?"

Mils? Did he have no clue how angry she was with him? "Heads."

"Come in, spinner."

She wanted to know what *come in, spinner* meant, but she refused to ask him, because she was mad at him and this game of pool wasn't about being friendly. This was war.

He caught the coin, slamming it down onto the back of his hand before saying, "Heads it is."

Good. "I'll break." She chalked her cue, leaned over the table, lined it up and shot. *Yes.* The thwacking noise the balls made when they hit on-center gave her a buzz, and she watched with hope in her mouth as the colored balls scattered out toward the pockets. The solid purple four ball dropped neatly into a corner pocket. *Great start.*

"Nice." Will's accent made it sound like *noice*, and admiration clung to the word.

I don't want you to be nice. I'm not playing nice. "I'll play solid colors." She moved around the table and adjusted her cue between her thumb and index finger before wrapping her index over the wood to make a closed bridge. "Red ball, side pocket."

Clack. The red ball raced across the felt and fell straight into the pocket before rolling loudly down the ball return trough. *Two down, six to go.*

"Shot," Will said amiably at the easy play.

She didn't want an amiable game. She wanted to sink every colored ball and leave him standing by the table holding a cue he couldn't use. She marched past him and repositioned herself on the other side of the table. The location of the maroon ball was a gift, and she sent it clear into a side pocket.

"Folks," Ty said, setting down his guitar, "Millie's on a roll, so I'm taking a short break."

A few of the guys in the bar had already drifted over to watch. "I'd bet on you, Doc, if I ever got to see you play," Trent Dattner said with a grin.

"You won't have to wait long," Will said confidently, his gaze scanning the table.

Not if I have my way, buddy. Studying the lie of the balls in relation to the pockets, Millie made a decision. "Yellow and green into the forward corner pocket."

Will laughed—a rich, deep, rumbling and sexy sound—clearly entertained by the notion. "So not going to happen."

The velvet effects of his laugh were still stroking her, tempting her to let go of her anger, but she wasn't buying. "Is that so?"

"Yeah." He rocked back on his feet as if he owned the floor space. "Those balls have my name on them."

This time she laughed. "I don't think so, *mate*." She hit the Aussie word with a distinctive diphthong, copying Will's accent. "But feel free to tell me why you do."

He stood slightly taller. "Green and gold are Australia's national colors."

She'd never seen him show any signs of patriotism before, and it surprised her. "Tonight they're two colors on Montana's flag. Watch me sink them."

She took her shot, confident she could do it.

Clack. Clack. Clack. Yes!

An enthusiastic cheer went up from the onlookers.

"That's a pretty good effort," Will said, sounding both impressed and perturbed all at the same time.

"Be afraid, Will. Be very afraid," Ethan said drily as he gave Will's shoulder a slap.

Three to go. Millie's heart hammered so fast in her chest she didn't know how it could be pumping any blood at all. *You can do this.* She walked slowly around the table, trying to shut out the many and varied suggestions the guys were calling out to her. Trying to shut out the way Will stood tall in the crowd with his left hand resting casually on his cue and his right knee bent, hips tilted—all easy grace, sexy and gorgeous.

He's not gorgeous. He's an ass, and I'm pissed with him. I'm proving a point.

Publicly humiliating him at pool isn't going to stop him from thinking about your diabetes.

Yeah, but it will make me feel better.

By now she'd sunk every easy and moderately difficult

ball, and things were looking decidedly tricky. Stalling, she re-chalked her cue.

Will stepped forward to take a closer look, and despite the twelve inches of air between them, her skin immediately heated and tingled.

You're mad at him, remember. So mad.

"Bastard of a shot," Will said laconically.

She stifled a smile at his first real attempt at trash talk. The man was worried. Good. He should be. She blew the loose chalk off her cue and out toward his face. "I've had worse."

He quirked one chestnut and disbelieving eyebrow and leaned in a little closer. "I find that hard to believe."

His softly spoken words sent a spark of hot, heavy, pulsing need into every part of her, and she gripped her cue tightly to stop herself from swaying toward him.

"You obviously haven't played as much pool as I have, hot-shot." She reached her arm out across him, being careful not to touch his shirt, and she pointed to the play. "White ball to blue, blue to cushion and then taking a forty-five-degree trajectory to orange and into the side pocket."

He snorted and appealed to the crowd. "Tell her she's dreamin'."

And she was, but she wasn't going to let him know that. Pulling some bills out of her pocket, she slapped them on the table's side rail. "Bet me."

He grinned. "You sure about that, Mils?"

"Millie only bets on a sure thing, Will," Ethan said, shooting her a look that said, *What's going on?*

She ignored him.

Will did, too, and instead turned his beautiful dark blue eyes onto her. An ache of longing started to slowly suck the oxygen from her anger, but behind the competitive glint in his eyes she glimpsed the same hint of worry that had been there all week. Worry for her. It refueled her anger at him.

She tapped his chest with her forefinger. "Oh, I'm very sure."

"Millie's kicking his ass," a cowboy muttered to Ty.

Will pulled out his wallet and matched her bet. "You're on. But know you'll be short on lunch money all of next week."

"Let me worry about me, okay." She moved to the right at

the exact moment he moved left, and the next second she was slamming into him, hard.

Her breasts flattened into his chest, his rock-hard thighs pressed into her softer ones and the simmering warmth that always ran just under her skin whenever they were in the same room coalesced into a fireball of need. It exploded into every cell, flooding her with a desire so strong it shut down all normal function. Her knees sagged, and she pressed more heavily against him. A faint voice in her head that sounded like it was coming from under water said weakly, *Step away.*

"Oops," he said, his voice raspy as his strong, wide hands gripped her hips. The next second, he'd spun her around and stepped back quickly. "I believe it's your go."

My go? Her mind had joined her body, and both were currently lying on their backs, panting.

Stop that. Sit up and behave, both of you. We're playing pool and beating the crap out of him.

She thrust out her hand and felt and saw it tremble as she closed it around the cue rest. "Dirty pool, Will," she muttered under her breath.

"Sorry, what?" He sounded slightly breathless and unusually distracted instead of fully prepped for trash talk.

Had she winded him? She realized with a bolt of shock that their collision must have been an accident and not part of his strategy to unnerve her. *Duh!* It was hardly a psychological play, because a lesbian wasn't going to turn into a basket case of brain-draining, chaotic lust from being pressed up against him.

Only, she wasn't gay, and right now her body was a puddly, uncoordinated mess. *Pull it together. You're not losing this.* The quiver in her body faded, and she carefully placed the cue rest in position.

"That's a bold move," Will said mockingly, all traces of his distraction gone.

She resisted giving him the finger. "Game on, Bartlett." With her left leg forward, knee bent and her right leg positioned behind her for balance, she leaned over the table, her elbows on the felt and her breasts pressed hard against the side rail.

"You can do it, Millie," Dane said encouragingly.

"Shut up, Dane," Ty said with a hint of exasperation.

Her concentration interrupted, she glanced up. Everyone's gaze was fixed on the cue ball in anticipation of her shot. Everyone's, that is, except Will. He wasn't looking anywhere near the ball or at her face or arms. His gaze seemed fixed on— Astonishment made her blink. Was he looking at her ass? *Oh please, as if. Just play the damn shot.*

"Sorry, Millie," Dane apologized.

"No need for an apology, Dane," Will said, squatting down next to her so his eyes were at table level. "A good player shuts out all distractions. Isn't that right, Millie?"

He was daring her to choke. "I'm not sure you'd know, Will."

"Boo-yah!" a cowboy yelled out. "Hey, Doc, you sure you've got the balls for this?"

"He hasn't got any balls yet," Ty quipped with a laugh.

"Remind me again, Ty, when do you need that prostate exam?" Will shot back.

The heckling went on around Millie, and she put her head down, trying to block all the extraneous sights and sounds— the clink of glasses, Dane's lurid T-shirt, the rap of cowboy boots on the wooden floor, but most of all the musky scent of Will that never seemed to leave her.

Visualizing the shot line, she drew in a long, deep breath. Without a doubt, this was the hardest shot she'd ever played, but then again, she'd never wanted to win so badly. She pushed her arm forward, and the cue moved smoothly against the rest, connecting with the cue ball.

White hit blue, which bounced off the cushion and sped into orange, propelling it into the pocket. Miraculously, blue immediately followed.

A roar went up. She'd just potted all seven balls in a row, and all that remained was the black eight ball. It sat alone, hers for the taking.

"You can hang up your cue now, Doc," Ty said. "You're well and truly screwed."

"It's not over 'til it's over," Will said, although resignation hung off every word.

Millie tapped the money. "Want to bet any more of your lunch money against me on this final shot?"

Will shook his head, a lock of his thick, sun-kissed hair falling into his eyes. "Thanks, but I'll pass."

"Wise move." She turned her back on him, trying to keep the flutters of excitement under control. She hadn't won yet. If she fluffed this shot, then Will could enter the game and do to her exactly what she'd done to him.

She remembered him suggesting the stroll. Hell, he'd probably bring her a parasol to protect her from the sun. Her determination came back in a steely rush, and she lined everything up, pictured the ghost ball just behind the eight ball and took the shot.

She'd gone for slow and steady, but as she watched the white ball roll, she instantly knew she'd underestimated the strength required. *Clack.* Her left hand rose to her mouth, and she bit her knuckles as she watched the agonizingly slow trajectory of the black ball. It crept forward, all the time losing momentum until it teetered very close to the edge of the pocket.

A collective gasp shot around the table.

Please. Please. Please.

The ball vanished into the pocket.

She squealed and threw her arms up in the air as the sound of clapping and cheering filled the bar. Her back was slapped, her shoulders pummeled, and suddenly she was looking up into Will's face. She'd expected to see humiliation, a dented ego, some loss of face, hell, even a modicum of anger, but instead he was smiling down at her, his face filled with happiness. It confused the hell out of her.

"Now *that* was incredible pool," he said, slapping her hand with a high five and pulling her in for a bear hug.

He was wrapped around her, his muscular arms crushing her against him head to toe. His chin pressed down on the top of her head, his heart thumped rhythmically and solidly against her breasts, and her cheek rested on the softness of his shirt with the hard play of taut muscle beneath. All of it felt so damn good it had to be a dream.

And then he released her, and as her feet hit the ground, his finger burned a trail of wonder across her cheek as he brushed a curl from her eyes. Her body vibrated with sensory overload of the very best kind, and she forgot she was mad at him. Forgot she'd wanted to make him squirm. Forgot just about everything, including the date and the name of the president.

He dropped his head close to hers, the warmth of his breath tickling her ear. "With all that excitement, you've probably burned up a lot of energy. We should eat."

Right then she remembered everything and she remembered it fast.

Chapter 11

Confused, Will watched Millie stomp out of the bar as if she was the one who'd had to stand by and not just lose a game of pool that he hadn't been able to participate in, but become tonight's entertainment for Leroy's. There was nothing a small town liked more than to see their lawyer, successful businessman or doctor lose face and lose money. Tonight, he'd done both.

As much as he hated that Millie had dominated the game to the point he hadn't been able to touch even one ball, he had to admire her skill. Who was he kidding? He'd admired more than that every time she'd leaned over the table. Fortunately, she hadn't noticed him checking out her ass, and although there'd been plenty of jokes from the blokes about him losing his balls, there thankfully hadn't been any references to him being a lesbro—a guy who hung out with gay women hoping they'd sleep with him. He was thankful for small mercies—that would be a lot harder to live down than losing a game of pool.

Given Millie had kicked his ass in more ways than one, he'd expected her to give him a chance to take a game off her after she'd eaten her dinner. Seems he was totally wrong about that.

Ethan appeared next to him, shoved a beer in his hand and pushed him toward a quiet table. "Man, I haven't seen Millie play like that since Mason Berkram, the physician's assistant, tried to pull rank on her." He rubbed his chin. "What the hell did you do to upset her?"

"Nothing. Jeez, I've only ever been nice to the woman."

"Yeah, well word from the wise," Ethan said, his mouth grimacing, "there's no benefit in being a nice and decent guy. They just hate you for it."

"Tell me about it," Will said, warming to the theme. "She just whipped me in front of everyone, but did I whinge? No, I was a good sport about it. Hell, I congratulated her, I offered to buy her dinner and then she gets all stroppy and stomps out." He sipped his beer, feeling better for having vented. "So who bit you in the bum?"

Ethan looked puzzled. "Excuse me?"

Will was used to people giving him odd looks, as if he'd just spoken to them in a foreign language, so he translated the Aussie. "Who got upset with you?"

"Oh, right." Ethan's confusion vanished. "Tara Ralston."

Will laughed. "I can tell you now, you're not going to get any joy there. She and Millie are dating."

Beer spurted out of Ethan's nose.

Will passed him a napkin in sympathy. "Sorry, mate. I didn't mean to surprise or disappoint you."

Ethan's coughing slowly subsided, and he took off his glasses, cleaning them before sliding them back on his face.

"Better?" Will inquired as he opened the menu. He was suddenly ravenously hungry.

"Will."

"Hmm." He was reading the specials and tossing up between ordering the prime rib or the shrimp dinner. Both came with soup and salad.

"Millie's not gay."

He glanced up at the poor, deluded guy. "Yeah, well that's what I thought about Tara, but it seems we're both wrong."

Ethan shook his head slowly. "I'm not wrong."

He tried to wrap his head around what Ethan was saying, but it didn't make any sense. Millie was definitely gay. "Some-times we think we know someone when really—"

"I've known Millie all my life, and I know for a *fact* that she's as straight as you and me."

Know. Fact. The words reverberated in his head like a sonic boom, and a chill whooshed through him with breath-freezing cold. Snatches of conversations with Millie poured out of his memory. *Totally out and proud. You're an ally. Tara, would you like to catch up for a coffee sometime?*

He shivered as the chill inside of him intensified. Millie had let him think she was gay. She'd let him try and set her up on a date. She'd lied to him.

The coldness in his veins exploded into white-hot, scalding fury, and he stood up abruptly, the legs of the chair scraping loudly on the floor. "Thanks for the beer, mate. I'll see you around."

Ignoring Ethan's urgent question of "Are you okay?" he strode through the bar in a haze of anger, pushed open the door and stormed into the warm, summer evening. Millie Switkowski had a hell of a lot of explaining to do, and she was going to do it now.

"Hey, Doctor Bartlett." Ray Finnemore, the aeronautical mechanic from the airport, walked over. "I was wanting to ask you about—"

"Is it a medical emergency?" he said curtly, climbing into his Jeep. Only a life-and-death situation would stop him from going directly to see Millie.

"No, it's about the maintenance contract for the helicopter."

"I'll talk to you about it on Monday, okay?"

"Sure, no worries." Ray slapped the top of the car. "Drive safe."

Five minutes later, after breaking the speed limit of the neighborhood, he pulled up outside Millie's parents' house and killed the engine. All he needed to do was take a quick walk down the drive, past the pool, and he'd be knocking on her door. As he got out of the car, he heard his name being called and, raising his sunglasses, he saw Millie's parents sitting on the porch sipping drinks. *Crap.* He should have used the back entrance. Now that they'd seen him, he could hardly march straight past them without stopping to chat.

He crossed the soft, spongy lawn, so very different from the dried, brown stalks of the summer grass at home, and tried to dredge their names from the recesses of his mind. "G'day, Susie, Danny. Lovely evening."

"Hello, Will." Susie smiled and extended a well-manicured hand. "What a lovely surprise."

Danny didn't offer up quite the same welcome. "I hear you've had an interesting evening."

Will fixed his smile in place and shoved his hands in his pockets. "Millie been bragging about her win, has she?"

"No, we haven't spoken to her yet. I saw it on the Twitter," Danny said with a touch of amusement. "Bethany used the hashtag NoBallsBartlett."

"Good old Bethany," Will said, trying not to grind his teeth. He knew he was going to be stuck with that moniker for the rest of the summer.

"Millie's got a good eye," Danny said. "I taught her to play."

"The jury's still out on whether that was a good thing or not," Susie said with an edge to her voice before turning her attention back to Will. "We're surprised to see Millie's home already. We thought she'd have stayed to celebrate. In fact, I was about to pop in and check on her to make sure she was feeling okay."

Susie had just gifted him a valid reason for being here. "That's why I'm here."

"So she is sick?" Susie's social smile faded to worry.

"No, I'm just bringing some insulin," he lied, hastening to reassure her and regretting he'd used the excuse.

Danny frowned. "It's not like Millie to run low on insulin."

"Something to do with an off batch. I should go."

"That's very kind of you, Will." Susie smiled at him gratefully.

None of this is about kindness. I'm furious with Millie. He raised his hand in a farewell wave and backed away, guilt kicking him that he'd misled Susie. "Enjoy the rest of your evening."

He strode down the side of the house, through the gate and into the yard. Millie's cat was curled up on a pool lounger, looking angelic. He wasn't falling for that trick again, and he didn't pause to pat the beast. The sound of loud music emanated from the guesthouse, and he banged hard on the screen door as much to make himself heard as to find an outlet for his anger.

Millie didn't appear, but as he knocked again, the volume of the music diminished.

"Come in, Mom," she said, sounding resigned. "It's open."

Will stepped through the doorway. "I'm not your mother."

She leaped from the couch to her feet, staring at him. "Will?" His name came out on a surprised squeak, and she cleared her throat, suddenly sounding cross. "What are you doing here?"

She'd changed out of her scrubs and was wearing those damn short pajamas of hers that, unlike every other outfit he'd ever seen her in, hid barely anything of her curvy and generous body. The body he'd spent hours fantasizing about and even more time fighting those thoughts because he'd believed she was a lesbian and unavailable.

Frustration and fury tumbled over and over, churning his gut. "You're. Not. Gay."

He heard the accusatory challenge that clung to the three little words, and like a slow-motion sequence, he saw the moment she did, too. She flinched. Her eyes widened, and the unique coppery ring in her irises vanished under the inky spread of her pupils. A pink flush flared on her cheeks, bloomed along her jaw and then raced down to stain her creamy décolletage. She wiped her palms against her shorts. Sweaty palms. Guilty palms.

Her bra-free breasts rose and fell as she breathed in deeply. "Ah no."

She'd never looked sexier, but for the first time, he didn't want to see it. "Ah no?" Incredulity spun around him like a web, choking him. "That's all you have to say?"

She swallowed. "Who told you?"

"Ethan." The red haze of fury behind his eyes suddenly changed to green. "He said he knew for a fact you're straight, which I'm taking as code for he's had sex with you."

"Not that it's any of your business," she said quietly, the words edged in steel, "but I've never had sex with Ethan. We're just good friends."

It was ludicrous that amidst all his anger and perplexity, that one fact made him feel somewhat relieved, but it didn't dent his outrage at her. "Millie, what the hell?"

He slapped the back of his right hand into the palm of his left. "First of all you don't tell me that you're diabetic and then you let me think that you're gay. What sort of a sick joke is this?"

"It's not a joke."

"So sue me if I don't believe you." The bitter taste of betrayal filled his mouth. "Jesus, Millie, I thought we were friends and then you go and do this?" And that was the crux of the issue. He thought she was his friend. Outrage dueled with embarrassment, and he could just imagine the talk in the town. "For fuck's sake, you let me try and set you up on a date. I bet you and Tara enjoyed a lot of laughs about that."

She sucked in her lips and shook her head. "I never mentioned anything to Tara. I didn't tell anyone."

None of this made sense. "I don't get it. If this isn't a joke and you didn't tell anyone that I thought you were gay, why didn't you have the common courtesy to tell me?"

"Hey." Her hands suddenly slapped her hips with a loud clap, and the quietness that had circled her disappeared. "I wasn't the one who sat down at a wedding and told me to my face that I was gay."

"What?" Her accusation burned him. "So now this is my fault?"

She nodded violently. "Uh-huh."

"You've got to be kidding me." He threw his arms out wide in disbelief. "What sort of a woman wears a man's suit to a wedding, anyway?"

"A woman who's the best man." Her voice rose. "A woman with a diabetic pump and a CGM that means she can't wear a tight-fitting dress." Her voice got even higher. "A woman who needs a purse that holds more than a lipstick and a phone." Now she was yelling. "None of it means I'm gay."

"Back then I didn't know you were a diabetic."

"You didn't need to know."

He was trying really hard to follow her argument, but like so many other women before her, he didn't understand her. "I'm the one who's been made to look a fool here, Millie. I'm the one who's owed an explanation." He ran his hand across the back of his neck. "Seriously, how hard is it to say, 'Will, I'm not gay.'"

Her chin jerked up and her eyes narrowed, but not before he'd seen a flash of hurt light them up. "About as hard as it is to hear you say you thought I was."

Aww, shit. This whole mess really was his fault.

———

DAMN it. Millie hated that her voice had just wobbled, but she hated even more the look of pity on Will's face. *Poor Millie.* All she wanted was for him to leave so she could mainline a tub of cookies-and-cream ice cream. Ice cream she shouldn't eat in those quantities, but some situations overrode all her healthy eating and good behavior. Some situations made her crave to be a normal woman who could eat comfort food with few consequences. This was definitely one of those times.

"Millie—"

She raised her hand. *You don't get to say anything.* "I don't want to hear it."

"—I've been a dickhead."

She blinked, not quite believing her ears or her brain's interpretation, and then she heard a hysterical laugh. It was hers. "Yeah, you have been."

He shrugged, his expression both contrite and perplexed. "Sorry."

She shrugged back. "I'd like to say it's okay, only—"

"Only it isn't close to being okay. I get it." He blew out a long breath. "Is it okay if I sit down?"

He looked so woebegone that she didn't have the heart to say no, and, truth be told, she didn't really want to. It was a unique experience to have a guy admitting to her that he was wrong, especially a doctor, and she planned to suck every bit of blood out of his apology. "Sure. Take a load off. Do you want something to eat or drink?"

He shook his head as he lowered himself onto the small two-person sofa and stretched his arm across the back, seeming to fill more than his share of the space. She sat carefully, pushing her back onto the sofa's arm and pulling her legs up underneath her so there was no chance she would accidentally touch him and embarrass herself. She could no longer hide her attraction to him behind pretending to be gay or pass off flushing bright pink as being hot. He knew she was straight, and she knew that wasn't going to change the fact he wasn't attracted to her.

Despite his casual posture, he looked ill at ease, which in turn made her feel uncomfortable. She half rose. "Are you sure I can't get you a beer or . . . ?"

He caught her hand, stopping her from completing her stand. "I don't need anything. Please. Just sit."

"O-kay." She sat and tried to slide her hand out of his, but he continued to grip it. "Um, Will?" She nodded toward their hands, but he didn't let go. Instead he fixed his hypnotic eyes on her, and she had to work at stopping a delicious shiver from consuming her.

"Do you have any idea how crazy I've been this last fortnight thinking you were gay?"

"Why would it even bother you?" A kernel of disappointment in him sprouted in her chest, and she tried tugging her hand away. "Are you telling me that you were just faking being supportive of me and the LGBT community?"

"No! Of course not!" His fingers closed more tightly around her hand, as if he wanted to emphasize his point. "I'm talking about how hard I found it helping you set up a date with Tara and trying to be a supportive friend when all I wanted to do was kiss you."

Her mouth fell open and she stared at him, her brain vacant of words. Surely he hadn't just said that? Surely she'd just superimposed her own insane fantasy onto his words. It wouldn't be the first time she'd pretended he'd said things to her that she'd wanted to hear.

He suddenly dropped her hand as a sad and wry expression crossed his face. "Sorry. I didn't mean to horrify you."

Say something. "I . . . you . . . it . . ." She swallowed. "Wow."

He laughed tightly, and tension coiled around his body like a preloaded spring. "Wow indeed. I gather you don't feel the same way."

"I . . . it's just . . ." *Focus, woman!* She finally managed to get her mouth to work, although her brain was spinning. "*You* wanted to kiss me?"

He smiled that lazy, twinkling smile. "Amongst other things, yes."

Tingling shimmers zipped through her before arrowing

down between her legs. *Take him, he's yours.* "Me?" She tapped her chest with her fingers. "Millie Switkowski?"

He leaned in close, gazing into her eyes, and slid his hand along her cheek. "Absolutely you, Millie Switkowski."

His deep, husky words played havoc with the shredded vestiges of her concentration, and she struggled to make sense of this totally unexpected conversation.

You don't have to make sense of it; you just have to kiss him. Kiss him like you've wanted to for a year.

A niggling thought hit her, and she eased back, breaking the contact. "I thought you wanted to be friends?"

"I did." He wrung his hands. "I do."

"And you're kind of my boss now."

"Not at all. Floyd's your boss. He's the one who decides where you work so that you meet the WWAMI requirements. I'm just a means to an end."

She felt herself frowning. "So, let me get this straight. You've never shown any interest in me other than as a friend, but now you've found out I'm not gay and you're in Bear Paw, you want to be friends with benefits and add me to your notches on the bedpost. Really classy, Will."

"No." Effrontery streaked across his handsome face. "It's not like that at all."

"How is it, then?"

Bewilderment played around him as if he was totally out of his depth. "Jesus, Millie, I don't know."

"Well that's reassuring."

He was quiet for a moment, staring at his feet, and then he exhaled a long, almost mystified sigh. "The truth is, Millie, you're the first woman I've wanted to have sex with for a long time."

Shock reverberated through her. "But you . . . you're always surrounded by beautiful women."

The left side of his mouth flattened. "Doesn't mean I'm having sex with them."

She remembered the times she thought she'd imagined him looking at her differently—the flare of desire in his eyes at the lake and the definite stare at her ass tonight. Had all those looks at work this week—looks she'd attributed to him seeing her only as a diabetic—been looks of longing? She found it hard to believe, because she was the plain Jane in this situation. She was the woman men overlooked. She was the woman men never saw as being sexual.

Not this time, baby.

She studied Will—this utterly gorgeous specimen of man who wanted her—and again glimpsed that cloak of loneliness that often dogged him. She scooted forward an inch as the long-dormant provocateur deep down inside her burst into life. "So being a playboy's overrated?"

He shifted slightly toward her, a wicked smile dancing on his lips. Lips she planned to explore very soon. "Frequently overrated."

"And you're on a dry spell?" She moved again and dropped her left leg down to entwine with his.

Every muscle in his body tensed. "I have been, yes."

She pouted her lips. "Poor baby."

His Adam's apple bounced up and down like apples in a water barrel on Halloween. "That's me."

The raspy words ran along her skin, calling up a carnal response that barely needed any encouragement. She knew without a shadow of a doubt that he wanted her, but she needed to hear it. "I've been driving you crazy?"

He placed one hand on her waist and flattened the palm of his other hand on her thigh, his thumb caressing her bare skin. She jumped at the deliciousness of it. At the anticipation of what would follow.

"Millie, you've been driving me crazy in ever-increasing ways from the morning I woke up in your bed surrounded by your scent."

She wanted so much to believe him, but she struggled to align the words with Will who could have any woman he chose. "What ways?"

"So many ways."

"Tell me."

His gaze soaked her in. "The way your curls bounce when you laugh, the way your whole face lights up when you smile"— he gently squeezed her thigh—"and all this gorgeous, soft, creamy skin that I've wanted to touch and taste for days. Let's not forget the way your scrubs tighten over your sweet, round behind when you bend over and . . ." His voice was now so deep it resonated in her chest. ". . . your utterly kissable plump bottom lip that's always in my mind when I close my eyes."

A silent squeal of wonder echoed through her. "I've been keeping you awake at night?"

His midnight blue eyes flared with heat. "Hell, yes."

She pressed her palm against his cheek, feeling the scratch of stubble. "So have you."

Relief flashed across his face, and with a groan of long-suppressed need, he pulled her into him, cradled her cheeks in his hands and ran his tongue along the seam of her lips.

She shivered in a thousand wondrous ways.

At different times over the past year she'd imagined this, fantasized about it, and she'd gone so far as kissing another man all the while pretending she was kissing Will, but none of it had prepared her for the real thing. It was as if fireworks were going off inside of her—colored lights lit up her head, booming noise sounded in her ears and hot, wondrous desire rained through her. She opened her mouth and sucked his tongue inside.

He flooded her with Will—the sharp taste of beer hops, the zip of mint, the hint of antiseptic and the red-hot heat of need. His hands moved into her hair, his fingers tangling with her curls as if he couldn't get enough of her, and all the while his tongue explored and stroked until she was breathing so fast she could barely catch enough air.

His tongue vanished. "Sorry," he panted. "Too fast."

"No—"

But he kissed away her protest with a sweet, chaste kiss on the center of her lips before dropping more of the same on the side of her mouth. The hungry need had gone, and a skitter of panic lanced her as he continued to kiss her across her cheek and down her neck. *Had he changed his mind?*

"Now to join the dots," he said in a deep rumble, and the tip of his tongue trailed between the points of each kiss.

With each stroke of his tongue and nip of each kiss a part of her melted. Her head fell back, then her shoulders, until Will's hand on her spine was the only thing holding her up. The sofa cushions pressed against her back, and she opened her eyes to see him leaning over her, his dark, dark eyes burning for her.

"Look at that, you're on your back," he said with mock surprise and a wicked grin as he whipped her pajama top up and over her head. A second later he was cupping her now tingling and aching breasts.

She laughed. "Is that a Will Bartlett signature move?"

"It might be, but I don't kiss and tell." He closed his mouth around her left breast and flicked her already-erect nipple with his tongue.

A streak of pure need tore through her, and she cried out, writhing underneath him. He did it again, and she wrapped her legs around his, needing an anchor against this delicious torment.

His hair brushed her face as he raised his head and kissed her again on the lips. "Enjoying yourself?"

She could scarcely see straight, let alone think. "I . . . um . . . ah . . . yes."

"Good." He winked at her before turning his attention to her right breast.

With each lick and suck of her breasts, she thought she'd lose her mind. She'd already lost control of her body—it had surrendered utterly to Will's ministrations and was a begging, panting, very wet mess.

He nipped her and she bucked against him.

He pulled back with a start. "Ouch. What the hell have you got in your pants?"

Holy crap. She'd tucked her insulin pump into the elastic waistband of her pajamas because who knew an hour ago she was going to be having sex. Not even in her wild, drunken party days had she had sex wearing her pump. She'd always removed it so no guy would notice. So she could pretend she was normal.

The wondrous, boneless feeling of being a sexy, desirable woman vanished, and she sat up so fast Will tumbled off the tiny sofa. "Oh God, sorry."

"All good." He sat up with a bemused look on his face. "I think this is a sign we need to—"

"Stop." She wrapped her arms around her naked breasts, suddenly embarrassed. The provocateur was now long gone and buried under the realization he was going to see all of her naked. Naked and with needles plunged into her belly. "Good idea."

He stared at her, a deep V carving into the bridge of his nose. "I was going to say relocate to a bed."

"Oh. Right."

He stood and then pulled her to her feet. Wrapping his arms around her so she was pressed warmly against his chest, he tucked her head under his chin. "A minute ago you sounded like you were about three seconds away from an orgasm, and now you want to stop. What's going on?"

She kept her eyes fixed on the stripes of his shirt. "Nothing."

He stroked her hair. "I'm not pressuring you, Millie. If you've changed your mind and you want to stop, we'll stop. Only it doesn't sound like nothing."

Seriously? Are you really going to let this get in the way of having sex with Will?

She closed her eyes and pressed her face into his chest.

He pressed a kiss into her hair. "I'm a good listener."

Just say it. One, two, three. "I just speared you with the corner of my insulin pump."

His hands gently gripped her shoulders so she had to look up at him. "Oh, is that what it was?"

"Yeah." She grimaced. "That's what it was."

"And . . . ?" He looked and sounded as if he had no clue why that was a problem.

"And . . ." *Oh God, this is so embarrassing.* "And you have this amazing body and I have—"

"A beautiful body."

She blew a curl out of her eyes. "You're just saying that so you get lucky."

He shook his head. "I've chosen not to get lucky for quite some time, Millie. Now I'm choosing to get lucky with you."

The sincerity in his voice made her brave. "My body . . . it's got red, angry patches from the pump tape."

He put his fingers under her chin. "It's beautiful."

"It's pinpricked and bruised."

"So now it's a competition?" He pulled off his shirt to reveal a large yellow and black bruise on his hip. "I walked into the EKG machine."

Her fingers traced the purple edges. "Ouch."

His eyes darkened again, and he said roughly, "You can kiss it better if you want."

She laughed and he kissed her before gazing down at her inquiringly. "Are we good?"

She bit her lip.

He groaned. "What now?"

"I don't have any protection."

A sheepish look crossed his face. "I do."

"Why am I not surprised?"

"What can I say?" He gave her that grin that melted her bones. "I'm a doctor and I always travel with a fully equipped medical kit."

"Oh, right, and condoms are so often required during medical emergencies." She started backing toward her bedroom, and he walked with her.

"You do realize that if I didn't have a condom, this would be an emergency situation."

"Oh my God, you're right. I take it back."

"Thank you." They'd reached the bed. "Can we stop talking now?"

"Good idea." She kissed him and her fingers reached for his belt.

Still kissing her, he somehow managed to kick off his shoes. When he pulled away to shuck his pants, she discarded hers and put her pump and Dex on the nightstand before leaping under the covers.

"No hiding." He whipped them back and leaned over her, kissing her until she forgot everything. Then he ran kisses down her chest and between her breasts and dallied at her belly button before kissing every single pump bruise, every needle stab scab, and every patch of reddened, angry skin until he reached her infusion set.

She tensed.

He brought his head back to hers. "Does it fall out easily?"

She shook her head. "No."

He grinned down at her. "Excellent."

Lightness flooded her and she wrapped her arms and legs around him before pulling herself up to face him. She immediately felt his arousal pressing against her. "Ready to have some fun?"

"Too right."

She ran her hands all over him, reveling in the wonder that

he was hers to explore. His chest rose and fell under her lips, his heart thudded against her palm, her fingers bumped over his ribs and tumbled into the spaces in between before splaying against his golden brown skin and savoring the feel of his taut abdominal muscles that lay below. She dropped her hand lower, wrapping it around his erection and glorying in its silken feel against her skin. She squeezed, wanting to wrap all of herself around it.

"Steady." He sucked in a jerky breath. "Remember the dry spell."

She hastily removed her hand.

His laugh rumbled around her as his hands did some exploring of their own. He started in her hair, his fingers massaging her scalp, and then he slowly moved them down her neck and across her shoulders. He wove a circular trail from her breasts back to her spine and then forward again to her abdomen, leisurely going lower and lower, leaving no place untouched.

His hand slipped between her thighs, and she sighed as he kneaded the soft skin there with perfect pressure. Still kissing him, her body rode the wondrously long wave of dreamy languor that his stroking elicited. She could let him do this to her forever.

His fingers eventually found her welcoming wetness, and his thumb moved in slow, tantalizing circles against her now-erect clitoris. Shimmers and tingles shot along her veins, promising her that so much more was still to come. When he slid a finger inside her, she gasped not from shock but from the jet of pure, hot pleasure that hit her, hit her so hard her head spun.

At that moment she forgot everything. Her body took over, and she lost herself to the glory of sensation. Nothing existed except his mouth against hers and the touch of his fingers and thumbs on her pulsing, demanding core. She clenched against him and deepened the kiss, urging him to drive her higher and higher while at the same time never wanting any of this to end. He made a guttural sound in the back of his throat as he flicked his fingers upward and increased the pressure of his thumb. The combination was a delicious form of torture that turned her body into a panting, begging being.

Oh, yes, please. This. One minute she was sitting on his lap kissing him and the next she was being hurled into a different time and place—floating over herself on a river of bliss that threatened to scatter her to all parts of the universe.

As the orgasm faded and she came back to earth panting, he kissed her, his eyes glittering with desire. "Think you can do that again?"

She laughed and realized she'd never laughed or had so much conversation during sex in her life. "I'm always up for a challenge."

"That's the way." He lifted her buttocks and lowered her gently and slowly down onto him, opening her bit by bit until he filled her to the hilt.

"Oh," she breathed out, tightening around him and feeling him everywhere.

"Is that a good *oh* or an I'm not sure *oh*?"

"Good. Really good."

He smiled a secret sort of a smile, as if he knew something she didn't. "Okay then."

Watching her face, he rocked into her and she rocked back. He did it again and she answered. She felt exposed by his gaze, but she didn't want to look away from him, so she went with it. She'd expected frantic, hot, bone-shaking, sweaty sex, but this was gentle. No, that wasn't exactly the word, it was— Oh God, she had no clue how to describe it except it was like the tantalizing opening of a present wrapped in layer upon layer of fine, handmade paper.

Unlike his fingers on her clitoris, this orgasm didn't explode unexpectedly; instead it crept up on her—delicately, deliciously, daringly—until a ripple became a riptide. As it pulled her up into the pleasure realms, her fingers dug into his shoulders and she screamed his name.

Will followed—his entire body tensing then shuddering against hers, his chest heaving. They sank into each other, waiting for their breathing to slow, and for a moment neither of them said a word.

Will moved first. "My legs have gone to sleep."

"Sorry." She rolled away from him, but he grabbed her and pulled her in close, spooning against her. "Don't be sorry." He kissed her shoulder. "That was amazing. Thank you."

"You're welcome." *Squee!* Will Bartlett had just thanked her for sex. What wondrous universe had she just entered?

She snuggled into him, her mind going a thousand miles a minute trying to process everything that had just happened. Rafts of giddiness shot through her every time she thought about Will being as attracted to her as she was to him.

Truth is, Millie, you're the first woman I've wanted to have sex with for a long time.

Did it mean anything more than friends having sex? She stopped the thought right there. It was way too soon to be thinking about that.

Behind her, his breathing deepened and she smiled. Obviously, Will wasn't overanalyzing anything. Perhaps she should learn from that and go with the flow. Only, going with the flow didn't exactly fit in with her diabetic life. She automatically reached out her hand and grabbed Dex off her nightstand. Two ominous arrows pointing down. *Shoot.* She'd eaten a healthy dinner, but she'd forgotten how much of a workout sex was, and now she needed more food.

Will will fuss.

And she'd get mad.

She didn't want to argue with him after the best sex of her life, so decision made, she lifted his arm and slowly moved away from him.

"All right?" he mumbled, his eyes closed.

"Bathroom."

"Hmmm. K."

Grabbing her handsets off the nightstand and sweeping up her pajamas, she left the room.

Chapter 12

Tara walked around the Bear Paw park surveying the lay-
out. It had been almost a week since the agonizingly
uncomfortable Fourth of July family fun day meeting, where
Ethan had been the perfect convener—on task, efficient and
excruciatingly polite. If her unexpected attendance after their
blackmail argument had surprised him, he hadn't shown it.
He'd merely noted down Mitch's apology on the official minutes and turned away from her.

The first time in the meeting when he'd been required to
direct a policing question to her, his gaze had been quick and
matter-of-fact. Initially, she couldn't put her finger on what the
difference was until he moved his attention to the parks and
recreation officer. That's when it hit her—before she'd accused
him of blackmail, his toffee-colored eyes had always looked
at her with warmth. Now there was a very noticeable chill.

She was used to men looking at her in a variety of ways—
with fear when she was in uniform, with sexual hunger when she
was not, and there'd been times during her military service when
the hunger had tangoed with disgust because she was a woman
in uniform in a country where women were hidden away. But

Ethan's gaze held none of those things that she understood. Instead, she read disinterest.

She'd told herself it didn't matter—in fact it was better this way. The few times she'd found herself drawn to studying him closely, she'd experienced dangerous sensations of attraction—sensations that she didn't trust, because they'd only ever led her astray. After her divorce, she'd vowed she was never giving in to attraction again, and now that she'd killed any interest Ethan may have had in her, she felt she'd gained some protection from her own feelings. Yes, it was definitely better things had turned out this way. After all, she wasn't in town to be liked—she was here to do a job.

You accused him of a crime. Again. You owe him an apology. Again.

The difficult truth had been like a prickly burr in her skin for almost a week. It pierced her sharply and often, reminding her that she was in the wrong and she needed to do something about it. She'd planned to apologize to Ethan after the meeting. She'd spent the entire meeting rehearsing it, but the moment he'd said the words *Meeting closed*, he'd risen and left.

Stressed, she'd gone directly to the ER to ask Millie for some advice, but when Millie had said, *What's up?* the thought of confiding in someone she didn't know very well was harder than making the apology to Ethan. So, she'd set another coffee date and left.

She'd stopped by the library on Thursday and Friday, but both times Ethan hadn't been there, and she left without leaving a message because what was she going to say? *Call me?* He wouldn't, and besides, she doubted the offhand Tahlee would actually pass on the message. Plans to find Ethan over the weekend were stymied when her time had been consumed by supervising three bored teens clean up the mess they'd created with their Friday night graffiti spree, and by then the time lapse since Wednesday had gotten both embarrassing and increasingly difficult to bridge. So here she was, another forty-eight hours later, and tomorrow she'd see Ethan again at another damn meeting.

She'd been putting off the park reconnaissance for the

family fun day assuming—desperately hoping—Mitch would step back into the role, but when she'd brought it up in this morning's telephone call, he'd said, "It's good experience for you." A week ago, she probably would have agreed with him. Now, not so much.

So here she was at the park at the technical end of her shift and ironically right outside the library. The building, with its glass-walled reading room, backed onto the park and over-looked a grove of large cottonwood trees that shaded the half dozen picnic tables. The children's playground and horseshoe pit were close by, and farther over, there was a covered BBQ area where the Lions Club would be cooking breakfast for the fun run participants and later in the day hosting the burger barn.

Consulting the map in her hand, she inspected the three entrances to the park—one came off Railroad Street, another off Main and the third off the smaller side street. With the Fourth of July falling on a Saturday this year, there wouldn't just be Bear Paw traffic coming through town but tourists as well. This meant detouring a sizable amount of traffic during the fun run and later for the parade. It would impact how many entrances they could use. She scrawled a note in the margin and wondered wryly if Mitch was up to directing traffic with his crutches from a wheelchair.

Using the map, she plotted out the proposed distance between the lines of vendors and the different community organizations' tents, making sure there was plenty of room for people walking in both directions. Many of the boxes on the map that represented tents were labeled with their planned occupants. Along with a variety of food and arts and crafts stalls, there was a sustainability and green energy tent, a story time and craft tent, a teen's tent, animal control adopt-a-pet, first aid and even a police department tent. She wondered why the PD needed a tent, let alone why it was positioned next to the petting zoo.

You have no clue how to work in a small town, Tara.

The same unnerving sensation that had been bothering her since her arrival in town ran up her spine. Had she done the wrong thing coming to Bear Paw?

Probably. Maybe. Perhaps.

Refusing to give any fuel to the unsettling thoughts, she

finished listing her questions for tomorrow's meeting before cutting back across the park toward her patrol car. As she passed the library steps, she automatically glanced up. She winced as a rush of delight shot through her and her heart rate kicked up.

Ethan had his back to her as he locked the library for the day. A leather computer satchel strap was slung across his slim-fit paisley shirt and brown vest, and the actual bag bumped off his mustard-colored jeans. Jeans that fit tightly and showed off his unexpectedly strong legs and taut behind. It was an oxymoron, because the guy dressed like a hipster and professed not to play sports, yet his body was remarkably toned. She instantly remembered how he'd risen to his feet when she'd handcuffed him.

Hauling her gaze away from his ass, she immediately noticed he was holding a black and red sports bag in his left hand with the words *Tae Kwon Do* stenciled across it in large white letters.

So that's how he does it.

Stop thinking about his buff body. Think about apologizing.

"Hello, Ethan."

Jeez, you're supposed to sound friendly, not like a suspicious cop.

He turned abruptly from the door and jogged down the steps, walking straight past her. "Officer."

She matched his stride and tried again, this time shooting for genial. "Call me Tara."

Now you just sound demanding. You totally suck at this.

He stopped and raised his brows. "Feeling appropriately guilty, are we?"

Yes. She launched into her well-rehearsed speech. "Ethan, I wish to apologize—"

"Yeah, stop right there." He held up his hand and ceased walking. "I've heard this speech once before, remember? Only last time it started with 'Doctor Langworthy' and the sentiment lasted all of nine days. This apology doesn't mean a damn thing. It's just standard operating procedure for you, isn't it?"

"Actually, police officers apologizing is definitely not standard operating procedure," she said decisively, thinking about her training. "In fact, they strongly recommend that you never do it."

He gave her a penetrating look that seemed to go on forever, and his silence jostled and bumped her with its antagonism. Then he did something totally unexpected. His tense face relaxed, his friendly mouth curved up, often-used happy lines creased the skin around his eyes and he laughed.

"I never picked you as having a sense of humor, Tara."

His laughter made her feel uneasy. "It's not what I'm known for," she said tightly.

"No kidding." A moment later, surprise chased away the laughter. "You're actually trying to apologize, aren't you?"

"Yes, I am."

His shoulders rose and fell as if to say, *Okay then.* "I'll shut up and let you."

She squirmed under his all-seeing gaze, and she nervously licked her lips, which was crazy, because she didn't get nervous around men. "What you said the other day. You were right."

"Can I have that in writing?"

Her chin shot up. "You really want to make this hard for me, don't you?"

"Sadly, a part of me really does," he said, as if the realization shocked him. "I much preferred being mistaken for a thief than being accused of blackmailing you."

Her gut churned. "I understand."

His intelligent brow creased in a frown. "Do you? Because it's important to me that you can make the distinction."

She heard a noise and was surprised to see she was frantically clicking the pen she still held in her hand—her thumb going up and down fast. She tried to stop. "I can make the distinction. I mistook your selfless deed and turned it into something self-serving and mean-spirited."

"You did." With his free hand, he adjusted his glasses on the bridge of his nose. "Although to be fair, I probably should have told you that I gave Judy the video as much for me as for you. I prefer having footage of me playing soccer badly and celebrating like a crazy man to a photo of me in a police cell."

From her perspective, both were embarrassing, but obviously for him one was more so than the other. "Another example of your moral stance?"

"You bet." He gave a rueful smile. "It also avoids the inevitable family interrogation and the headline *Son of Judge*

Arrested for Theft. I don't want to give the old man an early heart attack."

"No. Of course not," she managed to say, trying to sound like she understood, when she had no real experience of family expectations.

Far too often in her childhood, she'd had to be the mom. The only times Tara remembered being interrogated was when Lexie wanted more liquor and Tara had hidden the rent money where she couldn't find it. Problems like that probably hadn't featured in the Langworthys' home. Being shot at probably wasn't something he'd had to deal with, either, and it was a sharp reminder that his experiences of life both as a child and an adult were clean and sanitized compared with hers.

"Earth to Tara?" Ethan clicked his fingers in front of her face. "You okay? You seemed to vanish into another world there for a minute."

And she had—only that other world was the one she was familiar with while Bear Paw and people like Ethan were as foreign to her as her life was to them. *You're apologizing, remember? Get it over with.* She cleared her throat. "The other day you said I had no clue how to work in a small town, and you're right. I've spent the last few years working with people who shoot first and ask questions later. Actually, that was Detroit. In Afghanistan, they don't even bother to ask questions."

Her chin shot up as she reined in every emotion exactly as she'd been trained. "I apologize for judging you by that yardstick, and I'll endeavor to ensure it doesn't happen again."

"You served in the military?" Ethan asked, clearly stunned.

"I did," she said matter-of-factly, "and it was a natural choice to go into law enforcement when I de-enlisted." *But I don't want to talk about it.* "So, you do Tae Kwon Do?" she said, locking her gaze onto his gym bag. "Interesting choice in a town obsessed by baseball, softball, football, volleyball and basketball."

He smiled and again his eyes crinkled up in their friendly way. "As Judy told you the first day we met, ball sports aren't my thing."

"But you have to be coordinated to do martial arts."

"Yeah, but in a different way. I took it up at thirteen when I needed some street-cred to offset the fact I played cello."

"But you play it like a rock star," she blurted out, sounding like a fangirl and instantly regretting it.

"I do now, and thank you for noticing, but back in middle school I hadn't yet busted out my bad-boy cello riffs. I was still under the thumb of the classical music teacher."

She thought about her confusing middle school years when she still felt like a little girl but she'd developed the body of a woman. Not only had boys started staring at her, but men, too, and always with naked desire in their eyes. She'd craved to stay the child she'd been, but not even her mother had allowed her that, forcing her into clothes she didn't want to wear. "Middle school can be tough."

He shrugged. "It was a perfect storm, really. I was a weedy and skinny kid, I wore glasses, I played the cello and with a voice that was late to break, Mrs. Solberg, my well-meaning but deluded English teacher told everyone in class I had the reading voice of an angel."

Tara could picture it clearly. "You wouldn't have survived five minutes in my neighborhood," she said spontaneously.

He glanced at her with that intense look of his, and she immediately regretted what she'd said. What was wrong with her? First she'd mentioned Afghanistan to him and now this. She'd disclosed more about her life to Ethan in the last ten minutes than she'd told anyone else in her thirty-one days in Bear Paw. Or, for that matter, anyone else in a very long time.

But he didn't ask her where she'd grown up; he just continued with his story. "I ignored most of the stuff the kids did, like dressing my cello in a girls' basketball uniform and calling her my girlfriend, and making stupid band camp jokes, but one day Rudy Baker pantsed me and something inside me snapped.

"Before I knew it, I'd punched him in the mouth with the world's wobbliest left hook, but somehow it took him down anyway. Rudy was shocked speechless, the other kids were impressed by the copious amounts of blood, I bruised my hand so badly I couldn't play cello for two weeks and I got suspended for a few days."

"That really was very badass of you," she said, smiling for some reason.

"Oh yeah. Totally badass," he said wryly, "although as a police officer, I'm not sure you're supposed to say that. Anyway, my parents were horrified, mortified and every other 'fied in between. *Words not fists* was the tenet in our household, and I was marched over to the Bakers' house and made to apologize to a family whose philosophy was *Boys will be boys*. That almost undid the cred I'd scored with the punch.

"My mother talked at me nonstop for a week about how street brawling and using brute force wasn't something civilized people did. Dad didn't say quite as much, but his message was the same, only he added in a practical component. One night he drove me to Great Falls to a Tae Kwon Do class. There were no balls being thrown at my head, and unlike my usual *deer caught in headlights* approach to sports, I loved it."

"Your dad drove you to Great Falls and back once a week?" She couldn't stop her voice from rising on a tide of incredulity.

"Sure," Ethan said with a shrug, "and he drove me to the monthly weekend competitions. We even went to a couple of out-of-state meets. I think I loved the road trips with dad as much as the competitions. What about you? Did you do the whole traveling-for-sport thing?"

"I played soccer." *Until the other team mothers said it wasn't fair that Lexie wasn't on the schedule to drive.*

Again she looked at the bag, which was becoming her savior in keeping the conversation away from her. "So are you heading to Great Falls now?"

He shook his head. "No. I teach a kids' class here on Tuesdays to save the parents the drive."

"Wow, that's generous."

"No, it isn't," he said quickly as if being generous was something sordid. "The kids are great and it's good to see them learning that success doesn't hinge on the ability to catch, kick, hit or throw a ball. I get back way more than I give."

When she thought about what he'd done for her and the amount of work he was putting into the family fun day on top of his regular job, she tallied up that he gave a lot. He really cared for this town.

"I also teach an adult class at the gym," he said, starting to walk again.

"Bear Paw has a gym?" She hadn't noticed it on her numerous patrols.

He laughed. "Don't get too excited. It's really more of a

shed out back of Bear Paw Motors. There's kickboxing gear, some weights, an indoor rowing machine, and that's about it."

"I used to do kickboxing," she said with a rush of enthusiasm as she remembered how much she'd enjoyed it. How she'd kicked and boxed out her stress until she was a sweating, quivering mess. It had been better than sex.

"Cool." He gave her an encouraging smile, and the warmth was back in his eyes.

An errant tingle ran down her spine and finished between her legs.

Sex can be great with the right person.

How would I know?

Ethan continued, "You should come along sometime and use the equipment."

She felt the familiar walls rising up inside her. "Oh, I really don't—"

"Relax, Tara," he said with a sigh. "I'm not hitting on you. It's just you sounded like you missed kickboxing and I thought you might enjoy getting back into it."

They'd reached her patrol car and he stopped. "Besides, sitting at home every night must be starting to get mighty lonely."

She instantly bristled. "I don't sit at home every night."

"That's true," he said, a hint of irony in his voice, "you did come to Leroy's once." He glanced at his watch. "I have to go or I'll be late, but if you want some advice—"

Her chin shot up. "I don't."

"Yeah, you do," he said, giving her a kind and wise smile like the one an elderly man would give to a kid. "You took this job, so I'm figuring you wanted to come live here. It's time to find a way to get involved in the town."

She opened the vehicle's door. "I am involved in the town. I'm the deputy sheriff, and I bet you never told the sheriff he had to get involved."

"You're right, I didn't, because I didn't have to. Mitch Hagen plays golf and coaches Little League, and the deputy before you ran the model train club. By doing something outside of the job, you'll meet people."

"I meet plenty of people through work."

Ethan rolled his eyes at her defensiveness. "Yes, but they're not necessarily people you want to spend time with as Tara Ralston, private citizen."

Her mouth dried. *Tara Ralston, private citizen.*

She didn't even know who that was.

"I'm pretty stretched, and the women would love having a woman teach a kickboxing class, aerobics, hell, anything you can offer they'd happily accept. You'd meet people and it would help you settle in."

And that was the problem. She'd never settled anywhere in her life, and she wasn't certain she could do it here.

WILL walked into the ER whistling. "G'day, Loretta."

"Hello, Doctor Bartlett. You happy today," the cleaner said in her accented English as she swiped the squeegee over the automatic glass doors.

"It's a perfect summer's day," he said with a grin that hadn't faded in days. *And I got laid again last night.*

Discovering Millie was as attracted to him as he was to her had been the best Friday night he'd had in months. It had been a pretty awesome Saturday morning, too. The sunlight had roused him early, and he'd woken Millie the best way he knew how. If he'd thought Millie was sexy when she was alert and stalking around a pool table, it had nothing on the sleep-rumpled doe-eyed woman with the erotic and blissful sighs.

Just as he'd felt the pull of sleep again, she'd whipped back the sheets and jumped out of bed. "Sorry, but you have to go before my parents see your car's still out front."

Laughing at her joke, he'd reached for her, intending to pull her back to bed, but she'd dodged him and suddenly his clothes had been dumped on his chest. "I'm serious, Will."

"Your parents know you're not a virgin, right?" he'd asked, suddenly worried as he pulled on his shirt. "Your dad wasn't super friendly toward me when I arrived."

"They're fine with me having sex," she said almost irritably. "This is about me. I don't want my mother turning up for breakfast with that knowing smile on her face and demanding to hear all about it."

He grinned as he shoved one leg into his work pants. "Just tell her I'm fabulous."

She'd snorted and given him a shove. He'd fallen back on the bed, taking her with him. "You're dreamin'," she quoted back at him in a fair imitation of his accent, but her dancing eyes belied her words.

"We still good for a swim at the water hole?"

A small frown creased her creamy forehead, and he'd found himself holding his breath. "I guess because you're on call, that's our only option?"

He'd stroked her cheek, remembering his necessary lie. "It will be fun. I promise."

And it had been.

And so had Tuesday night and then again last night when he'd taken groceries over to Millie's place and cooked her dinner. It had been hard to leave her bed at midnight and return to the soulless motel, but he knew he needed to do that. He didn't want to jeopardize Millie's clinical rotation, and he had a feeling that if Floyd found out they were sleeping together, Millie would be kicked back to the clinic. He could hear her protests already, so things were easier this way.

"Anything happening on this fine Friday afternoon, Helen?" he asked the nurse unit manager as he rounded the nurses' station.

"We're still waiting on the surgical consult for Mr. D'Alba. It's lucky his appendix decided to give him grief on one of Doctor Meissner's visiting days or he'd be on the road to Great Falls right now."

"Let me know when Doctor Meissner arrives because we haven't met." He glanced around. "Is Millie still in the resuscitation room?"

"I think so. She's been practicing intubation on the mannequin."

He walked to the resus room. As her TRUST supervisor, he'd given her a medical emergency scenario and asked her to set up the resuscitation room with the equipment required to treat the patient. Pausing in the doorway, he took a brief moment to enjoy watching her before he had to separate from being her lover to being her boss. He loved that he knew the secret treasure that lay hidden beneath those baggy and utilitarian scrubs—smooth, silky, soft skin and a lush, fecund and responsive body.

His own body tightened, and he immediately moved his mind away from sex and concentrated on her face. Her curls were half tamed today—held off her cheeks with a hair band—and she was muttering intently to herself as she checked and rechecked a list.

"How's it going?" he asked from the doorway.

She looked up and immediately smiled, dimples spinning into her cheeks and lighting up her face. "Good."

"You had lunch?"

Her smile dimmed slightly. "Are you inviting me?"

"No," he said, confused by the snark in her voice. "We're at work and I thought we'd agreed—"

"Exactly," she said briskly. "We're at work and I have a fictitious patient arriving any minute. I think I've got everything I need."

He looked at the cluttered space. "You've got way more than everything."

She wriggled her nose. "But we always have this setup for a trauma."

"I'm not saying all this won't be needed at some point, but right now, I want to teach you about the feng shui of emergency medicine."

She laughed at the Chinese reference to flow, but when he didn't laugh with her, she sobered. "You're serious?"

"I'm very serious." He pushed off the doorway and walked into the room, loving that he had the opportunity to teach. "The difference between a well-run ER emergency and a total shambles is preparation and setup. Tell me about the patient."

She consulted her card again. "Nineteen-year-old male, agitated with a stab wound to the chest. Pulse 128, BP 80 over 60, respirations 36."

"What's crucial in that information?"

"He's bleeding and hemodynamically unstable."

"Sure, but your first problem is that he's hypoxic and a lack of oxygen to the brain is making him agitated. He's gonna fight you. He'll be lashing out, and this trolley—ah, cart," he translated as he moved it aside, "will be the first thing knocked over by him or by a team member trying to get to him to restrain him. You need three hundred and sixty degrees access to the patient and a buffer zone between the equipment so staff aren't falling over it."

"Okay." She stood for a moment surveying the room and then started moving equipment to create a space and at the same time creating order. "Clearly I need the blood warmer, the IV cannulation equipment, the video laryngoscope, the thoracotomy tray and . . ."

He loved the way her mind worked. "And in the second tier you need the ultrasound and, ideally, pre-gel it so you're ready."

She wrote on the back of the card. "You should run an in-service for all the staff."

"Good idea. I've also spoken to Floyd about clear color-coded signage for the emergency carts. Red for the crash cart, green for the difficult intubation cart, so that no matter who is in the department, they can find the correct equipment easily. And we're going to have labels for gowns in fluoro colors that say airway, circulation, et cetera, so I know which staff member is doing what."

"Doctor Bartlett?" A female voice sounded behind them and he turned.

A woman wearing bright blue scrubs and a tropically patterned OR pony hat walked into the room with her hand extended. "I'm Kelli Meissner. General surgeon."

"G'day." He returned her very firm handshake. "Good to meet you, and"—he moved his arm to indicate Millie—"this is Millie Switkowski, RN and medical student."

"Hi." Millie swapped the laryngoscope she was holding to her left hand so she could offer her right.

Kelli gave it a perfunctory shake, as if Millie was just another person in a long line of people she didn't really need to remember, before turning her attention back to Will. "I've added the appendix to my list for later this afternoon."

"Mr. D'Alba."

"Ah yes, I think that was his name, unless you have two patients with a rumbling appendix?"

"No, thankfully Mr. D'Alba's the only one," he said, stifling a sigh that she appeared to be a surgeon who saw everyone in terms of body parts. "How often do you operate in Bear Paw?"

"I come in for two days a month and operate on day one

and consult on day two in preparation for the following month. One night at the Glacier Park Inn's more than enough," she said with a shiver. "Helen tells me you're living there at the moment. Tough gig."

"It's not so bad if you eat elsewhere," he said conversationally. "Leroy's has a pretty good menu."

"Oh, I haven't been there yet." She threw him a smile that said I'm interested in going with you. "Seeing as we're both visiting physicians, perhaps we could have dinner together tonight?"

The laryngoscope Millie was holding clattered to the floor.

Kelli frowned. "That's an expensive piece of equipment, Switkowski."

"Ah, yes. Sorry."

Will was about to suggest Millie check that the light bulb hadn't broken when the MontMedAir pager and his phone beeped simultaneously. The buzz of adrenaline he always got when the pager went off kicked up his heart rate and cleared his mind of all extraneous thoughts and noise. "Will Bartlett," he said crisply as he took the call.

A minute later, he hung up and met Millie's and Kelli's questioning gazes. "There's been a multi-vehicle accident with up to eight people requiring medical assistance."

Millie raced for the door, calling over her shoulder, "I'll get the emergency packs."

"What can I do?" Kelli asked.

"Get your team marshaled, get blood, and get ready. I need you on standby for possible trauma surgery."

Helen appeared at the door. "How bad?"

"Bad bad. We'll be doing hot turnarounds between here and Great Falls. Copy Millie's setup in the second trauma bay."

Helen nodded. "I'm on it."

"Hey, guys."

Everyone turned in stunned surprise toward the new voices. Josh and Katrina strolled toward them, tan arm in tan arm, with wide honeymoon smiles on their faces.

"We just got back and thought we'd stop by and make you all jealous by telling you about fabulous Tahiti." Josh stopped walking, astonishment clear on his face. "Will? Good to see you. What brings you here?"

Will pulled him into a hard and fast bear hug, unable to believe the perfect timing.

"Hey, buddy, I missed you, too," Josh said, laughing and giving him a slap on the back.

"Tahiti stories will have to wait," he said, pulling gowns off the linen cart and throwing them at Josh and Katrina. "There's a multi-trauma car-versus-motorcycle on the Blackfeet Reservation, and I need you both in the ER."

The *whoop-whoop-whoop* of the chopper sounded overhead.

"Will." Millie stood in the hall dressed in her MontMedAir suit, emergency packs over her shoulder and helmet in her hand. "Let's go."

Chapter 13

Millie gasped as the chopper prepared to land. Below her in what was normally a serene, grassy plain, bodies lay scattered with limbs jutting at odd angles. A car rested on its roof, and a few feet away she could make out the crumpled wreckage of a motorcycle, likely T-boned by the car. It was as close to a war zone as she ever wanted to get. Farther over she could see two ambulances, a fire truck and a police vehicle parked in a half circle around the carnage.

"It's a shit-storm out there," Will said through the headset.

Surprised by the edge in his voice, she turned to look at him and took in his tense jaw and unexpectedly tight face. "You okay?"

"Fine." The clipped word had so much bass in it that it almost caused feedback. "You?"

"Fine." Her blood sugar was perfect—it was the unknown of what faced her out there that was making her feel a bit wobbly.

"The EMS have declared three patients as life threatening and two as critical," Will said, sounding more like himself. "Billings is sending a chopper, too, so we can clear the scene as fast as possible. Just follow my lead."

"Will do."

As the chopper landed, she undid her seat belt, opened the door and, bending low, got the gurney and equipment. Together, they ran toward the female EMT who was waving wildly.

The midafternoon light burned Millie's eyes, and the heat of her protective clothing combined with her adrenaline caused rivulets of sweat to collide and pool at her bra. The moment she got away from the noise of the helicopter, the gut-churning sound of low moaning and the bloodcurdling screaming hit her. It tore through her as the stench of blood and body fluids with a hint of gasoline drenched her nostrils. All of it combined into a firestorm that pummeled every corner of her senses.

This is not a drill. I repeat, this is not a drill.

She saw Will stop for a second and shake his head before running again.

"Thank God you're here," the EMT said to them, her relief palpable. "I've put on a neck collar and applied a tourniquet to his leg but . . ."

"We're on it," Will said in a reassuring tone, but as he dropped to his knees on the opposite side of the patient, Millie was struck by a look of resigned horror that flared in his eyes. It was as if he'd seen this before and it hadn't been good then and it wasn't now.

She looked at the face of their patient—smooth cheeks contorted in pain. He barely looked seventeen, and his ripped and torn jeans were soaked in blood. The EMT had cut the denim to expose his left leg or what was left of it. It was pulp.

She forced her stomach contents back down her throat. "Hey, buddy, I'm Millie and this is Doctor Will. What's your name?" she asked as she quickly attached him to the monitor so she could see his vitals.

"Ed." His fingers gripped her arm so tight it hurt. "Is my girlfriend okay?"

"Was she with you before the accident?" she asked in case Ed was suffering from concussion and talking about a different time.

"She was . . . sitting next . . . to me," he said slowly, obviously in a great deal of pain. "Why isn't she here now?"

"Because none of you were wearing seat belts," Will said savagely before sucking in a deep breath as if that would help him pull it all together. "Almost everyone was thrown clear of the car. We'll get you sorted and then we'll find your girl-friend." He wrapped a tourniquet around Ed's arm in preparation for an IV.

Ed tried to pull himself up using Will as a lever. "No!"

Millie glanced at the monitor reading the low BP, the rapid respirations and the pulse-ox of eighty-two, and she remembered Will saying only half an hour ago, *He's hypoxic and agitated, and he's gonna fight you.*

"I have . . . to see her," Ed said, tugging at the tourniquet.

"Millie, oxygen now," Will said, his voice low and urgent.

"On it." She turned on the oxygen tank and pulled the elastic of the mask out wide. "Ed, I'm just going to put this mask—"

"Jade." Ed's hands pushed at hers as she tried to strap on the mask.

"Mate," Will said soothingly as he looked up at the EMT with a nod. "I'm sending someone to find her, but my priority's saving you so that you can see her again. I need you to lie back so I can examine you."

"I'll be as quick as I can," the EMT said, breaking into a run.

The *chop-chop-chop* of the rotor blades of the Billings chopper deafened them as it flew over, hammering home exactly how serious the situation was and reinforcing the importance of the golden hour.

"Line in," Will said, pulling out the trocar, and she quickly connected the IV, hanging the bag on the gurney's stand. "Run it fast." He didn't need to say, *God knows how much blood he's lost*; it was written all over his face.

"You feeling dizzy, Ed?" she asked as Will proceeded to do a quick visual check of his chest and abdomen before commencing a thorough palpation.

"No. Just my leg."

But she knew the dizziness would come, because there was only so long the human body could keep a fast-diminishing blood supply diverted to vital organs. "Wriggle your fingers for me then your toes."

Ed did as instructed, easily moving his fingers on both hands and thankfully the toes of his right leg. "Has she . . . found Jade?"

Millie glimpsed the EMT across the pasture talking earnestly with another paramedic who was running his hands through his hair. Her throat tightened at the sight—it didn't look good. "As soon as we know anything, we'll tell you." Although, if it was really bad news, they'd be keeping that information from Ed until he was a lot more stable.

Will leaned over Ed's hips and said quietly into her ear, "No chest injuries, no complaints of abdominal pain and his abdomen is soft, so that's the good news. The bad news is the crushing injury to his leg, his plummeting BP, his risk of a fat embolism and his agitation. Treatment plan?"

Even in the midst of this carnage, he was still teaching her. "We need to protect his airway in case he arrests so, um, IM ketamine to sedate him? Then rapid sequence intubation?"

"Exactly." He gave her a tight smile. "Well done."

She drew up the anesthetic. "This is going to help, Ed," she said as she quickly administered it into his thigh. The guy didn't even flinch, which was a sure sign of the extreme pain he was experiencing from what was left of his leg.

"Let's do this." Will put out his hand for the laryngoscope. The moment he gripped it, he flicked it open and inserted it into Ed's mouth. "Visualizing the vocal cords. Tube." His fingers closed around the offered ET tube. A moment later it was inserted into Ed's trachea.

Millie was inflating the cuff with saline when one of the Billings team ran up wearing similar protective gear.

"Hey, Will," the guy said with easy familiarity. "We've secured the field."

"Tom." Will nodded his hello. "Is it as bad as it looks?"

"Pretty much. There's one severe head injury. A girl went straight through the windshield and it's not looking good. She's got CSF draining from her nose."

"Is she a teenage girl? Do you know her name?" Will asked abruptly.

Tom shook his head. "No, sorry. She's one of two teen girls. The other one has a flail chest and crush fractures to the left arm. We've also got two rigid abdomens, both with suspected ruptured spleens and one with a possible liver lac. There's one spinal cord injury with no sensation below the waist, a bilateral fractured femur with possible fractured pelvis and a male totally off his face on a mix of meth and alcohol."

"Let me guess?" Will said bitterly. "He's got minor cuts and abrasions and a possible concussion."

Tom sighed. "Sadly, you're right on the money. What have you got here?"

"Hypovolemic shock, risk of bleeding out and facing a probable above-knee amputation," Will said grimly as Millie took over bagging Ed. "I've got a surgeon on standby at Bear Paw Hospital, so we'll take the two rigid abdomens. You take this guy and the severe head injury to Billings. How bad is the flail chest?"

"We're inserting a chest tube, which will stabilize her for the second evacuation."

"Good. We'll pick her up on our second run along with the spinal injury and take her to Great Falls. That leaves you with the broken bones for your second trip." Will's voice suddenly got hard. "The police can take the meth head to the local hospital."

If Tom was shocked or surprised by Will's unprofessional use of derivative slang, he didn't show it. "Sounds like a plan."

"Great. The faster this bloke gets into the OR the better. Millie, meet me over at the other patients as fast as you can." Will stood and ran.

Millie quickly handed over Ed to the Billings flight nurse, and six minutes later she was back in the air with patients— Colton, a guy in his early twenties, and Lewis, a teenage boy. The trip to Bear Paw took four minutes, but as she bolused fluid into both of them in an attempt to maintain their blood pressure, it seemed like the longest four minutes of her life.

Will was multitasking—putting up another bag of Hartmann's solution while talking to Kelli on the radio, giving the surgeon an update on their patients. Millie tried not to think about the *Hello, I'm yours if you want me* look the female surgeon had given him just before they'd left. It had burst the beautiful bubble she'd been living in for almost a week—the bubble where only she and Will existed—and it had allowed the traitorous question of *Why does he want me?* to sneak back in and play havoc in Dolby sound.

I'm choosing to get lucky with you. She tried latching on to Will's words but immediately lost them to the duplicitous thought *He could choose to get lucky with other women.*

"We're coming in to land," Jay the pilot said, his voice loud in the headphones.

Through the swirling dust raised by the chopper's rotors, Millie saw the hospital's helipad with its distinctive red *H*. They touched down, the doors opened and Katrina's and Josh's anxious faces greeted them. The moment she'd handed over her patient to Josh, she ran and got new emergency packs and took half a minute to test her blood sugar. It was holding steady, but she unwrapped a protein bar anyway. She met Will at the front of the ER, and his eyes immediately narrowed at the protein bar in her hand.

She didn't need him suggesting she wasn't up to coming, and as much as she hated discussing her blood sugar with him or with anyone, she didn't want him kicking her off the flight. "All good." She thrust a bar at him. "Eat this."

He pushed it back at her as his long legs covered the short distance back to the helicopter. "I'm not hungry."

"Welcome to my world," she said wryly as she shoved it into his hand again. "You're probably hungry but the adrenaline's masking it."

He gave her an odd look as if she'd just solved a mystery for him. "You know, I'm always famished at the end of these retrievals."

She rolled her eyes. "So eat the bar." The irony of being a diabetic was that despite her body not always doing what it was supposed to do, she was tuned in to how it worked in a way other people never considered. Not that she wouldn't trade that knowledge in a heartbeat for a functioning pancreas.

Jay talked through his checks, the chopper rose and it seemed no time at all before they were landing again on the grassy plain. By now, some of the local community had arrived, their faces white with shock at the mess in front of them. The car, which looked like someone had taken a can opener to it and sheared off the side, told of the speed of the impact. A police officer was talking to a cluster of people and writing in his notebook. Some men stood stoically, shielding their eyes from the glare of the sun and holding weeping women close, while others wiped tears from their eyes when they felt no one was looking.

Millie's heart ached for them. An accident like this blasted through a small town like an explosion, leaving a crater of pain and a lot of very hard questions. As expected, they'd beaten the Billings crew back, and the EMTs had their two patients ready for loading.

A woman was sobbing over a teen girl who was propped up high on the gurney—a sure sign she needed help breathing.

Millie heard Will mutter softly to himself, "Jesus, are they all kids?"

It was true. The car seemed to have been full of teens out for a joyride—a ride that had turned tragic not just for them but also for the couple on the motorcycle.

"I'm Doctor Bartlett," Will said to the hysterical woman who was gripping the side of the gurney like it was a lifeline. "We need to load your daughter onto the chopper."

"Lily's a good girl," the woman said frantically, transferring her viselike grip to Will's arm. "She works hard. She's a good student, she helps out at the nursing home, she never acts up. She doesn't deserve to die."

Millie heard the fear in the woman's voice and recognized the start of the bargaining that always happened in traumatic situations. Bargains with God—*If she lives, I'll come back to church. If she lives, I'll give more to charity. If she lives . . .*

"Promise me, Doctor, that she'll be okay."

Will carefully and gently unfolded the woman's fingers from his arm. "We're doing our absolute best, and that means getting Lily to Great Falls as fast as possible."

"I have to come with her. She needs me."

Millie put her arm around the woman's shoulders and turned her toward the gathering crowd. "Can someone help us out here? Lily's mother needs to get to Great Falls."

The police officer came over and took the woman by the hand. "Leave it with me. I'm organizing transport for people to get to three different hospitals. Mary, don't you worry. We're gonna get you to Great Falls."

Millie turned her attention back to her patient where it belonged, and five minutes later, they were in the air again. Millie rechecked all of Lily's vital signs and then checked them against the EMT's last check. None of them made sense.

"Will?"

He turned from their paraplegic patient, who was sedated and still to best protect his spinal cord. "Problem?"

"Despite the chest tube, Lily's respirations are increasingly rapid. She's agitated and her BP's low, but I don't get it, because there are no signs of any internal bleeding."

He automatically checked the underwater sealed drainage, which was bubbling exactly like it was supposed to be doing, and then he looked at the Lifepak, reading the EKG. "Any abnormal heart sounds?"

"It's hard to hear over the noise of the chopper, but it's not a clear *lub-dub*."

A run of ectopic beats flashed across the Lifepak screen, backing up her words.

He ripped off his headset and grabbed a stethoscope. "Lily, honey, I just want to listen to your heart."

The girl nodded, her eyes wide above the oxygen mask.

Millie watched Will's brows snap down and deep lines of intense concentration dig into his forehead as he moved the stethoscope. She wondered what he could hear.

"Muffled heart sounds," he finally said, and his long fingers proceeded to explore Lily's neck. "Extended jugular vein."

"So her shortness of breath has nothing to do with her flail chest?" she asked, knowing she was one step behind him and hating it.

"That's right, which is why we missed this."

"What *this*?" she asked desperately.

His mouth twisted grimly. "She's in cardiac tamponade."

"Oh God." The sac around Lily's heart was filled with fluid and squashing her heart. "Thank goodness we're close to Great Falls."

Beep, beep beep. Another run of ectopic beats raced across the screen. The fluid around Lily's heart was compressing and stressing her heart.

He shook his head. "She could arrest on us before then. I need to do a pericardiocentesis and drain the fluid."

"Now?" Millie heard her voice squeak as she looked at their cramped space.

"Right now," he said in a voice that brooked no argument. "You find the heart on the portable ultrasound and I'll get a syringe and a large bore needle."

"Lily, this will feel cold, but it's all good, okay?" she said to the barely conscious girl. She squirted gel onto her chest and located the heart. She looked at Will. "Are you going to intubate first?" she asked softly.

His mouth flattened. "It's a catch-twenty-two. I'm calling removing the fluid first and hoping that's gonna work for us." He put his hand on their patient's shoulder. "Lily," he said gently, "stay with me. I have to put a needle in your chest to make you feel better."

"Preparing to land," Jay said routinely.

"No," Will said urgently. "I need a couple of minutes."

With the steadiest hand Millie had ever seen, Will carefully inserted the needle into the young girl's chest, his eyes fixed on the grainy black-and-white image of the ultrasound. "There, see?" He tilted his head toward the black image that the needle was reaching. "That's fluid."

"It seems back to front. I expected fluid to be white."

"Yeah, it's funny that way." He slowly withdrew the syringe's plunger, and blood filled the plastic. The EKG stopped screaming, and Will grinned at her, relief and the buzz of a win clear on his face.

A beautiful line of sinus rhythm beats with their neat and perfect PQRST sequences traced reassuringly across the screen. "That's incredible, Will."

He shrugged almost dismissively, and a dark look crossed his face. "It wouldn't have been necessary if a drug-affected moron hadn't gotten behind the wheel of a car."

Again, his intensity startled her. "Amen to that, but sadly it happens."

Will ignored her. "Jay, we can land when you're ready."

"Going down now, Doc."

The chopper banked, and Millie blew out a breath, never more thrilled to see the roof of the level two trauma unit and a team of waiting clinicians.

The Lifepak warning beep screamed again as Lily's heartbeat quivered.

Will swore. "She's in VF. Defib at one-fifty."

As Millie discharged the life-saving volts into Lily's body, the chopper touched down.

The Lifepak kept screaming. "Lily, don't you dare die on

me," Will said as he grabbed the paddles off Millie. He discharged two hundred and fifty volts into the teen, her body jerking under the assault.

"Sinus rhythm," Millie said as she sent up a *thank you* into the ether.

The chopper doors opened and Will yelled, "We need a cardiologist. She's in tamponade and she's already arrested once."

"We're on it," someone yelled, and then Lily was out of the chopper and being transferred onto an ER gurney and surrounded by the first Great Falls team. The second team took the handover of their paraplegic patient, and then Millie started walking toward the hospital doors, wanting to check on Lily.

Will's hand gripped her shoulder, stalling her progress. "Kelli needs us back in Bear Paw to transfer Colton to the ICU here. Apparently, when she opened him up, she found half his circulating volume in his peritoneum."

"What about Lily?"

He gave her a sympathetic look. "Our job was to get her here alive, and we did that." He shuddered. "Just. We'll check on her when we come back with Colton."

She wasn't used to such short patient contact, and she wasn't sure she liked having to hand them over so quickly. "What about Jade and Ed?"

"Both in theater in Billings," he said, sounding very Australian. "Sorry, they're both in the OR. We'll get an update when they're out. Come on." He spun around and marched straight back to the chopper with his shoulders rigidly straight—one hundred percent the ER physician.

She shoved a handful of fruit snacks into her mouth, along with some almonds and raisins, and ran back to the chopper.

———

"DO we dare believe it's over?" Millie asked Will, leaning into him as they walked into the guesthouse.

It was six hours since the first emergency call, but it felt like twelve. It also felt like it should be dark, but this was Montana in the summer, and it was light past ten. They'd flown five flights, but finally they were back in Bear Paw, and exhaustion clawed at her. She didn't want to think about what she looked like, although she had a fair idea, if Will was anything to go by. His hair stood up in jagged spikes, hauled up by frantic fingers seeking inspiration, and deep lines of concentration underscored his eyes, half buried in black smudges.

Will closed the door behind them and then stroked her hair. "We've been signed off until eight o'clock tomorrow morning. Any other emergencies tonight will be handled by another team."

She rested her head on his shoulder. "Thank God for that. I don't think I had another run in me. It was a tough day."

"I've had worse," he said in a clipped tone so unlike his usual relaxed manner.

She'd caught glimpses of a new Will today—one where the laid-back guy vanished momentarily, like when he'd stood stock-still in the pasture as if he'd been there once before. She guessed he'd seen a lot of awful stuff over the years. "What was your worst day ever?"

"You don't want to know."

"I do."

He shook his head. "Mils, it's been a shit of a day. Let's not add to it by revisiting past disasters, okay?"

Only it wasn't a question—it was a very firm statement, and his clenched jaw left her in no doubt that nothing she said would change his mind. As much as she was interested in hearing and learning from his experiences, she got his point and decided not to push it. "Another time, then."

"Hmmm." It came out low, sounding more like *I don't think so* rather than *Sure thing*. She was about to say something when his hand ran up into her hair, his fingers pressing firmly into her scalp in a recognizable prelude to sex.

She found herself pushing her head back against his fingers, loving the massage, and the pressure derailed her thoughts along with the faint reminder that now they'd been having great sex for a week, perhaps they should have the conversation, *Is this just a summer thing?*

She snuggled into his chest. "I'm so tired I can't decide what I want more: the hot tub, dinner or bed."

"I can help you make that taxing decision," he said, a sexy twinkle sparkling in his eyes, replacing his previous intransigent look.

"Can you, now?"

"Oh yeah." Gazing down at her, he cupped her cheeks with his large hands and gently moved his thumbs in small circles. The slight roughness of his thumb pad against her soft skin sent shivers of anticipation skating through her. Slowly, he lowered his mouth, his wide and generous lips seeking hers, but that was where slow stopped. His kiss invaded her mouth with urgency and a desperate energy that belied his fatigue.

Just like every other time he kissed her, half of her sighed and melted into a wide river of languid need while the other half of her sizzled with a desire that crackled and fizzed and demanded satiation. Now. Right now. Grasping his hand, she walked him down to her bedroom, pausing only to grab a condom from the nightstand drawer before stepping through the sliding glass doors and out onto the private deck. She pulled back the cover from the hot tub and started the jets.

"I like the way you think," he said with a grin before pulling off his shirt and shucking his pants.

She didn't even bother trying to stifle the low and appreciative *wow* that rolled out of her. She never tired of being able to see, touch and taste his beautiful body.

"Enjoy me. I'm all yours," he said as he lifted the top of her scrubs, pulling it easily over her head. He immediately paused, staring at her bright blue lace bra. "Noice." His accent rumbled and flattened the word. "Very noice, but as much as I want to admire it, the jets are bubbling and we're wasting electricity. The bra has to go."

"If it's in the interests of the environment and sustainability . . ." She undid the bra and attempted a sexy shimmy to wriggle it off her shoulders. Halfway through, she suddenly stilled, feeling very self-conscious. "I have no clue what I'm doing."

"It doesn't look that way to me," Will said appreciatively. "Keep going."

She still couldn't fully believe that this guy, who could have any woman he wanted, found her sexy, but he was standing in front of her with the evidence of his arousal hard and straight and beautiful. Laughing, she twirled the bra, stepped in close and placed it around his neck, pulling his head down to hers.

He made a hoarse sound and kissed her.

Her mind emptied of everything except Will.

When he broke the kiss so they could both breathe, she kicked off her pants, disconnected her insulin pump and stowed it on top of the towel shelf before joining him in the tub.

The warm water bubbled around them, and Will pulled her into his lap. His erection pressed against her, and she felt the familiar rush of anticipation and the wondrous, heavy throb of desire. She was ready.

Only, he didn't open the condom and lift her onto him. Instead, he surprised her by rubbing her shoulders, his strong, long fingers pressing and kneading, releasing the knots of tension that the draining afternoon and evening had put there. Under his expert ministrations, her muscles loosened and her shoulders dropped. He massaged her scalp before moving methodically down her neck and along her spine. His thumbs dipped between each vertebra with subtle pressure until they reached her hips. Suddenly, his hands were doing amazing things to her thighs.

Every muscle in her body sagged with bliss, and she leaned against him for support, her back resting against his chest and belly. Her eyelids fluttered closed. She was warm and relaxed, totally supported by him, and as much as she wanted him to fill her, as much as she wanted to impale herself upon him until all she could feel was him, a part of her never wanted to move from this warm, safe place or from the magic of his wondrous hands.

He dropped his head to her neck, his lips sucking and soothing, his tongue flicking and teasing her hot, wet skin, until every cell vibrated with lust and she was one banked fire of boneless need from tip to toe. Her breathing hitched as his hands moved to her front, massaging her belly in concentric circles, and then he was cupping her breasts with a pressure that was neither tender nor rough.

She heard low, guttural sounds and realized they came from her. They were moans of delight as slow, delicious pleasure meandered through every part of her like a lazy river on a hot summer's afternoon. She didn't know anything could feel this good. His fingers found her nipples, and a sharp bolt of need dived deep, imploding every languid feeling. With a throaty cry, she swung around fast to face him, her body aching and impatient for him. He smelled of salt, testosterone and sex, and his eyes were every shade of blue, just like van Gogh's *Starry Night*.

He reached for the small foil packet on the edge of the hot tub. "Ready?"

"Yes, please."

Panting, her mouth found his—wide and hot and greedy—and she claimed it with her own impatience, welcoming the flood of his hungry need tangoing with hers. She wanted to wrap herself around him so their skin overlapped and no space existed between them. Lifting her arms up around his neck, she linked her fingers and then she wrapped her legs around his waist until all of her was touching him.

Without breaking the kiss that threatened to suck the air from her lungs, his strong arms moved underneath her, gripping her buttocks, and then he lifted her over him.

A soft, high-pitched, involuntary squeal left her mouth as she anticipated the width and weight of him inside of her. *Oh. Yes. This.*

Beep, beep, beep, beep, beep, beep, beep.

Her breath caught. *No! No way! Not now!*

Will flinched and pulled his mouth from hers. "Is that Dex?"

"I'm fine." She kissed him again, flicking her tongue against his cheek in the way she knew made him kiss her hard.

Beep, beep, beep, beep, beep, beep, beep.

He pulled away again. "Millie, you either need insulin or you need to eat."

"I can do it in five minutes," she half panted, half sobbed as she felt the tip of his penis pressing against her and she clenched as if that was enough to suck him into her.

"Call me old-fashioned," he said tightly, "but I don't want to have sex with an unconscious woman." In a perfunctory movement, he lifted her off him and sat her on the hot tub's seat.

Shock dueled with desire. "Will . . ." But the rest of her sentence died under his granite gaze.

Sex in the hot tub—sex anywhere right now—was off the table.

Disappointment was far too tame a word to describe the feeling that stole through her. *Betrayal* came close. She hated her diabetes with a passion that threatened to rush her back to the dark days of the past. Not only had it totally wrecked the moment, it had just spectacularly reminded Will that she was faulty. Up until now, sex had been the *one* time he seemed to forget she was diabetic.

God, right now, any other woman would be humping him senseless. Rendering him utterly speechless, reducing him to a series of shudders and moans and watching ecstasy crawl across his face instead of this frown of consternation that came with a horrifying hint of paternal concern.

He stood up, shut off the jets, hauled her to her feet, flicked a towel off the waiting pile and wrapped it around her like she was a kid who needed help at bath time. With a rush of aggravation, she stepped out of the tub, needing to separate from him. She didn't want his help. She didn't want anyone's help. She just wanted to be treated like a normal woman—whatever that felt like, and she was utterly certain it didn't feel like this.

She grabbed the beeping Dex off the top of the towel cupboard. *Crap.* The numbers didn't lie—she was crashing.

Will wrapped a towel around his waist as he looked over her shoulder. "Hell, Millie. Why didn't you tell me you needed to eat the moment we got home?"

Don't blame me. She flicked her wet hair, showering him with water, and slapped her hands on her hips. "Because you distracted me by kissing me."

A contrite expression crossed his face. "My bad. I should have realized."

"No," she said tersely as she pushed past him into the bedroom, cross with Dex, cross with him, cross with herself. "You don't need to realize. That's my job."

As she pulled on some shorts, she felt the prickle of tears burning behind her eyes. *Damn it.* Hypoglycemia messed with her emotions, and she could lurch from irritable to angry to teary in a heartbeat. She would *not* cry in front of Will—that would be the ultimate humiliation on top of everything else.

Dex sounded again, and she grabbed some fruit snacks from her nightstand and raced for the kitchen. She'd just pulled some eggs out of the fridge when Will appeared. He stood tall in the doorway, looking damp and delectable, wearing a pair of sweatpants he'd forgotten to take with him the other night and Evan's old T-shirt. His expression was wary and alert—as if he wasn't sure if she was going to burst into tears or lunge at him and bite his head off.

So much for being sexy and desirable. She was certain that just like her family, he was starting to think that she came under the banner of *way too much hard work*.

He cleared his throat. "Can I make you an omelet?"

"I can do it." The double-crossing shakes chose that exact moment to set in, and the bowl she was holding clattered onto the counter.

He took that as his cue and swept into the kitchen as if it was his ER and she was the patient. He lifted her onto the counter like she was five years old, poured her a glass of juice, held it out in front of her and said, "Drink this."

She hated that she had no choice but to obey.

Chapter 14

"Please don't feel you have to stay."

Millie's tone managed to combine defensiveness, embarrassment and terse politeness. Confused, Will looked up from beating the eggs. "Do you want me to leave?"

Millie waved Dex under his nose. "I want you to see that the juice has kicked in and the shakes have gone. You've been looking after people all day, and the last thing you need to be doing now is looking after me."

You're wrong. But he wasn't dumb enough to say that to a woman who had the low blood sugar snarks. What he really wanted to say was, *Don't be embarrassed by what happened*, but he knew enough to tread very carefully around Millie when she was hypoglycemic. "Actually, I'm here for purely selfish reasons."

And in one way, he was. He'd been the one who'd kissed her in the hope of sex, because he'd wanted to lose himself in her and block out the events of the day. In far too many ways today had been like reliving the hell of Charlie's last few hours, except that no one had died. Yet.

All he wanted to do now was forget about drug-affected drivers, damaged young lives and a community reeling.

"Purely selfish reasons? Really?" she said, half grumpy, half teasing. "You have a passion for making eggs?"

He gently nudged her shoulder with his. "I have a passion for you."

A flash of skepticism lit up her eyes, and he hated that no matter what he did or said, she never seemed to fully believe she was sexy and desirable.

He leaned in and captured her lips, tasting the sweetness of the juice and the softness of Millie. "My despicable plan is to feed you, get those numbers up to a nice, solid level and then take you to bed so you can work off the calories until you're screaming and so is Dex."

"You got the stamina for that?" she asked, her eyes dancing.

And happy Millie was back. He let go of a breath he hadn't been aware he was holding. "I'll give it my best shot." He passed her a loaf of bread. "You make toast and I'll deal with the eggs."

Millie turned on her MP3 player, and they sang loudly and tunelessly to ABBA as they cooked. There was something soothing and reassuring about doing totally normal things after the day they'd been through. He was sautéing the bell pepper, onions and bacon when his phone vibrated and beeped on the counter.

He'd been getting updates on all the patients they'd evacuated, and he immediately tensed. The news about Jade wasn't good, and as much as he'd been hoping against it, he'd been half expecting bad news. "Billings?"

Millie picked up the sleek, fluoro red device—he'd deliberately chosen the color so he could always find the phone—and she offered it to him. He shook his head. "I don't want to burn this. You read it out."

"Okay." She swiped the screen and with eyes cast down read the text. "Oh."

His chest tightened at the sound, and he plucked the phone out of her hand, frantically reading the text, preparing for the worst. His brain lurched in his skull at the unexpected words.

"Exactly why is Doctor McBain asking you for sex advice?" Millie's bemusement tinkled in her voice.

"Because I'm the best," he teased, deliberately aiming to

divert the conversation away from the fact he was still helping the needy McBain. Women got funny about things like that.

"And you're so freaking humble." She pinched the phone back and scrolled up through the texts. "Oh my God, you've given this guy a step-by-step guide to seducing a woman."

"No," he said, feeling unusually defensive. "I gave him some dating tips in exchange for him covering my shifts so I could come to Josh and Katrina's wedding."

"So what you're saying is that you're not really a player but a generous guy."

He grinned at her cynical expression. "That's me. Generous to a fault, and I've been helping a bro out." He dumped the sautéed vegetables onto the omelet and flipped the other half over the top before slicing it in two and serving it onto the plates.

Millie spread sweet chili sauce over the eggs. "He's moved on from dating tips to foreplay."

He joined her at the table. "Yeah, that's crossing the line. The time has come for McBain to go cold turkey."

Millie kept scrolling while she ate. "Wow, some of these dating ideas are really good," she said, sounding begrudgingly impressed. She set the phone down and gave him a calculated and devious look. "Obviously, I put out way too early, because you didn't try any of these things with me."

"I took you canoeing and we had a picnic."

"*When* you thought I was a lesbian," she said indignantly.

"Yeah." The guilt swirled in his gut. "Sorry again for that major stuff-up."

She pushed her now empty plate away and twirled a curl around her finger, a calculating look in her eyes. "Given the psychological trauma that little mix-up inflicted on me, I think it's only fair you make it up to me."

He laughed, happy to oblige, because spending time with Millie was always fun. "Fair enough. Which scenario takes your fancy?"

"Flyboarding looks like fun."

His heart clenched. "We're choosing from the list. Flyboarding's not on that list, and it's not romantic. What about movies in the moonlight?"

She scrunched up her pretty face. "Yeah, but this is Bear Paw, so no such thing."

"I can set up a screen outside and we could have popcorn."

She shook her head slowly back and forth. "I don't think that will do it. No, I'm still thinking Flyboarding."

The idea of her blacking out at fifty feet in the air on top of a jet of water and then plummeting into a deep lake made his gut churn and his chest ache. He quickly scrambled for ideas. "I saw a poster advertising Montana Shakespeare in the Parks."

"Picnic rug, gourmet picnic hamper"—she consulted one of the text messages—"a bunch of wildflowers, chocolates and champagne."

"You don't drink alcohol, so I'll find something sparkling and low in sugar."

She got a stubborn look in her eyes. "What about the chocolates?"

"You know chocolates aren't a great idea."

She shrugged as if she didn't care. "Just this once, I can make an exception for Swiss chocolate balls."

He didn't want her to make an exception just this once or ever. He didn't want her blood sugar soaring sky-high or dropping dangerously low, because both came with risky consequences—loss of consciousness, kidney damage, retinal damage with eyesight loss, high blood pressure, gangrene—the list went on and on, and every item was tattooed onto every health professional's brain from the moment they became a student.

Almost as if she was making a point or flipping him the bird, she got out her lancet, pricked her finger and tested her blood sugar. "You know, Will, Flyboarding is probably safer than chocolate."

Like hell it is. "I think seeing *The Taming of the Shrew* in the park will be perfect."

"As long as you're not trying to tame me," she quipped, only her smile didn't quite reach her eyes.

"Never," he said, not wanting to argue. Not now. Not tonight. Not when he wanted to bury himself inside her luscious and welcoming body and forget the day.

"Do you have any photos of Australia on your phone?" she asked unexpectedly, her finger hovering over the photo icon.

"I think they're mostly of Montana, although mum sent a few the other day."

"Can I see them?"

"Sure."

She scrolled across and stopped at the one taken at Francois Peron National Park. "Oh my God, I want to go here. These colors are amazing. I've never seen cliffs that red next to a beach of golden sand, and the sea's so clear." She looked up at him, bemused. "The sky's the same blue as Montana."

He smiled at her, loving that she'd made that connection. "It is, and it's just as big and wide," he said, thinking of the shimmering heat of hot summer days in Murrinwindi.

"Do you get homesick?"

There was no point denying it. "Sometimes."

She scrolled again. "Oh, look at you, sexy surfer dude with your wet suit rolled down to your waist." She peered more closely at the photo, using her fingers to zoom in, and then she looked up, her expression one of confusion. "Did you used to have a tattoo on your left shoulder?"

His chest tightened so fast the pain radiated everywhere. *Charlie.* She must have scrolled through to the end of all the recently added photos and the phone had defaulted back to the start of the collection. He swallowed and tried to sound normal. "That's my twin."

Her eyebrows hit her hairline. "You have an identical twin?"

Had. But he didn't want to talk about Charlie in past tense. Not tonight. "Charlie."

Her eyes lit up. "He's gorgeous."

A streak of something green shot through him.

Dude. Charlie's laughing voice sounded in his head. *We swapped girlfriends all the time, so you must have it bad for this one if you're jealous of her admiring me. I'm dead, remember.*

As if he could forget. "Lusting after my brother in front of me isn't cool."

She laughed as if he was cracking a joke. "I want to meet him. He's got a look of fun in his eyes that makes yours look almost tame."

How had she noticed that? Most people couldn't tell them

apart when they were standing facing the two of them talking, let alone picking up on the biggest difference between them from a photograph.

"I bet the two of you together cause chaos."

"We used to," he said tightly, remembering how they'd each pretended to be the other and tricked their teachers, the girls they were dating and most of the town. "We've grown up now."

"Sure," she said, eyes dancing as she handed back the phone. "Is he in Australia?"

No. He stood and pulled her to her feet, wrapping his arms around her, loving the way she sank into his chest. "As much as I love Charlie, I can think of better things we could be doing."

He nuzzled her neck and then flicked his tongue into the hollow at the base of it. She shivered against him and pressed her lips to his chest. That was all it took to make him hard. He wanted her so badly it took everything he had not to rush her down the hall and push her onto the bed. He wanted to end this awful day with something good. He wanted to banish the vision of a field of pain with her crying out his name and her muscles spasming around him so tightly that it pushed him into the bliss of oblivion.

There he could forget. Forget today. Forget that awful day almost two years ago. Pretend that part of him hadn't shriveled and died with Charlie.

"Bed?" she asked, her eyes glazed with desire.

"Bed."

They ran to the room and leaped onto the mattress, rolling together, both vying to be on top. He tucked her under him, and she smiled up at him before wrapping her legs around him. God, it felt amazing. She felt amazing. He lowered his head, planning to kiss her until she writhed against him, bumping her hips against his and begging him to enter her.

Beep, beep, beep.

Millie sighed. "This time it's not me."

He groaned. "It's probably just McBain."

"A guy with sex on the brain will keep texting until you reply, so how about you turn the phone off for five minutes?"

"Sweetheart, it's gonna be off for a lot longer than that."

She laughed and swatted his shoulder. "You don't do modest, do you?"

He grinned down at her as he reached for the device. "Of course, if the lady doesn't want the full treatment, I can reduce the time."

She pressed her fingers to his lips. "That won't be necessary."

He propped himself up on an elbow, and as he went to push the power-off button he saw the words *did all we could*. He instantly rolled away from Millie, opened the text and read it. His hot blood chilled so fast it hurt.

———

MILLIE saw the moment Will paled under his healthy tan, and she automatically reached out her hand and touched his arm. "Jade?"

The young woman had been thrown through the windshield, and the human body wasn't designed for that sort of brutality.

He shook his head, his nostrils flaring. "Lily." His voice cracked on the young girl's name.

Millie sat up so fast her head spun. "But . . ." She tried to marshal her chaotic thoughts as shock socked her hard. "Two hours ago they told us she was stable."

"Yeah." He blew out a long breath. "It turns out she had an undiagnosed cardiac malformation, and the stress of the tamponade was too much for her heart. She arrested again, and this time they couldn't get her back." He tossed the phone onto the bed with a vicious flick of his wrist and then scrubbed his face with his hands. "I thought we'd gotten away with it. I thought we'd fought off death today and won."

His ragged words shocked her, because as an experienced emergency physician, he knew there were times when he couldn't save everyone. As tragic and as unexpected as Lily's death was, Millie knew that the only way to cope was to focus on the lives they'd saved, not the lives they'd lost. "In a way we did kind of win. We saved a lot of lives."

"She was sixteen, Millie!" He slammed his fist into the mattress, and then he was suddenly yelling. "And a moron high on meth stole her life. It's such a fucking waste."

The agony in his voice made her jump. It was never easy to lose a patient, but the intensity of his reaction seemed almost personal—just like the savagery of his voice when they'd landed at the accident site and he'd seen the bodies strewn across the field.

He stared at the wall with a haunted look on his face, and when he spoke, he sounded almost defeated. "The same thing happens at home. Country towns, bored kids, drugs and alcohol, fast cars and a belief they're invincible. They don't get that sometimes I can't pick up all of the pieces."

I? Surely he meant *we,* as in the medical community? Only now wasn't the time to ask or correct him. In fact, she got the distinct impression he didn't want her to say anything. Truth be told, nothing she could say would change a thing, but he looked so shattered that she needed to do something.

Wrapping her arms around him, she pulled him into her and held him close, his head resting in the crook of her neck. Stroking his hair with one hand, she rested the other on his ribs, feeling his chest expand and contract, and his breath rhythmically sweeping across her skin like a warm breeze. She rocked him slowly back and forth, wordlessly comforting him, while her mind jumped between the shock of Lily's death and the strength of Will's reaction for a patient he barely knew.

The rocking was hypnotic, and her eyes started to flutter closed when Will suddenly moved and pressed his lips gently against her throat. Slowly and steadily he trailed kisses upward until his mouth was on her cheek and his tongue was flicking in and out of her ear. Red, hot, fiery licks of desire arrowed straight down between her legs, making her gasp.

He lifted his head, and she caught a momentary shadow of something before the naked desire in his eyes obliterated it. "God, I want you."

His throaty words made her wet. "I want you, too."

He took her words as permission, grabbed a condom, and the next minute he'd rolled her under him without his usual finesse or gentleness, but she didn't care, because she was aching for him, too. With a searing kiss that sucked the breath from her lungs and made her see stars, he thrust into her.

Surprise made her clench. Not that it hurt—it didn't—it was just that every other time they'd had sex, he'd eased into her slowly and gently, opening her up little by little until she'd taken all of him into her and they'd started their rhythm together. This time, she felt like he was ahead in the game and she was playing catch-up.

Usually, he laughed and teased her, and he always checked with her that what he was doing was good for her. Now he was silent. He found her mouth again and kissed her as if he was inhaling her—as if he needed her breath to breathe. Leaving her panting, he tore his mouth away from hers, gripped her ankles and pulled her legs up over his shoulders. A moment later his hands lifted her buttocks.

With his chest heaving, he stared down at her, his navy eyes glittering and unfocused, and right then she knew he didn't see her. He thrust into her, his body demanding her orgasm rather than giving it, and her body responded despite a voice in her head asking what the hell was going on.

With each press against her G-spot, she felt herself being pulled higher and higher up the mountain toward the precipice her body craved, but as glorious, amazing and intense as this journey was, she and Will were out of sync. She felt torn between her need and his, as if they were on totally separate roads to the same destination.

Sensation upon sensation hammered her, and her fingers dug into his thighs as her body craved the prize. He tensed and then he was crying out and shuddering against her as his orgasm hit. It flung her out and over the edge as wave upon wave of pulsating, hedonistic pleasure rocked her.

When she fell back to earth, she realized that Will was slumped against her, a heavy, sweating, panting mess. She dragged in a breath and pushed at his shoulder. "Will. Can't breathe."

For a moment he didn't move, and then he mumbled, "Sorry," and propped himself up on one elbow. He stroked her cheek softly, and his eyes—twinkling again like they so often did—gazed down at her full of joy. "I take it from the state of the bed, that was your best orgasm yet."

And technically it was, but it felt oddly empty because of the disconnect that had existed between them. It left her feeling that she could have gotten the same effect from her vibrator. "Are you feeling okay, Will?"

He laughed and kissed her swiftly. "Why are you even asking me that after such amazing sex?"

It was a rhetorical question, and he rolled her onto the dry side of the bed·and pulled her in close, wrapping his arms around her and spooning in against her. A minute later he was snoring gently and Millie was left staring at the ceiling with a growing list of unanswered questions.

————

"MORNING, Will."

Damn. His hand stilled on the gate, and he turned around to see a smiling Susie Switkowski sitting by the pool sipping coffee. He wasn't embarrassed that she'd seen him, but he knew Millie wouldn't be happy. "You're up early, Susie," he said with a friendly smile.

"I love this time of day, and I find doing laps very relaxing." She picked up a cup. "Coffee?"

"Sure." There was no point rushing off now Susie knew he'd spent the night. "I don't have to be at the hospital until eight."

She passed him the cream and sugar and offered him a plate of summer fruits and some Danish pastries. "Danny and I often have breakfast out here in the summer, but this is the first time I've ever met anyone leaving Millie's." She took a sip of coffee. "How is she?"

"Still asleep."

"I meant how's her diabetes." A flicker of concern flashed in her eyes. "Is she stable?"

"I'm not her doctor, Susie," he said politely but firmly, "and even if I was, I couldn't tell you anything."

"I know that." Her sigh seemed to come from her feet. "I lost that right as a parent when she turned eighteen, but you're obviously spending a lot of time with her." A knowing smile slid quickly across her face. "It's just she doesn't tell Danny and me a thing unless she's admitted to the hospital, and even then I'm not sure she always tells us." Her face sagged and she suddenly looked her age. "We worry."

He frowned. "Millie's been hospitalized?"

She shuddered as if the memory was fresh. "She was in the ICU, and I know all those tubes and machines are normal for a medical person like you, but it was terrifying for us. That sort of fear never leaves you."

An image of his parents standing in the ICU next to Charlie's bed clutching each other for support and seeking reassurance from him that all the lines, tubes and machines would save his twin hit him hard. The thought of Millie in the ICU made it tough to breathe.

The doctor in him intervened. *Hospitalization is expected if the initial presentation of diabetes is a dramatic hyperglycemia.* "She's on top of things, and I'm keeping a close eye on her, Susie."

"Thank you, Will." She gave his hand a quick squeeze. "For a few years there her future looked so bleak that we didn't let ourselves think beyond just keeping her alive. Now she's studying medicine and the two of you are obviously getting along great."

A prickle of unease ran up his spine. He and Millie hadn't even talked about anything beyond tomorrow, and he couldn't see past this summer. Hell, he never looked very far ahead at all, because what was the point? You never knew what was around the corner waiting to explode the best-laid plans. "We're just having fun, Susie."

"Don't look so panic-stricken, Will," she said with a light laugh. "All Danny and I want is for Millie to be happy."

But underneath that light laugh, Will heard an edge of steel that said, *Hurt my daughter and deal with me.*

Chapter 15

Saturday morning started out with a bang, and Tara couldn't be happier. A student driver had reversed into a fire hydrant, sending a column of water high into the sky before it crashed down to flood Main Street. She'd detoured traffic while the fire department capped the hydrant and restored order. The moment that mess was cleaned up she'd gotten a call to attend to a domestic dispute.

She'd arrived to find Bethany Jacobs brandishing her silver crutch at her new neighbor after the guy's pet pig had gotten out and trampled all of Bethany's columbines and hollyhocks. After getting over the surprise that someone actually considered a pig a pet, Tara needed to draw on every mediation skill she had, along with her ability to make good coffee, before the situation had calmed. She still wasn't convinced that Bethany wouldn't follow through on her threat to turn the pig into bacon.

As Bethany lived on the far side of town, it made sense to do the morning patrol, and halfway through it she received a message from a tribal police officer on the Blackfeet Reservation asking her to put him in contact with Will Bartlett. As she was two blocks away from the hospital, she went straight there.

"G'day, Tara." Will greeted her with a smile that probably got him everything he ever wanted.

She explained the situation, and much to her surprise, he immediately made the call. While he was on his cell, Millie appeared from behind a cubicle curtain and gave her a welcoming smile. She immediately returned it. There was something open and engaging about Millie, and if Tara had been the sort of woman who made friends, she'd probably choose Millie.

"Hi, Tara. Social call?"

"Police business. Just passing on a message to Will from the reservation. They're having a meeting and a ceremony and wanted to get in touch with him."

Millie's smile immediately faded, and her gaze flicked to Will before returning to Tara. "It was pretty horrific, and they're all in shock. I think a community gathering is a really good idea."

"Talking won't change anything," Tara said tightly, thinking about the horrors of war and trying not to think about some of the awful things she'd seen growing up.

"Do you really believe that?" Millie's expression was one of stunned surprise. "Obviously, talking doesn't turn the clock back to the way things were, but it does give people a chance to grieve. It's an opportunity to navigate their way through the trauma and hopefully find a way of reconciling with it. Believe me, it's better than self-medicating and adding to the problem."

Tara immediately got a flash of her mother sprawled unconscious on the sofa with an empty bottle of vodka on the floor. "I guess you may have a point."

"But you're not convinced," Millie said with a wry smile. "Anyway, I'm glad you're here because it saves me a call. It's our street party tonight, and I'm hoping you'll come."

Tara got out her notebook. "Are you worried things might get out of hand?"

Millie's laughter echoed around the department. "No. I just thought you'd like to come along as my guest."

"Oh." She immediately felt foolish that she'd missed the invitation. "Right. Thanks."

"So you'll come?" Millie smiled encouragingly, her eyes bright with enthusiasm.

You have nothing else on and you need a friend.

Ethan's smiling face suddenly lit up in the back of her mind, and a shiver of longing shot through her along with something close to a lust chaser.

She tensed against it, trying to stop any ripple effect. *I meant Millie.* "I'll try to stop by. Do I need to bring something?"

Millie shook her head. "Mom and I are making enough food to cover our friends. It starts at six but it's totally casual, so just come when you can."

She nodded, turned to go and then turned back. Ever since Tuesday she'd been thinking about what Ethan had said, and she wanted Millie's opinion. "If I taught a kickboxing class at the gym, do you think women would come?"

Millie nodded vigorously, her curls jumping every which way. "I think you'd have to turn people away if you ran any sort of a gym class. We've never had a female personal trainer, and it would also help in other ways."

"What do you mean?"

She sighed. "Sadly, there are some women in our county who find themselves in domestic violence situations. It's my experience that they have to trust you before they'll confide in you. If they see you in a different role out of the uniform, it's only going to help."

"That's exactly what Ethan said."

"Eth's a smart guy," Millie replied with a huge amount of respect in her voice. "You should listen to him."

"Who's smart?" Will asked, sliding his phone into his pocket as he walked over and stood unusually close to Millie. "You talking about me again, Mils?"

Millie rolled her eyes, but her expression was soft and warm. "Your ego's bigger than Australia and the contiguous United States put together."

Their teasing was easy and familiar, and Tara would have had to be blind not to see the genuine affection that flowed between them.

They're having sex.

The thought hit her as fast as the unexpected slither of envy that snaked through her. Shocked by the envy, she immediately told herself she didn't have anything to feel envious about. She didn't miss sex—especially bad sex—and she certainly didn't miss having a lying, cheating man in her life.

It's not the sex. It's the tenderness.

She tried to shrug away the unsettling feelings—she was being ridiculous. It was impossible to miss something she'd never really known.

Feeling uncomfortable, she quickly made her excuses and left the hospital, driving directly to the safety of the police station. Here she could hide behind protocol and rules and keep all that emotional crap at bay. Even better, she was going to pass the afternoon by burying herself in the never-ending pile of paperwork.

She was surprised to find the LEC door unlocked and Mitch Hagen waiting for her. Before she could open her mouth, he said, "Ralston, you're off duty."

A jolt of panic hit her. "No, sir, I'm not."

He growled as he waved his crutch at her, and she was tempted to ask if he'd been taking lessons from Bethany. Then again, she valued her job.

"Yes, you are. Next weekend's the Fourth of July, and the weekend after that, Shakespeare in the Parks. You're gonna be working straight through, so you have to take time off now."

I want to keep busy. "But what if something happens?"

"If it needs two good legs, I'll call you. Otherwise, I don't want to see you back here until Monday morning."

She'd argued, but he'd pulled rank, and so here she was at four o'clock on Saturday afternoon, pacing back and forth in her now very clean and very tidy apartment with absolutely nothing to do. Rifts of edginess kept jagging through her, making her jumpy and unable to settle. Having nothing to do was pure torture, because it meant she had time to think, which was why she always kept busy.

Which begs the question yet again, why did you think moving here and taking this job was a good idea?

Shut up. Only she knew exactly why she'd done it—she'd wanted to start over and try living a normal life, whatever the hell that was. Other people seemed to be able to do it, but right now *normal* was giving her hives. She needed to do something to burn off all this agitation.

She threw on workout clothes, picked up her keys and

walked out the door. Five minutes later she was stepping inside the gym and her ears took a battering from the high-pitched shrieks of excited children. As her eyes adjusted to the gloom, she saw Ethan standing in the middle of the mats with six-year-olds running around him.

He suddenly clapped his hands, and they all stopped and bowed. He bowed back. "Say hello to Officer Tara, everyone."

How did he even know she was here? She hadn't seen his head turn toward her, but now ten kids were bowing at her.

"Hello, Officer Tara," they all chanted obediently.

She bowed back feeling self-conscious. "Hello."

Should she have said hello, boys and girls? Hello, children? Hi, kids? Argh! She didn't have much experience with children, and they made her nervous. Spinning on her heels, she stalked straight to the rowing machine and started exercising. She tried keeping her gaze fixed on the stroke rate, but it kept drifting to Ethan.

Ethan without his glasses. Ethan wearing his Tae Kwon Do uniform. He looked good in a *cross me and I'll bust your balls* kind of a way that contrasted sharply with his usual mild-mannered, hipster librarian look. A traitorous streak of heat pooled in her belly.

He's hot in all sorts of different ways and you know it.

I don't want to know it.

Too late, Tara. Way too late.

She rowed furiously, whipping her heart rate up to fast and her breathing to ragged, and all the time her gaze flitted between Ethan and the kids. They practiced kicking and did some simple patterns, and then the parents arrived, the kids departed and suddenly the gym was eerily silent.

"I'm glad you decided to come, Tara," Ethan said, walking over to her with a smile winding through his short beard. The same warm, friendly smile she'd missed the week he'd been angry with her.

A blip of warm, fuzzy feelings unfurled before she could stop them, and she immediately centered her gaze on his chest in an attempt to neutralize them.

Bad move.

A smattering of blond brown hair peeked out of the V of his uniform, and she immediately got an image of it winding down to his belly. "I . . ." She cleared her throat. "I thought you said you taught a kids' class on Tuesdays."

"I do. That was Wyatt Breckenbridge's birthday party."

"You do kids' birthday parties?" she asked incredulously. Was there anything he didn't do for the town?

He laughed. "Sure, if I'm asked. They're fun and I get the easy part. I run them around for an hour and then the parents take them to fill up on pizza, candy and ice cream."

She found herself shaking her head. "Kids bewilder me, but you're really good with them."

"Thanks." He looked as if she'd just bestowed upon him the best compliment he'd ever received. "You know, Tara, kids aren't that complicated. The more time you spend with them, the easier it gets. You'll learn that teaching the elementary kids bike safety."

"I have to do that?" she asked, horrified.

He threw back his head and laughed. "And there's that buried sense of humor of yours rising to the surface. You should let it out more often." He handed her a towel. "So, how are you?"

Nothing about his demeanor was sexual. If it was, she'd have known what to do, but she wasn't used to such open sincerity and real interest in her. Manic squads of butterflies unleashed in her stomach, hurling themselves against the sides. What on earth was wrong with her? Sure, feeling nervous before combat was normal, nerves in a difficult policing situation were expected, but a case of fluttering stomach from talking to a guy who was looking at her as if she was his sister? That wasn't something she was familiar with at all.

"Slowly going crazy." The words slipped out before her brain had censored her tongue.

He made a sympathetic sound. "Problems at work?"

"Only that there's not enough of it. I'm not used to having so much downtime."

"Must be a big transition for you coming out of the military."

She thought about the nights she found sleep hard to find and realized with some surprise that over the past few months they'd decreased from regular to occasional. "Actually, it's more the transition from working in Detroit to Bear Paw that's proving to be the problem."

Listen to yourself. You're doing it again—telling him stuff you never tell anyone. He'll take that as permission to keep asking you questions. Stop talking now.

"... kickboxing?"

"Excuse me?" She hadn't heard his question over the deafening volume of her own thoughts.

"Do you want to do some kickboxing? I promise I won't go easy on you."

This time she laughed. "I hadn't picked you as competitive."

"Ah, that's my power," he said as he picked up the kickboxing pads. "I'm an enigma."

And he was. He was unlike any of the men she'd ever known personally or professionally. He wasn't muscle bound and buff, and he didn't swagger or wield a weapon. He had a strong artistic side and a soft, caring nature, and yet with a black belt—second dan—in Tae Kwon Do, he was every bit as masculine as the hard-edged men who'd barreled through her life.

Accepting his offer, she climbed off the rowing machine, pulled on some gloves and joined him on the mats.

He bowed low to her and she returned it.

"Right cross, left jab," he said, holding up the pads.

She punched them hard, feeling his resistance.

"Add back leg knee," he instructed, moving the pad to catch her rising knee.

Three rounds later he barked, "Switch knee."

She kept boxing, alternating knees, feeling her heart rate pick up and her frustrations start to leave her.

"Left jab, right cross, back roundhouse."

As she swung her right leg up, he lowered the pad to his thigh and collected the hit.

She found her rhythm, adding the different combinations as he called them out to her and matched the pads to her jabs, uppers hooks and kicks. Her thoughts drained away and her mind emptied of everything except his instructions as she landed blow upon blow on the pads. Sweat dripped into her eyes and off her nose, and still his instructions rained down on her with no respite.

Her chest tightened as she panted, her breath straining to move in and out of her lungs. Every muscle in her body screamed as fire burned through her, and she now struggled to lift her arms and legs, which had turned into two-ton lead weights. Every part of her quivered with fatigue, her knees sagged and she felt herself folding inward. The mats called her, promising relief from pain and hard work. She almost gave in, almost sank down, and then a lightness swept through her, lifting her up with a white, vibrant energy, making her gasp.

She was floating. She was flying. Her arms and legs felt lighter, her kicks and hits sped up and she hammered the pads hard, each blow freeing her even more until she was a blur of motion.

"Stop," Ethan commanded, lowering the pads.

Nooooooo! It felt way too good to stop, but her hands dropped to her sides and she bowed to him before sitting down onto the mats.

He joined her, panting almost as hard but with a knowing smile on his face. "You got the rush, didn't you?"

She found herself grinning back at him, thrilled he understood. "Oh yeah. One minute I thought I was going to die and the next minute a surge of energy picked me up and threw me back in the game. It was like one part of me was boxing and the other part of me was soaring out of myself."

"I'm glad you enjoyed it."

"It was amazing," she said, still spinning on the high. "It was better than sex."

He made a strangled sound. "Granted, an endorphin rush is amazing, but better than sex? I don't think so."

She fell back so she was lying on the mats staring at the ceiling. "Believe me, it's better."

"Then I'm really sorry you've only ever had lousy sex."

She whipped her head to the left to look at him as an old embedded anger stirred inside of her. "Let me guess? You're about to offer to show me exactly how it should be done."

His eyes flashed the color of burnt butter. "And to think we were getting along so well there for a little bit," he said tightly as he wrapped his arms around his knees. "Seriously, Tara, after all our conversations, you really think I'm that sort of guy? Jesus, some asshole must have done a number on you."

She closed her eyes, trying to block out the hurt in his eyes and in his voice, but it stayed there, accusing her of being very unfair. She didn't want to tell him about the men in her life, but their legacy had just hurt him because she kept judging him based on her past experiences. Ethan didn't deserve that. He really was a good guy, and that alone scared her. Good guys confused her, and as much as she wanted to run from this, she owed him an explanation.

She returned her gaze to the ceiling, because it was easier than seeing the mixture of anger and pain on his cheeks. "One guy? I wish. It was way more than one."

ETHAN flinched as Tara's flat words punched him. She was the most beautiful woman he'd ever met, but she was also the toughest and knew every trick in the book of pushing, blocking and holding people at bay. Even when Millie had been struggling and out of control fighting her diabetes, she'd never been mean. Half of him wanted to hug Tara close, and the other half of him wanted to run. Falling for a difficult woman wasn't one of his life's goals, but despite how much she pressed his buttons, he was fast losing the battle to not want to care.

Watching her during her kickboxing routine had been blissful torture. She was fit and toned, and that glorious expanse of exposed belly between her black crop top and the bright red waistband of her black shorts was enough to make him hard for hours. She'd put everything she had into the kicks and punches, and he knew his arms would feel it tomorrow. As much as her athleticism attracted him, it had been the expression on her face that had held him captive. The ice queen had vanished, and along with her cool demeanor so had the tight control she kept herself firmly under. He'd watched as she'd slowly let go of her restraint and joy had snuck in and flared on her beautiful face. She'd not only dazzled him but she'd looked gloriously and blissfully happy.

He didn't know what shocked him more—the fact he'd never seen her look happy before or that he'd do almost anything to see it happen again. But right now, sitting next to her, that seemed like a long shot. She was coiled so tight that she vibrated with tension, and she was studiously avoiding eye contact. Not wanting to be higher than her, he lay down next to her, leaving enough room between them so there was no chance of accidental touching. He wasn't giving her any excuse to lash out again and leave. Not before he had a chance to try and understand her.

He cleared his throat. "Way more than one? I'm sorry to hear that."

She snorted, the sound derisive. "You sound like a counselor."

He swallowed his sigh. "Okay, then, I'm thrilled some guy has hurt you. That better?"

She turned her head, and her aquamarine eyes warmed a degree or two as her lips twitched upward for a split second. "See, this is the thing. You're so different from the men I'm used to that it confuses the hell out of me. I have no clue how to deal with you."

"Deal with me? Now you're scaring me," he joked, trying to relax her.

"Exactly," she said softly. "You frighten me."

Astonished, he rolled onto his side to face her. "Tara, absolutely nothing about me is frightening."

Her black lashes brushed her cheeks before rising again. "You're kind, caring and involved in your town."

"Exactly," he said, not remotely understanding where she was coming from. "I'm just a regular guy. Heck, the town's got a hashtag for me and broadcasts all of my dumb stuff on Twitter. If I was scary, do you think they'd do that?"

A flash of something hard and brittle lit up her eyes and then faded as fast as it had come. "You grew up very differently from me. You haven't fought in a war." Her fingertips scraped back and forth on the mat. "You see things from a totally different perspective, and that makes you not only frightening but as foreign as Afghanistan."

He didn't say anything, because he knew she'd have seen unimaginable things when she'd served, but he was starting to worry she'd seen as worse before she'd joined up.

"I'm going to tell you some stuff, Ethan, but don't interrupt."

"No, ma'am."

"I'm serious."

"So am I."

She looked back up at the ceiling and was silent for a moment, so he rolled onto his back and looked up, too. The only noise in the cavernous building was the rhythm of their breathing.

Tara sucked in a breath. "You know how your dad took you to Tae Kwon Do? Well, my dad took off before I had any real memory of him being around. He'd turn up every time mom and I'd rebuilt our lives without him in it, accepting yet again that he was never coming back."

She gave a bitter laugh. "He'd stay around just long enough to dismantle those foundations, lay new ones and then blow them up. Every time he left, mom went back to drinking and trying to find a man who wouldn't leave her. Unfortunately, she always chose worse men than my father. These guys not only abandoned her, they left far greater scars than dear old dad. As much as I hate him for what he did to us . . ."—she sucked in a breath—". . . did to her, when he was around he treated her well. *That* was the problem. If he'd been a total ass, we might have had a chance of creating some sort of a life without him in it."

He wanted to say, *Sorry*, but he'd promised not to interrupt; only he needed to do something to show her he felt for her. Taking a risk, he rested his hand very lightly on top of hers. Her fingers tensed under his palm, but thankfully, she didn't pull away.

"When I was younger, mom's boyfriends stuck me in front of the television and ignored me, but things changed when I turned fourteen. They started buying me clothes and things. Every gift came with an expectation."

This time Ethan tensed. He did not want to hear what he feared would come next.

"I got really good at making sure I was never alone with any of them. When a gym teacher at school offered kickboxing as an activity, I started training. I was tall and fit, which made grown men look at me in ways no teen should ever have to deal with, but it was also my safety net. I spent years sleeping with a baseball bat in my hand while my mother was passed out on the couch."

A growl rumbled deep from his chest, and his fingers automatically tightened around her hand as the remains of his lunch filled his mouth. He forced the acidic contents back down and wished he could break the necks of every single bastard that had ever tried to touch her. His anger spilled over to include a mother who'd left her kid exposed to that sort of danger.

"A couple of my teachers were amazing, and when things got really bad, I slept on their sofas, but school was finishing, and I knew once that happened, I'd have no backup. The night mom was too drunk to go out and her current boyfriend demanded I go in her place was the night I left home. With nowhere to go, I went to the diner and asked my boss if he could up my hours from part-time to full. He said no.

"I sat in a booth and ran through my options. My part-time waitressing job didn't earn me enough to rent a room, let alone feed me, and college, which had always been unlikely, was now impossible. An advertisement came on the TV for mouthwash, and I remember thinking, my life is falling apart and this white bitch with perfect teeth is worried about bad breath. I yelled at the screen.

"Then one of those moments happened, and if I was at all religious, I might say it was a sign, but really it was just another advertisement. It told me that joining the US Army would change my life, and it did. Two days later, I passed the aptitude test and I was a private on my way to boot camp." Her voice caught. "For the first time in my life I had a family."

"Except it was a family that sent you overseas and showed you even more horrors," he choked out against the clutch of gut-wrenching emotions that gripped him as tight as a lasso.

"But we had a common purpose," she said quietly, "and for the first time in my life, I had people looking out for me."

He'd only ever known the unconditional love and support of his family, and she'd never experienced anything like that from hers. Middle-class guilt struck him so hard, a burning hot pain lanced him down his side. "When you put it that way, I think I get it."

"Thank you."

She sounded grateful, which was both a surprise and a relief to him, and he felt it gave him permission to ask questions. "If you loved the army so much, why did you leave?"

"I got married." The flat and emotionless words hung in the air around them.

"Wow." It slipped out on a puff of amazement that she'd trusted a guy enough to marry him.

"Wow, indeed." She made an odd sound in her throat, which was half laugh, half anguish. "It still surprises me, but I met Tim overseas, and life in a war zone is surreal."

"I can only imagine."

"Don't," she said harshly. "Not even the worst imaginings come close to the reality."

"Noted." He slid his fingers in between hers, wanting to connect with her in a way she'd accept. "And I'm guessing you're not married now?"

"No." She blew out a long sigh. "Like I said, we were in a war zone, and on some level we probably thought committing to marriage would cheat death."

He flinched again. Without a shadow of a doubt, marriage was something he knew he wanted in his life. He'd always thought there'd be nothing better than publicly declaring his love for a woman, sharing his life with her and having a family. He'd never viewed it in terms of cheating death.

"That's . . ." *Interesting? Crazy? Understandable? Sad.*

If Tara noticed that his voice had trailed off, she didn't comment. She seemed lost in her memories and still needing to tell them. "Tim's proposal was unexpected, but I took it as a sign we'd work, because not one of the six guys my mother introduced into my life had ever married her. Not even my father."

She seemed to give herself a shake. "Anyway, after two tours of duty and one tour of Tim's infidelity, I divorced him. It was never going to be final for me unless I took an honorable discharge."

The burning pain turned to an ache, which spread through him. Every person she'd tried to love had let her down, and she'd not only lost her marriage and her trust in people, she'd lost the support of the army—the only family she'd really known.

The ache morphed into a slow burn of rage, and he wanted to take down every person who'd ever hurt her. He turned his head to look at her. "So you joined a new family in law enforcement?"

Her brow furrowed as if she didn't understand. "It was a skills match. I'm good at my job, Ethan."

"I don't doubt it." It was the one thing in her life she had a hope of being able to control.

They lay there with a wide space between them and their hands loosely connected. He kept replaying the conversation in his mind, rolling her words over in his head, trying to make sense of them.

You grew up very differently from me. You see things very differently from me.

He was a basically happy person. He had a positive outlook on life, and he knew that came from the dumb luck of his conception to parents who were positive and happy, too. Parents who'd given him opportunities Tara had never had. He wanted to share that outlook with her, show her the good stuff, and more than anything he wanted to see her happy.

He wanted to see her beautiful face light up with that joy again, but how did he make that happen with a woman who didn't trust and who took the first excuse to keep him at arm's length?

Sex won't do it.

As much as he'd love to work the magic he knew he was capable of if given the chance, as much as he wanted to watch her body suffuse with color and joy as she came, her bitter comment about sex carried a warning as loud as an emergency siren. Trying anything overtly sexual with Tara, even risking a kiss, would only give her an excuse to flee. He was determined to avoid that at all costs.

He swallowed an ironic laugh as a thought crossed his mind. If he took all those years he'd spent at high school and college being overlooked by beautiful women he'd lusted after and combined it with the discipline of Tae Kwon Do, he had the perfect training for this very situation.

He could hide his desire for her from her. Hell, he'd been doing it for almost a month already, so he could keep it going. He'd say and do nothing to even hint at how he felt until the day she gave him a sign that she felt the same way about him as he did about her.

Or not. He was used to the *or not* scenario, but he also knew that the key to any chance of success with Tara, of her trusting him and sharing his life, was friendship. That had to come first, but would she even accept his friendship?

She trusted you enough to tell you her story.

The thought steadied him and gave him hope. With it came an idea.

REGRET swamped Tara in suffocating waves as Ethan's silence rolled on. Millie was wrong. Talking didn't make things easier; it just made them worse. She should never have told him about her life in the trailer park—at worst it sexualized her in a way she never wanted men to think of her, and at best, it made people uncomfortable. It certainly highlighted their very different life experiences. She should have just hidden behind her failed marriage, because it made the other stuff look sanitized. Everyone had an experience of cheating, didn't they?

She sat up abruptly, pulling her hand out of his and hating how she immediately missed his warmth. "Well, this is embarrassing."

He stayed lying on the mat. "No, it isn't."

"Don't you dare feel sorry for me."

He sat up slowly, sitting cross-legged and facing her. His gaze was serious but supportive. "I'm feeling a lot of things right now, Tara, but sorry for you isn't one of them. I'm angry you had to deal with all of this shit as a kid. I'm furious at the useless adults who let you down. I have an overwhelming feeling of relief that you got out of a horrible situation that could have trapped you forever, but it absolutely kills me that you had to exchange one war zone with another to do it."

His mouth tweaked up slightly on one side. "And okay, you got me. I'm sorry you married a cheating prick, but my overwhelming feeling for you is one of utmost admiration. Most kids faced with that situation don't get out. You did and you've made a life for yourself." He raised his hand. "Go Tara."

She stared at him dumbfounded. She wasn't sure what she'd expected to hear him say, but she knew it wasn't this. After everything she'd told him, he admired her? The man never stopped surprising her.

He gave her a resigned look. "You going to high-five me or just leave me here with my arm up looking stupid."

A bubble of something that closely resembled fun welled up in her. "Well, now that you mention it . . ." She pretended to leave him hanging for a moment before slapping her palm against his. His fingers immediately closed loosely around her hand. She could have easily pulled away, but she didn't.

"Come dancing with me, Tara."

She gaped at him. "What?"

"Dancing." He rose to his feet and tugged her up with him. The next moment his other hand was on her waist and he was spinning her around. "The Switkowskis' street party always has dancing."

She stopped mid-twirl. "On a road?"

He sighed. "They close it off to traffic, Officer, so it's safe."

"I didn't sign a permit."

"Tara!"

"Sorry." The heat of his hand against the skin on the small of her back was screwing with her concentration. "Dancing sounds so . . ."

"Old-fashioned? Fun? Dorky?"

"Definitely all of the above," she said, trying to think if she'd ever been invited to go dancing and coming up blank. "But I was going to say *normal*."

He gave her his wide and enthusiastic smile that always tugged at her. "You need some normal in your life, so come dancing with me."

He twirled her out again, and when she spun back, she checked his face for clues that he had more than just dancing on his mind. Ethan was a nice guy, but he was still a guy, and guys expected sex. Despite the attraction she felt every time she was with him, she was hesitant to act on it.

"Is this a date?"

"There are no hidden agendas, Tara," he said with platonic friendship clear in the depths of his caramel eyes. "It's just dancing."

His reassurance should have filled her with relief, because like her mother, her attempts at relationships always failed. Tim had killed any illusions or delusions she may have had that she was capable of holding a marriage together, and when she'd filed for divorce, she'd promised herself she was keeping her life free of any emotional drama.

It's just dancing.

So why did she feel disappointed?

Chapter 16

t was 11 A.M. and Will's palms were slick with sweat—sopping wet like he'd plunged them into a bucket of water—as he stood facing the emotionally devastated community of Bison Creek. He recognized the people's pain, understood their loss and comprehended their rage that the accident need never have happened.

Two years ago, he'd been on the other side of a similar event with frighteningly familiar players. Back then, just like today, there was one family wracked with grief, another with guilt and a town reeling with people feeling they needed to take sides. Lesser things had been known to cause massive schisms in small towns—and this incident threatened to tear this tiny community apart.

He wanted to help, but the timing sucked. It was taking every bit of mental strength he had to hold it all together when his heart and mind screamed to be elsewhere. At the best of times he had a hollow space inside of him, but today he was struggling to paper it over and keep on going.

The *rez*, as Millie called it, was three thousand square miles of beautiful country that bordered Glacier National Park on one side and Canada on another. It belonged to the Blackfeet Nation and reminded him of the Australian aboriginal communities at home, only instead of vivid red dirt, they had acres of waving grass and a view of majestic mountains. When he'd accepted the grief counselor's invitation to attend today, he'd done some research so as not to inadvertently add to their sadness by doing something culturally insensitive. At home, in the outback aboriginal communities during *sorry business*, they never used the dead person's name, believing it would disturb their spirit. He'd been reassured that this didn't happen on the rez and he wouldn't be putting his foot into his mouth if he mentioned Lily.

Sadly, life on the rez was scarily familiar to home, with the indigenous nations sharing similar health and socioeconomic problems and a lot of it stemming from a current lack of employment for young people. Not that lack of employment was exclusive to the indigenous community—it was endemic in isolated country towns in Australia no matter the ancestry, and it appeared to be much the same here.

The community center was full, and the meeting had already gone beyond the planned hour as people kept asking questions, trying to make sense of the events. Trying to come up with ways to prevent such a tragic loss from ever happening again.

"What about Jade?" a teenager asked, her voice breaking on her friend's name.

"Jade remains in an induced coma," he said, immediately going on to explain exactly what that meant in words the girl could understand.

"And when she wakes up?" she asked.

If. Will tried not to wince. Situations like Jade's skewed the motor vehicle death figures, because technically Jade was still alive, but in oh so many ways, she'd lost her life. "Only time will tell how much of her brain function will return. I've seen it come back very slowly over time with a lot of hard work and determination."

"We can help," the teen said, glancing around encouragingly at her friends who all nodded their support.

They had no idea. "That will be great, and I hope you do." Will swallowed, gearing up for the hard bit. "I just want to let you know that the Jade who wakes up isn't going to be quite the same Jade you knew last week. Her personality might be different, and she may not remember everything."

The girl's mother squeezed her hand. "And the boys? How are they?"

"Ed and Bryce will have their own challenges as they learn to live their lives with a prosthetic leg and a wheelchair." He threw out an idea he thought might help the town come together. "Bryce will need a lot of expensive equipment to live at home. Ramps, rails, bars, that sort of thing. So having some fund-raising events would help."

"We could have a bake sale."

"What about a rodeo?" a man added.

"These are all good ideas," the grief counselor said, writing them down. "We can meet next week to discuss them, but right now, is there anyone else who wants to ask Doctor Bartlett a medical question?"

Will's head pounded, and his throat felt constricted as if his collar was too tight. He reached to loosen his tie only to find he wasn't wearing one.

Millie leaned in close and said softly, "It's already gone way over time, and you look beat. People will understand if you need to wrap it up."

He shook his head. He wasn't leaving until everyone who wanted to ask him a question had taken his or her opportunity.

"Swallow these, then." She produced some Tylenol out of her voluminous tote bag, which he'd learned over the past few weeks held a lot more than just her diabetes necessities. Passing him a glass of water, she pushed the tablets into his hand.

"Thanks." As he swallowed them around the lump in his throat, he saw some movement in his peripheral vision. A woman was trying to stand, and a man who had his head bent close to hers was holding her arm, as if he was trying to keep her in the chair.

"Do you have a question?"

The woman shook off the man's hand and shot to her feet, immediately stepping out into the aisle. Will recognized Lily's mother, and his gut rolled, spinning nausea through him. The grief counselor had told him Mary wasn't coming.

This is going to be tough, bro, Charlie's voice offered up. *Come find me when you're done.*

Mary pointed an accusatory finger at Will. "You took Lily and you . . ." Her voice cracked before rising with hysteria. ". . . you promised me she'd be okay."

Will's chest tightened. He knew he'd never said any such thing, because ER physicians never made promises, but denying her accusation wasn't going to help either of them. Neither was saying that he'd gotten Lily to the hospital alive, because the woman had just lost her child. The circle of life had been well and truly crapped on, and she needed to lash out at someone. He could at least give her that.

"Mary," Millie said gently, "Will said he'd do his best and he did. I was there. He—"

Will put his hand on Millie's arm, gripping it tightly, and shook his head. Two frown lines immediately appeared on her forehead, and her eyes filled with questions, but she stayed silent.

He walked up to Mary, and with his arms loose by his side, he bent his knees so he was closer to her height. "I'm so desperately sorry for your loss. More than anything, I wish things were different and you weren't living through this hell."

The grief-stricken woman made a strangled sound and then her legs buckled. Will grabbed her before she hit the floor, pulling her in against him as she sobbed uncontrollably. Great, wracking sobs that shuddered through her before transferring her grief to him. Two years ago he'd held his mother in the exact same way, and every rise and fall of Mary's chest brought those memories rushing back in 3-D and living color.

His breathing quickened, and he had to consciously force himself to take slow, deep breaths so he stayed the distance. He could not fall apart here. He would not. He slowly became aware of people forming a circle around them, and hands coming up to touch them both.

Lily's father squeezed his shoulder. "Thank you, Doctor

Bartlett." He gently eased Mary off Will's chest. "Come on, Mary, let's go sing our girl home."

The sobbing woman lifted her head and met Will's eyes with an anguished and imploring look. "You were one of the last people to spend time with her. Please come to the ceremony."

Every part of him yelled, *No, not today*, but he understood the need to hold on to tentative links—to try and keep someone's memory alive when memory was the only option left. "Sure."

Everyone moved outside into the bright, life-affirming sunshine, and under the huge blue sky, Will breathed more easily for the first time in ninety minutes.

Millie slid her hand into his. "Do you want to walk there?"

He appreciated the offer. "A walk would be great."

"I thought you'd say that." She squeezed his hand, her care and support flowing into him as they walked up the rise.

As much as he was thankful she was here, he kept his gaze fixed on the horizon, because if he looked at her, he'd only see questions in her eyes—so many unasked questions. Questions he'd been ducking all week. His usual tactics of teasing her, kissing her and burying himself deep inside her had dimmed them, but he'd seen them gain intensity during the community meeting.

"You okay?" Millie asked yet again, as if she was the poster girl for the annual Australian mental-health-awareness R U OK? Day.

"Yep," he lied yet again. "What about you? You must need some food?"

A flash of something in her eyes buried those damn questions for half a second. She patted her bag. "I packed sandwiches. What about you?"

"I'm not hungry."

"Doesn't mean you don't need to eat," she muttered quietly, sounding slightly ticked off.

He chose to ignore the comment, because the idea of food made him gag. They walked the rest of the half mile in silence before joining the circle of people on the hill. As Will sat, he plucked a blade of the long green grass and automatically started tying it as if it were suture thread—anything to keep his thoughts away from what this ceremony meant.

An image of Charlie's hand—so similar to his—slamming a textbook shut with a bang made his fingers drop the grass.

Bro, the sun's shining. Pull your nose out of that book and come outside.

The Blackfeet community started singing. It sounded to Will's untrained ear more like a chant of a few words rather than his own interpretation of a song. The rise and fall of voices filled with emotion circled him as the Blackfeet drew on their traditions to sing a young woman from her life on earth to her new spirit life on the other side. Just like the Aborigines had done at Jilagong.

Barely holding it together, Will didn't dare look at anyone's faces, so he fixed his gaze on the craggy mountains in the distance, seeking some sort of peace.

Which one of those are we going to climb? Charlie asked as clearly as if he were sitting next to him. *I reckon that middle one looks like the perfect challenge.*

Will pulled his mind back to the singing, but the more he concentrated on it, the louder Charlie's voice became. *Come on, surf's up and I've waxed the boards.*

Evie and Hannah want to double-date. Twins dating twins, let's try it.

Mate, your life would be so dull without me.

His heart rate picked up, thundering hard in his chest as if he'd just run the Olympic hundred-meter sprint. Pumping blood boomed loud in his ears, almost deafening him, but it didn't drown out Charlie's voice, which continued to gain volume and become more and more insistent.

I've signed us up for Tough Mudder. It's gonna be a blast.

I've taken the job at Jilagong. Come with me. I know we can make a difference.

I've met someone, Will. I want you to meet her.

The singing swirled around him, infused with sorrow, and memories hammered him relentlessly. His chest and throat were so rigid he could barely move air in and out, and every part of him screamed to get out of here.

He couldn't do this.

He couldn't stay here a minute longer without completely falling apart.

He grabbed the MontMedAir pager out of his pocket, stood up and strode down the hill.

———

MILLIE had assumed that when Will left the ceremony so abruptly, the MontMedAir pager must have vibrated and he'd politely removed himself to go take the call. Only that had been a while ago now. She checked her watch again—he'd been gone ten minutes and she was starting to wonder what was going on. If it had been an emergency, he would have come back and gotten her. If it wasn't an emergency, surely he would have explained that he couldn't talk, cut the call and returned. So why had he been gone so long?

The first song had finished, and she took the opportunity to go look for Will. He wasn't at the house where many people had gathered to share food, and although she doubted he'd be at the church, she checked there anyway. No Will. She stood on the steps of St. Anne's and called him on her cell. It went direct to his voice mail.

"Will, please call back. Oh, it's Millie by the way."

Duh, he will know that. Why do you even think he wouldn't?

But delving into that lack of self-belief was another project for another day.

As she walked past the community hall, she saw his Jeep parked in the lot, so he was still on the rez. Granted, that was a lot of area, although surely he wouldn't have taken off without letting her know?

Why? You're not a real couple, and he doesn't have to tell you his plans.

But he's a polite guy. He wouldn't just leave.

She kept walking, leaving the few buildings that constituted the small village, and her phone remained ominously silent despite the uncommon luck of it actually having plenty of reception bars. Her stomach churned with anxiety. There'd been times today he'd looked at breaking point, and it was the uncharacteristic nature of his disappearance that bothered her the most. She cursed herself for not having followed him when he'd first left the ceremony. Hated herself for not being brave enough this week to push him on his feelings about the accident.

She paused, squinting into the noon sun. Where on earth

was he? After scanning the area, she cut across the pasture, and drawn by the view of the mountains, she walked down toward the creek. In the distance, she saw the silhouette of a tall man with a familiar wide-legged stance. Relief made her dizzy. At least she thought it was relief, but she checked Dex just in case, because the last thing she needed was to arrive with a too-high or too-low blood sugar and give Will the excuse to focus on her instead of the other way around.

Dex was happy, so she kept walking. As she got closer, she realized Will had his back to her. Sunshine glinted on his hair, making it glow gold, and he was skipping stones into the slow-moving water. She didn't call out until she'd almost reached him, and she used the time to practice sounding casual rather than accusatory.

"There you are," she said with a smile. "I wondered where you'd gotten to."

She expected him to turn toward her, and she was already anticipating how he'd give her his lazy smile—the one that raced to his eyes and made her toes curl. He didn't turn. He didn't even reply. He just pulled his arm back, flicked his wrist and sent the flat oval stone skimming across the water, making seven jumps before it sank.

She closed the distance between them and stood next to him, near the water, making a conscious decision to go slowly rather than straight to the point of *What the hell, Will? I've been worried sick and why didn't you tell me where you'd gone?* "You've done that before."

"Once or twice," he said with typical Australian under-statement.

"Did you grow up near a creek?"

He skipped another stone. "River."

His monosyllabic response surprised her, because usually he drew verbal pictures of Australia whenever she asked about it. She put her hand on his arm. "You okay?"

"Yep." He bent down, picking up and discarding stones until he found another suitable one.

She didn't believe him. She'd had moments on and off all week when she was convinced something significant was bothering him, but whenever she asked, he smiled at her and denied it. Or he teased her. Often he kissed her until all coherent thought turned to mush and she was left wondering if she'd just imagined he had a problem.

You didn't imagine it the night Lily died.

The night they'd had sex and he'd looked like he was running from demons.

At first, all her insecurities had gone into overdrive and she'd automatically gone straight to *He doesn't want me anymore.* Except, if anything, he'd been even more attentive this week. And not just in bed. He'd helped her parents set up the street party, and although he'd been his usual charming and fun self with all the other women, keeping up a stream of banter, he'd danced almost exclusively with her. There'd been one exception—he'd asked Ethan to play a waltz on his cello, and he'd spun elderly but spry Mrs. van Dyke around with a skill that said he'd been taught how to dance. The look on the elderly lady's face was one of blissful wonder.

Millie knew exactly how she felt. Being held in those arms was pure joy. Later in the evening, Mrs. van Dyke had told Millie she'd met her late husband at a dance during World War II and that tonight Will had rekindled some lovely memories. Millie had instantly thought that come summer's end, memories were all she was going to have left as well.

Will's monopoly of her that night had been unexpected but wonderful. However, she refused to allow herself to read any more into it. What they had fell somewhere in between a one-night stand and a committed relationship. It was a gray area that neither of them had chosen to clarify. Clearly, they'd graduated from the one-night stand and she'd decided that as he was a guy with a moral compass, of course he was going to be faithful to her for the length of the summer. It didn't mean anything more than that.

But sometimes when he looked at her, those dark blue eyes of his filled with something so intense it took her breath away. It tempted her to believe he might feel more for her than a friend with benefits. More than a summer fling. When those moments happened, she forgot he could have any woman he wanted. Forgot that she was the woman men usually overlooked. Forgot the fact that her diabetes meant she came with a faulty equipment sticker and an expired warranty. It was a dangerous path to go down, but it was also deliciously addictive.

It's a summer thing. A. Summer. Thing.

And right now her gorgeous summer fling was skipping stones in a creek with the fierce concentration of a surgeon doing cardiac bypass surgery. Why was he skipping stones when he should be up at the ceremony?

He is so not okay. This time she wasn't accepting *Yep* or *I'm fine* as an answer.

"Will, you left kind of abruptly."

"Yep." He spat the word out, full of acrid bitterness that burned.

Even when he was in the middle of emergencies that were going pear-shaped, he always managed to sound upbeat and positive. So why the change? She was convinced it was somehow connected with Lily's death. "You're obviously not okay. Can I help?"

He hurled the stone he was holding so savagely that it didn't skip but sank into the water with an ominous plop. "Only if you can bring back the dead."

"Sadly, no one can do that." She slid her hand along his arm, showing her support. He shrugged off her touch, and his rejection chilled her all the way down to her toes.

"I just. Want to. Skip stones."

His terse, clipped words rained down on her like bullets, and his deep blue eyes—usually so full of fun—burned brightly with pain that reached out and threatened to choke her.

"Will, you did everything you possibly could to save Lily."

"I know that."

So? "Then you've got nothing to feel guilty about."

Another stone whipped across the water. "I *don't* feel guilty."

"Then I don't understand why you're down here"—she threw out her arm in the direction of the ceremony—"instead of being back up there."

"You don't have to understand," he said wearily.

"I do. We came out here today because you said you wanted to support the Blackfeet community. We could have returned to Bear Paw right after the meeting, but you accepted the invitation to go to the ceremony. Now you're down here with your phone turned off."

"Bloody hell, Millie," he ground out between clenched teeth. "Can't a bloke just take a break and skip some stones without being given the third degree?"

He'd never raised his voice to her before, but now he stood in front of her a totally different version of himself. His charm had vanished as easily as if it was a polite facade, leaving his handsome face fixed in an anguished rictus.

Leave it alone. You only have a month left of the summer before you have to return to medical school. If you push this, your summer fling likely ends right now. Why risk it?

Yes, but what am I actually risking?

Her gut rolled as the thought hit her and nausea clogged her throat. Was she really risking anything?

She didn't recognize this Will, so did she really know him after all? For six days he'd had moments of being detached. *It's been longer than that.* When she really thought about it, there'd been times right from when he'd arrived in Bear Paw—before they'd even had sex—when he'd looked utterly alone despite being in a crowd.

Had he been faking being happy all this time? Was the teasing, the kissing and the sex all part of that deception, too?

Her heart cramped—for him. For herself. "It's hardly the third degree, Will. I think me asking you why you're hiding out down here is a perfectly reasonable question."

The warm wind suddenly changed direction, bringing with it cool air. It lifted Will's hair, ruffling it gently. He suddenly ducked his head and raised his left hand as if he was a kid trying to dodge an adult's hand intent on tousling his hair.

"It's not fucking funny, Charlie." His yell echoed off the banks of the creek, strangled and full of distress.

Millie flinched at the raw sound, worried for Will's state of mind. Sure, she'd read twins were close, but why would he be yelling at his brother as if he was standing next to him. "Ah, Will." She stepped in close. "Charlie's not here. He's back in Australia."

He stared down at her, his eyes dark and empty of everything she was used to seeing there. "No," he said hollowly. "He's here."

"Here?" She glanced around, half expecting to see someone else farther along the creek while at the same time thinking that made no sense at all. If his twin was here, Will would be over the moon with happiness. "You mean he's in Bear Paw?"

Will shook his head slowly before resting his forehead on

the top of her head as if he was finding it hard to hold it up. She heard him suck in a long, deep breath.

He moved slightly and then looked down at her with a resigned expression. "You wanted to know why I'm down here instead of up there?"

"Yes."

"Because every time they chanted, Charlie's voice got louder and louder, and I couldn't deal with it."

He was hearing voices? A skitter of panic shot through her. "Do you . . . um . . . hear other people's voices in your head?"

"I'm not schizophrenic, Millie," he said with a hint of exasperation.

She was grappling to understand. "So it's a twin thing?"

He closed his eyes for a second as if he needed to force himself to speak. "Charlie died two years ago."

Chapter 17

Charlie's dead? A slow, dull pain started at Millie's toes, rolling through her until nowhere was free of its touch. The vibrant guy in the photo—Will's identical twin brother—had been dead two years? Wrapping her arms around Will's waist, she struggled to work through her shock and find the words to express her sympathy.

"I . . . that's . . . God . . ." Giving up, she just tightened her arms around him.

"Yeah. Exactly." His generous mouth twisted, full of sadness. "Today's the anniversary of his death, and up there with all those grieving people, it's like reliving that horrendous day all over again."

Unwrapping her arms from his waist, he slid his hand into her right one and sat on the pebbles, tugging her down with him. He stared out toward the mountains, looking pale and haggard. Thinking that he looked like he needed some sugar, she dug into her tote bag and offered him some jelly beans. He silently picked out all the black ones and put them in his mouth.

Watching him chew, she argued with herself about what she should do. Should she ask him what happened? Wait and see if he told her? She wanted to know how Charlie had died, but the fact he hadn't told her before now could mean he didn't consider their friendship worthy of that sort of closeness. The thought added an extra layer to the misery she felt for him.

This isn't about you.

"Charlie would have loved Glacier," Will finally said, his eyes still fixed on Heart Butte. "He'd have dragged me up every peak."

"I thought it would have been the other way around," she said, thinking how Will embraced every outdoor activity with one hundred percent enthusiasm.

He glanced at her, a faint smile hovering on his lips. "No. Charlie was the adventurous one." He flicked another pebble across the top of the water. "You know, I thought coming to Montana would make things easier."

She squeezed his hand. "Today was never going to be easy for you no matter where in the world you found yourself."

"True." He hung his head for a moment. "But I thought being out of Australia where Charlie was such a force in my life would help me on the other three hundred and sixty-four days of every year." Another pebble hit the water as his bitter laugh rent the air. "God knows why I was dumb enough to think that."

"I don't think it's dumb," she said, eager to reassure him. "I think it shows that you're trying to get on with your life."

"Get on with my life?" He snorted. "I'm not getting on with it. I'm getting by. Losing Charlie was like losing a limb." He hurled a rock into the water. "I spent thirty-two years with him, almost thirty-three if you count being squished up close in utero. He wasn't just my brother; he was my best friend. We were Team Bartlett, and then bam, he's dead and he's taken part of me with him."

She loved her brother, and if he died she'd miss him, but not anything like this, but then again, she wasn't a twin. She'd gone to school with the Perkins twins, who'd done everything together and occasionally finished each other's sentences. She'd thought that closeness was more of a girl-BFF thing than a twin thing, but listening to Will, she knew she'd been wrong. The pall of loneliness that often cloaked him suddenly made a whole lot of sense.

"How did Charlie die?"

"Fast."

That didn't tell her much, and a hundred more questions jumped up and down, impatiently waiting to be answered. She stalled them on her lips, swallowing them back down, hoping he'd elaborate.

Will tapped a pebble against another one, the clacking sound fast and insistent. "We both studied medicine, but after years in Sydney, Charlie craved the heat and dust of home and the warmth of the turquoise Indian Ocean. The plan had been to do our own thing for ten years and then open a practice together. Our great-great-grandmother on my mother's side was an Australian Aborigine, and Charlie always had an interest in indigenous health, especially as their life expectancy is ten years less than the white Australian population. Charlie was determined to make a difference, and he took a job as a medical officer working with outback, isolated aboriginal communities. He loved it, and he used to call me at all hours to discuss his plans and bounce ideas off me."

He ran his hand across the back of his neck. "God, I don't know why I'm telling you all of this. Sorry."

"Don't be sorry." She pulled his hand into her lap. "I want to hear it any way you want to tell it."

I want to know more about you.

He sighed, the sound resigned and tinged with sorrow. "It was my grandparents' golden wedding anniversary, Dad's parents," he qualified, "and everyone came home to the farm for it, including my younger sister, who was studying in Perth. Charlie drove the hundred K in from Jilagong, and we had the week planned, including me trying out his new wave board. On the Tuesday after the party, we went into Murrinwindi with Dad because he wanted to walk down the main street and show us off to the town."

"Proud parents?"

"Always." He glanced at her for a moment, as if he wanted her to understand. "In a lot of ways, Murrinwindi's similar to Bear Paw. There's no dashing in and out of a store, especially when a heap of cockies"—he immediately translated—"farmers are at the farm supplies store talking about the weather, when to sow the wheat and which harvester to use."

"Farmers around the world sound pretty much the same."

"Yeah." His gaze returned to the mountains. "After Charlie

and I had shaken hands with half the town, and I'd answered the obligatory questions about life on the east coast and been told I was a fool to have left the west, Charlie suggested we wait outside. That was code for *I've got something I want to tell you.*

He kept tapping the pebble hard against another one, creating white marks on the rock. "Sometimes Charlie and I had the same thought at the same moment, but I wasn't remotely prepared for what he said next. He told me he'd met someone. Miranda, an aboriginal health worker, and they'd been together for three months. He wanted me to drive out to Jilagong the next day and meet her."

Millie's heart lurched, although she wasn't sure if it was for Will or for the unknown Charlie or Miranda or for all of them.

Will's volume dropped into a deeper register. "Charlie lived large and he loved women, but he'd never once asked me specifically to meet a woman. I knew this was big, plus whenever he mentioned Miranda, he got this dopey look on his face. It was the first time in our lives that I didn't recognize him."

Because you've never been in love? But now wasn't the time to ask that.

Will kept talking. "The bugger had gone and fallen in love, and I had no clue how I felt about it. As it turned out, it didn't matter what I thought, because two seconds later it was all moot." His tapping hand stilled, the sound of the rock on rock faded to nothing and his voice dropped to almost a whisper. "A meth addict driving a car lost control of it as he came around the corner we were standing on."

And killed Charlie.

She bit her lip at the rush of feeling that hit her. Charlie had been standing with Will, talking about love and planning for the future when he'd died. It was devastatingly awful, made even worse by the total randomness of the event. Everything started to fall into place—Will's reaction last week at the accident scene and his devastation at Lily's death. It was all too eerily similar to Charlie's death. And surely he'd been hurt in the accident, too? She'd often wondered about how he'd gotten the jagged scar on his chin.

"And your injuries?"

His entire body tensed as if a whip had just slashed him.

"None," he said vehemently, his voice quavering with emotion. "I didn't even get a scratch. I was standing next to him with not even a meter between us, and he took the full impact." A tear rolled down his tan cheek. "I did everything I could, and the flying doctors evacuated him to Perth, but he was declared brain-dead soon after arrival. They kept him ventilated until we could all say good-bye, and then according to his wishes, they harvested his organs for donation.

His throat worked up and down fast. "Life teaches you that sick people die, not healthy ones. Charlie's dead and I'm still here. How unfair is that?"

She grieved for him, wishing more than anything she could do something—anything—to make this better, but she was impotent. She knew about the combination of random events and the distinct lack of fairness that was involved—she was the only person in the history of her extended family with an insidious and pervasive condition courtesy of her malfunctioning pancreas.

"There's no fair in random events, Will," she said, hugging him. "Sometimes life just sucks."

"You got that right." He shuddered against her. "Charlie loved life and embraced every new experience. I look in the mirror every day and see him staring back at me, reminding me that I'm still here living and breathing and he's not."

Survivor guilt was a very real thing, and everything inside of her filled with wretchedness for him. From what she knew of Will, he embraced life, too, and she didn't want him thinking he had any less of a right to be the twin that was alive. "There's no logic to random, either, and you'll make yourself crazy thinking like that. Maybe stop looking in mirrors?"

He made a strangled sort of a sound that had the hint of a laugh buried in it. "I'd have to grow a beard."

"That wouldn't be all bad." She stroked his cheek, thinking about the significance of the day and wondering how she could help. "What would you have done today if you'd been in Australia?"

"Gone surfing."

"Oh." She remembered the photo on his phone of Charlie in his wet suit, and she swallowed a sigh. "We're eight hundred miles from the Pacific Ocean. Do you want to take a hike, ride a bike, canoe? How can I help you honor Charlie today?"

He gave her a long look with eyes that hid more than they revealed. "Skip stones with me."

"Really?" It seemed such a tame activity compared with his usual pursuits and with the things he and Charlie had done together.

Charlie was the adventurous one. It was an odd thing for Will to have said, given he had a T-shirt for just about every extreme sport event on Montana's summer calendar.

"Really." He'd risen to his feet, and, with his hand extended, he was smiling down at her the way she loved. "Come on. I'll teach you how to do it."

She let him pull her to her feet, relieved he seemed a bit more together. "You do realize that a girl raised surrounded by glacial scree and with a competitive father and brother knows how to skip stones."

His eyes twinkled. "Challenge accepted. My record's seventeen."

"What was Charlie's?"

"He maintains it was eighteen, but as I wasn't there at the time, it doesn't count." He chose a pebble with the prerequisite flat surface and pressed it to his lips. "This one's for you, bro." He flicked it out, sending it flying across the water, counting as it went.

As it sank into the water on the sixth bounce, Millie sent hers skipping out over the water. "One, two, three, four, five, six, seven!" She jumped up and down, punching the air before glancing up into the sky. "I beat him by one for you, Charlie."

"Hey." Will spun around laughing and grabbed her by the waist, tugging her in close. "You're supposed to be on my team."

Do you want me to be?

She gazed up into his familiar face, recognizing the smile lines that bracketed his mouth and now understanding the origin of the deep lines around his eyes. She knew his body intimately—what made him ticklish, what made him hard, what made him make those little guttural sounds in the back of his throat before he came. At work she knew how he liked the ER organized, that he was calm in a crisis and that he was an excellent teacher.

But out of the bedroom and away from work, what could she really say about him? That he preferred to drink tea to coffee? That he craved fresh seafood and he liked his beef medium rare? That he called his parents once a week? That was a good sign, right? He was close to his family?

Even she knew she was grasping at straws. The only reason he'd told her about Charlie was because it was the anniversary of his death and he'd been hurting. There was still so much she didn't know about him, still so many conversations they hadn't had—conversations couples shared when they were committed to getting to know each other. Yet despite the logic telling her that she should know a lot more about him, despite the fact neither of them had promised the other anything, despite the fact they were only in Bear Paw for the summer, she stood on the brink—treacherously close to tumbling over the edge and loving him.

She stroked his cheek. "I am on your team."

"Good," he said emphatically, the word sounding distinctly proprietary.

He held her tight and lowered his head to hers, capturing her lips with his and kissing her. It wasn't hot, fast and furious, like it had occasionally been, nor was it playful, coaxing and seductive, which it often was—no, it was gentle. Kind. Caring. Grateful, almost.

She swayed on that unstable brink as his tenderness wove through her—all giving, no taking—and the soft edge crumbled like loose soil on a cliff top. She lost her footing completely. Closing her mind to all rational thought, she threw herself into the moment, tumbling headlong over the edge, down, down, down so deep.

For better or for worse, she loved him.

———

WILL'S parents' faces filled his computer screen. With the HD retinal display, the picture was incredibly clear and, sadly, despite their smiles, he could see the ravages of grief that had carved deep and indelible lines onto their faces. Hell, they could probably see the same on his. He guessed it was especially obvious today, given Charlie's anniversary had just passed and it was always an emotionally torrid day.

"How are things?" his mother asked.

He grinned at the sound of her accent, which he'd never considered broad before, but after a year and a bit away from home, it sounded very Australian. "Not bad."

She leaned forward as if it brought her closer to him. "What did you do on Thursday?"

Unwisely, he hadn't replied to the text she'd sent very early Thursday morning, and this was clearly the follow-up call to check he was still in one piece. He had no intention of telling his parents that he'd fallen apart, because they'd only worry, so he glossed over the finer details. "I spent it on an Indian reservation with Millie. It reminded me a bit of Jilagong."

His mother shot a surprised but hopeful look at his dad, which made his skin prickle. *You just named Millie.* He never once mentioned a specific woman to his parents—there was no point. Chances of him still dating her the following month were slim to none.

"Who's Millie?" she immediately asked.

"She's someone . . . I work with." An image of Millie sprawled naked across the bed, head thrown back and panting with her fingernails digging into his thighs, hit him hard, mocking his words.

"A doctor? Nurse?" his father chimed in, as his mother seemed to have gone unusually silent.

"Bit of both, really," he said, working on being offhand and casual. "She's a qualified nurse who's studying medicine."

"And today will be the Fourth of July over there if I've got the time change right. That's the Yanks' national day, isn't it? You got a holiday? Are you going white water rafting?"

He immediately relaxed. Good old dad—he was always a general conversationalist. "It's a holiday right up until someone drinks too much and does something stupid and I get called in. We're staying closer to town and going to the family fun day. I'm on a first responders' float in the parade."

"You and Millie?" his mother said, regaining her speech.

"Yes," he said, kicking himself. What the hell had he *not* been thinking mentioning her once, let alone twice?

"So you're seeing a bit of each other, then?"

"Little bit." This time his mind conjured up Millie listening to him talk about Charlie and then skipping stones with him. He had to hand it to her—she'd helped him through a really tough day.

She got you through last week, too.

He didn't want to think about last week. The week before Charlie's anniversary was always difficult, and this time it had been exacerbated by the accident on the rez, but now it was over. Thankfully and blessedly over.

"We saw Miranda on Thursday," his mother continued. "She brought a group of kids down from Jilagong for the surfing day. She says hi."

He didn't really know Miranda. Sure, he'd met her at Charlie's funeral, but she hadn't been anything like the woman he'd been expecting. In fact, she was nothing like the women they'd always dated, which had struck him as very odd, but his parents had embraced her as if she was part of the family. If he was honest with himself, he'd never been able to reconcile the idea of her and Charlie together, let alone being happy far into the future.

He asked the question that always niggled at him when Miranda was mentioned, as if he had to test her love for Charlie and check it was real. "Is she with someone?"

"No." Her mother sighed. "I wish she was."

Shock ripped along his veins. "How can you say that? It's only been two years since he died."

His mother's lips pursed. "I know exactly how long it's been, Will. I know you think you have a monopoly on grief for Charlie, but you don't. I lost a son and Miranda lost the man she loved."

His mother hadn't reprimanded him like that in years, and her censure crossed the thousands of miles that lay between them. *What the hell is wrong with you? You know what she's been through.* What they'd all been through. "Sorry."

She gave him a brisk nod, but her voice softened. "It's been an awful two years, and life will never be the same for us again, but the two of you seem to be putting your lives on hold and that isn't the answer. Miranda deserves to be happy again. So do you. Isn't it time you came home?"

A simmer of panic bubbled under his skin. "You're not suggesting that Miranda and I might get together, are you?"

She shrugged as if the answer was simple. "You both loved Charlie."

"Mum . . ." He gripped his temples with his thumbs. "I don't even know her."

"You need someone, and Charlie loved her," she said as if that was enough of a reason.

He didn't need anyone. "I'm not Charlie."

She muttered words that sounded something like *Charlie got it* before she said clearly, "What about Millie? You obviously like her."

"We're just friends," he said, trying hard not to let his rising irritation infiltrate his voice. What was wrong with his mother? She usually stayed out of his personal life, and she'd never tried matchmaking before. It suddenly occurred to him she was sixty-five now. Was her grandmother clock stuck in alarm mode?

He smiled into the camera, thinking about his sister, who'd been married for a year. "If you want a grandchild, tell Lauren and Alex to get a wriggle on."

She sighed. "This has nothing to do with your father and me wanting to be grandparents."

"What's it got to do with, then? You've never waded into my personal life before, so why start now? Where's all this coming from?"

"It's coming from you."

"Me?" He was fast becoming bewildered by the conversation and yet at the same time extremely wary.

She gave him an exasperated look very similar to the one she used to give him when he was a boy and he'd done something stupid. "Before Charlie died you'd never spent any real time alone. He was always with you either in person or on the other end of the phone, a text message or a video link. We can see how lonely you've been these last two years, and it's breaking our hearts."

She gripped his father's hand. "Life is better when you share it with someone, Will. You need to let someone in to share it with you."

"You mean like I used to share with Charlie?" Anger stirred at her total lack of understanding of the depth of connectedness he and Charlie shared. A connectedness severed by his death.

No one could ever come close to having that sort of bond with him. "I can't believe you just said that."

His father leaned forward. "We're worried about you, son."

"You don't have to be, Dad," he said tightly. "I'm fine. I have to go or I'll be late for the parade. Love you both. Bye."

He clicked his mouse and killed the connection.

———

"RALSTON!"

Tara's radio crackled with the not-so-dulcet tones of Mitch Hagen's gravelly voice. It was the Fourth of July, and the family fun day was in full swing. She'd been up before dawn putting the roadblocks in place for the fun run and the parade, and now both were over.

As she pulled her radio close to her mouth, the *boom-boom-boom* of the marching band was deafening. "Reading you loud and clear, Sheriff."

"You done dismantling the roadblocks?"

"Yes. I've just arrived at the park and I'm doing a foot patrol."

"I need you at the police tent with the police vehicle at noon for the Breaking Good show."

"The what?" she asked with a sigh. She'd thought it was too good to be true that her boss would just let her do traffic and crowd control.

"It's a first responder event. Kids get to see a police vehicle, ambulance, the medical evacuation chopper and get their photo taken with us. Make sure you've got your hat. Kids love putting on the hat."

"Next you'll be telling me there's coloring books and stickers."

"You got it," Mitch said, missing her sarcasm. "We've got a bunch of CSI for Kids booklets to give out. Don't be late."

"I'll be there."

"Oh, and, Ralston, nice job on the bacon offenders."

She smiled at the unexpected praise. The fun run first thing this morning had been uneventful out on the road but not so at the free breakfast. A minor altercation had broken out between two hungry runners and one last remaining piece of bacon.

"You want bacon?" she'd said, separating the two men who were old enough to know better. "Then you'll get bacon."

She'd instructed them to get into the backseat of her patrol car and had driven them to McDonalds, which was on the outskirts of town. She'd dumped them there without their phones or wallets, leaving them with plenty of time to think about their behavior on the one-mile walk back into town.

"Who told you about the bacon buddies, Sheriff?"

"Bethany put it up on Twitter. It's got more re-tweets than Ethan Langworthy striking out at the annual County versus Chamber of Commerce softball match, but that was pretty much expected. Happens just about every year. The guy should know better. I'll see you at noon."

"Over and out." She opened up the Twitter app on her phone, thinking about what Mitch had just said. Why did Ethan sign up for the team and open himself up for ridicule?

Because he walks his own line.

He didn't care what people thought about him; he just did what he enjoyed and took those along with him who wanted to join him. She admired that about him. She'd seen it in action when he'd taken her dancing. They'd danced so much it had been like a second workout of the day. From the Macarena to the twist with some line dancing thrown in and then an ABBA chaser, they'd danced it all. None of the dances had been slow, and none had involved much more touching that his hand in hers as he twirled her in and out.

Touch was a strange thing. With one person it could be threatening. With another it was reassuring. Ethan's hand in hers was both of those things, except the threat didn't come from him but from her heart. He was too easy to like, and that frightened her the most. He'd spent most of the evening with her, only leaving her when he'd answered a request from Will to play a waltz on his cello for Mrs. van Dyke.

Unlike the edgier music he usually played, the romantic tune had floated into the air—sweet and soft—like powdered sugar, and couples danced cheek to cheek. It had made her yearn for something she'd never known, but at the same time it had put her on edge. In the end, her overriding emotion was one of a lucky save—lucky he hadn't been free to hold her tight and waltz her around. She'd have been tempted to let him lead her anywhere while she rested her head on his shoulder.

"Excuse me, Officer," a nervous voice said. "Um, hi."

She pulled her mind back from her destabilizing thoughts about Ethan and noticed that a woman holding a little girl's hand was standing in front of her. "May I help you?"

"Um, I'm Carly, and Millie Switkowski said you're going to, um, run some women's only classes at the gym?"

"I was thinking about it. Are you interested?"

Carly nodded. "I'd like to sign up. Will there be child care?"

That idea hadn't even occurred to her. "I guess there should be, right?" She'd ask Ethan how to go about organizing it.

"That would be great. I know at least five other women who'd come."

Tara pulled a page out of her notebook and wrote down her cell number. "Get their names and numbers and text them to me. I'll get back to you all with a date and time."

"Thank you so much."

Carly's daughter, who'd been fidgeting next to her mother, suddenly squealed in delight. "Mommy, look! It's a lion."

Tara automatically turned and realized the library tent was right behind her. Standing outside was a two-legged lion with a shaggy mane and tail. With a brown nose and brown whiskers that seemed like they'd been drawn on with an eyebrow pencil, the lion looked suspiciously like Ethan.

Holding the costume's tail, he bobbed down to the child's height and said, "I've lost my roar and I can't remember what it sounds like. Do you know?"

The little girl's eyes went as round as saucers, and she nodded very seriously before scrunching up her face and yelling, "Raar!"

Putting his hand on his lion chest, Ethan fell back, pretending to be scared. "Wow, that's loud. But how did my roar end up inside of you?"

"It's my roar, silly," she said confidently as she spied the craft table. "Mommy, I want to go inside and draw a lion." She tugged her mother inside the tent.

Tara tried to imagine herself at age five again and thought she probably would have wanted to go inside, too. Lots of yellow and brown streamers and balloons festooned the roof of the tent, and posters of books featuring lions decorated the walls including *The Lion and the Mouse*, *When Lions Roar*, and *The Lion, the Witch and the Wardrobe*. One corner of the tent had beanbags and a sofa, and a few parents were taking some time out from the day's events and reading stories to their children. Diagonally opposite the reading nook, Tara could see Ethan's emo intern disinterestedly painting a child's face. It looked more like a Dalmatian than a lion, so perhaps Tahlee had gotten sick of painting lions.

Ethan gave her a welcoming smile, his caramel eyes alive with the joy of life.

Without a moment's hesitation she smiled straight back at him and immediately realized how unusual that was for her, because it wasn't something that came naturally. Often, she had to force herself to smile.

"I've lost my roar, Officer Tara, and I can't remember what it sounds like?"

"You've done an amazing job with the tent, Ethan."

The painted whiskers on his face wriggled as his cheeks creased with fun. "I've lost my roar, Officer Tara, and I can't remember what it sounds like."

Understanding dawned, and she suspected her eyes might be as wide as the little girl's. "You don't really expect me to roar, do you? I'm in uniform."

"I thought the police department helped lions to find stolen things." He tilted his head toward a group of children who'd gathered around them, and one of his costume ears flopped forward. He scratched his fake mane. "Do you think Officer Tara should help me find my roar?"

"Yes!" they all chorused, jumping up and down and clapping their hands.

She glanced at the parents, who were smiling indulgently at their kids. She really didn't feel comfortable roaring. "Open your mouth," she said pulling her flashlight from her belt.

He played along and opened his mouth wide and said, "Ah."

She shone the torch down his throat. "I can see your roar right there. It's just been hiding." She turned to the crowd. "When I count to three, if everyone roars, I'm sure it will come back."

"You have to roar, too, Tara," he said softly in her ear.

His breath tickled her skin, and a whoosh of delicious and addictive sensation whizzed through her, stirring up mayhem and leaving behind longing.

Just maybe you can trust this one?

She tried hard to shrug the thought away, but it wouldn't totally leave.

"Nothing bad will happen, you know," he said as if he'd just read her mind. "Other than perhaps you straining your throat. What do you have to lose?"

My reputation as a stern law enforcement officer. Every protective strategy I've surrounded myself with for years.

"It's just a bit of fun, Tara."

Fun. She really didn't do fun, and it certainly didn't come naturally.

But these kids were looking at her with a combination of anticipation, respect and a little bit of awe. "Okay, everyone, one, two, three."

Everyone roared and she opened her mouth and joined in, letting out the sound. It was loud, long and, going by the look of some of the younger children's faces, just a little bit scary. It felt absolutely amazing.

The roars came to an end and she turned to Ethan. "Everyone did a great job, so I think it's time for your roar to come out now."

He winked at her and roared. She snapped a photo and tagged it *Bear Paw librarian roaring for reading.* #OnlyEthan.

Chapter 18

As the band swung into action and people started dancing in front of the stage, Will sipped a cold beer, savoring the malty flavor as well as the fact he was now no longer on call. Now he could totally relax, and it was Josh's turn to care for the health needs of Bear Paw. As the evening involved people letting off fireworks after a day of drinking, Josh could be in for a busy night.

He deserved it. Midafternoon, Josh had asked him to judge the chili cook-off. When he'd excitedly sought Millie out at the first aid tent and told her he thought it was a real honor, she'd burst out laughing.

"What's so funny? You think an Aussie can't judge chili?"

She'd patted him on the arm. "I'm sure you're more than capable. Off you go and have fun."

The moment he'd arrived at the cook-off area, he'd realized being asked to judge wasn't an honor at all. Bear Paw took its chili as seriously as the women of Murrinwindi took their Lamingtons, scones and vanilla slice entries in the annual agricultural show. Josh had totally wimped out and hand-balled him a live social grenade.

Susie Switkowski had given him a nod, a smile and a wave

as if to say, *I know you're sleeping with my daughter and with that comes responsibilities.* When he'd been prevaricating between first and second place, Bethany had said, "Man up and make a damn decision," and the hospital team of Cassidy, Helen and Larissa had threatened to reactivate the NoBalls-Bartlett Twitter hashtag if he didn't give them first prize. Apparently trash-talking the judge was also part of the fun of the competition. He was in a lose-lose situation, and Josh Stanton owed him big-time.

As it turned out, the acerbic Bethany cooked amazing chili and had carried off the blue rosette—not that it had won him any favors.

"Doctor Bartlett, no one can understand that accent of yours," Bethany had said, plucking the microphone out of his hand and raising it to her mouth. "Attention, everyone. The winner of the prestigious Bear Paw chili cook-off is Bethany Jacobson. That's three years in a row, people."

The nurses had made it clear that he wasn't getting any favors from them anytime soon, which meant he was back to making his own coffee. Susie had given him a reproachful look, and Danny, shaking his head slowly as if Will's intelligence was under scrutiny, had said, "As a doctor, I thought you were supposed to be smart."

Oh yeah, Josh deserved to be frantic all night instead of being tucked up in bed with his new bride.

Thinking about bed made him think of Millie. She'd texted saying she was going home to get changed and she'd meet him later. He hoped later was soon. They'd spent the holiday passing each other rather than spending it together, which hadn't been his intention at all. After the parade, he'd assumed they would have strolled around the tents and then kicked back on a picnic rug in the shade, listening to the live music, but Bear Paw responsibilities had pulled them both in different directions.

"Hey, Will."

He turned to see Ethan looking more like his usual self, dressed in mustard skinny jeans, a floral shirt and a vest. "The lion's done for the day?"

"The lion sleeps tonight," he said as he showed his button to the bartender and picked up a beer.

"A-wimoweh." He raised his plastic cup to him. "Good day?"

"Yeah, it was." Ethan sipped his beer thoughtfully. "For the last few weeks, I've been trying to find something that excites my intern, and while I was busy being king of the little kids, she totally rocked the teen tent." His mouth turned up in a wry smile. "It seems her indifference is way less threatening than my enthusiasm. What about you?"

"We got a lot of interest in the chopper. People are always fascinated by how much state-of-the-art medical equipment we can fit into a confined space. And they were generous with their loose change donations."

"Would it even cover the cost of turning the helicopter on?"

Will laughed. "When you add together fuel, staff and wear and tear on the chopper, it works out about ten thousand dollars a minute to run, so not even close. But working with the flying doctors taught me that if the community feels a connection to the service, they support it, and we gratefully accept every penny." The band kicked up a toe-tapping number. "You playing tonight?"

"Ty and I've got the set just before the fireworks." He glanced toward the stage and grinned. "Well, will you look at that?"

Will saw three firefighters strutting their stuff on the stage. "You got a thing for guys in suspenders?"

"No. Look left."

Will followed his gaze and saw Millie dancing with Tara, hips bumping and hands waving. He didn't know what surprised him more—the fact Millie was still wearing scrubs or that the policewoman had metaphorically let down her hair.

"It's every man's fantasy," Ethan said appreciatively. "Two women in uniform dancing together."

The same green streak that had rushed through Will when he'd thought Ethan and Millie might have had sex shot through him again, only this time it hit faster and a lot harder. "Keep your eyes on the policewoman."

"Steady, there, Will," Ethan said mildly. "Millie and I are just friends."

Just friends. That's what he'd told his mother a few hours earlier, and given he'd spent two weeks lusting and fantasizing after Millie and another two weeks having great sex with her, *just friends* didn't reassure him one little bit.

He swung his gaze back to the librarian. "Friends have been known to have sex, Ethan."

"That's true, although you may have more experience with that than I do." For a librarian who wore glasses, he could lob an incredibly intimidating look. "And yes, we did talk about it once, but she was in a pretty bad place so I refused." This time his stare hardened to the color of brittle toffee. "I wouldn't do anything to hurt Millie."

The inference was clear—Ethan thought Will might. As much as that rankled, because he'd never intentionally hurt Millie, he didn't defend himself, because his brain was snagged, tangled and stuck on the words *a pretty bad place*.

A ripple of something closely related to apprehension ran through him. "What do you mean by a pretty bad place?"

Ethan shook his head. "It's not my story to tell, Will."

"Then why the hell did you say it?"

"I probably shouldn't have said anything, but you were going all territorial on me." Ethan sighed. "Look, it was a long time ago, and if Millie wanted you to know, she'd have told you. Forget I said anything." He put down his beer. "Come on, let's go cut in and dance."

Will watched him go, but dancing was the last thing on his mind.

———

ETHAN played his entire set on autopilot, his brain full of Tara dancing in uniform. Sure it had been one quick dance with a group of first responders as part of a fund-raiser, but she'd joined in and done it. Just like she'd joined in and played along this morning looking for his roar. He really hadn't expected her to go through with it, and when she'd opened that cherry red mouth of hers wide and let out that earsplitting roar, all he'd wanted to do was grab her, hold her tight and kiss her. Kiss her long and slow until she lost all her hard edges, softened in his arms and invited him into her bed.

Lucky for him and for the integrity of his plan, she'd roared in front of a group of little children and their parents, which had effectively stopped him from acting on impulse and doing something stupid. He was determined not to kiss her until she gave him an indisputable sign that she welcomed his touch.

Doing anything before that was way too risky and could undo all the small steps she'd made.

This past week had been a new kind of torture for him. Spending time with her was amazing, but the more time they were together, the more he wanted from her, and that was the problem. Given everything she'd been through, did she have anything to give? Did she even want to try? She'd tweeted a photo of him—did that count for anything?

She tweeted you in a lion costume, doofus, just like half the town.

The moment Ty played his last chord on the guitar, Ethan laid his cello down. "Good set."

Ty raised his brows. "You've played better hungover and with blistered fingers."

"Sorry." He pushed his glasses up his nose. "Bit preoccupied."

"You think?" Ty slid his guitar into its case. "Let me guess? You're about to ditch me to go watch the fireworks with the ice queen."

"Don't call her that," he said quietly but firmly.

Ty's hand paused on the case's locks. "Eth, be careful. Women rip out your heart, slice it up and hand it back to you in pieces."

"Katrina didn't deliberately do that to you, Ty."

"Doesn't make it any easier to deal with."

Worried for his friend, he slapped him on the shoulder. "Come watch the fireworks with us."

Ty snorted. "And cramp your style with the i— with Tara? I don't think so."

"There won't be any cramping. She's been through a lot, and I'm going more slowly than a turtle on sedatives."

"Thanks, but I'm good."

He didn't want Ty to be alone. "You sure?"

"Yeah. I'll watch the fireworks and then head home. I'm up early trailing cows first thing in the morning."

"If you're sure . . ." He said good-bye to the cowboy and made his way through the fast-fading light past the families who were cuddled up on picnic rugs waiting for the summer Montana sky to darken. Ten fifteen at night was way too late for the younger children, and many had already fallen fast asleep, curled up in their parents' arms. One year he wanted to be one of those families with a wife, a kid and a dog.

You're such a golden retriever, Ethan, Tahlee had said disparagingly yesterday. She'd been shelving the Spirit Animals series and he'd been telling her about his plans for today.

He'd thanked her for the compliment, which of course had earned him another eye roll, because Tahlee probably thought a retriever was pathetic and he should want to be a lion. But he valued loyalty, kindness, understanding and commitment, and if that was soft, well, so be it. He was who he was—he just wished he had someone to share it with.

And, moron, you've fallen for someone who's frightened of everything you want.

He found Tara pacing on the far side of the lake near the setup for the fireworks. In stark contrast to earlier in the day, nothing about her looked relaxed. "Hi. You look like you need to roar again and let it all out."

She gave him a small but rigid smile. "The fire department knows what they're doing, right?"

"For the fireworks display? Sure, they do it every year." As far as he understood, her job was to make sure that people were viewing from a safe distance, and she'd done that. All she had to do now was sit back and enjoy the show. "The town fireworks are as safe as they come. It's the DIY ones in backyards and out in the streets that usually cause the problems."

"Of course. Right." She checked her watch, her actions jerky. "Two minutes to go."

He liked the idea she was excited. "As a kid I drove my parents crazy waiting for the fireworks to start, and I still get a buzz out of them." He held his hand out toward her. "Come on, I know the perfect place to watch them."

"I don't want to watch them," she said flatly, her arms firmly by her side.

He dropped his hand, kicking himself that he'd even offered it. This wasn't like the time she was off duty and they'd gone dancing. The times they'd done kickboxing. "Why not?"

She looked almost apologetic. "Ethan, I hate fireworks."

"But they're spectac—" *You are a world-class idiot.* "Because of the noise?"

She nodded, anguish written all over her face. "It's like a

mortar attack. Every part of me wants to take cover, but I've got to be here until the show's over and the crowd's dispersed."

The event most everyone in town had been looking forward to all day was her worst nightmare—her and every dog in the county, and the display was about to start any minute. *Think.*

He caught her hand in his and squeezed it. "I've got an idea." Tugging her over to the hood of the police car, he climbed up and patted the space next to him. "Sit here."

"Ethan, that's—"

"No time to argue, Tara." He pulled his phone out of his pocket and quickly worked to untangle the earbuds. "Here you go."

He pressed the earpieces in her ears and scrolled through to a playlist of music that would be the perfect accompaniment for fireworks. Cranking up the volume, he hit play as the sky lit up with color—the tendrils of fireworks raining fire-engine red, dazzling white and royal blue high above them. A moment later, the first boom vibrated the air, thundering around them. Tara flinched. He turned the sound up higher, and the music was now so loud he could hear it spilling out from the earbuds. It felt as natural as breathing to listen to the music, gaze up at the sky, sling his arm around her shoulder and hold her tense body close.

———

THE operatic "Ride of the Valkyries," which always made Tara think of watching early-morning cartoons of Bugs Bunny being chased by Elmer Fudd, blasted into her ears, the orchestral instruments dominating all her senses. With the crashing symbols and the swell of the brass overriding most of the cracking boom of the fireworks, she dared to open her eyes to the sky. The music was a perfect match to the spectacle.

Balls of color bloomed across the inky darkness. Streaks of vivid white light tore up through the night as straight as a rocket before exploding and pouring back down like fluorescent hail. Ethan's shoulder pressed gently into her back, and she could feel the warmth of his arm through the sturdy cotton of her uniform. It should feel wrong. She should be leaning forward, but the touch had no agenda other than comfort, and she wanted it. Needed it for the next few minutes.

The music faded and her body jerked as she felt a boom vibrate in her chest. Ethan immediately pressed the phone's screen, and then soaring violins, the grand rumbling of timpani drums and the heralding sound of trumpets deafened her. She managed a weak laugh. "*Star Wars*?"

The light from the fireworks showed warmth and caring in his eyes. "It's perfect for fireworks. Rousing and grand."

"Got any John Philip Sousa?"

"I do, but I thought given the circumstances a military march might not be the best choice."

Her heart felt like it stopped for a split second before starting again, and her throat got ridiculously tight. "Anyone ever tell you that you're a really nice guy?"

He gave an exaggerated sigh. "Sadly, all of the time."

She didn't know what to say to that, so she listened to the music, and when Bruce Springsteen came on, she joined him in singing, "Born in the U.S.A." The moment the last trickle of light fell from the sky, Ethan dropped his arm.

Her back instantly felt cold, and all she wanted to do was lean back against him. Self-preservation made her slide off the hood. If she'd learned anything from her disastrous marriage, it was not to make any life-changing decisions under fire. She'd married Tim because she was scared. War was about survival, and what was needed to survive in war was very different from what was needed in peacetime.

The fireworks were over and so was this moment. She pulled the earbuds out of her ears. "Thank you. That really helped."

"You're welcome." He lifted his phone out of her hand and put it in his pocket. "I guess I should go and leave you to make sure the crowd departs peacefully."

He was right—she had another hour of work left before she was off duty, but that didn't stop a stab of disappointment catching her under the ribs.

He raised his hand and gave her a geeky robot-style wave. "Catch you later, Tara."

A crazy panicky feeling flipped her stomach as he turned away. One part of her was grateful that he didn't suggest she stop by his house after work or he stop by hers, but another part of her wanted to know exactly when *catch you later* was going to be.

"Ethan."

He turned back.

"Can you spot me tomorrow at kickboxing?"

"Sure."

"And I need to ask you about how I go about organizing child care for my exercise class."

Even in the shadows of the night, she saw a smile roll across his face. "You decided to run a class? That's awesome."

She tried to shut down the part of her that almost purred with his approval. "With you and Millie both thinking it was a great idea, did I really have a choice?"

"You always have a choice, Tara," he said softly. "I'd respect it whatever it was."

Suddenly it felt a lot like they were talking about something else entirely.

"SHUT up, Dex! I know already," Millie yelled at her beeping CGM.

The past week since the Fourth of July had been a great week for her diabetes, but tonight she felt like crap. Her blood sugar was three hundred, and her stomach cramped so hard she was lying on the sofa with her knees drawn up to her chest. Some days she hated being a woman. She'd exercised, she'd given herself extra insulin, but the hell if it was doing a damn thing to bring down her numbers.

She checked the time on her phone, and a sob gurgled out of her mouth. Will was supposed to be picking her up for Shakespeare in the Parks in fifteen minutes. She'd really been looking forward to the picnic and the play—his promised romantic evening—but she couldn't go feeling like this. She could hardly see straight, let alone concentrate on understanding old English. Experience had taught her that a blood sugar spike like this was always followed by a crashing low, which meant she had hours in front of her of pricking her finger and testing her blood sugar and feeling like death warmed up. Plus, she kept having to pee.

And you don't want Will to see you like this.

She reached for her phone. *He'll hear it in your voice.*

Bringing up the message icon, she typed:

Sorry! Something's come up. Enjoy the show and say hi to Katrina and Josh from me. Millie x

She summoned up enough energy to toss the phone back onto the coffee table and then lay back down, her head feeling like someone had opened it up and stuffed it full of sticky goop. She stared at her bare toes at the end of the sofa, surprised to see them, because she'd swear she was wearing lead-lined boots.

"Knock, knock, honey. I saw this in a little boutique in San Francisco when I was visiting Evan . . ."

Mom? Bloody hell. One of Will's expressions wove slowly across her sluggish mind, and she sat up before her mother got into the room.

". . . and I thought it would be perfect for—" Susie's voice faltered. "Millie, you look a bit pale. Are you sick?" Susie put the dress store carry bag on the coffee table and then automatically reached for Millie's forehead. "You feel warm. Have you taken your temperature?"

This was why she never told her parents her numbers. "Mom, I don't have a fever. It's just that time of the month and this one's a bit nasty. Please don't fuss."

"I'm your mother. Fussing comes with the job description."

Millie reached for the carry bag, hoping to distract her with the contents. "Show me what you found."

Susie smiled. "The perfect summer dress for you."

Millie doubted it. With clothing, her mother seemed to fight against Millie's diabetes as strongly as Millie had once fought it by trying to ignore it. "Mom, you know I don't wear dresses because they never allow for my—"

"Shush. You haven't even seen it." Her mother gave her an apologetic look. "I know I've always tried to push you into wearing dresses, and I've been thinking about what you said the night you wore the tuxedo, which is why when I saw this it said, Millie." Susie pulled the dress out and shook it free of the tissue paper. "It's the perfect color for you."

And it was. She took in the 1950s' princess-line dress with its modern overtones. The bodice had a low, square neckline and was the navy blue color of a deep lake on a cloudy day. Scattered over the blue was a fine pattern of white speckles, which spread across the sleeves and the bust. They faded to nothing at the point where the color slowly leeched to a summer sky blue and then to the same turquoise green as the ocean in Will's photo. The skirt flared and the white speckles recommenced four inches from the hem.

"Look," Susie said gleefully. "It's got lovely deep pockets, which are part of the dress and not stitched on as an after-thought, so the lines are smooth and flattering. What do you think?"

Even with her slightly blurred vision, Millie could see it would not only suit her, it would flow over her belly, allowing for Dex and her pump's insertion sites. "I love it."

Susie blew out a relieved breath. "Really?"

"Really. It's got all the elements I need in a dress. Thanks for thinking of me."

Susie smiled as if Millie had given her a gift. "I'm always thinking of you, honey. I thought perhaps you could wear it tonight. It might be a treat for Will to see you in a dress for a change and see those lovely legs of yours."

Given Will generally tried to undress her whenever they were alone, she wasn't sure he'd care either way. She was about to tell her mother she wasn't going to the play when Will walked in.

She stifled a groan. She really needed to start locking her door.

"Hello, Will," Susie said breezily.

"G'day, Susie." Will smiled and stretched out his hand in greeting.

Susie ignored his hand and presented her cheek for a kiss.

Will didn't seem to mind at all and brushed it quickly with his lips. "You're looking as lovely as ever."

"You're almost forgiven for giving Bethany first prize in the chili cook-off."

He grinned at her, all easy and relaxed charm. "What will put me back in the good books?"

"Come for family supper one night this week."

"Mom," Millie spluttered, but her lagging brain was a beat too slow. Will was already accepting the invitation.

"You kids have a good night," Susie said before disappear-ing out the door.

The moment it clicked shut, Millie watched Will's smile vanish. "What's going on, Millie? Your mother thinks we're going to the play, but you just blew me off with a text."

"I didn't blow you off. I—"

Beep, beep, beep, beep, beep.

Will picked up Dex and sucked in a sharp breath. "Jesus, Millie. Four hundred and ten? For a month you've been telling me you've got your diabetes under control. What have you been doing?"

His words punched her, opening old wounds from years past, and fury as hot as a furnace ignited. "What have I been doing? Obviously you think I've been bingeing on cotton candy and drinking beer."

He looked momentarily perplexed. "Have you?"

She threw a cushion at his head, feeling ridiculously betrayed. He should understand.

Why? He's an ER physician. You've had two endocrinologists who didn't get it.

But I need him to.

"You obviously think I've been mainlining sugar." She struggled to her feet. "Get out of my way. I need to pee, and when I get back, I want you gone."

Chapter 19

W ill wasn't going anywhere, but as he'd obviously already said a shitload of the wrong things, he stayed silent and stepped out of the way, allowing Millie past. He watched her disappear into the bedroom.

Four hundred and ten. Four hundred and freaking ten. All he could think about was the damage it was doing to her eyes, her kidneys, and her heart. To her. He wanted to magic the number down and down fast and fix this, but he couldn't. The fact ate at him, burrowing in like a dreaded tick.

How often did her blood sugar spike like this? How many hours had it been so high? When had she last seen her endocrinologist? Surely there was a plan to avoid situations like this. What was her A1C? The unanswered questions went around and around and around in his head, and then Millie was back in the room.

Her curls, usually so bouncy, sat limply on her head, and she looked nothing like his vivacious, energetic Millie. "I asked you to leave," she said curtly.

He smiled, shooting for conciliatory. "You don't know me very well if you think I'd leave you alone with a blood sugar this high."

She stomped past him and shoved her feet into her sneakers. "The reality is that we don't know each other very well at all. You only told me about Charlie because you had no choice." She wrenched open the door and walked outside.

He followed her, his temper rising. "Oh, and you're Miss-Share-Everything? You're a vault when it comes to your diabetes. Hell, you *texted* me to cancel the play without even mentioning it was because your blood sugar was out of control."

"It's not out of control, and your behavior today is *the* perfect example of why I didn't tell you." She marched through the gate and out onto the street.

His long strides easily caught him up with her. "So sue me for being worried about you."

"Worried?" Her eyes flashed every possible combination of green and brown. "I hear that a lot. I get it from my parents, from my endocrinologist and from everyone who knows I'm a diabetic, but what it really means is you think this spike is my fault. That the only possible way my blood sugar can be this high is because I've done something to cause it. Do you want to know what I did, Will?" Her voice shrieked then cracked.

"I did exactly the same thing that I did yesterday and the day before and day before that when my numbers stayed in the perfect range." She stopped suddenly, her chest rising and falling quickly as she caught her breath. "I wake up every morning a diabetic. It's a life sentence without any chance of parole. I never get a day off from juggling food and calculating carbs, analyzing Dex's data, fighting with the mail-order pharmacy and my insurance and working out insulin doses. Just a change in the brand or from cold to warm insulin can drop my blood sugar dramatically, and all the time I know that the drug I need to stay alive is the drug that can potentially kill me."

She suddenly sounded chronically exhausted and close to tears. "Some days, like today, my best efforts to keep my diabetes in check just aren't enough. I'm a nurse and I'm going to be a doctor, so yeah, on paper it looks like I should be able to avoid spikes like this, but this disease doesn't give a shit that I know stuff. This disease screws with me all of the time, and I don't need you pinning guilt on me, Will. I've got enough of that all on my own."

Her despair pummeled him, and he wrapped his arms around

her, wishing he could change things for her. Knowing he couldn't do a damn thing. He pressed a kiss into her hair. "I'm sorry. I didn't mean to make you feel guilty."

She met his gaze, her expression resigned. "No one ever does, but there's always an assumption that I'm doing the wrong thing. Eating the wrong foods, not exercising, exercising too much, not bolusing insulin early enough. All of it infers that in some small way I'm to blame." She pulled away from him and recommenced walking. "Once, that was true, but it hasn't been like that in a long time."

She was in a pretty bad place. Ethan's words had bothered him for a week. "How old were you when you were diagnosed?"

"Old for type one diabetes. Sixteen."

He sucked in a breath. At sixteen, he and Charlie had just gained height, lost their braces, discovered girls, alcohol and parties. "That would have been a tough time."

She gave a tight laugh that said *tough* didn't come close. "It was a triple threat. Take one chronic illness, add adolescent hormones and a desperate need to be just like everyone else, and BAM! No matter how hard I tried, I wasn't like everyone else. I was suddenly the freak who had to stick myself with needles, and everything changed.

"Mom and Dad went from being relaxed parents who said, *Have a good time* and *Be home by ten* to *Do you have your insulin, fruit snacks, orange juice?* and *We'll pick you up at ten.* All the freedom and spontaneity went out of my life. I couldn't just shove food in my mouth without thinking about it, and the town decided they'd"—she made air quotes—"*help* by doing useful things like swiping food out from under me, saying, *You can't eat that. Sugar will kill you.*"

"And I'm guessing Bethany led the charge," he said, thinking it was the sort of tactless thing the woman would do.

She shook her head. "Actually, Bethany was great. She's got rheumatoid arthritis, so she knows what it's like to live with a chronic illness. I know she's difficult, but deep down under all that bristle she's got a big heart."

"If you say so." He reached for her hand, and she closed her fingers around his. "So back to you?"

"Me?"

"Learning to live with diabetes?"

"Oh, that." She scrunched up her mouth and her nose wriggled. "For the first year, I wanted my old life back so bad I did *everything* my endocrinologist and my diabetes educator told me to do. I was like this goody-two-shoes, born-again diabetic. It made no difference to my blood sugar, which continued to fluctuate wildly. I was admitted to the hospital three times."

"Your mum mentioned that." The moment the words left his mouth, he knew he'd said the wrong thing.

Horror instantly combined with anger, tightening her cheeks. "You've been talking to my mother about me?"

"No." Her brows shot up fast, vanishing under her curls, and he hastily qualified, "Not really. One morning, she saw me leaving the guesthouse and she volunteered the information."

"Great," she said flatly.

He tried redirecting the conversation. "When did you get your first pump?"

"The following year when I went to college. Mom and Dad weren't happy about me being so far from home, but I convinced them the pump would solve everything, and we were all desperate to believe it. It didn't, and I was still having crazy swings, and then one day in a lecture about diabetes, they put up a list of things that affected blood sugar.

"Something inside me snapped. I wanted to stand up and scream at them that instead of the list they only needed one word. *Life*. Every damn thing that happens to me throughout the day affects my blood sugar. Being hot or being cold affects it. My monthly cycle totally screws with it, and today's a case in point. After that lecture, I was all *Screw you, diabetes*, and I started doing what every normal young adult at college does."

He thought about his early years at university. "Partied?"

"Oh yeah," she said, her mouth now a grim line. "I partied and I partied hard, because what was the point of doing everything right when none of it made a damn bit of difference?"

But he knew drinking alcohol would have made a huge difference to her blood sugar. To her health in general. The increasingly familiar dread that trickled through him whenever he thought about her diabetes intensified.

How long did you do this for? "But you don't drink now?"

"No."

Her sharp tone spoke volumes. She didn't want to tell him,

but he already knew bits and pieces, and he wanted to be able to connect the dots. "What changed?"

She tossed her head defiantly. "Almost dying makes a girl reevaluate her options."

His generalized fear for her coalesced into something far more real, and he stopped walking. "I'm glad you didn't die."

She gave him a sad smile. "So am I, and I thank Ethan every day that he had the presence of mind to know something was wrong. He called 911 and got me to the hospital."

"And?" Getting information out of her was like pulling teeth.

She glanced down at her feet before meeting his gaze. "I went into acute kidney failure and was in the ICU for a week."

Kidney failure. Kidney. Failure. No matter how he said the words in his head, *nothing* changed their significance.

She stroked his face. "Don't look so alarmed, Will. I'm fine."

He didn't believe her. "So how's your kidney function now?"

She sucked in her lips.

"Millie?" He heard the rumble in his voice he only ever used with difficult students and interns.

"I have some mild residual damage," she said quickly, "but it's all good and the labs prove it. I'm fit and healthy and careful with what I eat."

"That's great," he managed to say despite the thoughts careening around his brain. *You're diabetic and that's a risk factor all on its own. And what about babies? Pregnancy and diabetes is a lethal weapon for kidneys.*

Whoa! Stop right there.

What the hell was he doing thinking about babies? Before Charlie died, he'd only ever thought about kids in an abstract way—a vague possibility, or not, far out in the future. Since Charlie's death, he didn't think about the future at all, because planning was pointless when everything could be lost in a heartbeat.

I'm just thinking about babies in relation to Millie's future, not mine.

He thought he heard Charlie laugh.

"And we're back." She pulled her hand out of his, and he realized they'd power walked around the block. He followed her inside the guesthouse, where she waved Dex at him. "Yay, it's finally falling."

It was still too high for his liking. "You don't want to keep walking?"

She shook her head. "No. It can sit high for hours, but once it starts to fall, it tumbles fast. Now the challenge is to eat the right foods at the right time to stop a crashing hypo, so that's my night in a nutshell. If you leave now, you can still catch the start of the play."

"I don't care about the damn play, Millie," he said roughly, reaching for her. "I care about you."

She stilled, staring up at him, her beautiful eyes large in her pale face and brimming with emotion. "I care about you, too."

Her softly spoken words sent a slither of something close to uneasy agitation through him, and then it was gone.

FOUR hours later, Will lay in bed wide-awake with Millie asleep, her head on his chest. As she breathed in and out, her hair tickled his face, and he watched her. After the earlier pallor of her cheeks, they now had a healthy rosy bloom on them, and Dex, which he held in his hand, was showing a very satisfying one hundred.

They'd watched DVDs on the sofa, punctuated by Millie testing her blood sugar, counting carbs, eating, swearing, bolusing insulin and then eating again. Wrung out by the residual effects of the high blood sugar, she'd fallen asleep early. He should be taking advantage of an early night, too, and usually lying in bed cuddled up to Millie with her soft and generous body scooped into his, he fell asleep fast and slept soundly.

Not tonight. Tonight his brain just wouldn't shut up.

Trying not to wake Millie, he eased out of bed. She gave a gentle snore and rolled over, her hair a slash of brightness against the white pillowcase. An unbidden image of her head on a stark, white hospital pillow loomed large in his mind, and suddenly her face became Charlie's. He rubbed the tightness in his chest and padded out to the kitchen, making himself a mug of tea.

He sat down at the table to drink it and noticed Millie's laptop was open. He automatically reached out and touched the trackpad. The screen flickered to life open on the uploaded data from her CGM. The numbers stared at him. She'd always been tight-lipped about her blood sugar numbers. Despite the couple of exercise-induced hypos she'd had, which were pretty normal for a diabetic, and given how organized she was, he'd always assumed until today that her numbers were mostly good.

She's not your patient. Charlie's voice wafted through his head. *Mate, you're not seriously going to look at that.*

"That's rich coming from you," he muttered. "You thought rules existed to be broken."

I never breached confidentiality.

"I'm trying to help."

He scrolled through the data looking for patterns. She'd been stable through the winter and the spring with a regular spike once a month, but since the start of June there'd been some crazy swings. Swings that had nothing to do with her normal monthly spike. Was it the new job?

Sure, there was stress associated with learning new things, but she'd worked as an RN for a few years, so what she was doing now was not a hell of a lot different.

Some days, like today, my best efforts to keep my diabetes in check just aren't enough.

He stared at the figures, looking for clues, and his gut suddenly rolled. He'd arrived in Bear Paw in June.

He immediately ruled that out as being the cause, although there was an echo in his head about the human body's cocktail of massive hormone changes that took place when a person was attracted to someone. Lust changed body chemistry.

Life. Every damn thing affects my blood sugar.

Kidney failure.

He slapped the laptop closed against the accusatory numbers. Millie was a ticking time bomb, and it scared him senseless.

"THANKS, ladies," Tara said, holding up a drink bottle. "You've all worked really hard and it's hot tonight, so make sure you hydrate."

The women murmured their thanks and drifted away, chatting animatedly to one another. It was the third class she'd taught, and word was spreading. There were at least two new women at each class.

"Great session, Tara," Millie said, her face bright red as she gulped down some orange juice. "Once summer's over and school is back, you'll be turning people away."

"Or adding another class."

"Would you have time for that?"

She shrugged. "The sheriff will be back on the schedule by then, so it's doable."

Millie's brow creased in a slight frown. "That wouldn't leave you with any downtime."

"I like to keep busy."

"Remember to factor in some fun," Millie said, picking up her towel. "And talking about fun, you must come to my 'Millie goes to Seattle' party. I start classes in August, so it's coming up fast."

"Oh." A rush of disappointment hit her. She'd gotten to know Millie, and she really liked her. She hadn't realized she'd be leaving town so soon. "That's early."

"Yeah," she said on a sigh. "This year it's too early."

"I'll miss you."

Millie's dimples carved into her cheeks. "Thank you, but I'll be back at Christmas and again next summer. Meanwhile, if you want a coffee buddy, you've always got Ethan. He's got so many diverse interests that fascinating conversation's guaranteed."

The complicated tangle that was her emotions for Ethan tightened. "I guess."

"By the way, I saw the tweet you sent on the Fourth," Millie said with a knowing look. "Nice touch, and Bethany and Judy re-tweeted it."

"I thought it made a change from the usual funniest home video type," she said briskly.

"It's okay to like him."

"Of course I like him," she said, shoving her towel in her gym bag. "He's been very welcoming and helpful."

Millie hooted with laughter. "Oh, Tara, I saw the look on your face when you danced with him at the street party and again on the Fourth. There's a spark there, and although it's none of my business why you're holding back, if that sort of chemistry had ever flowed between me and Eth, I'd have snapped him up years ago."

"So there's no spark at all on either side?" she heard herself asking while her brain screamed, *Shut up! Shut up!*

"None at all." Millie gave an embarrassed smile. "Once, years ago when I was at a party and I'd drunk too much, I suggested we try, but even then I knew it wouldn't work. Eth being Eth kindly said no and in the process saved our friendship and both of us from excruciating embarrassment.

"I do love him, though, as a dear, dear friend, and I owe my life to him," she volunteered with unexpected candor. "He's special in so many ways, and I mean really good special, not weird special. He's the sort of guy who'd lay down his life protecting you while doing the dishes. Most women are too busy fantasizing about some alpha-macho guy who swoops in, guns blazing, and they totally miss the value in Ethan's kind of loyalty."

Tara's skin prickled under Millie's probing look. "I really don't need protecting," she said curtly and snapped her mouth shut before she added, *You know he could kill someone with one well-placed kick to the head.* She hated how Millie's words had stirred up all her confusing feelings for Ethan, and she wanted the conversation to stop now. "I need to lock up."

"Sure," Millie said, rolling up her floor mat and walking to the door. As she pulled it open, she paused. "Tara, no self-respecting twenty-first-century woman needs protecting, but it's kinda nice when someone loves you, cheers for you and has your back. Good night."

Tara watched Millie disappear out into the bright evening light, saw the door bang shut behind her and then was alone in the empty gym. It didn't bother her—she was used to being alone. Given a choice, she often chose her own company over people, because she didn't let herself down. She didn't cheat, use, abuse or betray herself.

Millie hasn't done any of those things.

Neither has Ethan.

For the thousandth time since the night of the Fourth of July, she thought about how he'd silenced the PTSD-inducing noise of the fireworks for her with music. How he'd wordlessly accepted her fear and found a practical way to help her deal with a tough situation, and in the process she'd avoided falling apart. He'd held her close and absorbed her initial flinches, provided agenda-free comfort, and then, the moment the last bang had vibrated the air and faded to nothing, he'd let her go. Not once in all their time together had he tried anything. He was her kickboxing partner, an occasional sharer of pizza and her key to finding her feet in small-town life.

He's my friend.

The thought shocked her. She didn't have many friends, and of those few people, none were men. Tim had been her lover and then her husband before becoming a lying, cheating betrayer, but he'd never been a friend. The men she worked with in the military were colleagues, not friends. A few weeks ago she'd have considered a platonic friendship with a man an impossible miracle.

It still is.

Millie was right. Nothing about her feelings for Ethan were platonic, but she didn't know how Ethan felt about her. She was used to overt displays of attraction from men—being undressed by their eyes, the *come on, baby* swagger of their hips, the not-so-casual brushes of their arms across her chest and the crudeness of their language when they told her what they wanted to do with her. None of it required a moment of puzzling out or interpretation.

The only times Ethan had touched her were with brief displays of support. Other than that, he was more restrained than the boys she'd known in middle school. God, they hadn't even kissed. She couldn't work him out. He was always friendly, always interested in her, always obliging, and yet he didn't take any crap and had on occasions pulled her up when he thought she was being difficult.

Duh! That's what a friend does.

Only, there'd been that *one* time after the fireworks when she wondered if he felt more for her than friendship. He'd looked at her, and his eyes, the rich, warm color of polished oak, had held a lick of heat, and he'd said, *You always have a choice, Tara.*

And then the moment had vanished and in the week and a half since had never been repeated.

You always have a choice. She'd replayed those words over and over in her head until she'd driven herself mad. She couldn't ever remember dithering. Decisions were her strong point, and she'd made a lot of them across the years. Some of them had saved her life. But this decision, this choice, was Sophie's choice—no choice at all. She'd rather pick up her weapon and take on a sniper than take on the emotional risk that both sides of this choice commanded.

———

ETHAN was mulling over his next move on Chess with Friends—his father was currently winning—and staring into the fridge. His current wish was that the contents would just mysteriously combine into something edible and bounce right into his hand. The pealing chimes of the doorbell made him start.

"Come in, it's open," he called, pulling two beers off the shelf, anticipating whoever the unexpected company was, he'd stay for a drink. He closed the fridge and looked up. One bottle slipped out of his hand.

Tara caught it and set it on the table. "Hello, Ethan," she said in her no-nonsense, throaty voice, her gaze direct as ever.

His shock at seeing her standing in his kitchen instantly morphed into fear. "What's happened? Who's hurt?"

She indicated her gym clothes. "I'm not in uniform. I'm not here on police business."

Relief swamped him. "Right. Of course. Sorry. Drink?" He handed her the beer she'd caught.

"Thanks." She took it and quickly spun off the top before tossing the cap neatly into the trash. She sat down at the table.

He did the same, but his thoughts were stuck on *Tara's in my house. Tara's in my kitchen.* It was the first time either of them had been in the other's home.

He realized it was his turn to talk. "Good day?"

"Yes." Her long, shapely left leg bounced up and down, tension washing off it in waves.

Usually after exercising she was relaxed—well, as relaxed as Tara was able to be. She always had an air of alertness about her that he figured was a constant because of her childhood and her time in the military. But she wasn't relaxed now, and she wasn't talking. That was odd, because if Tara had something to say, she just said it without preamble, coming straight to the point. He liked her directness, but it seemed to have deserted her tonight.

He smiled and offered her an opening. "I'm gathering you didn't stop by just for idle chitchat."

Her blue green eyes instantly snapped to his. "Are you attracted to me in any way?"

The unexpected question caught him mid-swallow, and he inhaled beer. Gasping and coughing, he struggled to empty his windpipe of fluid and pull in a breath.

Horror streaked across her face as she jumped to her feet, hitting him hard on the back. "Ethan. God, breathe. Do I need to call the EMS?"

He held up his hand, wheezing in and out—the sound not dissimilar to a strangled whistle. Eventually, the fire in his lungs eased, his breathing settled and he cleared his throat. He'd spent weeks sublimating his desire for Tara so as not to pressure her like the other bastards in her life had done. So as not to give her any excuse to run. Had he slipped up? Had she noticed something? Was she upset?

He glanced up at her. "Is there a right or wrong answer to that question?"

She swallowed, and all his blood left his brain. "Tara?"

"No."

"Okay then." He stood up and leaned against the table facing her. *Go slowly. Do not, I repeat, do not screw this up.* "Are you attracted to me in any way?"

Her shoulders squared but she met his gaze. "I've tried really hard not to be."

Yes, Virginia, there is a Santa Claus. "I think that has to be the best compliment I've ever been given." He pushed off the table and stepped in close.

Her soft floral scent enveloped him, and he slid his hand along her cheek. "You sure about this?"

She shook her head slowly from side to side.

He dropped his hand.

She grabbed it back.

It was the sign he'd been waiting so long for, and he took it. Weeks of thinking about this moment dissolved as reality took over. He cradled her face in his hands, leaned forward and kissed her. She was hard and soft, tense and pliant—she was Tara and she was amazing. Her lips tasted of fierce grape Gatorade and cautious restraint, and he pressed light kisses across the width of her top lip. When he'd fully explored it, he turned his attention to her bottom one, gently teasing its bountiful softness out with his tongue.

She made a mewling sound against his mouth and opened her lips under his. He tumbled inside that hot, wet, welcoming place and thought he'd died and gone to heaven.

———

TARA hadn't been kissed in a very long time, but even so, this kiss was unlike anything she'd ever experienced. How could Ethan kiss so gently yet so erotically? Nothing about it was him inflicting his will on her, but neither was it passive. Her body couldn't get enough of it.

She met his tongue with hers in a tango of exploration. She ran her tongue along his teeth, welcoming the rough and the smooth. She reveled in his fiery heat, and her taste buds exploded with his flavors of beer, salt and hunger—hunger for her. Weeks of locked-down and heavily bolted desire flooded her and instantly collided with his need for her. It detonated like fire on gasoline, making her breath hitch up and her heart race.

His mouth didn't leave hers, but his hands did, reaching around her shoulders for her braid. She felt the tug of the elastic come away, and then he broke the kiss and his fingers loosened her hair until if fell softly around her face, across her shoulders and down her back.

A smile of wonder broke across his face as he gently caressed her temples, smoothing her hair back behind her ears. "I've always thought you were beautiful, Tara, but with your hair down, you're absolutely stunning."

She was used to being told she was attractive—in both harsh tones and mild, but the tenderness and awe behind his words made her ache in places she hadn't allowed to feel. It made her want to believe.

He buried his hands in her hair, breathed deeply and then laughed.

"What's so funny?"

"Life's unexpected twists and turns. You, here in my kitchen with your hair down and gazing at me with slightly unfocused eyes."

She stroked his cheek. "You did that with your kisses."

He grinned as if she'd bestowed on him a priceless treasure. "Shall we keep doing it?"

"God, yes."

"My sentiments exactly." He pulled her back to him and proceeded to kiss her long, slow and thoroughly.

She ran her hands up into his hair, feeling the thick, silky waves slide through her fingers and breathing in the fresh zip of his wintergreen shampoo. Her hands molded to his scalp and then moved down to his neck and shoulders, imprinting the solid feel of him. Her fingers tingled and itched, begging to feel more than just the material of his shirt and demanding to touch his skin with hers.

She'd always been in control with men—always held a little bit of herself back. To a certain extent, sex had often involved her going through the motions, but as his mouth roved over hers, something inside her slipped. It threatened to give way completely, and she broke the kiss. With trembling fingers, she tried unsuccessfully to undo his shirt buttons.

"Damn it." Using both hands, she pulled, ripping the buttons from their cotton posts.

He laughed as she pushed the material off his shoulders. "You've never liked this shirt, have you?"

She had no idea what he was talking about.

He balled it and threw it in the trash. "I was wearing it the day we met. You made a small tear in the tail when you were hauling me out of the window."

"Sorry," she said automatically as she soaked in his tan and toned chest.

Heat lit up his eyes. "Don't be."

As his arms went around her and she pressed her lips to his shoulder, she felt his arousal pressing against her, and suddenly everything felt right. He wanted her. She wanted him. All the internal arguments and dilemmas she'd been wrestling with for days went blissfully silent.

His eyelashes fluttered butterfly kisses along her temple and across her cheek, sending rafts of wonder skimming through her. It was a light and playful touch, but she gloried in it, never wanting it to stop. His tongue darted inside her ear with a flick and lick.

Silver lights lit up behind her eyes, her legs buckled, and she sagged into him with a gasp.

"That's my girl," he whispered against her ear. "Want to take this out of the kitchen or christen my table?"

"My choice?"

"This time," he said, inferring there'd be a next time but it would be his turn to choose the venue.

"It's a perfectly nice table, but—"

"Good choice." He took her by the hand and ran her up the stairs. "I wasn't expecting company, so my bedroom's not exactly neat, but you've only got eyes for me, right?"

She pushed him down on the rumpled bed.

He grinned up at her. "I'm taking that as a yes."

With unfamiliar laughter dancing through her, she stared down at him, contemplating exactly which part of him she was going to kiss first. The hollow at the base of his throat? His clearly delineated pecs? The tawny line of hair that ran from his belly button straight down under the snap of his jeans? She shivered in anticipation of what lay underneath and decided she'd start by removing his jeans.

He moved just like he had the first day they'd met—sudden and lithe—and then he was back on his feet facing her. "I'm all for equality of the sexes, and as I'm shirtless and you're still wearing yours . . ." His hands gripped the hem of her T-shirt, and then it was off, up and over her head, leaving her standing in her plain white cotton bra.

"Plain packaging," he said with a smile as he flicked open the clasps of the bra. Her breasts tumbled out into his hands. "But there's absolutely nothing plain about the contents."

He lowered his mouth to her left breast and suckled her. Every particle of desire in her body shot downward, combining into a low, hot, heavy, throbbing sensation at the apex of her thighs, and her legs gave way. She fell onto the bed panting. "That's dirty pool. Your pants. Off now."

"Yes, Officer," he said with a smirk as he shucked them, and then he turned his attention to tugging her out of her Lycra workout pants.

"Wait." She grabbed them back just before he dropped them on the floor. Somehow, she managed to get her uncooperative fingers to pull the condom she'd brought with her out of the tiny waistband pocket. "We're going to need this."

"You bet." His eyes flashed with passion and appreciation as he joined her on the bed and he wrapped his arms around her.

Their mouths melded, their bodies bumped and wriggled— legs tangling, hands grasping—each finding the other's dips and curves until they fitted together. He kissed her like a man holding something precious but not breakable. He kissed her from her brow to her toes using his mouth and his hands to pleasure every place in between until she was boneless, shaking and screaming his name.

When he finally slid into her, she captured him, her muscles aching with relief that they could finally grip him. His rhythm caught hers, driving her forward and upward. Up, up, up, she spiraled, higher and higher to a realm she'd never been before. She shattered into a thousand tiny pieces.

Ethan followed, slumping against her momentarily before rolling onto his side and taking her with him. With one arm slung over her side and tucked up between her breasts, he pulled her butt into his belly and pressed a kiss onto her shoulder.

Peace stole through her, rolling languidly over all her defenses and laying them flat, until it reached and circled her heart. It glowed inside her like golden summer sunshine after rain, making her feel fresh, clean and new. She lay in Ethan's arms, feeling the steady rise and fall of his chest against her back, the thundering of his now slowing heart and the reassuring warmth of his skin. She was home.

Home.

She blew out a breath full of tumbling barricades and fortifications. *Home.*

She went to breathe in. Her lungs froze. Peace vanished.

Panic detonated like a grenade. *Get out. Get to safety. Go now.* She scrambled for her scattered protective armor starting with her panties.

"Ethan, I have to go."

Chapter 20

Ethan's body was wrapped around Tara's, but his brain was off soaking in a bath of bliss, kicking back, smoking a cigarette and planning on aging disgracefully with her.

She suddenly sat up. "I have to go."

What the hell? Cold air rushed across his body, jolting his brain back to the here and now. *Stay calm.* It took every ounce of discipline he had to remain lying down when every part of him wanted to rise up and grab hold of her arm. "Go as in to the bathroom or go as in leave?"

She didn't look at him but instead concentrated on fishing her panties up off the floor. "Leave."

He wanted to press his palm against the small of her back and feel her warmth, but survival told him that would be the worst thing he could do. That would give her more ammunition to leave. "I didn't hear your cell."

"No." She hooked her bra and swung it around before shoving her arms through the straps and pulling them up onto her shoulders—every action jerky.

"So why are you running?"

She didn't look at him. "I'm not running."

"I think you are." He rolled up off the bed and found his briefs. He was not going to be naked for what he knew was going to be one of the most important conversations of his life.

She shoved her legs into her activewear and cast her gaze around for her T-shirt. "It doesn't really matter what you think."

Ouch. His breath in stung, but he refused to play the *hurt Ethan so he leaves me alone* game, because far too much was at stake. He wanted Tara in his life, and now they'd gotten this far, he wasn't letting her walk away.

He picked up her T-shirt and folded it neatly. "We just had the world's best sex, Tara, so we've got that part of being a couple covered. Let's go downstairs and work on the rest of it."

Alarm bells rang in her eyes. "Give me my shirt."

He shook his head and tossed her his jeans instead. "You can have your shirt after we've talked this through."

"That's extortion."

He shook his head. "I don't think so. I've given you my jeans, so we're both in equal states of undress. Also, I'm not holding you against your will. You're free to leave at any time."

"In my bra?" Her voice rose, the pitch higher than he'd ever heard it. "Bethany would have that on Twitter in a heartbeat, and somehow I don't think the sheriff would be very understanding." Her eyes suddenly narrowed, and then she leaped toward his closet.

He got there first, barring her access to his shirts. He desperately wanted to touch her. He wanted to wrap his arms around her and hold her close, but that sort of intimacy was exactly what she was running from. He wanted her to trust him. He needed her to trust him, because unless she could do that, they didn't have a future.

"Tara, you came here to my house, told me you wanted me, had all of me and now you want to leave. If the roles were reversed, I'd be the world's worst bastard." He played his trump card—appealing to her sense of decency. "I've got feelings, too. All I'm asking is that you stay for a conversation."

And a chance. A chance for me to show you that taking a risk on us would be the best decision of your life.

He'd never wanted anything as much as he wanted Tara by

his side for the rest of his life. He only hoped he could pull it off, because the alternative didn't bear thinking about.

————

ALL I'm asking for is a conversation.

Tara's heart beat so fast she was in definite competition with a hummingbird, and right now, in betting terms, she was the favorite to win. Didn't Ethan realize what he was asking her? More than anything she wished she hadn't come over to his house in the first place.

The sex was amazing.

But it wasn't the sex she was running from.

She still couldn't believe that Ethan was using strong-arm tactics to make her stay. He wasn't that guy. He didn't do stuff like that.

You're free to leave at any time. Hah! That was a lie and he knew it because leaving in her underwear wasn't an option. She'd been in Bear Paw long enough to know that the flip side to a town that was mostly caring was that nothing could be kept secret. Whenever she walked up the path to her apartment she invariably met one of her neighbors. It was almost guaranteed that if she was shirtless, she'd not only meet someone, they'd have their cell phone out faster than a gunslinger at the O.K. Corral. Out of uniform and off duty, she was fair game.

Ethan had her over a barrel. "Fine," she said, stomping down the stairs, because looking at the bed and remembering what had just happened in it played havoc with her concentration. "You want to talk, you go right ahead." She had no intention of talking back.

Ethan followed her into the kitchen, but he didn't say anything. He did, however, put some cheese and crackers on a plate and pass her a fresh beer. It all looked totally normal, but it felt utterly surreal.

He pushed the plate toward her, and her stomach revolted at the thought of food. She steeled herself. "Can you just say what you want to say?"

"Sure." His finger followed a drop of condensation down his bottle of beer. "Tell me why you're scared."

Those weren't the words she was expecting, but they were

terrifyingly accurate. A fresh wave of panic hit her, and she shored up her protective armor. "I fought in a war, Ethan. I face down criminals for a job. I don't do scared."

He sucked on his beer, his expression bland. "I never took you for being a liar, Tara."

She hugged her arms over her chest, kept her gaze fixed on the ticking kitchen clock and refused to answer the accusation.

"How did you feel when you kissed me in the kitchen?" he asked quietly.

"Surely that was obvious."

He shot her a look that he used on difficult children. "Nice try, but I want you to tell me using your words, Tara."

"Aroused." It came out curt and hard.

His mouth pulled up on one side. "Besides that."

"I don't know."

"You do know." He blew out a breath. "Nothing bad is going to happen if you say it, Tara. In fact, something good might just come out of it."

A rush of anger spurted through her at his interrogation. "Hopeful, okay? I was feeling hopeful. Happy?"

"That you were hopeful? Absolutely." He leaned forward, his expression gentle. "Hopeful is a good thing."

"No, it isn't." Her heart banged so hard against her ribs she could feel the vibrations in her arms.

"Why not?"

"Because . . ." She closed her eyes for a moment against the pain that was piercing her. "You make me want to dream. You make me think that just maybe, I could have a normal life."

"You can."

She shook her head. "I already tried once, and it ended in tears and recriminations."

"That was a marriage in a war zone, Tara. Nothing about it came even close to being normal." He rubbed his chin as if he needed time to think. "Normal is way more dull, boring and blessedly predictable. First off, you and I are living in the same town. We'd be coming home to each other every night instead of having months and months of living apart. Second, chances of us being blown to smithereens are so slim they're not even a consideration."

His words ate into her resolve, and she immediately moved

to shore it up. "I don't have a clue how to be in a healthy relationship. My mother never had one, and if she couldn't do it then—"

"You are *not* your mother," Ethan said on a low growl as his cheeks hardened and his eyes flashed the color of peanut brittle. "She is not your yardstick. She was an alcoholic, which means she was sick and incapable of a functioning relationship."

She'd never heard him sound so adamant or look so determined. One part of her knew what he said was true, but the other voices in her head were so much louder.

He gave a heavy sigh. "Tara, you grew up not being able to depend on anyone, and I get how that made you fiercely independent. Hell, you needed to be to survive, but your life's moved on from survival. If you want to experience the next phase of your life, you need to let people in."

His gently spoken words fell on her softly like sprinkles of rain, but their message hit like hail—hard, cold and jagged. "But don't you see?" She wrung her hands. "That's the terrifying thing."

"Let me in, Tara. I want to be part of your life. I want to protect you."

"I'm a cop, Ethan. I carry a Taser and a gun. I don't need protection."

"I'm not talking about physical protection, Tara. I'm talking about your heart."

A sob rose in her throat and she fought it down. "Don't say that. You're asking too much of me. I have no clue how to do normal."

He reached across the table and picked up her hands. "You're already doing it."

She pulled away. "This isn't normal. How many women have you had sex with who've wanted to flee the moment it was over?"

"There may have been one or two," he said lightly with a typical Ethan self-deprecating tone. "But we're not talking about them. We're talking about you. You're holding down a regular job, and that's very normal."

"I'm the only female police officer in one hundred miles, so my job isn't all that normal."

"You've been having regular coffee dates with Millie and making friends."

"She's leaving town."

He rolled his eyes. "Okay. You're teaching gym classes."

She reached for a quick reason as to why that wasn't normal but drew a blank. "Actually, that is pretty normal, isn't it?"

He smiled. "Totally normal. Of course you do like to de-stress by trying to kick me in the head, which possibly isn't normal, but it could be healthy for conflict resolution in our relationship."

She immediately tensed at the word *relationship*. "This is so easy for you, Ethan. You grew up seeing what's normal behavior in a relationship and what's not."

"You obviously haven't met my parents," he joked before becoming serious again. "Tara, no relationship is easy. My parents love each other, but that doesn't mean they don't argue or occasionally yell at each other. Mom once got so frustrated with Dad arguing about where to store the trash can and referring to it as exhibit A just like in his courtroom that she threw an egg at him. Granted, it was hard-boiled, but he didn't know that."

An anguished laugh escaped her lips.

His thumbs drew circles on the tops of her hands. "I can't promise you there won't be times when I get frustrated with you or disagree with you and vice versa, but I can promise you this. I will never cheat on you or lie to you. I will never intentionally hurt you. I will always put you first, protect you, cherish you and love you." His gaze, filled with a mixture of hope and uncertainty, continued to hold hers. "Tara, none of what I just said can happen unless you take that massive leap of faith, trust me and let me into your life."

Let me into your life. Five little words, but their size was deceiving, because they could cause more damage to her heart and soul than a cluster bomb exploding on enemy installations. Sweat beaded on her hairline, her throat tightened so much she couldn't swallow and her blood rushed through her ears, deafening her.

She looked at Ethan's kind and considerate face, his warm eyes and the humor lines around his mouth. "You really love difficult, defensive me?"

"I really love challenging, clever, resilient you."

"I want to believe, Ethan, I do, but . . ."

"I know."

The fact he didn't say *Just do it* helped. "This has all happened so fast."

He shrugged as if six weeks wasn't fast or really an issue. "Moving forward we can take things as slowly as you like. There's no rush to move in together or get married, but we don't have a fighting chance unless you can commit to the idea of a future together and believe that it's possible. I want a future with you, Tara. One that stretches far into the years ahead."

A future. It called to her, pulling at all the reasons she'd decided to move to Bear Paw in the first place. Reasons she both craved and feared all at the same time. Could she really have what other people had? A man who loved her? A home?

Doubt rose to the surface. "You see children in your future, don't you?"

"Our future, Tara. Yes, I do."

"Is that a deal-breaker?"

He paled. "You don't want kids?"

Her heart squeezed even tighter. She hated that she was hurting him. "It's not so much that, it's . . ."

"Just say it, Tara," he said raggedly. "Believe me, you saying it out loud is going be easier for me to deal with than me imagining what you're thinking."

Say it fast. "You're so much better with kids than I am. I might not be any good at being a mother."

Relief crossed his face. "Stop being so hard on yourself. I'm just more relaxed around them than you are because I've currently got more experience, but you're already better than you think. When you first arrived in town, you would never have roared like a lion with them."

Warmth spun through her. "That's true."

"And if being an at-home mom isn't your thing, I'll happily be a house husband for a few years until they're old enough for school."

"You'd do that?"

He placed her T-shirt on the table between them. "Trust me, Tara," he said simply. "We're a team."

Trust me.

This man—this loyal, caring, loving man—wanted her in his life. She could continue to hold him at arm's length like she did with most everyone and continue to live the life she'd been living.

That horse has bolted. He's already changed your life.

Or she could step off the cliff and invite him in and share the future with him.

A shake started in her toes and radiated along all her limbs until she was shivering all over. "I trust you, Ethan. More than anything I want to be part of your team."

He was on his feet in a heartbeat, around the table and pulling her into his arms, wrapping them around her tightly. His love circled her and flowed into her, and an unwanted tear slipped out of her eye, followed by another and then another until she was sobbing and making a wet and sticky mess on his shoulder.

"I don't cry," she managed to gasp out.

He gazed down at her with eyes filmed with tears. "I do."

She continued to shake and cry and laugh as he held her and his heart thudded against her chest, each beat a testament of his love for her. She shot out a hand and grabbed her T-shirt, wiping her face with it before drying his eyes and drying his shoulder.

"I love you, Ethan."

His smile was wider than she'd ever seen it before. "I love you, too, Tara."

She laid her head on his chest, feeling his arms around her, and she knew that finally, after all these years, she was safe. She was truly home.

MILLIE was standing on top of Mount Brown, staring out at the spectacular view that surrounded her. The vivid blue of Lake McDonald lay far below to the west, and the boats on the water looked like toys. To the north was the craggy gray rock face of Heavens Peak, its majesty carved out by millions of years of ice and snow. She snuggled her back into Will's chest and wrapped his arms around her waist. "I told you it was worth the hard hike. Isn't it amazing?"

"You're amazing." He dropped his head into the curve of her neck and kissed her, his warm breath sending tingles shimmering through her. "Millie, I don't want this to end."

"Neither do I." She turned in his arms and pressed her hand to his cheek, loving the roughness of his stubble on her palm. "Come to Seattle with me."

He looked down her, his gaze full of love. "I'm way ahead of you. I've already found us an apartment and—" *Beep, beep, beep, beep, beep, beep, beep, beep.*

The noise pulled her hard and fast out of her delicious dream, leaving her struggling to work out where she was and what was happening. With sleep still fogging her brain, she shot out her hand toward the nightstand, feeling for Dex. Her fingers closed around her CGM, but it wasn't vibrating. Another level of sleep vanished, and she realized that Dex didn't even make that sort of sound. It was her phone.

God, she had too many devices in her life. "Hello." She thought she heard a muffled *Thank God.*

"Millie," Will said, his voice rumbling down the phone like a cozy hug. "You sound half asleep."

"That's because I was." She yawned, expecting him to apologize for waking her up.

"But it's after nine."

"So?" She blew a curl out of her eye. "I'm on the clinic schedule this week and I have today off."

"I know. You told me last night."

She thought about how wonderful last night had been, and her thoughts wandered off in that direction before she remembered there must be a reason for his call. "Are things busy? Do you need me to come in?"

"No, it's quiet. Kelli Meissner's asked me to scrub in on a bowel resection."

Why? Millie tensed. She hadn't warmed to the arrogant female surgeon, and Dr. Meissner's physician's assistant usually accompanied her. Even if the PA was sick, the surgeon still had the Bear Paw nursing staff. Why would she be asking Will to assist? He probably hadn't been in an OR since he was an intern.

Because the OR is her turf and she can show off and impress him there.

"I hope you can remember the difference between Babcock forceps and Mayo clamps," she teased, trying to cover her spurt of jealousy.

Will laughed. "It might be a bit of a challenge. Anyway, you good?"

"I'm fine. I've got my whole day planned." *Including a surprise for you.* She heard noise in the background.

"Sorry, Millie, I've got to go. I'll call you later. Have fun on your day off."

As he hung up, she realized he hadn't asked her whatever it was that had been so important that he'd woken her up. He didn't call her very often.

He doesn't need to.

Ever since the night they'd missed Shakespeare in the Parks and Will had mentioned that her mom knew they were sleeping together, he'd started staying for breakfast. Actually, he'd been having supper here the nights they weren't working, including two barbecues around the pool with her parents. In fact, when she thought about it, he was only going to the motel to get his shirts from the laundry service. Between work and home, they were pretty much together 24-7.

Not for much longer.

Don't think about it. You've still got a week left.

She thought about the dream instead. Odd that it was on Mount Brown. She and Will still hadn't managed to do the hike yet, but the rest of the dream she guessed was her subconscious verbalizing what she wanted to say to him. That wasn't quite accurate. She didn't expect him to change jobs and move to Seattle, but she wanted a sign from him that this wasn't all going to end absolutely on July 31.

Dex started beeping. The snack she'd eaten just after Will had left for his early-morning bike ride had done its bridging job, giving her a rare sleep-in, but now it was time to get up and have breakfast.

MILLIE was taking a break from her long list of errands and having lunch with her mom at the diner. In between mouthfuls of Shannon's pulled pork and apple flatbread, Susie was excitedly studying a map of Seattle.

"Oh, honey, your apartment's close by everything."

Her mom was planning on helping her move as well as

spending a couple of days taking her shopping. Since the success of the sundress, Susie was on a mission to find clothes that fit Millie's criteria and looked good. Millie, who appreciated Susie's new zeal to clothe her in a style she felt comfortable in, had conceded that there were special occasions like weddings and parties when she could strap her pump to her thigh and move her setups to her arms. Given the list of shops her mom had just suggested they visit, she was wondering if she should have kept that bit of intel about the setups to herself.

Millie's phone rang and she ignored it, because she knew how much it irked her mom if she took a non-urgent call at meal times.

"Honey, shouldn't you take that? It's Will."

"You sure? I guess the hospital might need me."

Her mother nodded and returned her gaze to the map of shopping precincts.

She picked up the phone. "Hi."

"G'day. What'cha doin'?" Will asked, his accent always more pronounced on the telephone.

Nothing about his tone of voice sounded urgent or harried. "Um, having lunch with Mom."

"Oh good. You're not on your own."

It seemed an odd thing to say. "Ah, no, but would it matter if I was?"

"It's nice for you to have some company on your day off."

"I guess." She thought about his call earlier. "What did you want to ask me?"

"Ask you?" He sounded confused.

"When you called before."

"I was just saying g'day."

Usually, they saw each other on and off during the day at work. Was he missing her? A warm feeling flowed through her, sparking hope. If he'd called her twice in the six hours since he'd kissed her good-bye this morning just to hear her voice, surely that meant something. Meant that he'd want to find ways they could be together when one of them was in Seattle and the other was in Great Falls. She didn't even want to think about the possibility of him returning to Australia.

"G'day, then."

He laughed at her attempt to sound Australian. "So you're having a good day?"

"I am. What's that expression you use? I'm kicking goals. The party preparation's almost done."

"So no highs or lows?"

Her tuna wrap curdled in her stomach. "All under control," she said overly brightly.

"Excellent. I'll let you get back to your lunch, and I'll call you around three about dinner plans. Say hi to Susie."

The line went dead.

Around three. It suddenly hit her. He'd been calling her today around the times she tested her blood sugar. Was he checking up on her? Her brain shied away from the thought. She was being ridiculous. Sure, he still brought in healthy food to the hospital, but as half the staff was now trying to lose weight, she knew it was no longer specifically just for her. He didn't check up on her at work, did he? *No.* She reassured herself those stolen kisses at random times across the day were just that—random.

He called you three times the other day when he was working at the clinic out at the rez. And he called Helen when you didn't pick up.

She started scrolling through her call log, checking the times while her thoughts fought each other. *They were work-related calls. He needed information each time.*

Information other people could have given him.

"No emergency?" Susie looked up from the brochures.

"No." She laid the phone down on the table, hating the information it was feeding her.

She thought back to the night she'd whipped him at pool, furious that he wouldn't take her white water rafting or go on a hike up Mount Brown—convinced he was treating her like a patient. Only she'd misread him, because those long looks had been about wanting her, nothing to do with her diabetes. Since that first night, life had been busy with work and community events in Bear Paw, not to mention having sex, so her plans to push him to go hiking had taken a back step. Surely those were the reasons they hadn't gone hiking, biking or rafting?

"Is everything okay, honey? You look a bit pale."

"Everything's fine," she said, giving herself a little shake to put everything in perspective. "He says hi."

"I think it's lovely that he just calls for a chat."

Her mother's expression was similar to the one she wore when she'd just finished watching a sappy movie. "From my side of the fence, he looks like a keeper. Have the two of you talked about—"

"No. It's complicated."

"Because of his work visa?"

I wish. Battling the bureaucracy of the INS would probably be a lot easier.

———

WILL checked his watch and willed the checkout line to move a bit faster. When he'd called Millie at three and said he'd be home at six with steaks, she'd said, "That just guaranteed a sick patient will walk into the ER at five and you'll be there until after seven."

She'd sounded a bit pissed off in general. It was hard to tell if it was from low blood sugar or if something else was bothering her. As much as he wanted to ask her if her blood sugar had dipped, it was up there with asking any woman who was snarky if they had their period. So he'd gone with the general, "Everything okay?" and she'd replied, "Just great. See you at six. I've got a surprise for you."

"Great. I've got one for you, too."

And now it was six and he was stuck behind Bethany in the late predinner rush at the grocery store. She was telling the young cashier about her new television, even though her groceries were bagged and she'd paid for them.

"Excuse me, ladies," he said with a smile. "I'm sorry, but there's an emergency, so if I could just . . ."

He justified the white lie to himself because there *would* be an emergency if Millie had bolused insulin anticipating that dinner was going to be when he'd promised. Another reason for him to tell her about his surprise gift to her.

Bethany narrowed her eyes at him, and he expected a volley of words, but all she said was, "Humph."

The cashier looked wide-eyed and grabbed his produce out of his arms. "Oh, sure, Doctor Bartlett, sorry."

He paid, ran to the car and texted Millie.

Sorry! Five minutes away.

Four minutes later he was kissing her hello and sneaking a peek at Dex, which was on the kitchen bench. "I'll start cooking."

"Mom sent over some dips she made, so I thought we could munch on those while we wait for the steaks. Do you want a drink? Beer? Wine?"

"Iced tea would be great."

Her hand paused on the refrigerator door. "I thought you said the only way to drink tea was steaming hot."

"You've corrupted me," he said, kissing her again before heading outside to the deck. He fired up the propane-fueled grill, letting it heat the way his father had taught him so when the steak hit the metal bars, it seared in the juices.

He set a timer on his phone to remind him when the grill would be hot enough and then sat at the outdoor table, which Millie had set for dinner. There was an envelope propped up on a candle with his name on it. "What's this?"

Her cheeks pinked. "Your birthday present."

"But it's still a week away." His birthday was just before she left Bear Paw for Seattle. He hadn't been thinking about either event, because since Charlie's death, he never thought much beyond the here and now.

She sat down next to him. "It involves some planning and a schedule change, so just open it and all will be explained."

A zip of excitement pulsed through him and immediately snagged on guilt. He was still alive and got to have birthdays. With more force than necessary, he ripped open the envelope and pulled out a gift certificate.

This certificate entitles Dr. Will Bartlett to an accelerated free-fall skydive. Enjoy the exhilaration of falling free through the BIG SKY COUNTRY skies.

The date was for set for his birthday.

Bro, we need to do something awesome every year on our birthday. Deal? Memories of Charlie making that pronouncement at sixteen and insisting they shake on it came rushing back to him.

Sadness tangled with something that could almost be called happiness, and that confused him, because his birthday was almost as tough as the anniversary of Charlie's death. He set the certificate down. "How did you know that Charlie and I always did something like this on our birthday?"

Her shoulders rose and fell. "I took a guess. From what you've told me about him, I figured the two of you would hardly have sat around playing board games."

"You got that right," he said, thinking about some of the things Charlie had dragged him into doing.

"You're not upset?"

He heard the tentativeness in her voice and moved to reassure her. "No. It's incredibly thoughtful." He kissed her cheek. "And it's the perfect gift. Charlie would have loved it, too. Thank you."

Relief crossed her face. "You're welcome."

He laced his fingers between hers. Since the day at the rez where they'd skipped stones, he'd discovered he liked telling her Charlie stories. Sharing him with her kept him close. "Over the years, we did all sorts of things on our birthday, but one of my favorite trips was snowboarding in the backcountry of the Victorian Alps." At her surprised expression, he added, "July falls in winter in Australia."

She laughed. "That's so weird. You know we might see snow on the Rockies when we jump."

His entire body jerked as if he'd been hit by 240 volts. "We?" The word wheezed out, and he immediately cleared his throat. "What do you mean by *we*?"

She squeezed his hand. "You didn't think I was going to let you jump on your own, did you? I'm jumping, too."

"No." The word came out so vehemently that the yellow breasted meadowlark on the deck railing ceased its twittering and flew away. The thought of her blacking out halfway through her descent haunted him. "That's not going to happen."

Millie stiffened, but sympathy played in her eyes. "Why?"

Dex chose that moment to beep, as if the device was saying it knew exactly why.

"Is this because I'm not Charlie?" she asked softly.

No. But so help him, he was using that thought as the reason. He stroked her face. "I'm sorry."

The sympathy in her eyes got pushed aside by hurt, and she released his hand. "Me too."

Guilt kicked him hard in the gut, but not enough to make him change his mind. No way in hell was he letting her skydive and risk her falling out of the sky. It had disaster written all over it. He kissed her and rose to his feet. "I need to cook those steaks."

She sighed. "Will, that beep is Dex reminding me that I need to change my sensor. It's got nothing to do with my blood sugar."

Thankfully, the timer he'd set on his phone sounded incessantly. "The grill's ready. I'll cook while you go change your sensor."

She opened her mouth as if she was going to say something, but she closed it, turned and walked away.

———

HAVING to eat no matter if she was hungry or not was one of the things that drove Millie crazy about being diabetic. Will's rejection of her offer to accompany him skydiving had vanquished her appetite. It had taken a great deal of effort to force down the tender, juicy steak and enough of the creamy potato salad she needed to eat to satisfy the amount of insulin she'd bolused.

She hated how much his rejection of her offer hurt. Right up to that moment, it had all been going well. She'd been so happy at the look on his face when he'd opened the envelope—*Boo-yah! Nailed that gift.* The warm and fuzzy feelings that had flowed through her because she'd known exactly what would make the man she loved happy had given her indescribable pleasure. It was like being on the top of the world. His *no* had plunged her into a deep, dark low.

Right gift, wrong date.

Stupid. Stupid. Stupid. She should have booked the jump for a less significant date, but it was his birthday present and they were running out of time to do things together. She'd honestly thought that after all he'd shared with her about Charlie, he'd be okay with her tagging along. Knowing she'd been way off target and he'd shut her out ate at her.

Over dinner, the conversation had lurched around the elephant in the room that was the skydive. They'd exchanged information about their day—Will overenthusiastically and she rather desultorily—and when she'd finally finished the meal, he'd insisted she go get comfy on the sofa while he cleared away. Usually they tidied up together, but she didn't have the energy to argue, so now she was sitting on the sofa, determined to rescue the evening when he joined her.

She heard the dishwasher start, and then Will walked into the room smiling. As he sat down next to her she noticed he was holding a small box tied with a silver bow. He rested it in his palm and held it out to her.

She blinked and her heart flipped in her chest like a fish on a dock. "Is . . . is . . . that for me?"

"You bet."

"But it's not my birthday."

"I know, but sometimes a gift just needs to be given. I was going to give it to you before dinner, but you got in first with your present."

"Sorry." Oh man, had she totally ruined his plans to propose?

He is not going to propose, but it might be a promise ring.

Zips of excitement rushed her. He was making the first move and talking about their future. This was the start of them committing to each other and making the three years she was tied to Seattle work.

"No worries," he said easily. "Now's probably a better time anyway, because we've got the rest of the evening to talk about it."

She waited for him to say something else, hint at what was in the box, tell her he loved her, but he just kept smiling at her, his blue-on-blue eyes crinkling around the edges. "Go ahead. Open it."

When she lifted the box off his palm, she realized that her imagination had been running wild and interfering with her visual perception. Although the box was a similar shape to a ring box, it was bigger. She neatly undid the bow and opened it. Her flipping heart stilled and then sank like a stone.

She stared down at a watch.

It wasn't a pretty, delicate piece of jewelry that would have suited her narrow wrist. No, it was bright fluoro green and black, a giant, clunky thing that was as tall as her wrist. "It's a watch," she said inanely, sounding stupid.

Will laughed. "It's a smart watch."

"Oh, like a sports watch that measures my heart rate?"

"Sort of, but it can do a lot more than that. You can link it to your phone and get your messages and e-mails."

She thought it was an odd gift, given that Mr. Fitness himself didn't wear one. "I'm not sure I need to be that connected."

He took it back off her and put it on the coffee table as if he needed her to concentrate on him, not the watch. "Millie, it's like a computer on your wrist. You can connect Dex to it so with the flick of your wrist you can easily see your blood sugar."

And with the size of the screen on the watch, so could everyone else in a ten-foot radius of her. She was about to say that getting Dex out of her pocket was really not a problem when Will said, "And the great thing is that with all of Dex's data uploaded into the cloud then other people can wear a smart watch and see your numbers, too."

Other people? She started at him speechless, her brain going around in circles. "What other people?"

"Your parents, me." His face was animated with enthusiasm. "This new CGM cloud is a game changer for diabetics."

She knew about the cloud, but she'd only ever thought about it in terms of children with diabetes. It gave their parents peace of mind and hopefully the kids more freedom, although information was a funny thing—sometimes it was used to confine. But she wasn't a kid—she was very much an adult, and this felt like a massive invasion of her privacy.

"Will, the only person I need or want scrutinizing my numbers is my endocrinologist. This would freak my parents out, and I spent years clawing out my independence from them and separating them from my diabetes, so why would I want to give all that up?"

He frowned. "This has got nothing to do with independence. This is all about keeping you safe." He leaned toward her. "For instance, say you have a hypo when you're asleep. I get a warning on my watch."

"I don't see the point. Dex wakes us both up anyway."

An odd look crossed his face, and he said gently, "This is for the time I'm not in bed with you."

Time. Her heart took a hit—pierced clean through from one side to the other—quivering wildly. He didn't say *times* as in the occasions when they'd be apart, but *time* as in the looming future. "What's the point of you knowing my numbers if you're in Great Falls or even Australia?"

"It's all part of your safety net," he said, not denying her claim he'd be somewhere other than Seattle. "If I couldn't reach you on your phone, then I'd contact someone in your building so they can go check on you."

She shook her head fast, curls flying. "I've been doing fine on my own for a long time now, Will. I don't need this."

"I think you do," he said firmly. "It's a way of keeping you safe."

She wanted to shake him. "You're not my doctor, Will."

A muscle twitched near his eye. "No, but I am a doctor, and I'm your mate, your friend. I care about you."

Friend, not lover. He'd just defined their relationship in his terms, and the words pummeled her so hard she wanted to put her hands over her head to ward off the devastating blows. She loved him with every breath she took, but despite their time together being the best weeks of her life, he only cared for her as a friend.

Good old Millie. Everyone's friend. Fun to have around.

Right at that moment she hated him. "You're my friend?" She spat the words out of her mouth on a rising tide of fury. "Have you conveniently forgotten about our weeks of sex and the fact you've virtually moved into the guesthouse?"

He flinched. "Of course not. It's been great, but you're leaving soon, and I just want to set you up so you're safe."

"It's not your job to keep me safe," she ground out between clenched teeth.

"I'm happy to do it."

She thought about her friends at grad school and of Ethan, Ty, Katrina and Josh. All of them loved her as a friend, but none of them would ever suggest that they get this intimate with her diabetes. Her skin prickled, and suddenly she needed to move away from his sincerity and caring before it suffocated her with everything that it didn't offer. Everything she wanted.

She stood up and started pacing. "I don't get it. You want me to share my blood sugar numbers with you but not my life?"

"Millie," his tone implored, "right from the start, we were always going to have an end date when you left for Seattle."

Her misguided hopes that he might feel differently took another knock, and she struggled to align being dumped with being spied on. It didn't match up. "But this idea of yours isn't ending us. It's keeping us connected in a way I don't want. It's creepy and it's stalkerish."

"The hell it is," he yelled, shooting to his feet. "Jeez, Millie. Don't you get it? I'm keeping you safe."

Safe. She blinked at him. How many times had he said that in the last few minutes? She thought about his phone calls today, all the times over their weeks together that he'd sought her out at work under the guise of wanting to see her, his verbal dodging and weaving whenever she suggested they go hiking, his almost obsessive response every time Dex beeped and just now, his reaction to her suggestion she go skydiving. Just like that, it was as if someone had turned the light up from a dim yellow to a bright white, all-revealing glare.

Her diabetes terrified him.

No way. He's an intelligent guy. A doctor. Rational. Scientific.

Life teaches you that sick people die, not healthy ones.

Will's words rushed back to her, bouncing and jostling in her head. He'd said them the day he'd told her Charlie had died. At the time, she hadn't thought much about it other than it being a fairly apt statement. Now it seemed a lot more personal. *I want to keep you safe.*

Did he think she was going to die?

No. It was such an irrational thought that she didn't want to entertain it. Nothing about it made any sense, especially not the part where he was breaking up with her but still wanting to be more involved in her diabetes than she would have wanted if they'd been together.

It was like being lost in a corn maze, and the only GPS she had was her love for him and a gut feeling. She'd stayed silent these last few weeks, waiting and hoping that Will might tell her he was committed to her beyond the summer, and when he did, she'd tell him she loved him. Only Will wasn't going to tell her, and the time had come for her to speak. Sometimes stepping out on a limb and taking a huge risk was required, and this was one of those times.

"I love you, Will, and I think you love me, too."

———

WILL heard Millie's heartfelt words and wished that he had not. Now he had no other recourse than to hurt her. He shook his head slowly. "I'm sorry, Millie. If it helps, you're the first woman I've spent so much time with in a long time."

Her eyes filled with pity, and it took him a moment to realize it wasn't for herself but for him. "And there's a reason for that, Will, and it's called *love*."

She waved her hand up and down her body. "Look at me. I'm a little bit heavy, I wear comfortable clothes and my makeup regime is a swipe of lip gloss when I remember. You could have spent the summer with much prettier and better dressed women than me."

He hated it when she said stuff like that about herself. "I did not slum it with you."

"Exactly." Her dimpled smile danced at him. "We're good together. I make you happy. You make me see a sparkling future of possibilities for both of us."

Her optimism bit into him, clamping down hard and reminding him exactly how everything wonderful could be lost in a heartbeat. "Millie, I can't give you what you want when it's not there to give."

She pressed her palm against his heart. "Tell me what's in there."

"A bloody enormous, empty space." The truth tumbled out before he could stop it. He closed his eyes, steeling himself for her reaction, hating the idea that raw and ragged pain would twist her beautiful face and take up residence in her eyes. When he opened his eyes, all he saw was empathy.

"I'm so sorry Charlie's dead, Will, but you can't live your life avoiding loving people in case they die."

His heart hammered hard and fast, beating the pain of memories through him. *Oh yes, I can and I will.* He had to, because he'd already lost half of himself.

He knew Millie, and if he committed to her, she'd want a child.

The idea of her body, compromised with some kidney damage, being pregnant and open to the ravages of all the other complications didn't bear thinking about. If he allowed himself to love her and something happened to her, he wouldn't survive it.

He tried to make her understand. "Charlie was fit and healthy, Millie, and"—he snapped his fingers—"he died."

A small frown creased the space between her eyes. "It was an awful thing, but it was a random accident." Her intelligent gaze sought his. "I'm not going to die on you, Will."

A spurt of anger burned him. "You can't promise me that. No one can promise anyone that."

She sighed as if he was a crazy person. "Let's look at this logically, then. You're fit and healthy, and you have the rest of your life in front of you. I'm fit and healthy with the rest of mine in front of me, so why don't we live it together?"

She didn't get it. His fear for her was a living, breathing thing in his chest, dealing out fingers of pain like a bartender with a bottle of Scotch. He'd tried to do the right thing so as not to hurt her. He'd organized the cloud so he could take care of her from a distance, he'd tried to be gentle and oblique, hoping she'd make the connections and understand so that he could use the reliable exit line of *They'd always had an end date.*

But she was pushing and pushing and pushing, and he needed it to stop. "You're not exactly healthy, Millie," he said quietly. "You have some kidney damage already."

She jerked as if he'd just slapped her hard, and her green and brown-flecked eyes darkened with amber shards of fury. "So you're saying that if I wasn't diabetic we'd have a future together?"

Her incredulity burned him from top to toe, and he wished more than anything he could change things, but this was survival. "I'm saying that I don't love you."

Her chest heaved like she'd just been running fast, and now it was hard to move air in and out of her lungs. Two pink spots of anger flared on her creamy cheeks. "This is *your* problem, Will, and I refuse to own it. I am done being the person who causes worry, because I work damn hard at managing my diabetes and living my life. I am *not* sick."

She sucked in another breath, but when she spoke again, her voice had lost its harshness. "Will, I get that losing Charlie was like losing a part of yourself, but tell me this. Would he be happy knowing you're walking away from a chance at happiness?"

Bro, you have to meet Miranda.

A simmer of unease bubbled under his skin. "Leave Charlie out of this."

"Why?" Her curls quivered. "Because you know he'd tell you that you're being a coward and a bloody idiot?"

At that moment he came close to hating her. "If you had any idea what it's like to lose the person closest to you in the world, you wouldn't be calling me a coward. Charlie was a doctor, too, Millie. He knew all the risks just like you and me."

She threw her hands up in the air. "And this is the problem. At first I thought that you being a doctor was handy in a boyfriend, because I didn't have to explain everything to you, but it's not good at all. I need you to let go of being a doctor and just be a regular guy. You're treating me like a patient, not a woman. You're focusing on all of the bad stuff instead of the good. Everything in life has an element of risk."

"And it can all be calculated."

She snorted. "You take greater risks with your life every time you do an extreme sport than I take with mine." Her eyes suddenly widened, and she said softly, "Charlie was the adventurous one."

The hairs on his arms stood up. "Charlie's got nothing to do with this conversation."

"I disagree. All these extreme sports you do, they're not naturally something you'd choose to do, are they? They're what Charlie would have talked you into, and now he's not here, you're doing them for him."

Beads of sweat broke out on the hair at the base of his neck. "That's bullshit."

"Will, live the life you want, not Charlie's."

Her words scalded him, and he instantly rejected them. "If I was living Charlie's life, I'd be working at Jilagong and married to Miranda, so I think that proves that I'm not living his life and that you're talking through your ass."

He wanted her to yell back so he'd feel less of a bastard, but she didn't. Instead, her round, pretty face sagged with resignation and she picked up the smart watch.

"This isn't a safety net, Will."

"Yes, it is."

"No, this is you wanting to control my life from the side-lines because you're too busy taking a rain check on your life. You're too damn scared to dive right in and live it with me."

Her words hit him with the jagged edges and weight of rocks. "That's enough. You've made your point. I think it's time I left."

She faced him down, hands on her hips and all her soft curves hard and tense. "Good idea. Take this with you." Her arm shot back like a pitcher's.

He whipped his hands up fast, catching the watch just before it hit him hard on the head.

Chapter 21

It was Millie's last day at the hospital, and she sat opposite Floyd Coulson, fingering the pages of her student appraisal.

"Doctor Bartlett's given you a glowing report, Millie."

And he had, but then Will didn't have any difficulties with their doctor-student relationship. He excelled at being a doctor. It was setting that aside and letting himself be a regular guy and just see her as an ordinary woman rather than a diabetic that was the problem.

Floyd continued, "Based on that report, WWAMI will be happy, and we're certainly looking forward to welcoming you back next summer for your next placement." He leaned back in his chair. "By then we might be in the position to offer you some surgical experience if Great Falls can spare Doctor Meissner for some extra days a month."

"Fabulous." Millie tried to sound enthusiastic. "Any chance of some OB-GYN experience?"

He tapped his nose. "Actually, the board's in negotiations. Bear Paw's never been in better shape for top-quality health care providers, and you know that we're hoping in three or four years' time, you'll be joining us."

"Just a few exams to get through between now and then," she said, trying to sound upbeat. *And a life without Will.*

Don't go there. She abruptly pulled her security tag over her head and wound the blue lanyard around the tag before placing it on the desk. "So I guess that's it for me for this year."

He rose and escorted her to the door. "We hope you enjoyed your summer with us as much as we enjoyed having you."

"Thanks." She managed to get the word out against a fast-tightening throat. "It was all great experience."

She walked away, taking in some deep breaths, and tried not to cry like she'd been doing every time she thought about the last two months. About Will. She loved him, but he wasn't brave enough to love her. She hated him for that. Hated that he of all people had defined her by her diabetes when there was so much more to her and her life.

The part of her that had been understanding of his grief for Charlie was now furious. Damn it, she was good for Will. He needed her, but she'd done everything she could—declared her love and fought hard for him—and it hadn't made a damn bit of difference. She wished she'd known Charlie, because she felt it in her very essence that he wouldn't have expected Will to put his life on hold. After all, he'd pursued his own work passions separate from Will, and he'd fallen in love.

But he'd still had his twin.

She'd spent hours online reading articles about twinless twins, and their stories of feeling like half of the person they'd been before their twin died resonated but didn't help her. Neither had reading the research that the grief an identical twin experiences at the loss of his or her twin is greater than for any other relative with the exception of losing a spouse. Will had convinced himself she was going to die early. Given his experience with Charlie, she had no power to fight that irrational belief, and they had no future while it existed.

This last week had been the longest in her life. Thankfully, she'd been scheduled to work with Josh in the clinic, which had avoided her worst nightmare of having to work with Will. She could just about hold it all together if she didn't have to see him.

That hadn't stopped her hearing about him, though. Josh

had a boy-crush on him after they'd worked together evacuating a cowboy with full thickness burns. Cassidy had mentioned in passing that a group of them had gone mountain bike riding after work one evening. Millie hoped he'd gotten stuck in the sucking mud of the west coulee. Even Bethany had betrayed her by saying, "At first I wasn't sure about that Doctor Bartlett, but I'm gonna miss him when he leaves. I won't miss that awful Australian black stuff he puts on his bread, though."

The hospital's automatic glass doors detected her presence and opened, and she walked out into the raging west wind. She never missed the wind when she was living away from Bear Paw, or the deep winter snow, but she wasn't exactly sure how she felt about Seattle's ever-present rain. She guessed she had three years to make up her mind. Opening her car door, she took one last look at the squat redbrick hospital building and the welcoming line of blue spruces. She blew out a breath. It was time to go.

Her phone beeped with a reminder, and she pulled it out of her bag. A tiny picture of a gold gift wrapped in a red bow appeared on the screen next to the words *Will's Birthday*. Her heart cramped. She'd forgotten she'd set the reminder, and with it came a surge of conflicting feelings. The excitement and thrill she'd gotten from planning the two-day event, booking the accelerated free-fall course and choosing the gorgeous bed-and-breakfast jostled in her chest along with the agony of Will's rejection of her. She'd cancelled the accommodations last week, but there'd been no refund for the course. She'd tossed the information packet into the trash, not wanting to think about what was supposed to have been a fantastic adventure but now represented everything she'd lost.

She glanced up at the cloudless blue sky, watching a flock of starlings fly over, their wings catching the airstreams so that occasionally they didn't need to flap. Did they feel free up there? She wanted to free herself of her last week—of her heartache, of her roller coaster of emotions that battered her and by default her blood sugar. More than anything she wanted to create a real break between her time with Will in Bear Paw and the next phase of her life in Seattle.

She suddenly knew the exact way to do it. Smiling, she clicked on a name in her contact list and made a call.

———

"HAPPY birthday, Will!" the ER staff chorused.

He made himself smile widely. "When you paged me saying there's a guy who put superglue in his eyes instead of Visine, it was really all about the cake?"

"You bet," Helen said, lighting the candles. "But Hector Rialdo actually did put superglue in his eyes last year, and Katrina ran a PSA on what not to keep in your medicine cabinet." She blew out the match. "Okay, everyone, sing it loud."

And they did. And off-key.

Cassidy handed him a knife. "Make a wish, Doctor Bartlett."

A wish? Bloody hell. He sliced the knife down into the soft, buttery yellow cake that was coated in coconut frosting and wished to get through the day. He'd chosen to work, because the idea of doing something else on his own had squirted acid into his gut and left him feeling exceptionally lonely.

Last year you were alone and you went dirt bike riding.

The thought sounded suspiciously like Charlie, and he tried to shrug it away. It stuck like a burr.

You should have gone skydiving, bro. It would have been awesome.

Skydiving made him think of Millie, and his stomach clenched. He missed her badly, but better to let her go now while he could still cope with being without her than get in too deep.

"I can see why you did your fellowship in emergency medicine, Will," Josh said with a laugh. "You're no surgeon with that knife."

He stared down at the section of cake, surprised to see how badly he'd mangled it, and handed the knife back to Helen. "Perhaps you could do the honors?"

While Helen fussed around the cake, slicing and serving it onto paper plates for everyone, Will concentrated on small talk with the staff.

"The team-building bike ride the other night was fun, wasn't it?" he said to Marissa.

She shuddered, and her thickly mascaraed eyelashes blinked

at him. "You can't be serious? It took me three showers to get all the mud off of me *and* I ruined a perfectly good T-shirt. Next time we have to do team building, we should go bowling."

Millie would have just laughed at the mud and pulled out a packet of wipes from her tote bag.

"That sounds like a plan," he said, shoveling cake fast into his mouth so he could finish it and leave.

"Doctor Bartlett." The new ER receptionist tossed her long blond hair. "I'm training for a half marathon. We should go for a run sometime."

"Great idea, Brianna, but I'm sorry, I'll have to take a rain check, because I'm finishing up in Bear Paw really soon."

Cassidy stuck her head into the room. "Will, we've got a woman with a nasty laceration on her arm. Lacey Converse. She's in curtain two, and her husband Mark's with her."

Thank you. "On my way." He dropped his plate into the trash and turned to the small crowd. "Thanks for the birthday wishes, everyone."

"Drinks tonight at Leroy's?" Josh asked, walking out the door with him.

"Sounds good."

Josh kept walking straight toward the clinic, and Will turned left, picking up the tablet computer. On his way to the cubicle he read Lacey's notes and her baseline vitals. She was sitting propped up on the gurney with her left arm elevated. Her husband sat next to her with one little girl on his knee and the other hanging off his arm.

"G'day, I'm Will Bartlett, doctor on duty. I hear you've been arguing with a chef's knife." He snapped on gloves and lifted the pressure dressing. Blood oozed from a deep cut that ran down the length of her middle finger and into the fleshy part of her palm.

She gave a wry smile. "And it won. We're vacationing at Saint Mary Lake, and I was filleting the trout Mark caught this morning."

"Mummy said a bad word," one of the little girls announced, her voice full of awe.

"I bet she did," Will replied, trying to keep a straight face.

"Madison's our manners' police," Mark said with an indulgent shake of his head.

"Daddy, I'm thirsty," the other child whined.

Will examined Lacey's hand, immobilizing all her other fingers, and asked her to bend the injured one. She couldn't shift it. "I think you've done some damage to your tendon."

"Can you fix it?" she asked anxiously.

"I can suture up the cut and give you a tetanus shot and some antibiotics, but I'm going to refer you to a hand surgeon who will repair the tendon at a later date. Are you allergic to anything? Any health issues?"

"Not allergic to anything that I know of," Lacey said, "but I am a type one diabetic."

He automatically glanced at the girls, who looked to be about six and four. "Any health complications because of your diabetes? Heart? Kidneys? Circulation?"

"Only red and itchy skin from the damn adhesive on my sensor."

Millie used Tough Pads. "I might have a tip on how to handle that, but first I'll get the nurse to check your blood sugar."

"No need," Lacey said firmly. "I can do it. Madison, honey, pass me my purse."

"It might be a bit hard one-handed," Will said as one of the little girls pulled out a familiar black zippered wallet.

Lacey laughed. "Nothing gets in the way of me testing my blood sugar, Doctor. I've already done it once since I arrived and it was one hundred ten."

"Daddy, I'm thirsty," the little girl whined again.

"Shh, Ellie," her father said. "I'll get you something soon." He glanced at Will. "I'm not real good with blood, so when Lacey cut her hand, we rushed straight here and left their snack packs at the camp."

You're married to a diabetic and you're not good with blood? The thought stunned him. "There's a vending machine in the hall. If you come with me, I can point it out to you on my way to the supply room."

Mark threw him a grateful smile. "Come on, girls."

"I want to stay with Mommy."

"Me too."

Mark sighed. "Only if you sit on the chair and don't move. Do that and I'll bring you both back something to eat and drink, okay?"

The girls murmured their acquiescence.

As he and Mark walked away, Will said, "They keep you busy."

"Yeah," he said with a resigned laugh. "We had them close together so they'd entertain each other, or that was the theory, anyway."

"Two pregnancies in two years must have been challenging for your wife and her diabetes."

Mark shrugged. "I leave all that stuff up to her and her doctors. My job's to argue with our HMO."

How can you sleep at night? Will couldn't believe Mark's casual attitude. "I guess that's one way of doing it."

Mark paused in front of the vending machine. "Yeah, well, the doctors are the experts, and Lacey's been diabetic since she was five, so she knows way more about it than me. No point worrying about what you can't control, right?"

Wrong. So wrong. There's every reason to worry.

Only Mark was feeding coins into the vending machine and not looking for an answer.

———

"HEY, Doc," the cowboys chorused, raising their beers in greeting as Will walked into Leroy's at the end of a long and lonely birthday.

"G'day, fellas."

"Millie's not here, Doc . . ." Dane called out.

An uncomfortable feeling settled under Will's ribs. He was both relieved and disappointed that Millie wasn't here, but he wasn't surprised. He hadn't seen her since she'd asked him to leave the guesthouse a week ago, and he knew that was deliberate on her part.

". . . And you know what that means, right, Doc? You're safe to play pool." Dane high-fived Troy.

"Guess I'll whip you later, then, mate," Will said, glancing around for Josh and Katrina and hoping they'd arrived first. He really didn't feel like bantering at the bar with the guys tonight.

He couldn't spot the Stantons, but Ethan stood up and gave him a wave as if he'd been watching out for him. Picking up a pitcher of beer and some glasses, he made his way over. "On your own tonight?"

"I am," Ethan said with a grin. "Millie stole my girlfriend."

Memories of when he'd first arrived in Bear Paw and his stupid misunderstanding about Millie and Tara came rushing back to embarrass him. "I think we're both absolutely certain now that neither of them is gay."

"Amen to that," Ethan said, raising his glass. "Happy birthday."

"Thanks." Will clinked his glass against Ethan's. "Hang on, how do you know it's my birthday?"

"I could say because Josh just texted to say he's running late and could I keep an eye out for you."

Something about the librarian's tone made him say, "Or?"

"Or . . ." He set his beer down neatly on the coaster. " I know it's your birthday because Millie's taken Tara skydiving."

"Jesus." He slammed his beer down, froth spilling out over his hand. "And you let her go?"

"Dude, Tara carries a gun. I'm not about to tell her she can't do something."

He had a crazy urge to grab Ethan's trendy shirtfront and pull him across the table. "I'm not talking about Tara."

"I know that."

For some reason his body itched under Ethan's direct gaze. "You've known Millie longer than me, so you know she shouldn't be skydiving."

"I know she's a grown woman who's more than capable of making her own decisions," he said reasonably.

"And you've seen her make some pretty stupid ones." He gripped his beer so hard his hand cramped. "She told me how you called 911."

"It was a long time ago now, Will."

"Yeah, well she's still diabetic. That hasn't changed, and the adrenaline involved in skydiving drops blood sugar faster than . . ." His brain sought an analogy and failed him. "Pretty bloody fast. You want her to black out at fifteen thousand feet?"

Ethan's shoulders straightened at Will's aggressive tone. "Of course not, and more importantly, neither does Millie. She's not stupid, Will. She loves her life too much to take dumb risks. I'm sure she knows what she's doing."

He thought of Mark Converse, who'd said much the same thing about his wife, and instantly rejected it. "I wish I had your confidence," he snarled, "given it's based on so much medical knowledge."

He felt a hand on his shoulder. "Sorry I'm late, Will," Josh said, glancing between him and Ethan. "Everything good?"

"Millie's gone skydiving," Ethan said as if it was an ordinary event.

Josh sat down and took a fistful of peanuts from the bowl. "Good for her."

What the . . . ? "You can't be serious?" Betrayal licked along Will's veins. Josh was a doctor. A colleague. A mate. "On which planet is this possibly a good thing?"

"Interesting," Josh said, as if Will was a science experiment. "I don't think I've ever seen you lose your cool before. You do know she wouldn't do anything stupid."

"I already told him that," Ethan added with one brow raised.

"Neither of you are helping," he ground out, his jaw so tight it felt like it might shatter.

"You can't wrap her in cotton balls, Will," Josh said, spinning his wedding ring. "That's one of the first things you learn in Love 101."

"I am *not* in love."

Ethan and Josh laughed so hard they spilled their beers.

"Very funny." Will sank the last of his beer, planning on leaving.

Josh sobered. "Think about it this way. Eth's known Millie for years, I've known her for a year and a half and you've been in town two months. You're the only one here who's bothered by the fact she's throwing herself out of a plane."

"Because she's diabetic!"

The bar chose that moment to go silent, and his frustrated words rang out loud and clear. Heads turned. Will poured another beer and wished he could slide under the table.

"There's way more to it than that, dude," Josh said sympathetically. "And seeing we're girling-up and talking about feelings, then I'll admit to you that I get it. Before I met Katrina, I'd never had this caveman response of wanting to keep a woman safe like I feel it for her. I want to stand on guard and club anything that might get close and hurt her, because the thought of anything happening to her makes it hard to breathe."

"Respect," Ethan said.

Will's chest burned as Josh's words rang terrifyingly true in his ears. "You both feel that way?"

The guys nodded.

"When it happens," Josh said, "you know you're in deep and you can no longer hide behind the *It's just good sex* excuse."

He wanted to say *I don't love her*, but Josh had just described his feelings for Millie to a tee. The need to protect her consumed him in a way it never had for any other woman.

I love you, Will, and I think you love me, too.

I love her. I really do love her. The full realization hit him with the impact of a two-by-four, and he rubbed his face with his palms. Without a shadow of a doubt, he loved Millie. "I thought that need to keep her safe was just me."

Josh gave a wry and understanding smile. "Welcome to our world. Of course, they'd kill us if we tried to stop them from doing anything risky, so you've got to tread carefully and find a balance." Josh squeezed his shoulder. "It's going to be harder for you because of Millie's diabetes. You can't slay that dragon, and the fact you know way more about the disease than the average Joe makes it worse."

"Her diabetes strikes terror into every part of me."

"And you walked away," Ethan said, his gaze fixed on Will's face as if he was looking down the sight of a gun.

"Listen, mate," Will said, his anger sparking as thoughts of Millie and Charlie charged around his head. "You don't know the full story. There are so many things that could go wrong."

"And there are so many things that could go right." Ethan didn't back down. "If you love her and she loves you, you can work everything else out. You just have to decide if you're man enough to step up."

Right then he hated Ethan, and more than anything he wanted to snot him one on the nose with his fist.

It's a fair call, bro, Charlie's voice chimed in reasonably. *I know it sucks for you that I'm dead, but life goes on. Millie told you that, too, and you'd be an idiot to keep shutting her out.*

How do you know? You've never even met her?

A laugh echoed in his head. *I know because you know. Oh, and, big brother, I knew it first.* Charlie flipped him the bird. *Millie's like Miranda. Real.*

"And their names both start with *M*."

Josh startled. "Excuse me?"

Will realized he'd just spoken out loud to Charlie or to his own thoughts—he was never totally certain, and it really didn't matter. "I'll explain it all another time."

"Sure," Josh said, flicking Ethan a worried look. "Listen, if you want a chance with Millie, you're gonna have to find a way of separating the doctor from the man. You need to trust her."

"That's easy for you to say."

"True, but it's the only way."

You're treating me like a patient, not a woman. You're focusing on all of the bad stuff instead of the good.

His gut rolled as he remembered some of the things he'd said to her. He stood up, frantic to get to her and fix things. "I'm going to talk to her."

"Not after drinking three beers on an empty stomach you're not." Ethan pushed him back in his seat. "They're a three-hour drive away, and arriving at midnight isn't going to win you any favors. We'll go in the morning and you can watch her jump."

He almost threw up.

Chapter 22

The buzz of the plane deafened Millie, and she was having second thoughts about this whole skydiving deal. Yesterday's training session had been great, but it had still been a buffer between her and the real thing of jumping out of a plane and tumbling into the sky.

Tara gave her the thumbs-up, grinning from ear to ear. The policewoman was in her element. Millie was not. What Tara saw as adventure and an adrenaline rush was currently freaking Millie out. Originally, she'd booked a tandem jump for herself and an accelerated free fall for Will, but on a shot of *I'll show him* fury, she'd decided to do his jump. Now reality had caught up with her, and it was a salient lesson that she should never make big decisions when she was bruised and hurting.

Her heart raced, her throat was drier than sandpaper and her body shook, but at least it wasn't from low blood sugar—it was just plain old dread. She'd read everything she could on the diabetes forums about what experienced diabetic skydivers did before they jumped, and she'd followed their instructions to the letter. She'd carbed up a few hours ago. She'd just had some candy. Her instructors knew about her diabetes, and someone was on the ground with D50 if she needed it. Going by the forum posts, it would be highly unlikely.

"See you back on terra firma," Tara shouted like the expert she was, and then she was barrel-rolling out of the plane, falling through the sky toward the green grass and blue lake that lay far, far below.

Oh. My. God.

"You ready to give me your pump?" Leon, one of her instructors, yelled over the noise of the plane. He held out a plastic container with a lid toward her.

"One more check, okay?"

"Sure. It's totally your call."

She pricked her finger and waited for the monitor to beep. 120. A nice, big safety buffer without being crazy high. She disconnected her pump and placed it in the container.

"You good to go?" Ted, the second instructor, asked.

She shook her helmeted head slowly back and forth.

Leon laughed. "Sure you are. You're gonna love it."

Millie highly doubted that. She loved canoeing, she loved hiking, she loved Will. *He doesn't love you.* She stood up, the parachute rig heavy on her back. "Let's do this."

The instructors edged close to the open door of the plane and beckoned her forward. The wind rushed her, and far below she saw mountains and trees and the crisscross jigsaw of crops and pastureland. She eased forward and then, just as she'd been taught, thrust her hands out in front of her. The next moment she was in the air, falling, falling, falling.

The wind captured her scream and threw it away as if it was insignificant.

In frog position and with Leon and Ted holding on to her arms and legs on either side, she looked up into the wide blue sky above her and then, with a gulp, down toward the green, gold, brown and gray of the earth below. Half of her brain was yelling, *You're falling at 120 mph*, and the other half was squealing, *This is incredible!* She was floating and flying, just like the birds she'd watched yesterday, and totally detached from her life far below.

The free fall seemed to go on forever. Leon pulled her arm down to the pilot chute handle a couple of times, checking she'd made contact, and then she was back, putting both arms out in front of her, bending them at the elbow. Leon tugged at her arm again—the third time was the sign. Her minute of free fall was over and it was time to deploy the parachute.

Leon let go of her. Her fingers gripped the handle and, remembering everything from the training, she tugged. Ted let go of her. Her body jolted upward for an instant, and then she was floating. She glanced over at the camera guy, who was clapping and showing her which way to pull the toggles to move the canopy.

Peace descended. She was wafting over the world and it was glorious. This was it. This was the separation from Will that she needed. She was landing a wiser woman, putting the summer behind her and getting on with her life without him.

Landing involved focusing on the big yellow cross on the ground. Pulling on the steering lines, she lined herself up with the target, and slowly but steadily the ground came closer and closer. She started moving her feet, and then the earth was hard against her soles and she sagged.

"Stand up, stand up," someone yelled.

And she did, and then she was standing on grass with the canopy streaming out behind her and she couldn't stop laughing. Whether it was from sheer relief or joy, she couldn't tell. *I did it!*

Her instructors, who'd landed just before her, gave her high fives and relieved her of her harness, and then Tara was hugging her and saying, "Go, Millie. You did great."

"I don't think I've ever been so scared in my life."

Yeah, you have been. Last week when Will walked away.

Protecting her high, she immediately shut out the thought. "Sorry, what were you saying?" she asked Tara as they commenced walking toward the hangar.

Tara was waving toward the entrance where people milled around, and she wore a secret smile on her lips. "Ethan's here. He came to see us jump."

Millie gave Tara a gentle elbow in the ribs. "I think it's more like Ethan came to see *you* jump."

Last night as they'd lain in their twin beds in the cabin, Millie had almost needed to pull the information out of Tara about her and Ethan. Tara hadn't wanted to tell her for fear of upsetting her. Despite Will's rejection of her, Millie could only be happy for Tara and her dear friend.

After Ethan had wrapped his arms around Tara and kissed

her thoroughly, Millie gave him a hug. "Hey, Eth. What a great surprise. It's so good to see you."

"I couldn't miss this, and what about you? You totally stuck that landing," he said, returning her hug. "I had a driving buddy come with me."

As he stepped back and she looked over his shoulder, shock ripped through her.

Will.

He looked like hell—his sun-kissed hair was standing up on its ends looking like he'd been electrocuted, and the grief lines around his eyes were deeper than when she'd last seen him. The guy whose social persona was one of relaxed charm looked exhausted and strung out.

Her heart did a treacherous flip, aching for him.

Stop it. I am not feeling sorry for him. He hurt me badly and he deserves to look like that.

She gave him a curt nod, unzipped her jumpsuit and stepped out of it.

———

WILL wanted more than anything to rush up to Millie, wrap his arms around her, hold her tight and never let her go, but the daggers she was firing at him from her eyes told him that would be a direct line to nowhere.

Ethan pressed a hand to his shoulder. "Tara and I are going to grab a coffee from the café. Come find us when you're done." He added softly, "Good luck."

If Millie's frosty demeanor was anything to go by, he needed more than luck. "G'day, Millie."

"Why are you here?"

Because I love you. He tried a smile. "I came to see you jump."

She snorted as she plunged her hand into her tote bag. "This from the man who forbids me to jump."

"Hey, Millie," one of the instructors called out to her holding up a plastic container. "I've got your pump and your test kit."

"Thanks, Leon."

She bestowed upon the guy one of her enthusiastic smiles, similar to the ones she used to give him. A smile that lit her up from the inside out.

Leon grinned and gave her an appreciative glance. "You did great out there. You let us know when you're good to jump again."

No. Only this time Will didn't know if his *no* was about the jump or because of the way Leon was looking at Millie. His Millie.

Leon walked away, and Millie lifted her T-shirt and reattached the pump before testing her blood sugar.

Is it high or low? Do you need insulin or food?

How are you feeling?

Will bit down so hard to stop himself from asking her the questions that he tasted the metallic tang of blood.

She fiddled with her pump, and he knew she was giving herself insulin. The words *How high?* beat a tattoo over and over in his head.

She looked up from the pump screen, her chin tilted high. "It's killing you, isn't it?"

He shoved his hands in his pockets and tried to look casual. "What?"

"Not knowing what my blood sugar is."

"No, not at all." But the statement he'd hoped would come out laid-back and calm sounded jerky and fake. He wanted to fix it. Wanted to fix everything. "Millie, I love you."

He blurted out the words, clumsy and loud, and a few people glanced around at them. When there wasn't a squeal of delight from Millie, they looked away, their embarrassment for him unmistakable.

Millie's hands had stilled on her tote bag, and her pupils were so large they almost obliterated her fascinating irises. She stared at him for a moment, and then she snapped out of her trance. "After what you said to me last week, I don't believe you."

That response hadn't featured in the scenario he'd played out in his head on the drive over from Bear Paw. He had to make her understand. "Millie, can we please go somewhere private and talk?"

She tossed her tote bag over her shoulder. "I've listened to you once already, Will, and it wasn't pleasant. Forgive me if I don't put myself out there again for a repeat performance."

Desperation clawed at him, and he touched her on the arm, not wanting her to leave. "Mils," he said automatically, using his nickname for her. "Please."

"Is this dude bothering you, Millie?" another instructor asked. "Because if he is, I can call security."

Will opened his mouth to object but quickly closed it, because getting thrown off the property wasn't going to help his cause. Or his visa status.

Only Millie wasn't objecting to the suggestion. In fact, she looked like she was seriously considering the security offer.

Will had never begged a woman for anything in his life, but he was doing it now. "Five minutes, Millie, please." Her gaze flickered away from him, and he held his breath.

"Thanks, Ted, but I'm fine."

"If you say so, but don't feel you can't change your mind." The guy pointed his fore and middle fingers at Will's eyes before pointing them back at his own and walked away.

Will breathed out on a long sigh. "Thank you."

Her eyes flashed. "The only reason I said no was because it would hurt your reputation as a physician."

Her words punched him. "Millie, I get that you're angry with me."

Her curls bounced wildly. "You have no idea."

He opened his hands out in front of her, seeking her forgiveness. "I know I hurt you and I'm sorry. So desperately sorry. You were totally right; I was scared. I'm still scared."

She frowned at him, her brow creasing up the way it did when she was thinking hard. "Let me get this straight. You just made a three-hour journey to tell me that you love me, but you're still scared."

"That's right." He smiled at her, his relief palpable that she finally understood.

"So really, nothing's changed." She crossed her arms over her chest as if she was warding him off. "It's a hell of a declaration, Will."

"That's not what I meant." Misery vaporized his short-lived relief and then rose up in his throat, ready to suffocate him.

"What do you mean, then?"

The tangle of everything that was his life tightened. "It's hard to explain."

Her hands slapped her hips. "Try me."

But there was nothing soft or forgiving about her request or her stance. If he wanted her in his life, he had to pull the scab off the wound that had cut deep into his heart the day Charlie had died, and then he had to shove his fist down deep into it. He had to bleed and plead and hope like hell that she'd understand and forgive him, because the alternative didn't bear thinking about.

"The last two years since I lost Charlie have been rough." He plowed his hand through his hair. "Scratch that. *Rough* doesn't even come close. They've been the toughest two years of my life. I dated women I knew didn't want anything more from me other than having some fun because I didn't want an emotional connection with anyone. I watched people being happy, and I didn't ever wonder if I could feel like that again, because I knew I never could. If I'm honest, I didn't want to, because it felt disloyal to Charlie."

She made a murmuring sound of agreement.

He huffed out a wry sigh. "Yeah, I know, you told me that, but that part's the easy bit. It's the kraken swimming underneath all of it that's the source of my nightmares and why I'm so scared." His voice cracked. "The thing is, Millie, if I lost you, it would be ten times worse than losing Charlie. The thought cripples me, and it's why I was the coward you said I was and why I walked away from us and hurt you so badly. I'm so desperately sorry, and if I had it to do over, I would do it all differently. I want to do it differently right now. Can you forgive me, love me and take a risk on me?"

She stared at him for a long, long moment.

He felt the loss of the battle in the desolation in her eyes and in the sinking of his heart even before she said, "I'm sorry."

———

THE raw emotion in Will's voice tore at Millie's heart and soul, and tears pricked the back of her eyes. Being told by the man you loved that he loved and adored you wasn't supposed to cause either of them this much pain.

"I'm sorry that I'm your worst nightmare, Will, but I can't change who I am."

He extended his hand toward her. "I love you exactly as you are."

She wanted to reach out so badly and slide her hand into his, but if she did that, she knew their inevitable parting would undo her completely. Best not to touch him. Best to stay the two separate people they were destined to be.

"I love you, too, Will, but I can't see how we can be together without both of us coming to resent each other. I understand the source of your fear, but the fear itself is suffocating me. I can't allow you to restrict what I do."

"You're right, and I promise you I'll wrestle the kraken and get better at controlling it."

"Words are easy to say," she said, thinking about the smart watch, the deliberate safe activities and the checking-up phone calls. "Can you honestly tell me you can step away from the diabetes stalking?"

He swallowed, his throat working overtime. "I watched you jump."

She didn't see the connection. "So you said."

He gave her a rueful look. "It almost killed me watching you come out of that plane, not knowing what your blood sugar was, but as two very wise blokes named Ethan and Josh told me, I have to trust you."

He hasn't asked you about your blood sugar. A tiny seed of hope shot through her. "Do you trust me?"

"Of course I do." His handsome face creased in regret. "Me wanting to know your numbers was never about not trusting you. It was about reassuring me that you were safe. I love you, Millie. I love you more than anyone else in the world, and I don't want to live my life without you in it. You're my best friend. Please help me make this work for us."

Both of his hands beckoned her now—hands that would hold her and stroke and caress her, but there were still too many important things that needed to be resolved before she could take hold of them. "Can you step back from being a doctor with me and just be my lover?"

He looked uneasy. "I know I've been way too much in your face about your numbers, but I can't go from that to being a totally disinterested guy, either."

She accepted his olive branch. "What scares you the most?"

He didn't hesitate. "You being asleep and alone and having a hypo when I'm not there because you're in the on-call room or I'm out on a retrieval."

If she was honest, being alone at night had always scared her a little bit, too, ever since she'd moved out of home. She extended her own olive branch. "Maybe that's a situation where the smart watch cloud thing can work, but I don't want you seeing my numbers twenty-four-seven, because you will drive yourself crazy."

"You know me too well," he said, his mouth curving into a half smile. "How about this? You decide when you're on and off the cloud, and you tell me when you're on so I wear the watch. Deal?"

The tiny shoot of hope expanded inside her. "That sounds like a perfect compromise. Hopefully, they'll have the cloud password protected soon, too, because I don't like the fact anyone could see my numbers."

"I get that." He rubbed his temple. "So, while we're defining my role in the diabetic part of your life and keeping the kraken at bay, I've got another suggestion I'd like you to think about."

She instantly tensed at his tentative tone, because he obviously thought she'd hate it. "What's that?"

"It's something a regular guy told me, but I won't do it if you don't want me to."

Her anxiety ratcheted up a notch. "Just ask me."

He tugged at his ear. "If it helps you, I'm more than happy to make those tedious calls to the insurance company and haggle for you. I thought it might be one less thing you have to do, because I know how hard you work at staying well."

A tear bloomed unexpectedly and slid down her cheek. She brushed it away, but another came and then another. It was ridiculous to be crying because he'd offered to make some telephone calls, but it meant so much to her that he wanted to support her in a way she wanted and needed.

She gave a very unsexy sniff and wiped her nose. "You'd do that for me? Help me try and avoid diabetic burnout?"

"Oh, Millie." He stepped in close. "I'd walk the ends of the earth for you."

And then she was making a weird honking sound and he was laughing and pulling her into his arms and burying his face in her hair and saying, "God, I love you so much."

He lowered his mouth to hers, kissing her gently but affirming his love for her and sealing his promises. When he finally released her lips, he said, "I was scared stiff when you jumped out of that plane, but mostly I was bursting with pride that you did it."

She slid her fingers between the buttons on his shirt, wanting to feel the warmth from his skin on her fingertips. "I was petrified," she said honestly. "It was your jump, not mine. I was only ever going to do a tandem."

He stroked her curls. "Charlie would have done the free fall laughing. I'd have been wetting my pants."

She stroked his hair. "You do know that you don't need to do everything Charlie would have done if he'd lived, right?"

"I know," he said quietly, "but sometimes I need to do some of those things to keep him close."

She pressed her hand to his heart. "I wish I'd known him."

"Me too. He was the smart one. He knew how amazing finding the right woman was, and he'd have loved you."

She smiled up at him. "Exactly how much?"

He grinned at her. "Nowhere near as much as I love you."

She was never going to tire of hearing him say that. "I love you, too."

"And I treasure that love and I treasure you." He suddenly looked serious again. "If you ever get pregnant, I might have to see someone to help me from not driving you crazy about your kidney function."

She stroked his face, moving to reassure him. "It's mild damage, Will, and I've never been advised not to get pregnant. Believe me, if we're ever that lucky, I'll be taking extraordinary care of myself."

He cupped her face with his hands. "Millie, I know we have a lot of stuff to work out, like me getting a job in Seattle for the next three years, sorting out a new visa, thinking about which country we're going to live in after you qualify, stuff like that, but someday in the future, will you marry me?"

Her heart somersaulted in her chest, and happiness followed. "You can see a sparkling future full of possibilities?"

"With you by my side, I do. Will you say yes?"

She threw her arms around his neck. "Yes."

He kissed her until her bones melted, her brain liquefied and she heard the sound of clapping and wooting.

"Get a room, people," someone yelled.

Will broke the kiss, and when her eyes came back into focus, she saw a crowd of about thirty people standing around smiling at them. He took a bow and grabbed her hand, holding it up like he was a referee in a boxing ring. "I'd like you to meet my fiancée, Millie Switkowski. Drinks in the café are on me, but as a doctor, my PSA is if you're jumping today, stick to soda, coffee or juice."

Everyone cheered.

Will grabbed Millie around the waist. "Come on, let's go get some tea from the café and plan the rest of our lives."

She couldn't think of anything she'd rather do.

———

Instant Message from Will Bartlett: Mum, can you and Dad jump onto FaceTime? There's someone I want you to meet. Will x

Instant Message from Liz Bartlett: Will!!!! Connecting right this second. Can't wait to meet Millie. Mum xxx

Tara Ralston @TaraR: Kickboxing class 8 pm. Child care and puppy care available with @DrE who excels at both. #OnlyEthan

Bear Paw @BearPaw: Golden retriever puppy has @DrE leashed & all wrapped up. See it here bit.ly /1tj3KhR #OnlyEthan

Ethan Langworthy @DrE: I might do dumb stuff occasionally @BearPaw but laugh all you want because I got the girl. Love you @TaraR.

Bethany Jacobs @Beth_J: No one likes a bragger @DrE. This Twitter feed's got way too mushy, people.

Bear Paw Heath Services @BearPawHS: Dr. Kelli Meissner, general surgeon, is accepting new patients.

Millie Switkowski @MillieSwit: Look out, Seattle! Will and I have arrived!

Read on for a preview of another
Medicine River Romance from Fiona Lowe

MONTANA ACTUALLY

Available now from Berkley Sensation!

The thirty cows blocking the road were a good indication to Dr. Josh Stanton that he was no longer in Chicago. That and the inordinate number of bloated roadkill with their legs in the air that he'd passed in the last few hours along Highway 2 as he traversed the north of Montana. Sure, Chicago had its fair share of flattened cats on its busy inner-city streets, but he'd stake his life no one living between North Halsted and North Wells streets had ever had to step over a deer.

He watched the cows lurch from decisiveness in their chosen direction to utter chaos as two border collies raced at their heels, barking frantically and driving them determinedly toward an open gate on the other side of the road. Josh's fingers tapped on the top of the steering wheel as they always did when he was stuck in traffic in Chicago's clogged streets. What was the collective noun for a group of cows? Bunch? Herd? He'd once seen a documentary on ranching in Australia and they'd said "mob" in their flat accent.

He guessed he'd find out the name soon enough, as he was close to finishing his 1,458-mile journey across Wisconsin, Minnesota, North Dakota and three-quarters of Montana.

When he'd left home three very long days ago, he'd thought the north woods of Wisconsin were as isolated as things got, but now, as he gazed around him and felt the howling west wind buffeting the car, he knew Menomonie was positively urban in comparison to the endless grass plains that surrounded him. Where the hell were the trees?

An older man on a horse, whose weather-beaten face told of a life lived outdoors, stopped next to Josh's low-slung sports car. Josh wound down the window, his gaze meeting jean-clad legs and horse flesh. He craned his neck.

"Taking a trip?" the cowboy asked conversationally, as if they had all the time in the world to chat.

I wish. "Relocating."

"Yeah?" His gaze took in Josh's Henley shirt and the computer bag on the seat next to him. "You're a bit far north for Seattle. Don't reckon you should risk the mountain roads driving *that* vehicle."

Josh automatically patted the dash as if the car's feelings needed soothing. Granted, his sports car wasn't the latest model this side of five years, but it was in great condition and he loved it. The buzz it gave him when he drove it more than made up for the extra money it had added to his outstanding loans.

"I'm not going over the mountains," he said, his mouth twisting wryly as he checked his TripTik. "I'm going to Medicine River County and a town called Bear Paw."

A town that was wrenching him from his home and staking a claim on his life that went straight through his heart. A town that Ashley had refused point-blank to even consider visiting, let alone living in.

The cowboy called out an instruction to his dogs, who immediately raced behind a recalcitrant calf, and then he lifted his hat and scratched his head. "Bear Paw. Okay."

Josh wasn't certain what to read into the statement. Sure, he'd seen a photo on the Internet of the small hospital, but short of that, he didn't know much else. "My cell's out of range, so I've lost my location on the map, but I think it's about twenty miles away. Do you know it?"

"Oh yeah. I know it. What takes you there?"

Debt half the size of Montana. "Work. I'm the new physician."

The man nodded slowly. "Ah."

Unease skittered through Josh's belly. What did the cowboy know that he didn't? "What the hell does 'ah' mean?"

He laughed. "Relax, son. Your trip's over."

As the last cow finally conceded the grass was indeed greener on the pasture side of the fence and had moved through the gate, Josh looked down the now clear road and saw nothing. Nothing if he discounted some sort of a crop and a hell of a lot of sky. He squinted and just made out what looked like a communications tower. "So where's the town?"

The older man pointed down the dead-straight road. "Three miles gets you to the outskirts and another mile to the traffic signal. Two miles past that, you're done with the town and heading to the mountains."

That distance in Chicago wouldn't even get him from his apartment to his favorite deli. How small was this place? "What if I turn at the traffic signal?"

"Right? Now that will take you straight to Canada, eh." He grinned at his own joke.

The town couldn't possibly be so small. "According to Wikipedia," Josh said, "it's got a population of three thousand people."

The cowboy scratched his head again. "I guess if you include the ranches, it does. It's surely bigger than Bow. Mind, just about everywhere's bigger'n Bow."

Disbelief flooded Josh as he remembered passing a rusty town sign. "That place with the tavern and nothing else?"

"Yup, that'd be Bow." He shoved his hand through the open window. "The name's Kirk McCade. Welcome to Bear Paw, Doctor."

Josh gripped his hand. "Josh Stanton."

Kirk slapped his hand on the roof of the car. "No doubt this baby is a sweet ride, but once you've settled in, best buy yourself an outfit."

"A what?" Surely the cowboy wasn't talking about clothes.

"A truck, a pickup. Winter here's tough on vehicles."

A slither of indignation ran up Josh's spine. He might not

be used to wide-open spaces, but he knew weather. "I've just spent two years in Chicago, so I know all about winter."

Kirk laughed so hard Josh worried he'd fall off the horse.

———

KATRINA McCade loved her family dearly, but there were some days she wished they didn't have her cell phone number. Today was one of those days. Every time she got the paint roller primed, raised and in position, ready to paint the living room walls of her cottage, her phone beeped. Over the last hour, almost every member of her family had contacted her.

Her father had been the first—brief and to the point—calling to confirm that she was cooking supper tonight for her mother's birthday. She'd reassured him, and the moment he'd hung up, her mother, who had no clue about the surprise birthday supper, had called. She'd wanted Katrina to check the menu at both Leroy's and the Village Lounge and book the one with the best steak special because her father loved his beef. Even on her birthday, she was thinking of others. Ten minutes after that, her phone had vibrated with the sound of a motorcycle, which meant her younger brother, Dillon, was texting her.

Please buy gift for Mom that looks like I chose it. Also wrap it cos I suck at bows.

The moment that missive had pinged onto her phone, her younger sister called wanting dating advice.

Dating advice? Hah! Katrina gave the roller such a hard push that it skated across the wall spreading paint in a wide arc instead of the even vertical plane she'd intended. When Megan, her twenty-one-year-old baby sister, had asked her opinion on the best way to hook up with her latest crush, it had taken all of her self-control not to blurt out that *all* men required a police check, marital status verification and blood tests before the first date. Only such a caustic comment would have invited questions she didn't want to answer. Instead, she'd suggested Megan invite a friend to go with her to the Jack-Squat bar.

Her sister had hinted that maybe Katrina might like to come along and meet the guy in question and give her opinion, but the thought of driving an hour and a half south tomorrow night and spending time in a loud and noisy bar with a group of college kids was the last thing Katrina wanted to do. It made her feel old. No way did she need any more reminders that her thirtieth birthday was bearing down on her as fast as the Amtrak that ran through Bear Paw every day at noon. Heck, since coming back to her hometown a few weeks ago after working away for eight years, she'd deflected so many questions about her lack of a boyfriend and her future plans, she could teach a course.

A fine spray of paint dusted her as she found a rhythm, and a sense of satisfaction built on seeing her progress. Her phone buzzed again and she sighed. The only person in her immediate family whom she hadn't spoken to so far this morning was her older brother, Beau. Technically, he was her cousin, but for as long as she could remember, Beau had lived with them and she considered him a brother as much as her parents considered him their son. He preferred to text rather than to talk, but he'd probably just realized the date and wanted her to buy a present for their mother as well. Men!

Wiping her hands on her paint-stained shorts so that she didn't swipe paint onto the phone's touch screen, she hit accept, not recognizing the number. "Hello?"

"Trina." A familiar voice—one that had made her heart flutter for months and now made it cramp in anger and betrayal—came down the line. She could hear the sound of a code being called over a PA in the background.

"Brent." She sighed, closing her eyes and automatically calculating the time zone change. She hated that her mind immediately pictured him coming out of surgery wearing his monogrammed scrubs and distinctive red clogs. She quickly opened her eyes and stared out across the plains toward the Rocky Mountains in the distance, desperately seeking calm. "I thought we'd agreed to no calls."

This time he sighed. "I agreed you needed time and I've given it to you. You've made your point, Trina, I get it, but it doesn't change the fact we still love each other. With some compromise and understanding on your part, we can still make this work."

Still. His arrogance astounded her, although it shouldn't be a surprise. She still whipped herself for having been oblivious to that particular character flaw. His tone said everything was her fault but she was being forgiven.

She pinched the bridge of her nose, welcoming the pain because she had no clue how to even go about explaining that no amount of trying was going to make them work. *Ever.* "Nothing's changed, Brent."

"I miss you."

Her throat tightened as the quietly spoken words caressed her, reminding her of the wonderful times they'd shared. Her resolve wavered.

"Trina, I just want to reassure you that you can get me on this number anytime."

This number. Her brain jolted her back to reality so fast she got whiplash. He'd gotten another phone. Another number just for her. Again. Her knees wobbled and she gripped the doorjamb to hold herself up. Wet paint squelched around her fingers. *Shit.* She pulled her hand away and found her voice. "Good-bye, Brent."

She cut the call, hurled the phone onto the sofa as if it were radioactive and then ran fast and hard on the spot, letting out a scream that came from the center of her being. A deer grazing at the edge of the now weed-choked garden took off at a run. All the feelings she'd spent weeks letting go of surged back, buffeting her like the frigid and biting arctic winds that swooped in from Canada. Anger at Brent. Even more anger at herself and at her own stupidity. Anger period. She hated how it dug in, making her feel so powerless, desperately foolish and immensely sad all at the same time. She bit the inside of her cheek to try and stall the shakes that threatened to send her into the fetal position on the couch.

She never, ever wanted to feel like this again, which was why she'd come home in the first place, effectively putting two thousand miles between her and Brent. Closing the door to temptation and poor judgment.

Her old border collie, Boy, heaved himself off his rug and came over to her, licking her hand. He was deaf and half blind but he always knew when she was upset. She rubbed his ears and buried her face in his coat, thinking about how her life had changed so much. A few weeks ago she'd had a great job and a clear vision of her future firmly set in Philly. When it all came tumbling down, she'd bolted back to Bear Paw, telling herself it was only temporary. A breathing space. She'd even made some calls about doing some health care volunteering in Ecuador, because at least that was a plan of sorts and it reassured her that her time in Bear Paw would be short.

She hadn't told her parents the real reason for her return, because she didn't need to see or hear their disappointment that she'd failed, especially as she'd been heard to say more than once that she preferred living in the city. Instead, she'd skirted the truth and told them she was burned-out from her high-pressure unit manager job and she was taking a break to visit with them and work on the cottage. They'd immediately suggested she work at the Bear Paw hospital like she'd done when she'd graduated, but she was determined to avoid anything to do with doctors and hospitals. Instead, she'd gotten a part-time job at the diner and at Leroy's. Although her parents had never been thrilled she'd left Bear Paw and they'd been the ones to urge her two years ago to buy the cottage, they'd silently accepted her decision, but she caught their troubled gazes on her from time to time. She hated that. Hated that her inability to make the right choices in her life had landed her back at home.

Giving Boy a *thank you but I'm fine* rub around the ears, she grabbed the roller with a jerk and quickly made short work of the rest of the walls. By the time she'd finished and was surveying her handiwork, she'd found a modicum of hard-earned calm. The new paint had gotten rid of the nicotine stains left by the stressed-out accountant who'd run from town the moment tax season was over. He'd been a lousy tenant despite Walt, her Realtor, promising her six months ago that he came with great references. After the mess he'd left behind, Katrina was convinced the previous landlord wrote the glowing report just to get rid of him.

The fact that her tenant had broken the lease was timely, because as much as she loved her family, she'd lived alone too long to go back to living in the ranch house. Coming home for short visits was one thing, but there was something about moving into her childhood room that turned back the clock. She ceased being Katrina McCade, independent career woman, and became Katrina—dutiful daughter, sibling mediator and general go-to person. It was all wrapped up with a distinct lack of privacy and it was wearing her out.

The moment the paint fumes had vaporized, she was moving in, and she'd repair the other damage that had been inflicted on the house. She'd even use some of her savings to renovate the kitchen. After that, she might go to Ecuador and be useful or she might head to California or . . . She had no clue. All she knew was that her plans were open-ended.

You've never done fluid. Her mind went straight to the very scheduled life she'd shared with Brent over the past eight months. She immediately hauled it back. She could do fluid. She could try and go with the flow with one exception. Lesson learned—no matter how much she enjoyed being in a relationship, she was not getting involved with another man anytime soon.

She pulled a screwdriver out of the tool belt around her waist and levered open the paint can containing the lavender paint for her bedroom. She suddenly smiled. At least Bear Paw didn't have a surgeon with devastating charm, or for that matter a physician under sixty. She was totally safe on that front, and for that small mercy, she was truly grateful.

———

JOSH drove down a long gravel road seriously doubting the directions the hospital administrator had e-mailed him. Surely, the house that came with the job would be in the town and close by the hospital? Only he'd passed the hospital, two miles back, where he'd be reporting tomorrow morning at eight. Now Main Street, with its mixture of flat-fronted brick and clapboard shops, was well behind him, too. He appeared to be heading for Canada.

He hit a pothole and his front fender scraped the road. *Shit.* He slowed his speed and zigzagged his way around another four potholes before he pulled over to face the intensive stare of a jackrabbit, whose large ears mocked him. This was ludicrous. It was one thing for his student loans to have mortgaged his life, bringing him to a small town in the middle of nowhere, but surely the hospital wouldn't have rented him a house way out here. He must have missed the turn back in town.

At least he now had one bar of service on his phone. He plugged the GPS coordinates of the house into the app. The melon-colored exclamation point magically appeared one-quarter mile away from his current blue location dot. He looked to his left. He needed to turn onto a driveway that had never seen blacktop or gravel.

"You've got to be kidding me," he muttered as he threw the gear stick into first. No wonder the hospital administrator had said the house would be open and not to worry about a key. It was in the middle of damn-well-nowhere.

Five bone-shuddering minutes later, he pulled up outside a house or a cottage—he wasn't sure which, and he wasn't certain the builder had known, either. It was a mishmash of design and was neither attic cottage nor log cabin. One section was cladding and the other logs, and he thought he glimpsed some exposed house wrap between the two. The eaves extended over a door that was offset, in fact the whole side of the house he was facing looked as if it had been tacked on as an afterthought. A small satellite dish clung precariously to the roof, and Josh was surprised it hadn't been blown away and taken the house with it.

The property screamed first homeowner's dream, renovator's delight or student housing. It had been a very long time since he'd been a student, and the gloss of living in a house that had seen better days had well and truly lost its shine. A few scraggly trees attempted to survive to create a much-needed windbreak, but most looked like they'd given up on the job. Weeds dotted the short path to the house, and a rusted-out truck was parked outside, possibly abandoned. Just fabulous.

The property was wrong on so many levels that it had to be a mistake. Reaching for his phone, he prepared to call the hospital administrator to complain when he remembered he'd gotten a message from him saying he was out of town today. Reluctantly, Josh pushed himself out of the car, locked it behind him and walked directly to the door. He knocked and waited but no one came, so with a firm grip, he turned the handle. Surprise jolted him when it opened smoothly and without a squeak.

He had to duck his head as he walked through the small entrance with its coat hooks and a boot box, before stepping into a pine-clad kitchen. Circa 1970, it came complete with faded lime green counters and a breakfast nook. It was a far cry from the granite countertop kitchen with all its modern stainless steel appliances back in his Chicago apartment.

Her Chicago apartment.

Not wanting thoughts of Ashley to creep into his mind, he decided that even though there was no way in hell he was going to live here, he'd explore the house and list all the reasons why the place was unsuitable. Paint fumes hit him the moment he crossed into the living room, and moving carefully, so as not to get paint on his chinos, he soon found himself facing a small, steep staircase.

Years of experience running between floors of the many different hospitals he'd worked in had him taking the stairs two at a time. His head suddenly slammed into the sloped ceiling. "Jesus."

His vision swam and he rubbed his scalp, already feeling a lump the size of a golf ball rising under his fingers. He mentally added another reason to his mounting list. Not only was the house in the boonies, it was built for dwarfs. Moving decidedly more slowly, he took the rest of the stairs one at a time with his head bent low. He didn't risk straightening up until he was well and truly on the landing.

Raising his head, he realized there was no landing—he was standing in a room. A dormer bedroom. He blinked in surprise. An old dog lay sleeping on a rug, and a short woman stood on a ladder with her back to him and with white earbuds in her ears. She was carefully painting the area where lavender walls met the white ceiling. Her heavy leather work boots gripped the second-top step and thick, bright red socks peeked out over the top. A paint can perched precariously on a board near her knees.

He almost called out but he didn't want to startle her and risk her falling off the ladder and breaking something. Plus, his gaze seemed fixed on her bare legs. They weren't model-long, but the calves were muscular and sculpted as if they worked out often and were strong for the effort. And the skin was tan. A beautiful, golden tan from sunshine, not the orange tint from a bottle like he'd noticed on some patients after the long Illinois winters. Just as his mind and gaze slid upward, hoping to glimpse what he imagined would be the sweet curve of her ass, denim cutoffs rudely broke the view.

Damn. Still, the shorts hinted that the naked view might well be a good one. A bright blue paisley blouse that didn't remotely match the shorts—and reminded him of his grandmother—flowed over the waistband at complete odds with the wide black band of a tool belt. His brain jolted, trying to merge the juxtaposing images of modern meeting old-fashioned. His gaze had just reached short, glossy black hair when she turned and saw him.

Before he could raise his hands to show her that he came in peace, her enormous green eyes—the color of spring—dilated in shock.

The dog barked.

She moved abruptly, her actions jerky, and her knee caught the edge of the board, sending the paint can flying.

Two seconds later, Josh was wearing lavender paint.

LOVE
ROMANCE
NOVELS?

For news on all your favorite romance authors, sneak peeks into the newest releases, book giveaways, and much more—

"Like" Love Always on Facebook!
LoveAlwaysBooks

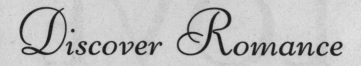

Discover Romance

berkleyjoveauthors.com

See what's coming up next from your favorite romance authors and explore all the latest Berkley, Jove, and Sensation selections.

See what's new

~

Find author appearances

~

Win fantastic prizes

~

Get reading recommendations

~

Chat with authors and other fans

~

Read interviews with authors you love